# WESTERN

*Rugged men looking for love...*

## The Cowboy's Forgotten Love
### Tina Radcliffe

## The Cowboy's Inheritance
### Julia Ruth

## MILLS & BOON

THE COWBOY'S FORGOTTEN LOVE
© 2024 by Tina M. Radcliffe
Philippine Copyright 2024
Australian Copyright 2024
New Zealand Copyright 2024

First Published 2024
First Australian Paperback Edition 2024
ISBN 978 1 038 93534 2

THE COWBOY'S INHERITANCE
© 2024 by Julia Bennett
Philippine Copyright 2024
Australian Copyright 2024
New Zealand Copyright 2024

First Published 2024
First Australian Paperback Edition 2024
ISBN 978 1 038 93534 2

MIX
Paper | Supporting responsible forestry
FSC® C001695
www.fsc.org

Published by
Harlequin Mills & Boon
An imprint of Harlequin Enterprises (Australia) Pty Limited (ABN 47 001 180 918), a subsidiary of HarperCollins Publishers Australia Pty Limited
(ABN 36 009 913 517)
Level 19, 201 Elizabeth Street
SYDNEY NSW 2000 AUSTRALIA

Cover art used by arrangement with Harlequin Books S.A.. All rights reserved.

Printed and bound in Australia by McPherson's Printing Group

# The Cowboy's Forgotten Love

## Tina Radcliffe

# MILLS & BOON

**Tina Radcliffe** has been dreaming and scribbling for years. Originally from Western New York, she left home for a tour of duty with the US Army Security Agency stationed in Augsburg, Germany, and ended up in Tulsa, Oklahoma. Her past careers include certified oncology RN, library cataloger and pharmacy clerk. She recently moved from Denver, Colorado, to the Phoenix, Arizona, area, where she writes heartwarming and fun inspirational romance.

### Books by Tina Radcliffe

### Love Inspired

### *Lazy M Ranch*

*The Baby Inheritance*
*The Cowboy Bargain*
*The Cowboy's Secret Past*
*The Cowboy's Forgotten Love*

### *Hearts of Oklahoma*

*Finding the Road Home*
*Ready to Trust*
*His Holiday Prayer*
*The Cowgirl's Sacrifice*

### *Big Heart Ranch*

*Claiming Her Cowboy*
*Falling for the Cowgirl*
*Christmas with the Cowboy*
*Her Last Chance Cowboy*

### Love Inspired Suspense

*Sabotaged Mission*

Visit the Author Profile page at LoveInspired.com for more titles.

God is my strength and power:
and he maketh my way perfect.
—*2 Samuel* 22:33

## Acknowledgments

Everything comes full circle. As Lucas Morgan's book ends my journey to Homestead Pass, Oklahoma, a big thank-you to Deborah Clack, who lit the flame that ignited this story idea. Thanks to Sherry Peters Photography and Bradbury Lane for the print of the Morgan boys. I am grateful.

A final thanks to reader Kim Church, who helped me research Lawton, Oklahoma.

# CHAPTER ONE

DESPITE THE HEAT of Oklahoma's last days of summer, Harper Reilly opened all the windows of her truck and let the hot afternoon breeze blow through the cab and whip through her hair. She turned the radio louder and grinned. Life was good.

After a lifetime of being Lucas Morgan's bestie, she might finally be moving out of the friend zone. She'd mustered the courage to tell him she cared for him three weeks ago at his brother Trevor's wedding and was nothing less than stunned when the cavalier lady's man admitted he felt the same way.

Since then, they'd been separated by rodeo circuit obligations. Friday, she'd joined him in Lawton for the Lawton Rangers Rodeo, and she couldn't stop smiling. Luc was the partner she'd prayed for. The man she longed to settle down with for whatever the future held.

Their performance at the rodeo provided a sweet preface for them to reconnect and discuss where they would go from there on a personal level. On a professional level, she had a list of important things to discuss with him regarding the training center the two of them hoped to launch next year.

Harper had placed first in cowgirl's barrel racing, and Luc had done well in saddle bronc riding, taking the number two spot after gaining ground on his competition. It was good to see his name on the leaderboard. Following a year riddled with injuries, things had begun to turn around in March. Luc had stayed on the leaderboard ever since. She couldn't be happier for him. He wanted to go out on top, and that dream was coming true.

Harper checked the dash clock. She'd left her trailer with plenty of time to head into town for Saturday dinner. She and Luc were supposed to meet at Milano's Italian Restaurant for a romantic meal. He hadn't said the word *romantic*, but she'd already checked the place out online. It was definitely romantic.

She smiled again. Was she getting ahead of herself? She hoped not.

They'd shared many meals over the years, but tonight—tonight was like a first date. The rodeo events were over, and they would have a chance to really talk. Yes, there was a lot on the line tonight and she was ready to make serious plans for the future.

As she rounded a bend in the road, the red and blue flashing lights of emergency and police vehicles glowed in the overcast sky. The chatter and intermittent static of a police radio and the crunching of tires filled the air as vehicles slowly moved past the scene on the left side of the road.

Though she couldn't tell exactly what had happened, Harper sent up a silent prayer for whoever might be involved in the mishap that had caused the two-lane road to be funneled to a single lane with traffic stopped in either direction. A police officer in an orange reflective vest waved her on, and she moved cautiously past the emergency vehicles.

Then the accident scene became visible. A truck had hit a tree. Its front fender and the hood were crumpled, and the front window was shattered.

A black Ford truck. It was a popular vehicle. Back home in Homestead Pass, all the Morgan boys had black pickups. Yet goose bumps raced down her arms, and her heart rate picked up. Harper's gaze landed on the license plate depicting a white scissor-tailed flycatcher against a blue landscape.

LAZYM#4.

*Luc!* The fourth Morgan sibling. The man who held her heart.

Her stomach dropped and she nearly hit the brakes. Catching herself at the last moment before she caused another accident, Harper checked her rear mirror, signaled and pulled off the road once she'd cleared the accident perimeter. She jumped from the dually and stumbled when her feet hit the asphalt. Realizing she wore heels and not her usual boots, she regained her balance and raced across the street toward the ambulance, her sundress billowing.

Two uniformed emergency medical responders loaded a person through the open rear doors just as she reached the vehicle. One of the techs climbed into the ambulance while Harper strained to get a look at the person on the gurney. All she saw was the soles of boots and an IV bag suspended on a pole swaying gently.

"My head is killing me," the patient moaned.

Harper startled at the sound of Luc's voice. Her heart clenched. This couldn't be happening.

"Wait. That's Luc," she called.

"Lady, we gotta go." The second tech stood with his hand on the door, his body effectively blocking her from getting any closer.

"Please. Is he going to be okay?"

"Are you immediate family?" he asked.

"A close friend." *Not family. I'm his almost girlfriend.*

The tech looked at his partner inside the vehicle and exchanged a silent communication. He leaned closer. "His condition is serious though stable. Your friend is confused at the moment." The tech raised a hand and met her gaze. "You didn't hear that from me, or I'll lose my job for sure."

Harper nodded. "Thank you. Which hospital are you taking him to?"

"Southwestern Medical Center. Lee Boulevard."

The door slammed and the tech jumped into the driver's seat while Harper stood on the side of the road, wrapping her arms around herself as the wind began to pick up. The faint smell of burning rubber reached her nose and she shivered. Overhead, the darkening sky had become more ominous as sirens and flashing lights escorted the ambulance toward town. The wail and yelp blared over and over until it faded out of earshot.

"Ma'am, may I help you?"

Harper whirled around at the voice. A kindly faced police officer in a blue short-sleeved uniform peered at her.

"Lucas Morgan. He's… He's a close friend."

"Ah. This must be quite a shock," the officer returned. "But he's in good hands." He stared at her for a moment. "You look familiar. What's your name?"

"Harper Reilly."

"Reilly. Barrel racer. I saw you take the big prize on Friday. Congratulations."

"Thank you." Heat warmed her face at the unexpected recognition.

"I'm sorry about your friend. Do you need directions to the hospital?"

"My truck's guidance will find it. But thank you." Harper wiped away the moisture sprinkling down on them as they stood on the side of the road.

"Ma'am, would you happen to have a number for his next of kin to notify them about the accident? I asked Mr. Morgan for that information, but he was a bit confused. Head injury and all."

Harper straightened at the words and searched the policeman's face. "Head injury?"

"That's not a diagnosis, mind you. It's what I gathered from the scene." He waved an arm at the truck. "You can see the vehicle hit a tree. Though the airbag deployed, it didn't protect him from the tree branch that shot sideways through the windshield."

Stepping closer to the truck, Harper assessed the scene. Her eyes followed the tire tracks from the road to the grassy area. She blinked at the sight of the branch and the webbing of broken safety glass and began to process what she saw. Luc had been headed for the rodeo grounds, not into town. Why? The plan was to meet at the restaurant. He'd said that he had errands to run first. Perhaps Luc finished early and thought they could take one vehicle?

Either way, assessing the angle of that tree branch, she realized that Luc was fortunate to be alive.

"Do you know what happened?" Harper asked.

"An eyewitness headed in the other direction saw a deer run in front of the truck. Your friend's quick thinking helped him avoid hitting the animal, but he lost control on the wet pavement."

A horn beeped and the officer took her elbow, gently guiding her across the street. "Tow truck needs to get in here."

"Where will Luc's truck be taken?"

"To an impound lot." He pulled out a card and wrote a number on the back. "Call them on Monday."

"Thank you. I will."

Harper offered the officer the Lazy M Ranch number and turned to leave. Though she let the officer know she would be contacting the family, he'd advised he was required to call them in an official capacity as well.

Rain chased her across the road and to her truck. Hands trembling and her heart beating overtime, she fumbled with the door handle and maneuvered inside the vehicle. She wiped the moisture from her face once more then pulled her phone from her purse and hit Call on the familiar number.

The Morgan boys had suffered many losses in the past, including the death of their parents when they were young. She'd known the family since high school. It would be better if they heard the news from her first.

"Morgan." Luc's eldest brother answered on the first ring.

"Drew, this is Harper Reilly."

"Hey, Harper. How are you?"

"I'm f-f-fine…" she stammered. "It's Luc. I'm calling about Luc." Harper stared out the window where rain tapped against the windshield, blurring the scenery.

There was an intake of breath and then silence for a moment. "Is he okay? What happened? I keep telling him it's time to retire from the rodeo."

Harper hesitated, searching for a gentle response. It wasn't fair that they had to hear the news over the phone. "A deer ran in front of his truck. He hit a tree." She swallowed. "The ambulance is taking him to Southwestern Medical Center in Lawton."

"You're in Oklahoma?"

"Yes. We finished up the Lawton rodeo this morning and planned to head to Montana for the Fallon County Rodeo tomorrow."

"You're close by. That's good. How bad is it?"

"I'm not family, so I couldn't get much information. Head injury. Serious but stable."

"You weren't with him when it happened?"

"No. Fortunately, I stumbled upon the scene as the first responders loaded him into an ambulance. They tell me he was conscious but confused."

"Okay." Drew paused as if thinking. "Okay. We'll be there right away. Thanks, Harper."

"Drew, you're two hours away, and it's raining here. Drive safely," she said. "I'll be praying."

"Yeah. Prayer. Good plan."

Harper disconnected the phone and worked to stay calm. "Lord, You've had Your hand on Luc for thirty-six years. I trust You to continue to protect him and his family. Amen."

"HARPER!" LUCAS WAVED his friend into the hospital room. Finally, he had a visitor who wasn't dressed in scrubs or a white lab coat. His best friend carried a raincoat over her arm and wore a pink floral sundress as she hesitantly stepped through the doorway and looked around the room.

"Raincoat?" Lucas asked.

"It's pouring out there." She hung her coat on the back of the door and smoothed her long, russet hair.

"Is it?" Huh. He didn't recall rain. Lucas smiled and the simple movement started off a chain reaction of pain radiating from his jaw to his temple. Pain aside, his heart warmed at the sight of his best friend in a dress, no less, and heels. Tall and willowy, she filled out the dress nicely.

"Look at you all gussied up," he said. "Got a new fella?" A spark of jealousy jumped to life, but he tamped it down. What was he thinking? Harper was his best friend. Lucas raised a hand. "Kidding. Just kidding."

Harper frowned, confusion on her face, her green eyes concerned. "Are you okay?" she asked. Worry lines marred her golden freckled complexion and concern shadowed her gaze.

"Okay? Well, that's a matter of opinion." He'd spent the last two hours being poked and questioned. All the while, his life had flashed before him on a loop. While he didn't remember the rodeo accident that had put him in the hospital, he did remember the ambulance ride. All he could think about was what a mess he'd made of things.

It occurred to him that he'd been on the circuit so long he'd missed half the important things in his life. His brothers had settled down. He'd blinked and all three of them had fallen in love with amazing women. Each of his brothers was involved in some capacity with running the Lazy M Ranch they'd all inherited when their parents died. Yep, they'd all found their path except him. Thirty-six years old, and he hadn't figured out what he wanted to be when he grew up. He wasn't any closer to finding someone to share his life with now than last year either.

"Luc?"

"Huh?" He looked at Harper. "Did you say something? Sorry. I was thinking."

"I said that I was here earlier. Your nurse told me you were getting an MRI."

Lucas scoffed. "I'm certain I've had every test there is. MRI. CT. They took a gallon of blood too." He laughed and then winced. "But you know me. I've got a hard head. I'm fine. Takes more than a mean bronc to keep me down."

"What?" She stared at him as though he had two heads instead of the one that had been knocked around in a blender.

"You know what I mean." Despite the shooting pain, Lucas laughed again. "How do you like this outfit?" He shot a disparaging look at himself in the trendy blue-and-white-patterned hospital gown and grimaced. "They won't give me my Wranglers and boots back. Believe me. I tried. I don't even know where my phone is."

"It's probably in your truck. I'll find it." She grimaced. "How are you feeling? That's quite a black eye you have. And there's a knot the size of Oklahoma on your forehead."

"Is there?" He touched the bandage at this brow line. Three stitches. The nurse in the emergency room had told him he was fortunate to not have lost his right eye. "I'm not sure what happened, but I have a wicked headache and my nose feels like I was sucker punched."

"Your nose is definitely swollen. Did they give you anything for the pain?"

"Nope. The nurse said they don't want me sedated."

He ran his fingers over the worn silver watch on his wrist. His galloping heart had settled some when he'd realized the memento, once his father's, was untouched.

"I called your brothers," Harper said.

"What?" He spit out the question and then bit back the ensuing pain. *Note to self, chill out. It hurts less.* "Why would you do that, Harp? I'll be out of here shortly, and we'll be on our way to Tucson."

"Tucson?" Her jaw sagged.

"You're still going, aren't you?" He was aware that Harper had obligations at home. The Reillys were Homestead Pass royalty thanks to Reilly Pecans, and Harper regularly pitched in during pecan harvest. Plus, her grandmother's deteriorating health had her going home often now that her folks had moved the matriarch to the Reilly ranch.

"The Tucson rodeo is held in February, Luc."

"Yep. Arizona in winter." He leaned back against the pillows and focused on that solitary cheerful thought. "I'm so ready for sunshine and saguaro cactus. Maybe we can take a side trip to Sedona again? It's out of the way, but why not? All work and no play and all that. What do you think?"

"Sedona? Let's slow down a minute here," she said. "Do you know where we are?"

Luc narrowed his eyes. Why was she asking silly questions? "I'm in Fort Worth. We've been here all week." He paused. "Are you okay, Harper? You look confused."

A disturbance in the hall had both Harper and Lucas turning toward the door. It burst open and the entire Morgan family poured into the hospital room, their boots clacking on the linoleum floor as they entered. A harried nurse followed right behind, admonishing them to be quiet before she left.

His older brothers, Drew and Sam, along with his fraternal twin, Trevor, and their grandfather all stared at him.

Lucas did a double take. Why was his entire family here?

"Well, thank the Lord," Gramps said. "You're in one piece."

"No worse for wear, as you can see. But if you're all here, who's watching the ranch?" Lucas asked. "And how did you get here so fast?"

Gramps stepped closer to the bed with a newspaper under his arm. He pulled off his Stetson and hugged Harper. At eighty-four, Gus Morgan could easily be taken for a man ten years younger. Beneath his Stetson, his brown hair was barely touched by gray.

His grandfather turned to Lucas, the sharp blue eyes assessing. "It wasn't fast. I wanted to go south and pick up Highway 62, but Drew said the back roads were faster." Gramps scowled and rolled his eyes.

"It *was* faster," Drew said.

"My truck's suspension will never be the same," Trevor muttered.

"We took two vehicles, but your brothers wouldn't even stop for a Dr Pepper break," Gramps groused.

"What are you talking about?" Lucas asked, looking at his family. "It's four hours from Homestead Pass."

His grandfather's eyes rounded and he inched closer to the hospital bed. "In what world? It's two hours from home to Lawton."

"Lawton?" Pain surged behind Lucas's eyes as he processed what Gramps said. Then he sank back onto the pillows.

"You okay, Luc?" Trevor approached him.

"I'm fine. A little banged up, is all. I feel bad you all came out here on a Sunday."

"Sunday? It's not Sunday," Trevor said.

"Sure it is. We got into Fort Worth a week ago. That was February fifth. Do you want me to recite the alphabet backward too?"

"Easy there," Gramps said. He unfolded the paper tucked under his arm and placed it on the bed. It was an issue of the *Homestead Pass Daily Journal*. "Son, it's the middle of August. Not February. And it's Saturday night."

"What?" Lucas closed his eyes and then opened them. How could that be?

Gramps shook his head. "Mayhap, I spoke too soon. Sounds like you're having some issues with your head, son."

Lucas stared at his grandfather, trying to ignore the dizziness that threatened. For the first time since he'd arrived at the hospital, he was worried about his prognosis. How had he lost such a chunk of time? He worked to string together his memories of the events from February to now, without success. Panic simmered in his gut.

"Have you talked to a doctor?" Gramps asked.

"Talked to a couple of them in the emergency department. They asked me a bunch of questions, including what day it is, and then they sent me for tests." He shrugged, working to shake off his growing concern and his grandfather's. "I don't see what the big deal is. I've hit my head before."

Gramps shot Sam a pointed look. "Go find that nurse and tell her we want a doctor in here pronto, would you?"

"Yes, sir." His brother gave a solemn nod and left the room.

Minutes later, a different nurse rushed in. The petite young woman assessed him and then his visitors. "Dr. Gradeless will be here shortly. I apologize for the delay. He's tied up in the emergency room."

"Can you tell us what's going on with my grandson in the meantime?" Gramps asked.

The nurse looked at Lucas. "Mr. Morgan? Do you agree to share information about your medical condition with your visitors?"

"They aren't visitors. This is my family. Whatever you have to say, you can say in front of them."

Again, her gaze spanned the room. "Aside from the head laceration and bruised ribs, I can tell you that he's suffering from a concussion."

Lucas scoffed. "Is that all? I told everyone in the emergency department that I've had half a dozen of those. That's old news."

"Yes," the nurse replied. "I believe that is the doctor's concern."

A phone trilled and Harper scrambled to pull the cell from her pocket. "Excuse me. It's my father. I'll be right back."

When she slipped out of the room, the nurse gave his brothers and his grandfather a stern look. "It's past visiting hours. If you keep your voices down, you can stay until the doctor arrives. Otherwise, I'll have to speak to security and have you escorted out." She nodded and wove her way around his brothers and out of the room.

"Huh. Would never have called that," Sam said. "She looked like such a sweet little thing."

"Those are the ones you have to look out for. Trust me. I married one just like her," Trevor quipped.

"Married? When did you and Hope get hitched?" Lucas frowned, trying to sort dates in his mind without success.

"Luc, we got married on the first Saturday in August. You were my best man." Bleak concern filled his brother's blue eyes.

"Nah. Really?" Why couldn't he remember his brother's wedding? "Did I have fun?"

"You always have fun," Trevor returned. "Though, except for dancing the polka with half the church ladies, you mostly hung out with Harper."

"Could we focus here, boys? Luc here has amnesia," Gramps said. "I'm guessing there's more going on than another concussion."

"I've taken worse spills," Lucas said. That was the truth. Except this time, he didn't remember what had happened to land him in the hospital. He held up his right arm. "Remember last summer when you met your wife, Trev? Sixteen stitches up and down my arm."

"You aren't helping yourself here, Luc," Trevor muttered.

Gramps shook his head. "I don't like it. Don't like it at all." He turned to Harper, who'd entered the room again. "Sure appreciate you calling us about Lucas right away."

Harper nodded, her lips a thin line. Lucas noted the anxiety in her eyes and the tension in her slim frame. The two of them had a long history of supporting each other through the dark times and the good. He longed to hug his buddy and tell her everything would be okay.

Today, for the first time in his life, he wasn't sure everything would be okay.

The room fell silent, except for the quiet beep of the IV pump, the sound of patient call buzzers echoing from the hall and the muffled squeak of shoes on linoleum.

His brother Drew walked to the window, brow creased as he took in the night sky. Lucas hated worrying his family. The Morgans had had a rough past. Drew was the oldest, and things had fallen on his shoulders when their parents had died until Gramps moved in. Luc and Trevor had been thirteen. It hadn't been a good time, and Luc hadn't made it any easier. While his brothers were stoics who'd swallowed their grief, he had been inconsolable for over a year.

Minutes later, a light tap at the door frame proceeded the entry of a physician in a white lab coat. A tall man with a generous smile glanced around the room. "Good evening. I'm Dr. Gradeless." He took a moment to shake hands with everyone in the room and exchange introductions before approaching the foot of the bed.

Lucas tensed, his fists opening and closing as he waited for the impending diagnosis.

"Doc, what's going on?" Gramps burst out. "Luc's lost months of his life."

"I understand. The scans show a traumatic brain injury. It appears he has retrograde amnesia."

"Can you explain that so I can understand it, Doc?" Gramps asked. "What's the difference between a traumatic brain injury and a concussion?"

"A concussion is a type of TBI. The brain moves and is bruised. In your grandson's case, it's led to retrograde amnesia."

"'Retrograde amnesia,'" Drew repeated. "What can we do?"

"Rest is the most important thing right now. It's a wait-and-see situation," the doctor said. "The symptoms usually go away on their own in hours or weeks, sometimes even months."

"Wait and see?" Gramps shook his head. "No offense, Doc, but you spent all that time in medical school and that's the best you can do?"

"Point well taken." Dr. Gradeless gave a nod of acknowledgment. "Unfortunately, there is no definitive answer with head injuries. The good news is that, according to the paramedic's report, the good Samaritan who observed the crash reported that Lucas didn't lose consciousness for long. Your grandson is alert and shows no other symptoms except a headache and mild dizziness. We'll provide acetaminophen for the headache. He needs to rest for the next twenty-four hours while the staff monitors him for any worsening symptoms."

"Then I can get back to work?" Lucas ran a hand over his chin. Maybe things weren't as lousy as he'd thought.

The physician narrowed his gaze. "What work is that?"

"Rodeo. Saddle bronc riding."

"Oh no." The doctor's face reflected surprise. "That is precisely the activity you must avoid. Rest from mental and physical activity is what I'm prescribing."

Lucas stared at him, hope fading. "For how long?"

"The plan is to take things one day at a time, gradually resuming regular nonjarring activities."

"And then I'll get my memory back?"

"Once again, there are no definitive answers when it comes to a brain injury. There are various kinds of memory and a range of types of memory loss and recovery."

Dr. Gradeless eyed the group. "All of you should be observing Mr. Morgan for neurological changes as well. I'll provide a guidance handout at discharge and a referral to a neurologist in your area. He should follow up with an office visit as soon as possible, and head to an emergency room if his symptoms worsen." The doctor paused. "In the meantime, rest is the prescription."

"Rest," Lucas muttered at the offensive takeaway from the doctor's spiel.

"Think of it as an opportunity to do some of the things you've put off."

"Like what? Basket weaving?"

Gramps snorted.

The neurologist shot Lucas a disapproving glance. "Mr. Morgan, I don't think you appreciate how fortunate you are. That accident could have been fatal."

"Yeah, I'm sorry, Doc," Lucas apologized. "I know you're right, but this is an adjustment."

Dr. Gradeless scanned the room, his eyes coming back to Lucas. "Here's the best advice I can offer. Don't push yourself. If you are pressed to recall those missing memories, you're going to increase your stress and the likelihood of headaches. Additionally, that stress can lead to depression." He paused. "This isn't a race to remember the past."

Lucas stared at him, a bit stunned by the words.

"I'd like to recommend a therapist to work through how you're feeling."

Lucas nodded at Gramps. "My grandfather is the family therapist."

"Oh, I wasn't aware." Dr. Gradeless looked at the Morgan patriarch.

"He's being facetious," Gramps inserted. "But I can tell you that we're on it. Fact is, he has a sister-in-law who's a registered nurse. You can be sure he'll have plenty of care." He eyed Lucas. "Whether he likes it or not."

Lucas barely resisted groaning aloud. His gaze met Harper's. She was the one person in the room who really understood his struggles the last year. She lifted her hands as if in prayer and mouthed, *It's going to be okay.*

In that moment, he relaxed a bit. Things were messed up,

all right, but he knew to keep his eyes on the Lord, no matter what. He looked at Harper again and sent up a prayer, thanking Him for his best friend.

# CHAPTER TWO

HARPER STOOD AT the foot of Luc's bed and assessed his bruised eye. The colors had transitioned from black and blue to black, blue and purple, and they stood out against the butterfly bandage that had replaced the gauze on his temple. His nose seemed somewhat less swollen and pronounced. Still, seeing the six-foot-tall cowboy in a hospital bed, wearing a blue-dotted gown and connected to an IV shook her each time she walked in the room. His wavy, caramel-colored hair could use a visit to the barber. A lock fell over his forehead and she fought the urge to push it back.

"How do you feel?" she finally asked, working to keep her voice calm and even, though she felt anything but. Last night at 3:00 a.m., while she'd stared at the ceiling of her trailer, Harper decided she would not let her own fears about Luc's memory loss and what it meant for their future take priority over his recovery. No stress, the doctor had said. Right now, it was her job as his friend to do whatever she could to be there for him. She wouldn't press him to pull up memories.

"The headache rages on." Lucas shrugged. "Got a few new aches today, including my ribs. Though my ego isn't quite as bruised now that I know a tree hit me and I didn't fall off a horse." He looked at her. "Why do you suppose I lost control of the truck anyhow?"

She studied him. Had he forgotten what she'd repeated on Saturday and Sunday already? "The policeman said a deer ran across the road. It wasn't your fault, and there wasn't anything you could have done differently. There was a car behind you and vehicles approaching in the other lane."

"I could have *not* hit that tree. A bronc, I can understand, but a tree?"

"It was raining. Everything was slick. Cut yourself some slack."

"I guess," he muttered, his attention on the IV tubing.

Harper checked her watch. "I'm going to head over to the impound lot. I called Les Farley and someone from Farley Towing is meeting me there," she said. "They'll get your truck back to Homestead Pass."

"Harper."

She looked up and met his stare. "Thank you. I appreciate it. Thank Les for me, would you?"

"I will. Are you going to be okay until your family gets back from breakfast?"

Luc offered a bitter chuckle. "Yeah, sure. I'm surrounded by babysitters here." He nodded and then hesitated. "Thanks, Harp. You're a good friend."

A good friend. Yes, she was. Twenty-four hours ago, she'd been certain that she was moving toward more than that.

"See you back in Homestead Pass," she said.

Harper mulled over the situation with Luc as she drove to the lot. She'd hardly slept last night, tossing, and turning as she contemplated the uncertain future. All she could do was pray that his injured brain healed.

She recalled the moment everything had changed between them. It was July at the Colorado Cattlemen's Days in Gunnison. The minute his score lit up the leaderboard, Luc had raced from the arena to find Harper. He'd picked her up and whirled her around. And for the first time since they'd met, Lucas kissed her.

She lifted a hand from the steering wheel to touch her lips. *It was the sweetest kiss.*

One that made her realize that, after years content as Luc's best friend, she wanted more. Harper had been forced to admit to herself that she'd denied her feelings for Luc for far too long. Perhaps had been fearful that if things played out, one day she'd be relegated to a long line of Lucas Morgan's ex-girlfriends. She wanted it all and the kiss had given her hope maybe that wasn't a dream. After the kiss, Luc had apologized nonstop for the next twenty-four hours.

In the weeks after that, they'd pretended it hadn't happened. When she couldn't hold back any longer, she'd blurted out her feelings after Trevor and Hope's wedding. Luc's responding admission that he cared about her had knocked her boots off.

That moment was real, wasn't it? Or had he been caught up in the emotion of his brother's wedding? After seeing the tenderness in his eyes, Harper had left Homestead Pass that weekend with a full heart, and hope. Now, she wasn't certain. Had she imagined things?

The ringing of Harper's cell phone jarred her from her thoughts. The dashboard display connected to her cell flashed her father's number.

She let it go to voice mail. Harper wasn't up to another grilling. Colin Reilly had been pressing her about the family business lately. The discussions always seemed to end with a word about Luc.

Her father blamed the cowboy for turning her away from Reilly Pecans and leading her astray to the rodeo circuit.

Sure, he liked Luc. Everyone liked Luc. But he also thought he was a man without a plan. He'd told her more than once that Lucas Morgan needed to settle down, stop being a jokester, and claim his place as part owner of the very successful Lazy M cattle ranch.

Her father was wrong, Luc had a plan and once the bank loan was approved, they'd be able to share that plan. That is, if he remembered.

Luc had a single-minded need to prove himself, and he intended to do that by opening a riding school and rodeo training facility on the ranch when he retired in January. Though she never really understood what drove Luc, she immediately knew she wanted in on the venture.

Rodeo was a young person's sport, and at thirty-two, she was already thinking about a future beyond the circuit, though she hadn't shared those thoughts with anyone but Luc.

Harper was ready for a future where she was her own boss. Not just another barrel racer or the daughter of the CEO of Reilly Pecans. She was also ready to start thinking about settling down and maybe having a family.

It had taken her months to get Luc to see past his ego long enough to convince him to let her partner with him on his plan. Come January, they'd both retire.

After all, with her skills in barrel racing and team roping, and his background and reputation in saddle bronc riding, they could combine their talent and double the potential of a training school.

Once Luc had agreed, she'd wasted no time getting the paperwork together and contacting the bank to present their strategy in hopes of funding.

They'd been turned down the first time but, unwilling to take no for an answer, and unbeknownst to Luc, Harper had resubmitted the paperwork. She'd planned to explain to Luc over dinner how she'd tweaked the financials to ensure approval this time.

The dinner that never was.

Her breath caught in her throat. Would he remember what had already been set in motion? Should she even discuss the venture with him after the doctor's warning about stress? The last thing she wanted was to endanger the healing process.

Harper slowed down as she approached the facility. Surrounded by a chain-link fence, the gated entrance to the parking lot was open. She drove through, parked, and headed to the small office.

"Hi. I'm here to pick up a truck," Harper announced.

A female clerk looked up. "Are you the registered owner?"

"No. He's in the hospital. I have a notarized letter and all the required documents. I also brought cash for the fee." Harper slid the paperwork across the counter.

"Cash. Now you're talking my language." The woman shuffled the papers, examining each one before she started typing on a keyboard. "Says here the vehicle needs to be towed."

"Yes. Farley's Towing out of Homestead Pass will pick it up today."

"The gates are locked at five sharp. If the tow isn't here and gone before then, you'll owe for another day."

"They'll be here shortly."

The clerk offered a short nod and slid the keys, attached to a tag, across the counter. "Space sixteen."

"Thank you."

The August heat radiated from the asphalt parking lot as she strode to space sixteen. Harper assessed the truck from all angles and shook her head.

Luc spent a ridiculous amount of time washing and waxing the dually, which he'd paid for in cash from his winnings last year. He was going to be one upset cowboy when he saw his baby.

In her opinion, the insurance adjuster would consider it totaled. Still, it had to be removed from the impound lot either way. Harper opened the driver's-side door wide enough to release the heat and stepped back for a moment. Then she searched for his phone beneath the driver's seat, without success.

A peek into the cab's back seat revealed his duffel, a pair of boots, a saddle and riding tack. Harper grabbed everything and put it on the ground. Luc's duffel was open, the contents a jumble of clothes scattered with glass. She'd empty the glass out before she transferred his belongings her truck.

She moved to search the passenger seat, which was also decorated with a layer of glass. She pulled a bandana from her purse and wiped the upholstery. After emptying the glove box, she carefully reached into the space beneath the center console cupholder.

*Ugh.* Wet carpet, an overturned disposable coffee cup and, yes, Luc's phone. His very wet phone. Harper retrieved the cell, wiped it off, and examined the cracked screen. She played with the buttons for a minute, attempting to reboot the device. When that didn't work, she removed and reinserted the SIM card. Still no sign of life.

She gave up and gathered Luc's belongings. Making several trips, she hauled his tack, boots and saddle to her truck.

At the rumble of an engine, she turned to see a Farley Towing truck enter the yard. Les Farley jump from his vehicle and look around.

"Hey, Les." Harper waved and crossed the parking lot. "Thanks for making the drive." She knew it was a big deal that Lester H. Farley himself had driven clear from Homestead Pass.

"Oh, I owe Gus Morgan more than a couple favors. This will make us about even."

As he spoke, the passenger door of the tow truck opened and a pretty blonde stepped down. When she cleared the door, Harley recognize the woman. Kit Farley Edwards. Les's oldest daughter and Harper's friend from childhood. A very pregnant friend.

"Kit?" Harper exclaimed. "You're pregnant?" Kit's was one of the many weddings Harper had attended over the last few years. It seemed everyone was getting married. Everyone but her.

Kit's smile lit up her face and she grinned with a glance at her father. "Yes. Due at the end of summer. First grandchild for my dad."

Les pushed back his worn ball cap and beamed at the words.

"Congratulations. I'm so happy for you. What are you doing back in Oklahoma?" Harper asked.

"Joe accepted a position teaching at the high school, so we packed up and left Arizona at the end of the school year.

"That's wonderful. Let me know when the baby shower is. I definitely want to attend."

"My mother-in-law will send the invitations out soon."

"Perfect." Harper frowned. "What are you doing out with your father today?"

"Joe had a training seminar, so Dad took me to Oklahoma City to pick up a crib. When the call came in, I came along for the ride."

Harper nodded. Kit had gotten married eighteen months ago and now had a baby on the way. The bliss on her face said it all, and Harper couldn't deny her envy.

"Where's Luc's truck?" Les asked.

"The black one, there all by itself," Harper said.

Les strode across the parking lot, leaving Kit and Harper alone.

"How is Lucas?" Kit asked. "His accident is all everyone's talking about in town."

"Improving. Some memory issues, but Lucas is strong and stubborn. He's on the road to recovery."

Kit put a hand on Harper's arm. "We'll be praying."

Harper nodded. The heartfelt words staved off the despair of not knowing what the future held. "Thanks, Kit."

The other woman cocked her head. "I always thought that when Luc eventually settled down it would be with you."

"I, um…" Harper swallowed, unsure what to say.

"Whoa!" Les interrupted, sparing Harper from answering her friend.

Grimacing, he removed his cap and slapped it back on his balding head. "That truck is in bad shape."

"Yes. The insurance company said someone will be out to your place to assess the damage tomorrow."

Harper handed over the keys. "I sure appreciate this, Les."

"No problem. Friends take care of each other."

Harper and Kit stood to the side as the rollback tow truck backed up to the black dually. Once Les connected the winch, it only took a short time to load the disabled vehicle and lock down the wheels.

"Looks like he's about done," Kit said.

"I'll be sure to call you now that I know you're back." Harper hugged her friend.

"Are you home for a while as well?" Kit asked.

"Probably," Harper said. She wasn't going anywhere until Luc recovered, though she wasn't sure what that looked like.

Harper's cell buzzed as she waved at the departing tow truck. She reached into her pocket and glanced at the caller ID. Gus Morgan?

"Gus. Is everything all right?"

"This is Lucas. Gramps lent me his phone. We're halfway home. I thought I'd check and see how you were doing."

Lucas.

Images of the Kit's swollen belly flashed through her mind. Longing pressed on Harper's heart.

"Harper? You still there?"

"I'm here." Her voice cracked with emotion.

"You sound sort of odd."

"Do I? No, I'm fine."

"Everything go okay with the truck?"

"Yes, Les was here, and your truck is on its way home. I grabbed all your stuff, too."

"Thanks. Any chance you found my phone?"

"I did. Unfortunately, the phone bit the bullet."

"Bummer." He sighed. "Thanks for doing all that."

The muffled sound of Gus's voice could be heard in the background.

"Gramps says he owes you Sunday dinner."

"Tell Gus thank you." She hesitated, there was so much more she wanted to ask him about what he remembered, but she held back.

"Are you sure everything is all right?"

"Yes. Of course."

"Okay, well, I have an appointment with a neurologist in Oklahoma City tomorrow afternoon. Trevor's wife pulled a few strings and got me in. Think you can take me?" He paused. "I know it's a big ask, but you're the only one who isn't making me claustrophobic right now."

"Absolutely." Asking her to help was a positive thing.

"Thank you." He paused. "It's a long drive, and I've a lot of questions. Maybe you can help me fill in the blanks on my life since February."

Harper rubbed the throbbing spot on her right temple as her eye twitched. Right now, she had as many questions as he did.

"Harper?"

"Yes. Sorry. Um, no problem. I'm sure I can help." Once again, she tried to focus on the positive. Maybe she could gently find out what he recalled about their joint venture and their relationship.

"I can always count on you, Harper. I appreciate that."

Yes, she'd be there for him, like she had dozens of times before. But, for the first time in her life, she began to question the wisdom of her devotion. Kit's words came back to her.

What if Luc would never be able to settle down? Was she destined to always be waiting for him?

THE VIEW FROM the front porch rocker extended all the way to the graveled entrance drive of the Lazy M Ranch and was illuminated by the full moon. Though the sun had set, the mosquitos hadn't noticed Lucas on the porch, so he continued to sit and stare into the distance.

Twice, the Good Lord had spared his life.

*Why him?*

He thought back to the last time he'd seen his parents alive. It had been late August then as well. His mother had been sitting in the truck, digging in her purse for her sunglasses. Lucas recalled that old pickup his father drove. He'd always said the vehicle's dents and scratches gave the old Ford personality.

Drew had graduated from college and had been working full-time on the ranch. Sam, then seventeen, had spent most of his summer working with a new horse. Trevor had been at junior high football practice that particular day.

Lucas hadn't made the cut for football and the endless months of July and August had been filled with long days helping on the ranch.

"Are you sure you don't want to come with us?" his father had asked Lucas one last time. "We're getting ice cream in Elk City. You could use a treat."

"No. I'm gonna stay and watch Sam practice. He promised to let me ride that mare he's training."

"Okay, but you wear a helmet. You hear?"

"I will." Excitement rushed through Lucas as he'd started for the corral. Then he remembered the watch his father had lent him this morning. Lucas had turned and called to his father, "I didn't give your watch back."

"Keep it for now. I'll collect it from you later."

Lucas had grinned. "Thanks, Dad. Love you."

"Back at you, kiddo."

His father'd waved and his mother had blown a kiss as the truck tires crunched over the gravel, and rumbled down the drive, leaving a wake of dust behind.

Lucas bowed his head and sighed. A deep ache crushed his chest, nearly sucking the air from his lungs as it always did when he remembered that day. He could barely swallow past the pain that was still so raw after all these years.

*Why, Lord?*

The creak of the screen door startled him and he turned his head to see Gramps standing on the porch, his hip on the rail.

"What are you doing out here in the dark?" his grandfather asked.

"Thinking."

"Easy there. That doc said no strenuous activity."

Lucas chuckled. "Ever think about a second career as a standup comic, Gramps?"

"Pshaw. Not nearly as much fun as harassing you and your brothers."

They were silent for minutes; the only sounds that of the ranch at night. The cattle bellowed as a horned owl hooted to the humming white noise of the air conditioner unit.

"What's out there that has your interest?" Gramps asked.

"Thinking about the folks." He paused. "Gramps, how did you make it through that time? You lost your only child. How were you so strong?"

"We were all strong in the Lord, Luc."

"No." Lucas shook his head. "I wasn't. I cried myself to sleep for a solid year.

"No shame in that." He put his hand on Lucas's shoulder. "The Lord gave me a job to do. Didn't mean I forgot my son." Gramps tapped his heart. "I carry him in here. Then and now."

Once again, silence stretched. Then Gramps gave a slight smile. "Remember how your daddy could laugh?"

Lucas nodded, finding himself smiling. "Yeah. Dad laughed until he was short of breath. I do remember that. I've forgotten lots of things, but I'll never forget that."

"There you go. Your daddy is with you. And someday we'll all be reunited." His grandfather pinned him with his gaze in the semidarkness. "What's eating at you?"

"I want to make Dad proud, and I feel like I'll never get there." The words spilled out of him in a rush.

"You're thirty-six. What's the hurry?"

"Gramps, my brothers have already made something of themselves. This accident has made my path to where God wants me so convoluted, even I'm not sure where I'm headed." Lucas made a face, thinking about the training school he'd hoped to open next year. A training school in honor of his father.

"All you gotta do is keep your eye on your Maker, son. I learned a long time ago not to put boundaries on what God can do in my life."

"Am I?"

"Sure you are. This accident don't mean nothing in the grand scheme of things."

There was silence between them for minutes, though the katydids continued to fill the night.

"Gramps, do you ever think things would have been different if I'd gone with them that day?" Luc finally asked.

His grandfather sucked in a breath and stumbled a step. "Playing what-if is a bad idea." Gus turned and stared at him.

"They wanted me to go. Maybe I could have done something."

"There's nothing you could have done, son. It was a drunk driver. Plain and simple." He shook his head, suddenly looking his eighty-four years. "All this time, you've had that bottled up inside you?"

"Hitting that deer. Losing my memory. Realizing I slipped by death again… It's made me think about my life. Why was I spared?" Lucas shrugged. "If He has a plan, I want to get things right."

"Relax. You're doing fine. Just keep taking the next step. You'll get to where He wants you to be if you keep listening to that still-small voice."

"I sure hope so, Gramps. I sure hope so."

"Getting late, and I need my beauty sleep," his grandfather said.

"I'll be in shortly. I have an early morning as well. Harper is driving me to OKC for my neurology appointment."

"We're blessed to have Harper in our lives. Hope you know that."

Lucas cocked his head to look at his grandfather. "Why do you say it like that?"

"Like what?"

"Like I'm two cans short of a six-pack."

Gramps chuckled. "You said it, not me. Don't overlook what's right in front of your eyes, Lucas."

The door bounced softly and creaked again before it closed behind Gramps.

Lucas stared into the distance once again, mulling his grandfather's parting words. Right in front of his eyes?

He eased up from the chair. Yeah, he was blessed to have Harper Reilly in his life. He'd never take his best friend for granted.

"I REALLY APPRECIATE you taking me to this appointment." Lucas gingerly pulled on his seat belt, careful not to disturb his healing ribs. He looked over at Harper in the driver's seat of her truck and shrugged. "Not sure why there's such a rush to get me in here. This doctor didn't tell me anything new. I'm supposed to come back in two weeks. That'll be September."

"Great. I can take you if you stop thanking me." She glanced over her shoulder, signaled, and pulled into traffic.

"I can't help it. I'm grateful." He released a breath of frustration. "And I don't know why I can't drive. It's an hour and forty-five minutes each way. I hate inconveniencing you like this."

"Luc, you have to take this seriously. You've had a traumatic brain injury. What if you're driving and you have vision issues? Or a seizure?"

"Oh, I'm taking it seriously. All I can think about is that I can't remember over six months of my life and can't get on a horse." He heaved a sigh. Life as he knew it was officially over.

"This is only temporary," Harper said.

"Harper…" His voice dropped. "It's possible it could be permanent. I may never remember, and I might never get medical clearance to return to the circuit."

When she didn't answer, he looked over at her. Harper's hands were tight on the steering wheel and her face had paled.

"I'm sorry," he murmured.

"Why are you apologizing? You haven't done anything wrong," she said.

"I'm whining." He sighed again. "Nobody likes a whiny cowboy."

"Did the doctor say anything encouraging?"

"I guess. We talked about what I can do." He began to count on his fingers. "I can help Trevor with the Kids Day Event. I can paint and work in the garden. Fishing is allowed. Oh, and I can bake." He laughed and then groaned at the pain it caused. "Is that hilarious or what?"

His high-octane life was no more, and now he was reduced to baking cookies. He'd cry if the situation weren't so laughable.

"That's all he said?"

"He said I might experience emotional outbursts." Lucas chuckled. "Would this qualify as an emotional outburst?"

Harper's lips twitched. "Nope. You'll have to try harder." She shot him a quick glance.

Lucas nearly laughed out loud. Harper would let him vent, but she wasn't going to help him throw a pity party. And she was right. That would get them nowhere fast.

"How's the headache?" she asked.

"Comes and goes. Currently present. Doc said it could last up to a year or longer." He looked at her. "More good news, right?"

"You're alive and in one piece. That would be the good news."

"Yeah. One piece," Lucas murmured. "One piece who's missing more than half a year of his memories and has no idea what he's going to do with the rest of his life. I knew I was heading toward retirement, but this wasn't how I saw things shaking out. There's no way I can start a rodeo training school in my current condition. As it stands, I've been barred from riding a horse."

"You don't have to do it alone. I'm here."

"We already talked about that. You're a rising star. You can't retire now. Besides, I want to do this without you propping me up." Without anyone propping him up, for that matter. People had coddled him ever since his folks died. He'd started on the circuit to prove himself. Lucas felt the same way about the training school.

"Luc, I'm retiring in January. Period. I may hit the circuit in my spare time, but I'm ready for the next chapter of my life."

"Since when?"

"Since we already discussed this."

"We have?"

"Let's change the subject for now. Okay? The doctor said not to push yourself to recall."

He glanced over at Harper. Once again, her jaw was set and she had a death grip on the steering wheel. "You okay?"

"Yes. Why wouldn't I be?"

"I don't know." Lucas paused. "You seem…upset."

"I'm fine."

Silence stretched for a moment as he tried to figure out what was going on. It wasn't nothing. He suspected her reticence had something to do with the missing pieces of his life.

"Maybe this would be a good time for you to tell me what I've been doing since early February," he said.

Harper sighed and gestured to the glove box. "Open that up and grab the papers on top."

Lucas reached inside and removed the neatly folded sheets. "What is this?"

"One page for each month since February. I wasn't sure what the last thing you recall is, so I went back to a few days before we arrived in Fort Worth last February."

"I do remember Fort Worth. We pulled in on Sunday." He waved the papers. "This is a great place to start. Thank you."

"You're welcome. You hit close to forty events in the last six months. I didn't do nearly as many."

"Huh? Did I? I hope my bank account shows I'm in the black if I was that busy." His eyes rounded as he flipped the pages. "My placements are here too."

"I looked them up last night."

"You did? Wow. This is above and beyond." He glanced at her and then down at the paperwork again. "Thank you, Harp."

"You're welcome. I thought that if you remember the circuit, it might be easier to recall...other things."

"What 'other things'?"

Harper shrugged. "I was generalizing."

"What's this?" he asked, tapping the paper. "You even noted where we ate on the road?" Lucas laughed. "Apparently, you twisted my arm and got me to go to that horrible Tex-Mex place again?"

"It's not horrible." Her lips twitched. "They have the best chili relleno in three states."

Lucas chuckled. "So you say."

"You remember the restaurant. That's good."

"You're right. That is good. Too bad I don't recall eating there on this occasion." He looked at her. "What did I order?"

She laughed, and it was a soft, sweet melody. Ah, Harper's laugh. The sound buoyed him. She was always upbeat, even when he was fighting demons. "What you always order," she said.

"Fish tacos." They answered at the same time, and he laughed again.

Lucas examined the rest of the notations for February, pushing past the throbbing of his head. "Not bad. I took the number two spot, right behind Jasper Leonard. Respectable standings for an old guy."

"You're not an old guy," she said. "Look at each month—you can see how you're killing it."

"Aw, thanks. You've always been my biggest cheerleader." Gramps was right. He was blessed to have Harper in his life.

"Because you're one of the best saddle bronc riders out there, Luc."

*Used to be,* Lucas mentally corrected. He turned the pages slowly. "What happened in April?"

"I'm not sure what your schedule was since I was home much of the month. Gram had surgery."

"Surgery? What for?"

"She broke her hip. Trevor's wife, Hope, managed her home care for a while. She didn't bounce back like your grandfather did after his hip surgery," Harper continued.

"Her hip. Seems there's a lot of that going around." Gramps had hip replacement surgery over a year ago as well. "How's she doing?"

"We lost her, Luc."

Lucas snapped to attention, his heart hammering. "Bettie is gone?" He'd had a soft spot in his heart for Harper's maternal grandmother. The woman had insisted that he call her Bettie, and she'd always sent Harper off with home-baked treats for him.

He reached over and squeezed her hand on the steering wheel. "I'm so sorry. I'll miss Bettie. She was the best." He couldn't imagine losing his grandfather. Lucas stared at Harper. "Did I at least attend the funeral?"

"You did." Harper swallowed, her eyes glassy with unshed tears.

"I'm so sorry, Harp."

He'd gone to the funeral and couldn't even remember. How lousy was that?

Lucas stared silently at the papers in his lap. After the news about Bettie, his focus was shot. He stopped and closed his eyes for a moment. "I'm not doing too well with reading right now, but I appreciate you putting this together."

"No problem." She slipped on her sunglasses.

"Anything else important happen that I ought to know about?"

"I…um…" She turned her head for a quick second and then stared straight ahead, her lips a thin line.

Lucas stared at her profile. The mahogany-brown tresses, highlighted naturally with red, were pulled back into a low ponytail. It was difficult to see her dark moss-green eyes behind the opaque sunglasses perched on her nose.

Moments like this, he appreciated how beautiful she was. Inside and out. Then he'd have to remind himself that they were friends.

Just friends.

Girlfriends came and went. But friends were forever, and he wanted Harper in his life forever.

"Is that a no?" he asked when she didn't answer.

Harper nodded, her eyes firmly fixed on the road.

Goose bumps ran down his arms and his gut said something was up. Yep, they'd been friends long enough for him to recognize the signs of trouble brewing. All he had to do was wait it out.

Trouble was, he suspected it had something to do with his missing memories. The more he thought about what it could be, the more his head hurt.

*Not good, Morgan.*

Not good at all.

# CHAPTER THREE

"HARPER ELIZABETH REILLY is in the kitchen."

Harper turned from the stove to see her father enter the room. Tall, with a build like a wrestler and a mop of red hair graying at the temples, Colin Reilly was an intimidating sight unless you looked close enough to see the laughing green eyes.

As the youngest of the three Reilly daughters, Harper had a special relationship with her father. She'd always been daddy's little girl.

"Are you making your famous chicken casserole for lunch?" he asked.

"No. This is to take to the Lazy M."

He opened a cupboard and grabbed a glass. "How's Lucas?"

"Not much has changed. He saw the neurologist yesterday. You know how much energy Luc has. Being sidelined is challenging."

"Your mother and I are praying for him."

"Thanks, Dad. Where is Mom, anyhow?"

"In her studio."

"What's she working on?" Harper had learned as a child that the downside of having Maureen Reilly, prominent sculptress, as a mother was that she couldn't be disturbed during studio hours unless it involved broken bones or blood.

"Your mother is completing a piece commissioned by a bank in Tulsa."

"That's impressive."

"It is." He filled his glass with water and then turned from the sink. "How long will you be home?"

"It depends on Luc's recovery."

"Luc's recovery." Her father was silent for a moment. Then he cleared his throat. "Your dear mother warned me to keep my mouth closed. But you're my baby girl, and I can't stand by and let you get hurt."

"Dad, please," Harper groaned. "Not another lecture about waiting around for Luc. We're friends. That's all."

That was the truth. The bitter truth.

"Now, Harper, I like Lucas. You know that. I just don't understand why a smart gal like you has followed that boy around for over twenty years."

*Here we go again.*

Annoyed, she turned back to the stove and added salt and pepper to the pan of sizzling chicken with a tad bit of force. "I've only known him for fourteen years."

"Huh. It sure seems like twenty years."

"I'm four years younger than he is. We went to different colleges. When I was in grad school, he'd gotten his business degree and hit the circuit full-time. It's not like I've been his shadow all my life."

"You have a marketing degree, but you tossed that aside to race a horse around barrels and follow Lucas around the country."

"Luc and I have different schedules. I don't follow him around." Indignation rose again and she dared to meet her father's gaze head-on. "Besides, I've made a nice living thanks to the rodeo. Far more than I would have in a midlevel marketing position."

She didn't like to brag, but she'd managed to parlay barrel racing into some lucrative ventures. There'd been magazine interviews and, last year, she'd been part of an endorsement deal with a popular women's boot line.

"I'd expect nothing less." He saluted her with his glass. "You're a Reilly. I'm proud of your horsemanship skills. But I paid for all those private riding lessons because I thought it was a hobby. Not a career path."

"It's what I enjoy doing right now. Don't you want me to be happy?"

"Apples and oranges. Of course, I want you to be happy. But you've run out of excuses, Harper."

*"Dad."* She knew what was coming next. Her father was about to launch into how she'd evaded what her parents believed was her destiny.

"You're home, and we're about to have an opening in the marketing department. And it isn't a midlevel position. How's that for a coincidence?"

Harper took a deep breath. Her father was a self-made man who had built the Reilly Pecans empire from nothing, and he expected his children to participate in the family business and give back to the community, as he did.

"Dad, I'm home because Luc is hurt. No other reason."

"I appreciate your concern for Lucas's welfare, but your mother and I raised you to make decisions about your future based on what's right for you as an independent young woman."

She opened her mouth to protest and he held up a hand.

"I've been upfront about my expectations, and I've given you far more leeway than your sisters. But it's time."

Time. Well, that was all well and fine for her sisters, who were delighted at the doors Reilly Pecans had opened for them. Both were married and happily settled into corporate life. Her oldest sister, by ten years, Madeline, a senior vice president, managed the various value-added products divisions of Reilly Pecans. Dana, five years Harper's senior, was another vice president. Of what, Harper couldn't recall.

The corporate office for Reilly Pecans was a five-minute drive from Maddy's home and Dana's condo in Oklahoma City. OK City would be an hour-and-forty-minute drive for Harper from Homestead Pass. She'd be forced to move if she took the job. That meant finding a place to board her horse too.

Retiring from the rodeo circuit was definitely on her radar. But going directly from a saddle to a desk chair was not part of her plan.

Harper grimaced. "You want me to sit in an office in Oklahoma City and market pecans."

Her father pulled out a kitchen chair and sat down at the table. "I want you to market your family business."

Pecans. Harper couldn't escape them.

"And you don't have to sit in an office all day," her father continued. "Plenty of my employees are hybrid. I'm hybrid. You'd know that if you paid attention."

She looked at her father. "Dad, I—"

He raised a palm. "Pecans have been good to you, Harper. They bought this house. The biggest house in Homestead Pass. Pecans fed our family. Paid for college, your horses, and those lessons. We're more than blessed because of those orchards." Her father offered a sad smile. "There was a time when you were proud of the business."

"I am proud." Harper lifted the lid on a pan on the back burner and stirred the cream sauce. "Do we have to discuss this now?"

"Take a guess how many résumés have already come in for the position I want you to fill."

Apparently, they did have to have this discussion now. She gave a slow shake of her head as her father kept talking.

"Over fifty, Harper. Fifty on the rumor that I'll have an opening when one of our employees goes on maternity leave in November."

"How long would this arrangement be?"

He took a long drink of water and then met her gaze. "Six

months. Just like your sisters. We'll start you as an intern learning from the ground up. Then ease you into the marketing position."

"Six months!" She blinked. "That's through February. Next year." Harper envisioned the life being sucked from her.

"Didn't you just say you were sticking around for Lucas? This seems like the perfect time to fulfill your obligation to your family." He narrowed his eyes. "Unless you have other plans."

Harper hesitated.

"As a matter of fact, I'm exploring several options," she said.

That was the truth. She'd heard through the circuit grapevine that she had been shortlisted for a big endorsement deal. Nothing concrete yet. Then there was the training school. Working with Luc, training riders, was her real passion. But that option was on hold until the bank approved the loan, and she could talk to Luc about the plans already in motion. Plans he didn't recall and might not be so happy about the second time around.

"Be that as it may, I want you to give the family business a shot. That was our arrangement."

"An arrangement made when I was a kid."

"You were eighteen and headed to college, as I recall. You understood the expectations. I'm asking no more of you than I did your sisters. Give the business a chance. If it isn't a good fit, you're free to step away."

"Are you saying that if I do a stint with Reilly Pecans and decide to go back to the circuit or any other career path, I'd have your blessing?"

"Absolutely." He offered a tender smile that reminded her that despite their differences of opinion, she loved her father dearly.

"I look at you, Harper, and I see potential. You can do anything. *Anything.*"

When he paused, Harper realized he was about to deliver the final blow.

"Maybe if you came to work for the company, you'd meet someone besides cowboys."

There it was. Arrow to the heart. Complete disapproval of the man she cared for.

Wounded, Harper turned to the stove. She added the browned chicken to a casserole dish before carefully pouring the sauce over the pieces. Silence stretched as she opened the oven and slid the baking dish inside.

"You hate the business that much?" her father asked quietly. Sadness laced his voice.

"Not at all. I haven't missed a harvest since I was six years old. That's the part of the business I enjoy. Not management."

"We can always find a place for you driving a tractor."

Harper chuckled and looked at him. "I don't doubt that."

"Your mother and I love you and want only the best for you." He paused. "This is an opportunity to secure your future."

His phone rang, saving her from responding. He glanced at his cell and cocked his head toward the hall. "I have to take this. Then we can finish this conversation."

Harper swallowed past the lump in her throat. The pragmatist in her whispered that her father had made some valid points. There was no escaping the fact that she wasn't getting any younger. Her days on the circuit were numbered. And now? Now, Lucas didn't recall that they'd created a plan for their future. Harper worked to push away the despair. Didn't the Lord have a hand on her?

She shook her head, refusing to allow circumstances to get her down. Her thoughts went to the flood story her father had once told her. There was a man sitting on a roof as the floodwaters rose. A boat and a helicopter came by to save him, but the man dismissed them as he waited on God. The man drowned and found himself standing before the Lord. It was the Lord who had sent the boat and the helicopter.

Maybe she ought to at least check out the position with Reilly Pecans. She didn't want to find herself with zero options. Even as the thought crossed her mind, a part of her cringed at the idea of even a day not spent out in the sunshine.

Minutes later, her father stepped back into the kitchen with expectation on his face. "Where were we?"

"Marketing Reilly Pecans."

"And your answer?"

"Two months. I'll know by the time your marketing person leaves what I want to do. And I'll only commit if I have the flexibility I'll need if Luc needs my assistance with medical appointments."

Two months was plenty of time to fulfill her obligation to give Reilly Pecans a chance, and hopefully enough time to bring Luc up to date on the training center plans without pushing him to remember.

Her father arched a brow, clearly surprised. "I'll consider your offer if you go into this with a smile on your face instead of acting like there's a noose around your neck."

Harper chuckled. "You have a deal."

The conversation with her father echoed as Harper drove to the Lazy M Ranch. This was not how she'd expected the last quarter of the year to unfold. She and Lucas were back to square one, thanks to his accident, and pecans were about to unseat her dreams.

Luc was part of those dreams, and it pained her to realize that everything she wanted had been within reach and was now very uncertain.

She'd met Luc Morgan when she was a senior in high school, and he'd come to talk to the graduating class at Homestead Pass High School.

His speech had been about going after your passion in life. Harper had taken his words to heart, knowing that despite the trajectory her parents planned for her, what she really wanted was a career in professional rodeo. She'd dared to approach him after the talk and ask for pointers on following that dream.

He'd encouraged her to complete college, as he had, and to sign up for events in her spare time. Sage advice that she'd followed.

That had started her segue to the circuit and her infatuation with the tall, charming cowboy. With Luc's career guidance, she'd entered competitions on the weekends and during college breaks. And they'd become friends. Good friends.

She shook her head.

*Good friends.*

The words weren't nearly as satisfying as they used to be.

Harper pulled up to the Morgan ranch house. She juggled the casserole in one hand and a gift bag in the other and pressed the doorbell. After minutes, there was no response.

Her soft knock on the door was promptly answered by Bess Lowder, the Morgan family cook and housekeeper. The woman was responsible for managing the Lazy M household since Luc's parents' passing. Dressed in her usual denim shirt and rolled-up blue jeans uniform, Bess held open the screen door.

"You don't need to knock, sweetie. You're just like family. Come on in."

Harper glanced in the living room as they moved down the hall in the direction of the kitchen. She stopped and did a double take. Every single surface was filled with plants and flowers. There were artful arrangements, freshly cut flowers, plants with big bows, even containers of succulents. The almost sickly scent of flowers overwhelmed Harper. She coughed and stepped away from the room. "What happened?"

"Oh that. All for Lucas. In the words of Gus Morgan, 'this place has been busier than a twofer sale at the Green Apple Grocery.'" She chuckled. "Smells like a flower shop as well."

"It does," Harper said.

Bess took the casserole from Harper's hands and dipped her head toward the kitchen. "I'll show you what else they brought." She opened the refrigerator door and Harper nearly gasped. Every inch was stuffed with casserole dishes and covered bowls. Glass and plastic storage containers lined the normally clutter-free countertop. Each had a label on top.

Taking a step closer to the counter, Harper read one of the labels. "Claire Talmadge? He dated her in college. I thought she was in New York City."

"Claire had her mother drop that off with a note that promised she'd be in town soon to see Lucas." Bess practically rolled her eyes.

The Homestead Pass grapevine whispered that Claire had asked Lucas to marry her the night of college graduation. Harper had never actually verified the validity of that story. Now she wondered, and her stomach knotted at the thought. She and Luc didn't cross the line to discuss personal relationships after a few missteps in the past.

More and more, Harper was beginning to think she had imagined the shift in her relationship with Luc.

Humiliation raced over Harper. "Who else?" she asked.

"Oh, honey, I have a list." Bess wedged Harper's casserole into the fridge and then turned to the counter. She opened a drawer and pulled out a legal pad. "I had to start documenting everything so that I can return the containers to the right gals."

"Gals? All this is from Luc's female friends?" Stunned, Harper took the legal pad and skimmed the list before placing it on the counter.

Bess nodded. "Former girlfriends, except for Ben at the barber shop."

Harper glanced around. "Where is Luc?"

"It's been a nonstop parade here since sunrise, which I suspect is due to Gus initiating the Homestead Pass chatter line yesterday."

"Is Luc okay?"

"Tired, is all. He's trying way too hard to figure out what happened between now and last February."

"But the doctor warned him about that."

"Yes. Gus told me about the doc's admonition." Bess clucked her tongue. "I called Trevor's wife, and she came by, checked his vital signs and did a quick neurological exam. She prescribed disconnecting the doorbell followed by a nap. That went over as well as you can imagine."

"Uh-oh."

"Yes. There may have been bribing with the promise of cinnamon rolls."

"Oh, Bess. I'm so sorry. I should have called first."

Bess gave a shake of her head, setting the gray curls in. "Nonsense. I told you. You're family." She smiled and ran a hand through her gray curls. "Gus says you're coming to Sunday dinner, right?"

"I hate to impose."

"I'm not here on Sundays, so it's not an imposition." She chuckled. "Olivia usually cooks." Sam's wife was a local chef and Luc had often raved about her cooking. "But not this week. There's too much food in this house that needs to be eaten."

"Good point." Harper held up the small bag in her hand. "I'll leave this for Lucas. It's that black licorice he likes so much. I stopped at the Hitching Post yesterday and picked up their last two packages."

"You are the sweetest."

A sharp knock at the front door had them both turning.

"More company. I'd better get that."

Harper scanned the kitchen counter when Bess left. A sinking feeling began in the pit of her stomach.

Once again, she questioned whether she had read the situation between herself and Luc all wrong. She thought what she'd seen in his eyes had meant there was something special between them. Now she wasn't certain of anything.

Harper eyed the names on the list again. Twenty women. She had zero intention of becoming number twenty-one on this list.

It occurred to her that her father was right about one thing. She knew better than to pin her dreams on a man. It was time to take back the reins to her future and fight for what she'd worked so hard for.

"FIVE THOUSAND DOLLARS!" Lucas put a hand to his aching head. "Are you sure? Maybe we should call the bank."

"Easy there," Sam said. "You're not supposed to get excited. As for the bank, it's after five p.m. The bank is closed."

Closed. Right. He should have remembered that.

After all his visitors yesterday, followed by mandatory napping, Lucas was ready to get on with his life, however limited it might be. An hour ago, he'd sat down behind the computer in the office at the Lazy M Ranch's main house to review his checking and savings account and realized the computer screen was only making his head throb and his vision blur. When he'd called Sam, who held the distinction of being a part-time accountant, his brother had come right over.

"What did I do with five grand?" Lucas paced back and forth across the hardwood floor of the office.

"I'm sure there's a simple answer. We'll laugh once we figure it out."

"Sam, you just reviewed my bank records. I withdrew five thousand bucks and I don't know why. I am not laughing."

"I'll lend you money if you need it. Now relax."

"Thanks, but I don't want your money and that doesn't help me figure out what happened." He rubbed his temple. "Why didn't I use my credit card?"

"Maybe you didn't want to max it out. Don't you use the credit card on the road?"

"Fair conclusion," Lucas agreed.

"It's showing as a withdrawal, but you didn't write a check. My guess is that you paid for something with a cashier's check." Sam continued to stare at the bank statement on the screen. "The only way to track that is to call the issuing bank. We can't do that until Monday."

Lucas dropped into one of the wingback chairs in the office. "What did I buy with five thousand bucks?"

"You've been talking about getting a trailer with living quarters."

"A trailer." Lucas perked up. "You're right. I have been talking about a trailer for a long time, so maybe I put a down payment on one." He scowled. "So where's the trailer?"

Sam shrugged. "Could be in Lawton. Harper would know."

"Okay, so if we go with that scenario, where's my copy of the cashier's check?" Lucas cocked his head and looked at his brother.

"Have you checked your wallet?"

He pulled out his worn, brown-leather wallet and examined all the folds and crevices. "Nothing but a receipt for burgers."

"What about the Wranglers you wore to the hospital?" Sam asked.

"I threw them in the washing machine when I got home, after I showered." He knit his brows together thinking. "Then I put them in the dryer. Haven't seen them since."

"I saw Bess folding towels when I came in," Sam said.

"Bess!" Lucas called. He scrambled out the door and down the stairs, with Sam thundering right behind him. At the bottom of the stairs, Lucas nearly collided with the housekeeper. He put a hand on her arm to steady them both.

"Slow down! Those stairs aren't a rodeo chute," Bess warned. "And you're supposed to be resting."

"Have you seen my laundry?" Lucas asked.

The housekeeper eyed him with a chuckle. "This is a laundry emergency?"

"Yes, ma'am," he said. "In a manner of speaking,"

"I couldn't dry the towels with your clothes in the dryer, so I pulled them out. Goodness, that was three days ago. They're still in a basket on top of the washer, waiting for you."

Bess did more than her job description spelled out, but she wisely never set foot in Lucas's room. Said no matter what she did, his room looked like a tornado hit the place the next day.

She wasn't wrong.

"Don't suppose you found anything unusual in the dryer?" Sam asked.

"Stuff that was in my pocket," Lucas added.

"Stuff in your pocket has been a given with your laundry since you were fourteen years old, Lucas." Bess smiled fondly. "There's a twenty-dollar bill, some change and a receipt that got washed." She pointed to the laundry room.

"A receipt!" Lucas pressed a kiss to her cheek. "I love you, Bess."

She eyed him suspiciously. "It's laundry."

"Today it's an answer to prayer," Sam said.

Racing into the laundry room, Lucas grabbed the basket and then headed for the kitchen. Hopefully, they'd solve the mystery of the missing money.

When he put the laundry on the kitchen table, Sam plucked the twenty off the pile while Lucas grabbed the folded piece of paper.

"You took my money."

"My accounting fee," Sam said. "Now, easy with that paper. Watch what you're doing. Maybe you should use tweezers."

"Have you got tweezers?" Lucas pulled open the kitchen drawers one after another, rattling utensils, before he closed each drawer quickly. "Nothing."

Sam leaned close. "Just be careful."

Lucas slowly unfolded the rectangle until it was in two pieces. "What's that say?"

"It's your portion of the cashier's check, all right. The ink's pretty faded, but it looks like it says Keller's Family Jeweler in Lawton, Oklahoma."

"Keller's Family Jeweler." Lucas could barely get the words out.

"Bingo," Sam said. "Looks to me like you bought jewelry."

"Where's the jewelry, and the box, and the paperwork that usually comes with a five-thousand-dollar piece of bling?" Lucas pulled out a chair and sat, his head spinning. "Sam, do you think it's a ring? Like an engagement ring?"

Nah, that couldn't be right. He would remember something like that.

He stared at his brother. "Could I have really asked someone to marry me?"

"Far-fetched as it may sound, I can't think of another plausible conclusion," Sam said. "Looks like you fell in love, little brother."

Lucas released a whoosh of air as reality hit like a punch to the gut. "Somewhere out there is a woman who has that ring, and I don't have a clue who she might be."

"Surely, Harper will know. Ask her."

"No way. That's not the kind of humiliation a fella goes looking for. Besides, Harper and I have a strict policy about mixing personal stuff into our friendship. I crossed the line once and almost ruined everything."

"What do you mean?"

"A couple of years ago, she dated some yahoo bull rider. They broke up and I let her cry on my shoulder and told her what I thought of him." He grimaced. "Big mistake. The next week, they patched things up, and she was mad at me for bad-mouthing him. She didn't speak to me for a month."

"That's not enough reason not to talk to her about this."

"Oh, there's more. I asked Harper's advice when I dated the Pawnee rodeo queen last year. Out of the blue, she blew up and kicked me out of her trailer. Told me if I couldn't see that the woman was only interested in changing her name to Mrs. Lucas Morgan then I was too dumb for her to be friends with." He whistled. "That was something else. Nope. I care too much about our friendship to risk alienating her with talk about another woman again."

"Fair enough," Sam returned. He glanced at the containers on the counter, turning to examine the labels. Then his brows shot up. "That's a lot of containers. From a lot of women. For the record, how many women have you dated?"

"I can't do that math. If you recall, I have retrograde amnesia. I can't remember the last six months."

"Ballpark then." Sam opened the fridge, pulled out a Dr Pepper, and flipped the tab. "How many exes can you remember?" He took a long swig from the can and eyed Lucas.

"In Homestead Pass or all together?"

"Seriously?"

"I'm a popular guy. Is that a crime?"

"Maybe." Sam counted containers. "More than five?"

Lucas raised his thumb to indicate more.

"Ten?" Sam jerked back as he said the word.

"More like a couple of dozen." He shrugged without apology. "I'm friends with all my exes. Doesn't that count?"

"You're going to have to reach out to them and see what you can find out."

"Aw, no. That will be downright embarrassing." Lucas stared at the receipt, his stomach twisting.

"Not as humiliating as it will be when your fiancée catches up with you."

"I guess I could call a couple of buddies first. If I can locate their numbers."

"Did Harper find your phone?"

"Dead."

"You know that you can pull data from a dead phone. Right?"

"No, I can't. It's an old model with a SIM card. A damaged SIM card."

"What is it? A flip phone?"

"No. Not a flip phone, wise guy."

"Well, you have the number for the jeweler. Call them on

Monday and see if you can get any information. Maybe your fiancée picked out the ring."

"Brilliant." Lucas nodded and then grimaced. He had to stop shaking his head. "This receipt is for last Saturday. I must have gone to the jeweler before the accident."

"Yep. Last Saturday in Lawton. I think you'd better find a way to ask Harper without her catching on. She knows more than you think."

"*Harper?* Wait a minute." Lucas jumped up. "Harper dropped off my saddle and clothes." He raced out of the office and up the stairs, with Sam following. "Maybe the paperwork is in my duffel."

"Slow down. You're supposed to take it easy."

"You don't walk when the house is on fire," Lucas called over his shoulder. He grabbed the duffel and turned it upside down on the bed.

His clothes fell out, followed by a leather binder.

Sam grabbed the binder. "What's this?"

"Paperwork and schedules. Stuff I need on the road."

His shaving kit plopped onto the bed, followed by a black beribboned shopping bag that landed right on top of the duffel.

"Whoa. What's that fancy bag?" Sam asked.

Lucas snatched the bag and peeked inside. His jaw sagged at the sight of a jeweler's ring box. Hands shaking, he sank to the bed and pulled out the small black-velvet box. He stared at it for a full minute, unable to open the thing.

Sam grabbed the box from his hand and flipped open the lid to reveal a sparkling engagement ring. His brother whistled long and low. "I believe they call this a marquise diamond."

"Do they?" Lucas squeaked out the question.

"How did you manage to fall in love and buy a ring without telling your family?"

Lucas leveled him with a glare. "If I knew the answer to that question, or any of the two dozen you've asked since you showed up, I wouldn't be in this predicament."

"I'm going to go over your credit card transactions. Maybe you sent flowers or something, and I can figure out who you're courting."

"Flowers. I never thought of that." He paused. "Sam, you're not going to tell anyone about this, are you?"

"Who would believe me?"

"Good point. If this gets out, I'll be the laughingstock of Homestead Pass." Lucas frowned. "Gramps can never find out."

"You're getting a little paranoid, aren't you?"

"You know what Gramps calls me? The ice cream man. Says I have a new flavor each month."

"He isn't wrong. Though I sure don't know how you manage it." Sam looked him up and down. "You need a shave and a haircut."

Lucas ran a hand over his two-day growth. Wasn't any point in being a bronc rider if he had to shave every day. "Says who?"

"Everyone." Sam chuckled. "Although maybe we should rethink that. Apparently, there's a woman out there who wants to be your wife just the way you are. Or at least you think she does."

"So where is she?" Lucas asked. Where was his almost fiancée?

"I don't know. Out of the country? Or sitting home waiting for you to call."

"I guess that's possible." He let out a breath. "It's a relief to have found the ring. All I have to do is find the woman."

"Like that's going to be easy, given your history." Sam picked up the leather binder and unzipped it. "What's this?"

"I told you. Paperwork. Nothing special."

"Maybe there's information on your mystery woman in here." His brother flipped through the papers, a frown on his face. "Luc, this is a business plan for a rodeo training school. An extremely thorough and well-executed plan. The kind you show a bank loan officer." Sam shuffled through more papers. "Yep. That's what it is. And this is a copy of the bank loan application. All six pages worth. Signed by you and Harper."

Stunned, Lucas reached for the binder. "Let me see that." His gaze landed on the date the application had been signed. It matched the time they'd been in Homestead Pass for Trevor's wedding.

What was going on here? Why hadn't Harper said something on the way home from the neurologist? He'd asked if anything important had happened.

This seemed pretty important. He'd formed an official business partnership with his best friend and couldn't remember doing so. How did that happen? The plan had always been for him to go into business solo. He'd turned down her offer to collaborate numerous times and for good reason.

The training school was his opportunity to prove himself to his family.

"Good for you," Sam said. "You've talked about retiring next year. Guess I never thought you'd actually do the deed."

Head pounding, Lucas looked at his brother. "I have no idea where these papers came from."

"You don't remember this?" Sam asked.

Lucas put a hand to his throbbing head. "I remember thinking I ought to put a plan in motion for January. I sure don't recall doing it." Once again, things felt surreal, like he was living someone else's life.

A buzz sounded and Lucas stood and pulled a cell from his pocket.

"I thought your phone bit the dust," Sam said.

"This is Gramps's cell. I've ordered one online. Should be here this week." Lucas stared at the text on the screen. "It's Harper. She's checking to see what time she should be here on Sunday."

"Sunday. Perfect. You can grill her then."

Lucas looked at his brother. "You're right. I need to figure out what's going on with this business plan."

"Business plan? I want to know about the ring. The ring that's missing a fiancée."

"Get real. I'm not going to mention the ring. Not yet."

Sam started laughing.

Lucas tucked the phone in his pocket and glared at Sam. "What's so funny?"

"It just hit me that this is exactly like the prince searching for his princess, getting women to try on glass slippers." His brother grinned. "You know. *Cinderella.*"

"You're comparing my life to a fairy tale? That's not funny at all."

"Come on, Luc. You hit your head, lost your memory, found an engagement ring in your gym bag. You have no idea who your intended is, and you're launching a business without your knowledge." Sam nodded. "Oh yeah. It is kind of funny, and it could only happen to you."

Lucas cringed at the words. His brother was right. It could only happen to him. He'd lost his memory of the last six months. A life where he'd made plans for the future that included settling down. Somehow he had to figure out exactly what had happened.

# CHAPTER FOUR

"PASS THE BROWNIES, Gramps." Lucas nodded at the plate in the middle of the kitchen table where he, Gramps and Harper still sat after his brothers and their families had departed only a short time ago.

"Not so fast." His grandfather held up a hand. "Those look mighty tasty, but they're deceiving."

"What do you mean?" Lucas cocked his head and assessed the square tin of frosted brownies.

"Son, no disrespect intended, but truth is, not all your girlfriends ought to be let loose in the kitchen." He looked at Harper, who snorted and then covered her mouth.

"They aren't my girlfriends," Lucas protested with a sharp glance at Harper. "And you can't mess up brownies."

"Ex-girlfriends then." The elder Morgan pushed the tin out of Lucas's reach and slid the plate of Bess's cinnamon rolls across the table. "Trust me on this."

Lucas examined the pastries and chose a plump roll thick with cream cheese frosting dripping down the sides over ribbons of buttery cinnamon filling. The Lazy M Ranch housekeeper had a secret recipe for cinnamon rolls that brought grown men to their knees. That included him.

In turn, Lucas slid the plate to Harper. "Here you go."

"Seriously?" She held up a hand. "I'm still full from dinner."

"I'm never full," he returned. "And did I mention that your chicken casserole was delicious?"

That was an understatement. They'd reheated half the casseroles in the refrigerator for Sunday dinner and, hands down, Harper's was the favorite.

"He's right." Gramps offered an enthusiastic nod in Harper's direction. "Obviously, present company was excluded from my comment. You aren't one of his exes."

Lucas blinked at the comment. No, she wasn't. His glance moved to Harper once again. She seemed to be preoccupied with her coffee cup.

Why was it he and Harper had never dated? At first, it was because he was her mentor, and it wouldn't be right. Now, after years as close friends, he wouldn't do anything to risk that friendship. His girlfriends lasted a few weeks at most. Harper's friendship was for a lifetime. He couldn't imagine her not being in his life. Didn't want to even think about it.

"Nice to have a meal with the entire family." Lucas put on a smile and hoped his attempt to change the subject would work.

"Sure was." Gramps shook his head. "Woo-ee. Never thought the day would come I'd have so many great-grandchildren. Drew and Sam have two each. Trevor one." He looked at Lucas. "What are you waiting for? You aren't getting any younger."

Lucas jumped up. "Would you look at the time. Didn't you say you had to call Jane, Gramps?"

His grandfather checked his watch and stood. "You're right. We best get those dishes done before Bess finds them in the morning. Olivia started the dishwasher already, so we'll have to do these by hand."

"Harper and I can handle the dishes," Lucas said.

"Harper's our guest," his grandfather protested.

"It's only a couple of mugs and dessert plates. We got it. Besides, Harp and I have a few things to discuss."

"Okay. You twisted my arm," Gramps said. "I'll excuse myself then. Jane and I have book club meeting details to finalize."

"Who's Jane?" Harper asked when his grandfather had left the room. She picked up dessert plates from the table and moved to the sink.

"Jane Smith. Retired librarian. Remember her from Homestead Pass Middle School? She manages Sam's woodcraft showroom."

"Mrs. Smith. Yes. I do remember her. She and Gus are dating?"

"I thought so, but Gramps flat-out denies any such thing. Says they've been friends for years. He claims men and women can be friends without romance." Lucas raised a brow. "I suppose so. Look at us."

"Right," Harper murmured. "Look at us."

He turned at the undertone in her response. Had he imagined it? Harper didn't play games. Generally, she was an open book. So why did he sense red flags left and right of late?

They had lots to discuss tonight, but a part of him cautioned to take it slow. Something was definitely going on with Harper.

Familiar with the Morgan kitchen, she filled the sink with a squirt of dishwashing liquid and water and began to wash the dessert plates. Her attention remained focused out the large kitchen window overlooking the front porch and gravel drive.

Lucas finished off the rest of his cinnamon roll, picked up his plate and brought it to the counter. He grabbed a towel and plucked a mug from the dish drainer. "Everything okay in your world?"

"Me?" A musing smile touched Harper's lips. She looked at him. "You're the one with a shiner and a two-inch dent on your forehead. How are you?"

"A little better every day. My ribs are healing. Doesn't hurt as much when I laugh. I'm functioning on the hope that one day—" he snapped his fingers "—all my memories will be restored."

"It's only been a week, Luc. The doctor specifically said you weren't supposed to push yourself to retrieve your memories."

"But we can talk, right?"

"Talk? Is that what you were referring to when you told Gus we have something to discuss?"

Lucas opened a cupboard and put several mugs away. "How long are you staying in Homestead Pass? You're headed to Pasadena, right?" He clucked his tongue. "I'm sorry to miss that one. They've got a nice purse."

She eyed him. "You didn't answer my question. What did you want to discuss?"

"I'll get there. This is the scenic route." He looked at her. "Cali next?"

"No. Right now, it looks like I'll be Homestead Pass for a bit."

"Why?" Contemplating her answer, Lucas dried a dish, adding it to the stack before he turned back to her. "You're not hanging around because of me, are you?"

"Yes and no." She cocked her head to meet his gaze.

"What's that mean?"

"It means that's why I'm here now. You're my friend, and I won't leave if your health is compromised."

"I appreciate that, but I don't want to stand in the way of your career."

"You aren't."

"We can agree to disagree on that point." Lucas picked up another plate from the drainer. "You said yes *and* no. What's the no?"

Her hand skimmed the water, and she pulled out two forks. "I'm interning at Reilly Pecans starting tomorrow."

"Whoa! What?" The plate he held clattered onto the counter.

"Careful, Luc."

"Interning? Mind explaining that bombshell?"

Harper sighed and pushed her sweeping bangs away from

her face with the back of her hand. "It's a Reilly rite of passage that I've been able to dodge for nine years. I may have mentioned it to you."

"I never thought you were serious about that."

"My father is very serious about Reilly Pecans." Harper sighed. "Traditionally, it's expected after college. Since I was busy with grad school and the rodeo, I dodged the bullet. Until now."

"I don't get it. Why intern?" Lucas asked.

"Because my father read me the riot act." She blew out a breath. "The plan has always been for me and my sisters to intern, fall in love with the business, and never leave." She shrugged. "You know. Happily ever after. The end."

"You agreed to this?"

"Agreed? If only it were that simple." She gave a small chuckle. "My sisters complied long ago. I don't have much choice. I'm home, and my father took the opportunity to remind me of my obligation."

"This is my fault," he said. "You're home because of me."

Harper waved a hand. "Not at all. This was inevitable. Besides, it could be worse. I talked him down from six months to two."

"What about competing?"

"On hold for now. I told you, I'm inching toward retirement."

"Give me a break," he groaned. "You're only thirty-two. You're not eligible for the senior category yet. The current two-time barrel racing champ is thirty-nine, and she's setting arena records left and right."

"Absolutely true." Harper looked at him and then away as pink touched her cheeks. "But maybe I'm getting a little tired of living out of a trailer after almost ten years of nomadic life."

He raised a brow. "Your trailer is nicer than most folks' homes."

"It's still a trailer. The thing is… I'd like to get married and start a family soon." She peeked up at him and then quickly looked away. "I'm trying to stay positive about all this. Who knows, maybe this will be a growth opportunity."

Lucas doubted that. What Harper liked was being in control and she thrived in wide-open spaces. Just like him. He was silent for minutes, thinking.

*Marriage and kids.*

Sure, of course. He couldn't expect things to stay the same forever. Didn't he want that too? A partner in life? Someone to fill the void in his heart? Wasn't that why he had an engagement ring in his duffel bag?

Harper deserved the best, and if that's what she wanted, he prayed the Good Lord brought her just that. Yeah, and he'd have to repeat that a few dozen times before his chest stopped aching at the thought of them going their separate ways someday after so many years as close friends.

She shot him a wary look. "Are you going to tell me what you wanted to talk about?"

"Ah, yeah. Um…" He cleared his throat. "I discovered that we've launched plans to go into business together. Going into business is a huge deal. Why didn't you tell me?"

She released the plug from the sink and dried her hands on a towel as the water and suds circled the drain with a sucking sound. "I suspected you didn't remember, and in truth, I dreaded having to convince you a second time."

"Convince me a second time? That sounds like we've had this conversation before."

Harper opened her mouth and closed it as though she had something to say but was holding back.

Lucas nodded at the table. "Let's sit down and talk. Okay?"

The chair legs squeaked as they moved on the oak floor. Harper sat and folded her hands on the table. There was silence between them, the only sound the hum of the refrigerator.

He looked into her eyes, searching for an answer. "I really want to understand."

Harper lowered her gaze, concentrating on her hands before finally looking at him. "If you recall, you gave me 'the speech' in the truck when I took you to your doctor's appointment."

*"The speech?"*

"Yes. The one about how you have to do this yourself."

"Now you make me sound pigheaded."

She arched her brows. "You started talking about the training center two years ago. I asked to partner with you, and you flat shut me out."

"I do recall a few discussions, but I wouldn't say I shut you out."

"Please, all I've ever heard is how this is *your* project."

He looked at her. "You're telling me that at some point, I agreed to partner up with you."

Harper offered a solemn nod, her eyes on the table.

He'd been clear from the get-go that this was his venture. A project he'd kept to himself for a long time. It was an opportunity to build something that said Lucas Morgan wasn't just a pretty face with a brass buckle.

Sure, he'd made a go of the rodeo, but he wasn't a star, like Harper was.

Besides, this was the chance to step out of the shadows of his talented brothers. Though he was a fraternal twin, he'd always been the baby of the family. The baby who had to be protected because he'd worn his feelings on his sleeve when their parents died. Now, at six foot three, standing as tall as his big brother Drew, he still felt that he didn't measure up.

"Luc, I know how hard this is for you—not only are you injured, but you lost your memory. Grasping to remember details to fill in the blanks has to be the worst nightmare. But for a moment, think about how it affects those around you. It's a domino situation, and we're all struggling to understand what this means for the future."

Yeah, Harper was right. He was thinking. Thinking about the woman out there who might be expecting a ring.

"Luc? You okay?" Harper asked quietly.

Lucas rubbed his chin, still trying to understand.

"So that's why you've mentioned January several times."

She nodded.

"Why would I change my mind about taking on a partner?" He knew he was being a jerk, yet he seemed unable to keep his mouth shut.

Harper straightened her shoulders, breathed deeply, and looked at him straight on. "Oh, I don't know, Luc. Maybe because we're friends, and you can't do everything yourself." Irritation laced her voice and her green eyes sparked with anger. "Clearly, you found the business plan. Did you read it in its entirety?"

Lucas swallowed. "No. Reading triggers headaches. Headaches start the whole cycle of dizziness and nausea."

"I'm sorry." She paused. "But if you had read it, you'd have realized that it's a good business plan. An impressive plan. I put in hours of research on that paperwork."

"I have no doubt that you did. Thank you." He ran a hand over his chin. "Look, I'm sorry, Harp. It's just there are so many puzzle pieces missing."

She nodded again. This time, her face reflected misery. Then she released a slow breath and looked away.

Well, he felt miserable too. It hadn't been his intention to hurt her.

"Where do we go from here?" he asked.

"That's up to you, Luc. The first loan application was rejected."

"Rejected?"

"Yes. You knew about the rejection. I took the liberty of tweaking the application paperwork and submitting it again. They advised me it might take longer to receive a response because the department manager was on medical leave. I'll check on things this week."

"What happens if it's approved?"

"You tell me." She gave a slight shrug.

He frowned. "I must have had a good reason to go against everything I laid out in my head for years. Too bad I can't figure out what it is."

Harper slowly turned her head and looked at him, her jaw sagging. "Excuse me?"

"That didn't come out as I'd intended."

"What did you intend?"

"I intended to express my confusion, and I'm trying to understand." He scrambled to move past his awkward and harsh comment. "If the loan is approved, how do you suggest we proceed?"

"We hadn't planned to start until January, but with you out of commission and both of us in Homestead Pass, we could begin now. Slowly. You're still in recovery mode and I have an obligation to my father."

*We. We. We.* How had things gone from a solo act to a team project? And how would he figure it out without alienating Harper?

"So, what does getting started look like?" His head began to ache from thinking, working to capture any scrap of a memory that would explain how this happened.

"We can discuss moving forward with contractors, if we get a green light from the bank."

Lucas nodded, trying to find the upside in the information. "Starting now will put the project a good six months ahead of schedule. That's an advantage. If I start the project in January, I wouldn't be able to start construction until spring. And, with calving, late spring."

"I forgot about calving," Harper said.

"Yep. Absolutely another advantage to starting now." He paused. "What happens if the loan isn't approved?"

She looked at him. "I think you should focus your energy on what will happen when the loan is approved."

"You're so certain it will be?"

"Nothing is certain, but I'm confident I provided an excellent business plan outlining a path to success. It will be up to you to decide if you can proceed with the project as a team."

"I don't like you leaving the circuit. I can tell you that much." He looked at her. "You have records to break. Buckles to win."

"That's moot. I already promised my dad. I'm here for two months. Besides, I told you. I'm ready for a change too."

She was in the right place for change. There were so many changes going on right now, he could hardly focus on one before another jumped out at him. "Harp, what if we get this project launched, and I can't ride again? Ever."

"The plan isn't dependent on you, or me, for that matter. Your name, yes. But not necessarily you in a saddle."

"That doesn't make any sense."

"Sure it does. If you recall... Oops, sorry. You can't recall." She took a breath. "We expanded the scope of the business plan to allow us to bring in other specialty professionals during the quarterly training sessions."

"Quarterly?"

"Yes. That's what we decided..." She looked at him. "You know. Before."

Lucas nodded. It made sense. Too bad he couldn't remember deciding to make sense.

"When the facility is not in use, we're going to allow other instructors to rent the facilities for private lessons."

Lucas jerked back with surprise. "Who thought of that? It's genius. We'll be making money outside of our scheduled training school. Passive income. I love it."

"Right?" A smile turned up the corners of her mouth. "And with an outside arena and an inside climate-controlled facility, we have functionality year-round and the potential for twice the revenue."

"Two arenas? How can we afford two when there's equipment to purchase, not to mention horses?"

"We start slowly. It's all in the paperwork."

"Okay. Give me some time to process everything and get through the paperwork."

"Of course. Take your time, but you ought to know that I'm not walking away from this project because you can't remember. My future is at stake here."

He met her solemn gaze and nodded. This wasn't what he'd planned, but the Lord had other ideas. And if he had to have a business partner, who better than his best friend?

"I'm sorry, Harper. The last thing I want is to hurt you. This whole memory thing is overwhelming. It's like there are two of me, and the guy previously running my life forgot to sync his calendar with me before he went on hiatus." He paused. "Then there's the headaches and the vision issues on top of that."

"Sure. I get that. I hope you know that I'm praying every day for you. So are my parents."

"Thank you."

She stood. "I better get going. Thanks for dinner."

"Don't forget your casserole dish." Lucas stood as well.

"Yes. Right. Casserole dish." She picked hers up from the assortment of pans and plates that had been emptied and washed. "You sure have a lot of female friends."

"I guess so." His gaze followed hers to the counter. "Haven't seen most of them in a while."

"No?"

"Correction. I don't think I have." He paused. "Do you know something I don't?" Maybe Sam was right. Maybe Harper knew the woman he was going to ask to marry him.

"I don't know anything, and I do not want to know anything." Harper held up a hand and backed away, looking everywhere but at him.

"Just asking." Lucas shrugged. "And by the way, I've decided to throw a little barbecue to say thank you and get all these dishes back to the proper owners."

"That's an idea. All your exes in one place at the same time. Sounds like fun." She made a gagging sound.

A phone began to buzz and Harper pulled hers from the back pocket of her jeans. She glanced at it and frowned.

"Everything okay?"

"Something is up at home. Dana and her husband just showed up at my parents' house." She looked at him. "Want to stop by and say hello?"

"Yeah, hard pass. Your dad doesn't like me."

"That's not true."

He rolled his eyes. It was true. Colin Reilly didn't have anything positive to say about their friendship, especially after Harper had joined the rodeo circuit. He didn't believe Luc was good enough for his daughter, and he was right. Too bad the pecan baron hadn't figured out that Lucas wasn't in the running for his daughter's hand. They were friends. Only friends. A mantra that was starting to wear thin.

"You better get going," Lucas said.

For a moment, she stared at him, her lips a thin line. "When's your next neurology appointment?"

"Next week or the week after. I have it written down somewhere."

"I'll go with you."

"You can't do that. You have a day job now."

"My father still owns the company. I can slip out early."

"We'll see." Today's conversation made him realize how much he relied on Harper. Was that a good thing? Especially in light of her declaration to move on and settle down. Whoever the fortunate fella was, he sure wouldn't want Lucas hanging around.

He grimaced at the thought of being a third-wheel around his best friend.

"Are you okay?" Harper asked.

"Yeah. Headache."

She nodded. "I'll see you at the Kids Day Event on Saturday?"

"Yep. I'm going to assist Bess in the snack tent. If I'm really fortunate, I'll be able to pass out juice boxes and carrot sticks."

"Oh, stop."

"You have a good day tomorrow on your first day in corporate America. Play nice with the other kids. Make good choices."

She laughed. "I always do."

Yeah, she always did, which was why he didn't want to be the one who kept her from achieving everything she deserved in life. And as it stood, he wasn't happy about their business arrangement. Wasn't sure if he could handle his project becoming their project.

What could he have been thinking? Didn't matter. For now, he'd let things ride and pray the arrangement the other Lucas Morgan had made wasn't the biggest mistake of his life.

And Harper's.

HARPER BIT INTO her apple and stared out the window of the Reilly Pecans' employee lunchroom. Rain pelted the glass, creating a blurry gray visual that matched her mood. She found herself replaying the conversation with Luc over and over in her head and becoming more annoyed each time.

She'd thought they were on a trajectory to a shared future in more ways than one. Now, not only had the relationship been kicked into the red dirt, but he had reluctantly let the partnership stand in an effort to protect the only thing that really mattered. Their friendship.

That wasn't what she wanted. She wanted to go into the venture on equal footing, with the assurance that they both brought skills and dedication to the table that would ensure the success of the project. The way the situation stood left her unsatisfied, and she didn't like it at all, especially since she'd put so much into the training center plans. This project was her baby too.

She hadn't expected such a strong reaction from Luc about

the partnership. Now she dreaded what would happen when he found out about the collateral attached to the second loan application. The one she'd planned to tell him about over dinner in Lawton the night of the accident. After their first loan application had been rejected by the bank, she had submitted the second application using land she'd inherited as collateral.

Harper held the title to a prime piece of property outside Elk City that she'd inherited from her grandmother. It was an option guaranteed to secure the loan without asking either Reilly Pecans or the Lazy M Ranch to back the venture. She had a spreadsheet all prepared to illustrate how they'd pay off the loan and remove the lien in their first few years.

Harper shook her head. Old Luc would've understood the rationale and have agreed in a heartbeat. New Luc would surely object. The last thing she wanted was to stress him and worsen his condition.

She hated being in this position.

Fortunately, she'd been going nonstop since morning, leaving her little time to mull over yesterday or to even think about the fact that new Luc didn't remember that they were at the precipice of a relationship before his accident. At least, she'd thought so.

Harper had gotten up at dawn to give her horse a workout, then showered and driven to the city.

Her new job kept her busy with paperwork and introductions. Everyone she met had been pleasant and welcoming. Of course, she was the boss's daughter, so they had to be nice. Harper had run into that dynamic often. As she nodded and smiled, it occurred to her that some of the employees she met were no doubt hiding resentment that as a nepotism baby, she was first in line for a coveted marketing position that others had worked years to qualify for. She couldn't blame them for being unhappy.

"Why aren't you eating in the executive dining room?" Her sister Dana slid into the chair across from Harper.

Harper shrugged. "You want me and my peanut butter and jelly sandwich and apple to eat in the executive dining room?"

"The chef in the executive dining room prepared turkey tetrazzini with porcini mushrooms. You could have eaten your pitiful lunch another day."

"Does Maddy eat in the executive dining room too?" Harper asked.

"Yes, though not today. She's working from home. One of her kids has a bug."

Harper nodded. "So where's Allen?" Dana's husband, a Reilly corporate attorney, had been by her side last evening when they'd announced the decision to celebrate their anniversary with a party at the Reilly mansion.

Dana sighed, her eyes overflowing with love. She held out her left hand and admired the diamond eternity ring on her finger. "He's in Tulsa for the day."

"That's quite the piece of jewelry." A beautiful ring, not unlike her sister's extravagant engagement ring. Harper knew when the time came, she'd opt for something simple.

"I'm so happy, Harp." Dana grinned, her eyes glowing. "I can't wait for our anniversary party."

Her sister's words brought Harper out of her musings. Looking at Dana was like looking at a petite version of herself. They both had the same wavy red-brown hair and green eyes. Dana, however, took after the maternal side of the family and was tiny and dainty.

Harper, at five foot eight, was all Reilly. She used to mourn her height, longing to be tiny instead of towering over boys in high school. Now she embraced her long legs and ability to reach the top shelf of the grocery store.

"I'm glad you're happy. But why do you need another party?" Only five years ago, the gardens of their parents' classic stone Colonial mansion had been transformed into an intimate wedding venue for two hundred. Harper's left eye twitched as she thought about the event and what she considered a waste of money.

"Oh, Harper, you wouldn't understand. Gathering our friends and family together for our anniversary allows us an opportunity to declare our love."

Harper bit back a snarky remark. Wasn't the eternity ring on her sister's finger a screaming declaration of their love? Dana was right. She didn't get it. To her, love was in the small unsaid things. It was actions, not words or diamonds.

And it was possible that Harper couldn't see things from Dana's point of view because she found herself a bit envious of her sister. Declaration of love. She sighed. Right now, all she could declare was that Luc was her best friend.

"I already spoke with Mom," Dana continued. "She's going to hire Moretti Catering."

Loretta Moretti. That was the first positive thing she'd heard since Dana had sat down. Sam's wife, Olivia, and her aunt Loretta were both phenomenal chefs. Harper would follow Moretti Catering anywhere.

Dana pulled out her phone and slid her finger across the screen. "Allen is out of town for most of September, so I'm thinking this Saturday. Loretta has an availability."

"This Saturday? Isn't that kind of short notice?" Harper shook her head. "That won't work for me."

"Oh, come on. This is Homestead Pass, population ten thousand. What pressing engagement could you possibly have?"

"Don't bad-mouth your hometown. Homestead Pass made Reilly Pecans. And, as it happens, I have a charity event over at the Lazy M."

Dana sighed. "You can't get out of it? For your sister's party?"

"I won't leave them short-handed. I honor my commitments."

"Honestly, you're just like Daddy."

"I'll take that as a compliment." Harper smiled and tucked her apple core in her lunch bag.

"The only other date that works for everyone is three weeks from now. Tell me you aren't folding bandages for the Red Cross then."

"Very funny. I'll make the other date work." Harper paused. "How does Allen feel about a party?"

Dana shrugged. "Whatever makes me happy."

How different Dana's husband was from Luc. He'd never want to be obligated to the boss. Was he prideful or merely determined to be self-made? Probably both, though the latter sounded like her father. Maybe her dad and Luc had more in common than either of them realized.

"Is that your phone buzzing?" Dana asked.

Harper reached into her purse. "Yes. It's Luc. I better see what he wants."

"Lucas Morgan. The love-'em-and-leave-'em cowboy." Dana shook her head. "I spent quite a few of my college weekends at the rodeo trying to get his attention. He never noticed."

"You did? Really?" The words gave her pause. Luc and Dana? Her sister was much too high maintenance and Luc far too low maintenance. Was it wrong that she was pleased that Luc hadn't asked her sister out?

Dana laughed. "Yes, really. Oh, and I'm inviting Allen's cousin to the party. Also an attorney. He has potential. I'll introduce you."

"No. I do not want to be set up."

"You'll thank me later."

*Oh, I doubt it.*

Dana stood. She glanced at the industrial clock on the wall. "Benefits meeting in fifteen minutes. See you there."

"Yes, ma'am."

Harper dialed Luc's number and he answered immediately. "Luc, did you need something?"

"I left a voice message. You weren't supposed to call me back. I didn't want to interrupt your first day at work."

"I'm on lunch break."

"Oh." He released a breath, his voice hesitant. "I got a letter from the bank."

Her heart began to trot. "Open it." She'd rather find out now if it was bad news and move on to plan B. Not that she had a plan B.

"No. I'll wait until you can come by."

She swallowed, more nervous than she expected. "Okay, I'll be there as soon as I can."

"Take your time. I'm not going anywhere. I'll save you some dinner. Bess is making macaroni and cheese from scratch."

"My favorite. See you then."

Harper stood and cleaned up the table, tossing her lunch bag in the trash as she headed to the conference room. She had to give her father credit. The corporate headquarters was state-of-the-art, with every convenience at the disposal of the staff. If she hadn't grown accustomed to fresh air, the scent of horse and hay, and the dirt of a training arena, she might think this environment had merit.

Life would be a lot simpler if Reilly Pecans was her destiny. When Harper was six, her mother had signed her up for ballet lessons, as she had when her sisters had been the same age. Harper had hated ballet. She'd begged for horse riding lessons. Those lessons had set her on the road to meeting Luc. After that, she'd always thought horses and Luc would always be her future.

Was she wrong?

# CHAPTER FIVE

LUCAS DID A double take when Harper left her truck and approached the steps of the Morgan ranch house. His boots hit the ground to stop the movement of the rocking chair. He stood to greet her, doing his best not to stare at the woman before him, tall and regal in a gray suit with a white silk blouse, her hair pinned to the back of her head.

"Harper Reilly. Is that you? Can't say I've ever seen you looking like the boss before." *Or looking so good. Period.* He tamped back that remark and focused on a potted begonia instead of her long legs.

She walked up the steps, her heels tapping on the cement, and then stopped to swat at a fly. "What are you talking about? You've seen me in a skirt plenty of times."

"This is different. You've gone all corporate."

"Oh, stop giving me a hard time. I'm cranky from fighting traffic, and I'm starving. Feed me, or I'll get a burger at the diner."

"Yes, ma'am." He held open the door, allowing the cool air to welcome them into the house and out of the humidity.

"Has Bess already gone home for the day?" Harper asked.

"Yeah, but I told her you were stopping by, so she made chocolate-chip cookies."

"I love that woman. I'm surprised someone hasn't stolen her away from the Lazy M."

"Don't even whisper such a thing." Lucas pulled out a kitchen chair. "Sit down and relax."

"Let me wash my hands first." Harper kicked off her shoes and put her suit jacket on the back of the chair before moving to the oversize farmhouse porcelain sink. "I'm not sure I can handle dressing up every day for work." She scrunched up her face. "And the commute. Ugh."

"Not much you can do about it, right?" He put a serving bowl of macaroni and cheese in the microwave and set the timer.

"I'll have work-from-home options after this week." She sighed. "If I make it that long. I didn't appreciate how blessed I was to have a career in wide-open spaces until now." Harper glanced at the counter and pursed her lips. "The stack of containers to return to your girlfriends is taking over the kitchen."

"Yeah, Bess said the same thing. And they're *ex-girlfriends*. I don't know why no one can remember that part."

"Potato. Potahto."

"The point is, I'm going to take care of the situation."

"And how will you do that?" She turned on the water and sluiced the liquid over her hands before reaching for the soap dispenser.

"I told you. A barbecue party. I'm thinking next Saturday. Got any plans?"

"Me?" She eyed him. "Why would I want to come to a barbecue featuring your ex-girlfriends?"

"For moral support. That's what friends do."

Harper's eyes rounded and she smiled. "Oh, is that what they do? Well, then have I got a deal for you."

He cocked his head. "What kind of deal?"

"Dana and Allen are celebrating their fifth anniversary in late September."

"Not sure I get the connection but tell them congrats from me."

"Or you could tell them yourself. My parents are hosting an intimate party. If you agree to attend as moral support, in return, I'll come to your party."

Lucas grimaced and let out a loud groan. "That is not a fair deal. We're talking jeans and barbecue versus church clothes and unidentifiable stuff on water crackers." He shook his head. "Nope. Nope. Nope."

Harper shrugged and reached for a dish towel. "It's not unidentifiable stuff. Olivia's aunt is catering."

"She's catering my event too," he returned.

"Is she making cannoli? My sister specifically requested cannoli."

"No. We're having hand pies. She said cannoli doesn't go with shredded pork and ribs."

"Oh well. Maybe next time."

He couldn't help but smile. Loretta Moretti's cannoli. That sure changed the equation. A fella could put up with a lot for homemade cannoli.

"What is it you need me to do at this soiree?" he asked.

"Keep me from falling asleep. Create a diversion when my family tries to set me up with anyone they deem a suitable match. You know, the usual."

For a long minute, Lucas debated, finally capitulating when he thought about the cannoli again. "Fine. I'll do it."

"Wonderful." Harper smiled sweetly and then turned to the microwave without missing a beat. "Oh, that smells lovely."

Clever gal. Move on quickly so he can't change his mind. She knew him too well.

Harper glanced at the plate and silverware already on the table. "How can I help?"

"I got this," he said. "Bess made cornbread muffins too. Don't suppose those might be of interest?"

"Absolutely. I earned them today."

"Was your first day at the office that bad?"

"Not bad, simply not what I'm accustomed to. Actually, the morning zipped by. It was the afternoon that was terminal." She walked to the table and sat down. "I was with two other new hires. We sat through hours of presentations. At one point, my legs started twitching from sitting still so long."

The microwave beeped and Harper shot up from the chair. "I'll get that."

"Harp, I got it." Lucas grabbed potholders from the counter.

"You've never waited on me before. No sense starting now."

"Sit," Lucas said. "You're tired, and you're my guest." He carefully removed the serving bowl, bubbling with buttery cheesy noodles, and placed it on a trivet in the center of the table. "Want a rundown of my day?"

She eyed him cautiously and unfolded the cloth napkin on her lap. "Do tell me about your day, Lucas."

"I organized and filled goodie bags for the Kids Day Event. Stickers. Pens and pencils, notebooks, and little Bibles. I filled more than one hundred bags. Then I stocked the prize booth."

"Prize booth?"

"Yeah. The kids get tokens when they arrive, and they can earn more at each activity. The tokens can be turned in at the booth for prizes." He pulled plates from the cupboard as he spoke and placed them on the table.

"What a great idea. Who thought of that?"

Lucas bowed as he put a tin of golden-brown cornbread muffins and a tub of butter on the table. "Me. I saw something similar at kid's rodeo up in Montana and told Trevor about it."

"That's really genius." She glanced around. "Do you have any honey?"

"Sure do," he said. "Do you want a salad with that meal?"

"No, thanks." She shook her head. "I prefer languishing in carbs."

Harper added a healthy amount of macaroni and cheese to her plate before slathering butter and honey on a muffin. Then she said, "Let's pray. Fast. I'm starving."

She took his hand. "Lord, thank You for Your abundant blessings, for our new ventures, and for patience. Lots of patience. Bless this food to my body. Amen."

"Amen," he murmured, slowly releasing her soft fingers.

She wasted no time digging in. Lucas had never seen a woman enjoy food like Harper. Despite her appetite, she never gained an ounce. His glance skimmed over her trim figure before he quickly looked away. *This is Harper*, he reminded himself. *No checking out your best friend.*

"Mmm. This is amazing." Harper held a spoonful in the air. "I need to get the recipe. We eat macaroni and cheese from a box at my house."

"You're joking, right? I thought you had a chef."

"We've had a few over the years. My father always fires them, and my mother is hopeless in the kitchen." She licked her lips and glanced around. "Don't tell her I said that. She's a fabulous sculptress and a wonderful wife and mother, but a terrible cook. Once, she lost track of time in the middle of a piece and nearly burned the kitchen up."

Lucas chuckled.

"Time…" Harper repeated. Her spoon clattered to her plate and she wiped her lips with the napkin. "I nearly forgot why I stopped by. Where's the envelope?"

Lucas stood and pulled a slightly wrinkled, thick white envelope from his back pocket.

Eyes round with excitement, Harper clasped her hands together tightly. "Come on. Open it, Luc."

"Okay," he said on a sigh. He wasn't nearly as excited as she was. No matter what the letter said, there were decisions to be made.

Lucas slid a finger under the flap. He tore open the envelope and pulled out the papers inside. The cover letter was short and to the point.

"'Dear Mr. Morgan and Ms. Reilly. I have good news. Homestead Pass Bank has approved your loan for the proposed training center.'" Lucas skimmed the other papers. "Looks like approval conditions and financing numbers."

Harper released a short gasp. "May I read it?"

"Sure. Your eyes are better than mine right now. I'm still getting headaches when I read." He handed her the letter, along with several other papers. For minutes, she intently read each page and then looked up at him.

"I'm thrilled, but I don't want to get ahead of myself, Luc. Have you been praying about this?" she asked. "Do you want to proceed?"

"Sure. Ah, yeah."

Harper dropped her head. "I don't want your grudging acceptance of a partnership, Luc."

"It's not grudging acceptance." No. That didn't describe what was going on in his head, because he couldn't even pinpoint those emotions. Once again, the guy he used to be had stolen how he was feeling now, leaving Lucas confused. The same question rattled around in his aching head. Why had he agreed to a partnership in the first place?

"Right. Hold back that enthusiasm, pal." She pushed her plate away and looked around. "I'll take those cookies now."

Lucas grabbed the plastic container from the counter and put it in front of Harper.

"What about you?" he asked.

"What do you mean?" Harper asked.

"How can you start a business when you have a full-time job?"

"A temporary full-time job," she said. "Besides, I'm good at juggling."

"Why do you want to do this, Harper?"

"Why?" Her gaze moved from the cookie to him and then away.

"Yeah. You have lots of options in the equine community, not to mention Reilly Pecans can open any door you choose. Why a training center with a broke-down cowboy?"

"You are not a broke-down cowboy. And I already told you why. Retirement is in the not-too-distant future. I want to choose that future instead of having it decided for me." Harper tensed. "And I certainly do not want my father's name granting me opportunities I haven't earned."

She lifted her head and eyed him long and hard with hooded green eyes. "I've earned this opportunity, Lucas. And I believe that we can create a training center that will prove to be something we both can be proud of."

He raised his palms. "Easy there. I'm simply trying to figure out where we go from here."

"If you want to proceed, we should meet with an attorney who can help us file the appropriate documents."

"An attorney. Do you know any?"

"Naturally, Reilly Pecans has quite a few on retainer, but I'd rather not involve my father."

He looked at her. "Have you mentioned any of this to Colin?"

"Not yet. I will eventually. I'd rather tell my father after the internship is completed. I promised him I'd give Reilly Pecans a chance. I don't want to hurt his feelings. He's convinced I'll fall in love with the company." She looked at Lucas. "I'm sort of between a rock and a hard place."

Lucas ignored her murmured words. "He's not going to be happy that you and I are doing business together."

"My father is not complicated. He has a plan for Reilly Pecans. Anything that obstructs that plan makes him unhappy."

She was right. The wrath of Reilly was unavoidable. Her

dad would no doubt blame Luc for keeping his baby girl from her true destiny.

"How about you?" she asked. "Have you spoken to your family?"

"No family discussion, if that's what you mean." He raised a hand. "Sam stumbled on the business plan in my binder. Any reason why I can't tell the rest of the family?"

"No, of course not. We agreed not to involve family in the financing, that's all."

"Sam's a certified public accountant. What if he recommends someone he's worked with?"

"That'll be fine with me."

"What about registering a name?" Luc asked. "Got any ideas?"

"Luc you already chose a name. Homestead Pass Training Center." She looked at him. "You know. Before your accident."

"Huh. Well, glad I'm doing something besides losing my memory." He looked at her. "So no Morgan and Reilly in the name? We decided on that?"

"If we put Reilly on there, someone is bound to think it's something to do with pecans. We didn't want to confuse anyone with Morgan Ranch or Reilly Pecan references."

"Wish I could recall that conversation. I might be a tad more enthused about things if I could." He rubbed his head.

"I'm sorry," Harper said. "I feel bad that every time we discuss this your head aches and you look stressed. That's exactly what the doctor said to avoid."

"Don't apologize. None of this is your fault." Lucas slid into a chair and worked to find something to say that might make them both feel better.

"Who died?" Gramps walked into the kitchen, his boots clomping on the wooden floor.

"No one died," Lucas said.

"Then why the long faces?" He moved across the room to

the coffeepot, where he removed the carafe and examined the liquid, his face contorting with pain. "Who made this swill?"

"Bess did before she left," Lucas said.

"I suppose I'm forced to drink Dr Pepper." Gramps pulled open the refrigerator, grabbed a can and approached the table. "What's going on?"

"Remember back when I talked to the family about someday using my parcel for a training school?" Lucas asked.

"When you retire. Yeah, that's the same as when pigs fly, right?" His grandfather took an empty chair.

"No. I'd been thinking of retiring in January. With this injury, the timeline has been moved up."

Gramps popped the lid on his soda. "That's great news."

"That's not quite all the news," Harper said. "Luc and I are going into business together."

"Oh." Gramps frowned.

"What do you mean? What does 'oh' mean?" Lucas asked, anxiety rising.

"Many a friendship has been torn asunder because of a business deal, son."

"'Torn asunder'? Did you make that up?" Lucas asked.

"No. That's pure Gus Morgan."

"Mom and Dad started Lazy M Ranch together, and it was a very successful venture. What about that?"

"Aw, that's different," Gramps said. He took a long swig of soda. "Your momma and poppa were married. Committed."

"We're committed." He looked at Harper, searching her wide green eyes. "Aren't we committed to this plan?"

"I am. I don't know about you." She opened the plastic container once more and reached for another cookie.

"I'm committed," he said a little too loudly.

"Well, there you go," Gramps said. "You're both committed. Sounds like your dreams are going to come true."

Lucas slid his glance to Harper once again. She looked at him and then focused on the cookie in her hand, but in the brief moment they connected, he'd seen confusion in her eyes. Maybe because she'd seen the fear in his.

Sam's wife, Olivia, had once told him that the best dreams should scare us. Starting his own business was a dream come true. A business with Harper, however, terrified him. What if he failed and took her with him? What would happen to their friendship?

He couldn't let that happen. He wouldn't.

*Show me what to do here, Lord. Show me Your will for this situation.*

GRAVEL CRUNCHED AND the smell of diesel filled the air as the second of three yellow school buses, rented for the Kids Day Event, rumbled toward the Lazy M Ranch exit. Harper chuckled as she waved to the elementary-aged children on the last bus. In return, they smooshed their little faces against the glass and waved back, laughing and giggling.

"This was a good day. It was so much fun helping those kiddos ride the donkeys." She pushed her bangs back from her slick and sweaty forehead and turned to Luc. "Eighty degrees of heat and humidity that only August in Oklahoma can offer, and yet a perfect day." She sniffed the air. "Except that I now smell like donkey."

Luc pushed his straw Stetson back and leaned close. "Aw, not too bad."

"It was worth it. I haven't had that much fun since I helped out with Sunday school class when I was in high school. Today reminded me how much I enjoy working with children." She looked around the grounds, where white tent peaks dotted the landscape. The bright-colored Kids Day banners that had been stretched between the tents moved back and forth in the breeze.

"Trevor has quite the ministry with this event," Luc said. "This is the third year, and they doubled the number of kids bused in from Oklahoma City. Pastor McGuinness is tickled at the success."

"That's fantastic."

"It is. My brother is making a difference in the community. In the world." He paused. "I want to do that."

His response had Harper's mind whirling. "You know, the training center will be open well before next summer. I'm sure we can find a way for our training center to be part of the next Kids Day. I'd like that. Wouldn't you?"

"What do you have in mind?" Luc asked.

"A small rodeo might be an option. Mutton busting and roping. I'd be up for a barrel racing demo."

"Hmm."

That was all he said as half a dozen more ideas popped into her head, but she held back. She recognized that her enthusiasm could be a lot to handle. Blame it on the Reilly genes. The old Luc had understood that and it had never bothered him. The new Luc's expression said that he needed more processing time.

She missed the old Luc.

"Care to check out the training center property?" he asked Harper.

"Sure." They'd already checked out the property a dozen times when they'd been home for the wedding, but Luc didn't remember that. She'd take his interest today as a good sign. Maybe being in the space would trigger his memories.

"Hey, you two."

Harper turned to see Trevor, Luc's fraternal twin, approach. His adopted young son, Cole, trailed behind with an energetic brown-and-white border-collie-mix pup.

The cowboy certainly had changed in the last year. She would have labeled Trevor solemn and circumspect in the past. No longer. A smile lit up his face, and love shone in his eyes when he turned and nodded at something Cole said.

Yes, that's what falling in love did to a guy.

A mere two weeks ago, she thought she'd seen something in

Luc's eyes. She shot him a quick sidelong glance and sighed, more confused than ever.

"Thanks for your hard work today," Trevor said as he stepped closer.

Luc grinned. "We had fun, Trev."

"Ditto that," Harper added. "Now, how can we help with cleanup?"

"Oh no. You've done plenty," Trevor said. "Cole here has a whole cleanup team ready."

"Way to go, Cole," Luc said with a grin. He offered the shy thirteen-year-old a high five. "I knew I liked you for a reason."

"Thanks, Uncle Luc," Cole mumbled.

"Who has the keys to the UTV?" Lucas continued. "I want to take a ride over to my parcel with Harper."

Trevor pulled a jangling ring of keys from his back pocket and tossed them to Harper, who caught them easily. "Here you go. Don't let him in the driver's seat."

"Nope. I won't," she said with a wink.

"Well, you're no fun," Luc said.

"And proud of it." Trevor smiled at Harper. "Good to see you, Harper. Are you coming to the battle of the exes?"

"Battle of the exes?" Harper snorted and burst out laughing. "Oh yes. I'll be there. I'm bringing popcorn and a lawn chair."

"Oh, go on, you two," Luc grumbled. "It's a barbecue party. A polite gesture to thank my friends for their kindness when I was down, that's all."

Trevor's lips twitched. "Anyone else notice that the guest list is all women?"

"Not true," Luc protested. "The ranch wranglers, including Slim Jim, will be there. Ben from the barbershop is coming as well."

"Ah, Ben. Cole and I were there last month." He ran a hand over Cole's summer buzz cut. "You know he cuts hair, right?"

Luc pulled off his straw Stetson and pushed back his waves

of brown hair. "I have that on my to-do list. I clean up real nice. Don't I, Harper?"

She stepped back. "I am not incriminating myself." Nor would she admit that she liked Luc's disreputable brown shaggy hair as is.

Trevor laughed as he pulled a cell out of his pocket and read the screen. "That's Hope. She saved us cupcakes." He looked at Harper and Luc as he looped an arm around Cole's shoulders. "See you two later."

Harper turned to see Gus Morgan heading in their direction, his boots kicking up dust as he strode across the compact red dirt.

"There you are," Gus called. "I've been looking for you." He gave Harper a nod of greeting as he approached.

"Me or Harper?" Luc asked.

"Lucas Morgan is what the boxes say. There's at least ten of them, and they're filling up the kitchen."

"Boxes. What boxes?" Luc asked. "Where did they come from?"

"I surely don't know the answer to that question," Luc's grandfather returned. "Didn't look close enough."

"Do you want to go up to the house first?" Harper asked.

"Nah, it's probably ranch supplies accidentally sent to the house. Sometimes they put my name on them instead of Trevor's. I'll check it out later." He turned to his grandfather. "Thanks, Gramps."

"No problem. I'm heading to Jane's. She picked up my book club read from the library, and I'm anxious to get started. There's leftover meat loaf in the refrigerator." Gus laughed. "If you can get to the fridge."

"I'll get the boxes cleared out."

Harper matched her steps to Luc's as they strode to the equipment barn where a UTV waited for them outside the building.

"I've always wanted to drive one of these," Harper said. She examined the olive drab color of the doorless off-road vehicle.

"Don't you have one at the orchards?"

"Several. But only the staff are allowed to use them."

"No perks for being the boss's daughter?"

"Oh sure. Perks aplenty. All the pecans I can crack. Cinnamon-roasted pecans come autumn, and from the added-value division, there's pecan divinity at Christmas."

"I love Reilly pecan divinity," Luc said. "I'm also partial to the pecan praline." He smacked his lips.

"I remember," Harper said. It was tradition for her to bring pecan treats to the Morgan household every year between Thanksgiving and Christmas.

They slid into the side-by-side seats and fastened seat belts before she backed up the vehicle and headed across the pasture toward the gravel and dirt road that cut through the Lazy M. A billow of red dirt followed them once she maneuvered the UTV onto the road.

"Easy there," Luc said. "I'm feeling every last bump."

Harper let out a small gasp and lifted her boot from the gas. "Oh, so sorry. I forgot."

At the fork in the road, she slowed and turned left. Straight ahead was where Drew had built a house for his family at the top of the hill. Sam and Olivia's place was to the right and along the eastern pasture. This was pretty land covered with bleached summer grasses that extended to a rolling backdrop of fir trees.

They were headed to a paved private road that separated two halves of the property. Luc's parcel bordered the road. Minutes later, an aged one-story log cabin came into view. The notched horizontal logs had faded to a dull gray. A porch and railing surrounded the cabin, though the railing had fallen down in several spots.

If possible, the building seemed sketchier than the last time she'd been here, no doubt due to the summer storms of the last few weeks.

"Did you ever decide what you want to do with the cabin?"

"Was it under discussion?"

Harper shot a glance at Luc. "For some reason, a discussion came up at Trevor's wedding. Drew had mentioned razing the place, and you said you wanted to think it over."

"The cabin stays. I should have made that clear right away." He narrowed his gaze. "I don't know why I would have said that."

She parked the vehicle beneath the canopy of a huge oak tree and got out. Luc followed. He approached the cabin slowly, hands in his back pockets, and stopped and stared. "My dad took Trevor and me on great adventures in that cabin. It holds a lot of memories."

Luc normally spoke only in generalities about his parents. He'd never shared much about their death, and she hadn't pried, recognizing the Do Not Enter signs he'd erected when she'd ask a question or two. Yet, after all these years, she longed for him to let her in, if only to understand him better.

She sensed that today was different. Or maybe it was that Luc was different. "What kind of adventures?" she asked.

"Overnight camping trips. Just the three of us." A soft smile touched his mouth. "Taught us how to pitch a tent right there." He pointed to a grassy area to the left of the cabin. "One time, Trev and I were about ten years old, and we insisted on doing it all ourselves. I remember that night like it was yesterday. The mosquitos were biting, and the air was thick. We rushed to set up the tent and get inside…" His voice trailed off.

"Fun night?"

"Oh sure," Luc nodded. "We played Go Fish and board games until we fell asleep. There was a rude awakening when the tent collapsed in the middle of the night. While we scrambled around trying to figure out what to do about it, the skies opened up and the rain decided to teach us another lesson."

"What did your dad do?" Harper asked.

"Dad laughed." Luc smiled, his eyes glassy as he continued to stare at the cabin. "Said there was very little in life that wasn't worth laughing about." He cleared his throat and turned to her. "I seem to have forgotten that lesson."

Harper nodded slowly. Now she understood why he'd chosen this parcel. Because it reminded him of his father. Sure, there was pain associated with this land and the cabin, but there was joy in the memories as well.

"I have no doubt we can salvage the place," she finally said. "Make it part of the training school experience."

"Part of… I don't follow."

"The cabin. How about a merch store?"

"Merch?"

"Yes. Training center merchandise. You were the one who originally mentioned ordering merchandise. T-shirts, hats, saddle blankets. Then there's mugs and water bottles." She grinned. "Think about it, Luc. Visitors could purchase popcorn and soda and snacks at the cabin to take to arena performances."

"Merch, huh?" Luc cocked his head, confused. "Be nice if I could remember my brilliant ideas so I could take credit for them."

"Your memory will come back eventually." She started for the cabin. "Come on, let's take a look and see how much work it's going to need."

"Slow down there, Harp. Those steps aren't as trustworthy as they used to be."

Harper raced up the wooden steps before Luc's warning registered. A crack sounded and both of her booted feet dropped through the aged and splintering boards. Her balance off, Harper waved her arms, struggling to regain her stability before she face-planted forward.

She froze when strong hands circled her waist, both keeping her upright and startling her.

"Don't move," Luc commanded, his breath soft in her ear.

"Oh, that's not going to be a problem."

"Are you hurt?"

"No, my boots and jeans protected me." She worked to raise her legs. "What I am is stuck." Stuck and dazed from Luc's touch.

"Hang on. I'll get the tire iron from the UTV."

He returned a few minutes later and knelt next to the steps, pounding at the boards, randomly removing the rotted and dusty pieces one at a time. "Okay, yank your feet up."

Harper glanced at the boards scattered around her and then at the remains of what was once a railing. "I need something to hold on to."

"Right. Right." He examined the situation. "Put your arms around my neck and I'll haul you out."

She grimaced at the potential humiliation the solution held. "Couldn't you just give me your arm?"

"What? That won't work. Put your arms around my neck, would you?"

"Fine," Harper muttered. Though she turned her head as she slipped her arms around his neck, she couldn't help but inhale a combination of Luc's aftershave and a healthy dose of awkward embarrassment.

He pulled her free from the steps and whirled around, dropping her lightly on the ground. Harper stumbled away from him as though she'd been zapped by a cattle prod. Goodness, she'd never been that close to Luc in her entire life. His arms around her seemed foreign and somehow yet right. Too right.

Then she recalled that she wore eau de donkey perfume and looked like a hot mess. She nearly groaned aloud.

"Thanks," Harper said. Avoiding his gaze, she bent over to brush the dust and debris of the ancient wood planks from her jeans and inspect the material for splinters, praying he wouldn't notice the embarrassment burning her face.

"Are you sure you're not hurt?" he asked. Concern laced his voice.

"I'm fine. The porch isn't, but I am."

"Guess this place needs more work than I wanted to admit.

I'll start repairing the cabin as soon as possible. The doc didn't tell me I couldn't do a little carpentry."

"Sam's a carpenter. Maybe he has time to help."

"Aw, I don't want to bother Sam. He's already helped me out a lot since I got back. He's plenty busy with his woodworking projects and obligations at the ranch."

Harper shook her head at Luc's stubbornness. "He's your brother," she finally said. "In fact, Drew probably has a thought or two about the cabin as well."

"That reminds me. What about the plans for the training center? I recall seeing the drawings in the business plan. Who did we hire?"

"A friend of Drew's, but he's had to pull out of the project due to a job move. We talked about hiring Drew."

"Good idea. I'll talk to him. Oh, and I meant to tell you that Sam's attorney friend can fit us in late Wednesday afternoon. His office is in Oklahoma City. Sam is going to drop me off for another appointment earlier in the day. Think I can hitch a ride home with you?"

"Sure, but what do you mean he's going to drop you off? Drop you off where?"

"I was referred to a neuro-optometrist in the city for evaluation." Lucas shrugged and gave a chuckle. "Maybe I'll need glasses. Think that will make me look smart?"

Harper turned her attention to Luc's face and took in the two-day beard, the straight nose and his blue eyes the color of a calm summer sky. It was the face of a man you could count on.

*Look away*, she commanded herself.

"Luc, you are smart. You graduated from college with a business degree."

"If I was smart, my life wouldn't be upside down."

"Stop that. None of this has been in your control. Now tell me, what does a neuro-optometrist do?"

"They specialize in vision rehab from traumatic brain injuries. I'm not sure what he can offer me, but after over two weeks of living someone else's life, I'm ready to try anything."

"A specialist. That's encouraging."

"It is if I can start using the computer and reading without triggering a headache."

"That would be huge," she agreed. "So, you have an appointment and then you'll meet me at the attorney's office?"

"Yeah. That work for you?"

"Absolutely. Maybe we could have dinner afterward and discuss our progress."

"Good idea."

"Thanks, Harper." Luc gave the cabin a long look. "I'd really like it if we could make the cabin have a purpose in our plans."

"I don't see any reason why we can't make that happen."

Harper stared at the structure for a moment. It seemed that all of their steps of late were coming together to create something bigger than she and Luc had imagined when they'd started uniting their dreams. She could only pray that Luc saw that too. And perhaps it might help him to recall that they'd been on the path to uniting their hearts as well.

# CHAPTER SIX

LUCAS REACHED FOR the door handle to exit the attorney's office at the same time Harper did. When their hands tangled, he stepped back. Quickly.

"I've got it." He placed his palm on the door, doing his best to avoid accidentally brushing against Harper as she moved past him onto the sidewalk.

Saturday's incident at the cabin continued to haunt him, the feel of Harper in his arms distracting him at odd moments.

This was Harper. His friend. The revelation that he was attracted to his buddy had startled Lucas to his core. More than that, it confused him. And he sure didn't need any more confusion in his life. So, yeah, he'd avoid the whole touching thing from here on out. Or at least until he figured out what was going on.

A car horn had him glancing at five-o'clock traffic backed up on the street. He was grateful they would have dinner before heading back to Homestead Pass. There was something to be said about living in a town where heavy traffic meant five cars waiting for the light at the intersection of Edison and Main.

"That went smoothly," Harper said.

"Hmm?" Lucas looked down at her.

"The attorney," Harper said. "Where were you?"

"I'm here. Lots on my mind." He nodded as her comment registered. "Thanks to your meticulous planning and preparation, everything has gone smoothly."

"Not a big deal," she demurred. "I wasn't looking for a pat on the back."

But it was a big deal. Despite his memory loss regarding how they'd gotten to where they were right now, and his misgivings, one thing was obvious. Harper had all the chops of an astute businesswoman. Sure, he might toss in a few good ideas here and there, but Harper held the reins that directed the operation.

It's not that he'd thought Harper was just a pretty face. That wasn't it. Long ago, he'd realized she was smart as can be as well as the consummate athlete on the circuit. Over the last three weeks since the accident, he'd discovered that she was a lot like her father as well—a leader with a natural head for business.

"You're wrong, Harp. It is a big deal. The guy was impressed with how you had everything ready to go. Dotted all your i's and crossed your t's is what he said. You made us look like we know what we're doing." He paused. "I know I've given you a lot of grief, but old Lucas and new Lucas both agree that you're doing a bang-up job."

She cocked her head and smiled, her green eyes sparkling. "Was that a compliment?"

"Yes. Absolutely a compliment, and you know what? It occurs to me that you're a lot like your daddy."

Harper rolled her eyes and started walking down the long stretch of sidewalk, her heels clicking on the pavement. "I am not even going to ask what that means."

Lucas shrugged and matched his steps to hers, taking note once again of how different she looked. Today she was all corporate in a suit and heels. Different in a way that messed with his head.

"All I'm saying is that, despite my issues, I appreciate what you've accomplished."

"I'm starving," she returned, shutting down the topic. "Are you hungry?"

"Oh yeah. My stomach has been rumbling for an hour. Where are we eating?"

"How about Italian, since I never got my ravioli? There's a cute little place around the corner and a block over that looks promising. Somewhere between fancy and a dive joint. Dana says the tiramisu is almost as good as Olivia's bistro."

"I'm in," Lucas said.

Harper looked at him. "Do you mind walking since the weather is so agreeable?"

"Not at all. Lead the way."

The aroma of sweet basil, oregano and tomatoes teased Lucas mercilessly as they settled into a soft pleather booth with menus. A smiling server took their beverage orders and placed glasses of ice water dripping with condensation in front of them.

Lucas grabbed a crisp grissini from the basket in the middle of the table and perused the menu. Thankfully, the lighting in the place wasn't too subdued, and the font was legible. Reading had become increasingly challenging lately. His glance landed on ravioli, and he looked up at Harper. "What did you mean you never got your ravioli? Were you talking about Olivia's restaurant?"

"No." She leaned forward. "We arranged to meet for dinner the evening of your accident."

"Saturday? We did?"

"Yes. Milano's Italian Restaurant in Lawton."

"Milano's," he murmured. Sort of a fancy place as he recalled. Maybe celebrating?

She scanned his face as though searching for a sign that he remembered. He didn't, though he sensed from her expression that this was a critical piece of information.

Lucas closed his eyes for a moment and could almost grasp the edge of a memory dancing on the periphery of his mind.

Milano's Italian Restaurant.

With Harper.

*Almost.* Then it was gone.

He looked at her and shook his head at the expectation in her eyes, which confirmed his gut intuition. There was something important about that dinner they were supposed to have. Lucas desperately longed to figure out what he couldn't remember.

"Sorry, Harp." Lucas released a long breath. "I have nothing."

"It's okay." She said the words softly.

"Is it? I feel like there's something off between you and me." He reached into his pants' pocket, pulled out two black pens with white script, and placed them on the table. "It would be real nice if I could recall stuff like ordering ten boxes of merchandise."

"The boxes? I take it they weren't farm supplies?"

"Nope."

Harper picked up a pen and rotated the barrel to read the print. "'Homestead Pass Training Center.'" She looked at him. "You ordered pens?"

"Oh, so much more than pens." Lucas began to count on his fingers. "There's also notepads, mugs, water bottles and ball caps." He shrugged. "I even got the name right."

"What? No T-shirts?" She gave a small laugh.

"Maybe they'll arrive next week. You were right. Apparently, I was very excited about this project when I placed the order."

*Excited when I placed the order.*

Lucas paused to mull his choice of words, sneaking a quick peek at Harper. She hadn't noticed. The date on the invoice was June. Yep, less than three months ago he'd been so enthusiastic about their joint business venture that he'd spent what amounted to a night's prize purse on swag.

Fast forward to now and he couldn't even recall how she'd become his partner. Once again, he was left feeling like he'd been dropped smack-dab into the middle of someone else's life.

"Seriously?' Harper chuckled. "Ten boxes? Where are they?"

"After Gramps tripped over them, I shoved them in the empty guest room."

"I like the colors you went with," she said. "We talked about colors and logos a few months ago."

"Did we talk about ordering pens?"

"No. But think positive. You now have merchandise for our cabin store." She took a sip of water. "How's that going? The cabin, I mean. Did you talk to Sam?"

"Ah, not yet." He studied the menu, hoping she'd let it slide.

"Not yet as in 'I can do it myself'?"

"Something like that." This time he met her gaze, silently pleading for her to let it go.

Harper opened her mouth and closed it as if she, too, wasn't looking to argue.

When their server interrupted with mugs of fresh steaming coffee and prepared to take their food order, Lucas made a mental note to leave a large tip.

"Butternut squash ravioli sounds good to me as well," Lucas said as he relinquished his menu.

He and Harper sipped coffee in silence for a moment. Good coffee. Lucas looked around. Nice place too. Not as nice as Moretti's Farm-to-Table Bistro, of course. He couldn't help but wonder about Milano's again. He and Harper usually favored hole-in-the-wall places on the road. Authentic and low-priced cuisine.

"Did I thank you for taking off work early to pick me up?" Lucas asked.

"You did. Twice." She set down her cup. "Tell me about your appointment with the neuro-optometrist," Harper said.

"Turns out I probably needed reading glasses all along, but

the doc isn't going to prescribe them until I've had at least four weeks of visual rehab."

"Visual rehab? You mentioned that before. How does that work?"

"I'm about to find out. All I know is that they tossed a lot of information at me today. Doctor speak. Words like *neurological event, visual motor balance* and *optometric visual therapy* were thrown around. The gist of it is prism lenses and eye training exercises. Once I get started, I'll be able to do some of the exercises at home."

"That's good, right?"

"I sure hope so. The goal is to eliminate the headaches, dizziness and anxiety when I read."

"Anxiety?"

Lucas looked around and then leaned closer. "Yeah. I get pretty anxious when I start to read, and my vision doubles or the headaches start and I get nauseous. It's a hamster wheel I haven't figured out how to dodge."

"It must be frustrating. Did he offer anything promising regarding riding?"

"I'll progress to riding with a helmet at all times once the vision issue is under control. I can drive then as well." He paused, his eyes wandering to the wavy grain of the wood tabletop. "But I'll never be going back to the circuit. I know I'm retiring and all, but it's different when you walk away on your own terms as opposed to not being able to get back in the arena because someone else has put the nail in your coffin."

"I'm sorry, Luc." She reached out and touched his hand.

Lucas grimaced at the jolt. There it was again. His pulse shot to Mach 3. He slid his hand away and studied his water glass.

"Thanks. I'm trying to focus on the positive. I'll be back in the saddle eventually, and I won't have to drive with Gramps." Lucas chuckled. "Have you ever driven with my grandfather?"

"I don't think so. I'm like you. I rarely relinquish my driver's seat."

"Well, let me tell you, it's like being on a tour bus. He stops to chat with everyone he knows. The man randomly signals, pulls over and rolls down the window. Yesterday, it took us an hour and a half to go from the ranch to the grocery store." Lucas shook his head. "By the way, Mary McAfee at the inn is having a bunionectomy next month. Her second. Winnie at the post office has a cousin whose son joined the army. And keep it under your hat, but Pastor McGuinness has a suspicious mole on his back."

Harper's laughter spilled out. "That's more news than I got from yesterday's *Homestead Pass Daily Journal*."

"Right?"

"Harper Reilly? Is that you?"

Harper swiveled quickly in her seat, eyes rounding with surprise. "Dallas!" A grin split her face as she jumped from her seat and flung her arms around a tall cowboy. Slightly embarrassed, she stepped away a moment later and motioned toward Lucas.

"Luc, this is Dallas Pettersen." She turned to the cowboy. "Dallas, meet my good friend, Lucas Morgan."

Slowly unfolding himself, Lucas rose to his feet. He narrowed his gaze and gave the young cowboy a slow assessment. The kid could have modeled Western clothing for a magazine with his crisp short-sleeved checkered shirt, razor-creased Wrangler jeans and spotless white-straw Stetson. The glossy buckle at his waist had been polished bright enough to blind a person in the sunlight. His face was clean-shaven with no stubble to be seen, emphasizing the angles of his jawline.

Though annoyance had Lucas frowning, he offered the other man his hand. "Pleased to meet you."

"Lucas Morgan? In the flesh. Wow, I've been following your career since I was a kid. I consider it an honor to meet an old-timer like yourself. Why, you have more time in the saddle than I have on the earth."

*Ouch. That hurt.*

"That might be a slight exaggeration," Lucas muttered. Even if it were true, men had been challenged to a duel at noon for less in the old Western days. He cocked his head. "How is it you two know each other?"

Harper looked at Dallas and they both laughed. "I know his parents. Family friends. I babysat Dallas and his sister when I was in college." She smiled. "I remember many a night helping you with sixth-grade algebra."

Dallas grimaced. "Don't remind me."

Lucas did the math as he ran a hand over his two-day beard. Dallas was somewhere around twenty-one or twenty-two. No way Harper would be interested in a kid that young.

His glance went from Harper to Dallas as the two old friends grinned at each other.

*Or would she?*

And why did it matter to him? They didn't interfere in each other's romantic life. Yep. That rule had been established years ago, he reminded himself. Harper was looking to settle down. He ought to be happy.

*I'm happy for her*, he repeated over and over in his head.

Lucas unclenched his fists and eyed the other cowboy while working on his happy face.

"What are you up to these days, Dallas?" Harper asked. "I heard you graduated from OSU last year."

The kid nodded. "Yep. Took the LSATs in the spring and sent off applications to law school. Now I'm hitting the circuit while I'm in wait mode."

"A cowboy lawyer. I love that." Harper turned to Lucas. "Very cool, right?"

"Oh yeah. Love it," Lucas returned. *Almost as good as a stick in the eye.*

"What about you? What are you doing in the city, Harper?" the cowboy asked.

"In town for business."

Dallas nodded, offering the full wattage of his smile. "Well, it's really good to see you."

"You too." Harper lifted a brow in Lucas's direction. "Would you like to join us for dinner, Dallas?"

*Nope. Nope. Nope.* Lucas willed the kid to refuse the offer.

"Oh no. I don't want to interrupt." Dallas nodded and gestured to the back of the room. "I've some buddies waiting for me. Wait until I tell them who I met." He shook his head slowly. "The two of you are like rodeo royalty."

"Not quite. But thanks for that, Dallas," Harper said with a laugh.

"Now, be sure to give me a call, Harper. I'd love to jaw about old times."

*Right. Old times.* Lucas glanced around. Where was that ravioli?

"I'll do that," Harper said and gave Dallas another hug.

"Nice to meet you, sir," the younger cowboy said.

"You, too, kid." Lucas sat down and gave a short laugh as the cowboy strode away. "Old-timer? Seriously?" he grumbled.

Harper slid into the booth. "Come on. We are getting old."

"Not me. I don't ever plan to get old. I'll be like Gramps. Frisky and sassy until the Good Lord takes me home."

"I don't doubt that." A soft smile touched Harper's lips. "Still, time keeps moving, pal. Though it seems like I was babysitting Dallas only yesterday."

"And now he's six foot tall and flirting with you."

"He was not." Eyes averted, Harper folded her napkin on her lap while her face turned pink.

Lucas laughed. "Yes, my friend. He was."

"Dallas is much too young for me."

Lucas glanced across the room where the young cowboy

sat with his friends. After a minute, Dallas turned and met Lucas's stare.

"Too young for you, huh? Maybe you ought to tell him that."

The icy stare he leveled at the cowboy had the kid offering a quick nod before he turned back around. Yeah, the youngster was definitely crushing on his one-time babysitter. And Lucas wasn't quite sure why it annoyed him so much.

"THERE'S A CONDO for sale in our community," Dana said.

Harper chased the last crumbs of mocha-chocolate birthday cake from her plate and then looked up at both of her sisters who sat across the family dining room table. It seemed she was always outnumbered at family events since Gram passed—Harper on one side of the table and her sisters and their spouses on the other.

"Did you have a nice birthday, Maddy?" Harper asked.

Her eldest sister chuckled at Harper's dodge of Dana's words. "I did. We left the kids with a sitter. Edgar and I had a lovely dinner at a new restaurant in the city before we came here for dessert."

Edgar nodded absently while he shot stealth glances at his smartwatch. Harper didn't quite understand what her sister saw in the tall, silent, tax attorney, but apparently there was someone for everyone.

"Hello. Did you hear me, Harper?" Dana persisted.

Harper smiled politely and reached for her water glass. "Were you speaking to me?" She tried not to sigh too loudly. The trouble with being the youngest was that everyone seemed determined to run her life.

"Yes. I said there's a condo on the market in my community. It's five minutes from work. There's a wonderful workout facility in the member's center, and we're only steps from the golf course and the country club." Dana turned to Allen. "We love our place. Right, honey?"

Allen glanced up from his dessert plate, looking confused for a moment. "Right. Right."

"You and I could commute to work together when Allen is out of town," Dana continued.

"Dana, I agreed to a two-month internship. Let me take things one day at a time," Harper said. She had zero desire to move to the city.

"Your father and I are so excited that you're working at the company." Her mother tucked a lock of short blond hair behind an ear and beamed at her youngest daughter. "Have you made a decision about the full-time position?"

"Not really." Harper cut herself another small wedge of Maddy's birthday cake. This was her third piece. If the conversation didn't detour to someone else soon, she wouldn't fit into her jeans. "Who made the cake? It's yummy. The raspberry jam filling is sublime."

"Mom special ordered it from a new bakery in Elk City," Dana said. "I've ordered our anniversary cake from there."

Undeterred, Harper's mother waved a hand in the air. "Sweetheart, you're going to have to give me a little more than that. Are you at least enjoying yourself there?"

Harper blinked. She disliked being in this position. Her parents were so certain two months at Reilly Pecans would change her career path. "Well, um…the training program is comprehensive. At the end of the month, I'll start working with the gal who's leaving. As her assistant."

"That's wonderful. You wouldn't be placed in such an important position if you weren't smart and talented."

*Or the boss's daughter.* Harper bit her lip. She hated contradicting her mother, especially when she was the parent who asked so little of her.

"Maureen, I know our girl will to be a force in the company." Colin looked at his wife and then around the table, his expression tender. "Won't it be wonderful when all our girls are part of Reilly Pecans?"

*Oh terrific. Now she was going to break her father's heart.*

Harper searched for a topic to divert the direction of the current train wreck. "You'll never guess who I ran into this week." She grinned and glanced around the table. "Dallas Pettersen."

"Dallas?" Her mom smiled. "How is he?" She shook her head. "Now you've reminded me, I should reach out to his parents. It's been so long."

"What's Dallas up to?" Maddy asked.

"Prelaw," Harper said.

"Dallas was always a good kid," her father said. "You could do worse."

Harper's jaw sagged. "Dad, I am not dating Dallas."

"Why not?"

"Oh my goodness. He's at least ten years younger than me, and I thought you didn't like cowboys."

"Age is only a number," her father said. "And you mentioned prelaw. Another attorney in the family couldn't hurt."

*"I am not dating Dallas."* She shoved another bite of cake into her mouth, savoring the sickly-sweet buttercream.

"What's the story on the construction that's about to begin at Lazy M Ranch?"

"What?" Harper's head popped up and she stared across the table at the ill-timed comment from Maddy's husband.

Edgar, of all people. The man never spoke at family gatherings. Tonight he chose to break his vow of silence? Harper swallowed hard and prayed that no one could see how unnerved she was.

Eyes on her plate, she responded. "I, um… What construction?"

"A friend of mine is consulting on a project that's about to break ground out there this autumn. I'm certain he said the Homestead Pass Training Center on the Lazy M Ranch."

"Oh that." She gestured with a flip of her hand. "Lucas is retiring and launching a rodeo and equestrian training center."

Dana blinked and leaned forward, hands clasped, elbows on the table. "That's huge news, Harp. Why haven't you said anything?"

"What's to say?"

"What do you mean 'what's to say'?" Dana continued. "Normally, all we hear is Lucas this and Lucas that."

"You're right, Dana. You should talk to Lucas about the project." Harper eyed the exits and picked up her fork again.

"Did I understand correctly that you're half of this project?"

*Edgar!*

Harper gripped the fork tightly. She glared at him. So much for sharing the news about the training center in her own time. Preferably, after the internship was completed.

"I'm more like a silent partner until my obligations with Reilly Pecans are met."

"How silent?" her father asked, his stare piercing.

"Maybe this isn't the place to discuss Harper's personal business," Maddy offered.

Harper glanced around the table. Despite Maddy's attempt to toss her a life preserver, all eyes remained on the youngest child.

"Harper, is all this true?" her mother asked.

"Ah… Yes."

"So this was the other option you were talking about?" her father asked.

"One of them. Yes. Financing has been up in the air. We only just received the green light from the bank."

Folding her linen napkin and placing it on the table, Harper worked to keep her voice level and calm. They couldn't see her hands shaking, could they?

"When did all this come about?" her mother asked.

"Oh, we've been kicking around the idea for some time." *That's right, Harper. Keep it casual.* "We both planned to retire in January. When Luc injured himself in August, the timeline was accelerated."

"You didn't tell your mother and I you were going to retire in January," her father said. "I would have remembered that."

Harper looked from her father to her mother. "I would have told you once all the details were ironed out."

"The details." He shook his head. "And how did you two finance such an undertaking, anyhow?"

Harper hesitated. "Dad, do we have to have financial discussion now?"

"I don't see why not. We're all family here." He glanced around. "We don't have secrets. Do we?"

Her eyes followed his, only to find everyone following the conversation with way too much interest.

"I used the property Gram left me as collateral," she finally said.

"Without discussing it with your mother or me?"

The dining room was silent, the tension uncomfortably thick and awkward.

"It's her inheritance, Colin," her mother interjected. "And she's thirty-two years old. You started Reilly Pecans at that age. I don't recall you asking anyone's permission. Don't you think we should be proud of her initiative?"

Relief flooded through Harper at the words. She mouthed a thank you to her ally as the odds shifted in her favor.

Colin released a sizeable harrumph. "I hope you feel the same if she loses that inheritance, Maureen." He turned to Harper. "I'd like to see your business plan, young lady. And I'd like to know how your commitment to Reilly Pecans fits in with this project with Lucas."

A slow pounding started at Harper's temple. "I'm happy to have you review my business plan when I have the opportunity, Daddy. As for my commitment to the family business, it remains unchanged. I promised you two months, and I intend to keep my promise."

The answer failed to soften her father's expression.

"I can't believe you're leaving the circuit," Dana said.

"That's up in the air as well. I might still rodeo on the side." She cleared her throat. "As I said, retirement was on my radar for next year. The timeline for the school has been moved up with Luc's injury."

Edgar gestured with a hand as if ready to add to the conversation. Before he could, Maddy stood. "Not another word, Edgar." She glanced at her watch. "The babysitter is on a tight schedule. We're going to have to wrap this party up."

Dana stood, as well, and looked at everyone. "Don't forget. My anniversary party is coming up."

"How could we forget, Dana?" Maddy murmured. "You've reminded us a dozen times."

"Now, Madeline," Colin said. "Be nice. Your sister is very excited."

Harper's phone buzzed amid the intensifying white noise of family discussion. She stared at the device, grateful for the diversion.

It was Luc. Oh boy, could she use a dose of Lucas Morgan right now.

"I have to get this. It's very important." She pushed back her chair and dashed out of the room and out of the house to the front portico with its massive pillars.

She pressed the answer button. "Luc, what's up?"

"Am I interrupting anything?"

"Not a thing." The warm breath of evening embraced her as she spoke. Harper relaxed against a column, hidden from the tall windows of the dining room.

"Are you sure? You sound…funny."

"Just another night at the Reilly's. We celebrated Maddy's birthday. Edgar threw me under the bus. Oh, and my father is furious about my life choices, as usual."

"Why furious?"

"He found out about the training center and doubts my commitment to the pecan business."

"Furious sounds pretty serious."

"I don't want to talk about it." She paused. "What's up with you?"

"Did you show him the business plan? Colin will be impressed if you show him the paperwork."

"We didn't get that far. And I really do not want to talk about it." Further discussion would only stoke Luc's belief that her father didn't like him.

"Okay. Sure."

"You called because…"

"You didn't RSVP for the barbecue party tomorrow night."

Harper chuckled. "It's not like you sent out formal invitations or RSVP requests."

"No, but we made a deal, and I'm verifying that you're still coming, thus upholding your end of our bargain."

"Getting nervous?" she asked.

"You have no idea. I haven't had a party since Trev and I turned eight."

"That's not true. You told me that Gus threw you a graduation party after college. Mini golf in Oklahoma City."

"Not the same thing. Besides, I'm the host. I've never hosted an event before. It's a huge responsibility."

"Loretta Moretti is catering. There's nothing for you to do but smile and enjoy your guests."

"Easy for you to say."

"Absolutely. Because never in a zillion years would I throw a party for all my exes."

"How many exes do you have?"

"Not many, and yet I still wouldn't ever be so foolhardy." She paused. 'I'm not sure I understood your rationale for this event in the first place. A party to return dishes?"

"Think of it as a giant thank-you card. Besides, I'm fortunate to be alive, and I want to celebrate that."

"Gratefulness. Okay, I can get on board with that. Embrace it for the next twenty-four hours and you won't be nervous." Harper paused. "'In everything give thanks.'"

"Sounds familiar."

"First Thessalonians 5:18." A verse she ought to embrace as well. Life was all upside down right now. Despite how things appeared, the Lord never changed. That was what she should focus on.

"'In everything give thanks,'" he repeated. "I like it. Short and to the point." Luc paused. "Are you sure you don't want me to talk to Colin?"

"No. Absolutely not." Luc talking to her father could only add fuel to a simmering fire.

"Alright. If you say so." He was silent for a moment. "See you tomorrow, Harp."

"Yes. Thanks, Luc."

"Thanks? For what?"

A smile escaped as Harper imagined Luc's intent gaze upon her. His blue eyes concerned.

"Thanks for being my friend," she answered.

"Any time, buddy. Any time."

Harper slid the phone into her pocket and moved closer to the windows that framed the front of the house, revealing the dining room and hall. Maddy and Edgar stood in the foyer, saying their goodbyes, along with Dana and Allen.

She reached for the doorknob, praying the bell hadn't rung on round two of dinner with the Reillys.

"'In everything give thanks,'" she whispered.

# CHAPTER SEVEN

TREVOR POKED HIS head into the kitchen. "Luc, there's a guy outside who wants to talk to you about a horse."

"Is that the start of a cheesy joke?" Lucas laughed, picked up his coffee mug from the kitchen table and took a long swallow.

"Nope. There's a guy outside with a mare. Says you bought her."

Lucas glanced at the wall clock. The barbecue party kicked off in less than an hour. "I knew it. Everything's been going so well up to now. Of course, the other boot had to drop."

"Howdy, Ms. Moretti," Trevor called.

Loretta Moretti turned from the counter where she and a catering assistant reviewed notes on a clipboard.

"Trevor, lovely to see you. Will all your family be with us tonight?"

Gramps stepped into the kitchen. "Yes, ma'am. The boys and their wives got babysitters so they could be here tonight to support Lucas."

"Wonderful," Loretta said. "I haven't seen your handsome grandsons all together since Trevor's wedding."

Trevor smiled and put a hand on his grandfather's shoulder, leaning close. "Are you sure they aren't here for the entertainment portion of the show, Gramps?"

"That too," Gus chuckled.

"Is there entertainment besides the band?" Loretta asked. "I wasn't aware."

"No," Lucas said. "That's just Gramps being facetious. No worries."

Loretta nodded. "What about these containers on the kitchen table? Could you remind me why they are here?"

"They belong to our guests and, hopefully, they'll claim them before the night ends," Lucas said.

"I see." She smiled and waved a hand at the stack of dishes on the counter. "Well, if you'll excuse me. There's some last-minute preparation to be done. Guests will be arriving any time now."

"Oh sure." Lucas nodded. "I gotta see a man about a horse."

He stepped outside with Trevor behind him to find a gray-haired cowboy, wearing a smile that lit up his leathery face, approach the house.

"Son, let me apologize for taking so long to get here. I tried to call you half a dozen times, but your voice mail was full, and I couldn't get through. I plain gave up. Good thing you drew me that map to your ranch."

"Thanks for coming out. When was it I bought the horse?"

The cowboy blinked at the question. "Early August."

Lucas nodded. "As it turns out, shortly after that, I hit a tree with my pickup and lost a good bit of my memory."

Pushing back the brim of his worn and yellowed straw cowboy hat, the older man cocked his head. "So you've got amnesia? Like in the movies." He clucked his tongue. "Well, ain't that something."

"Yes, sir. It surely is," Lucas agreed. Though "something" didn't even begin to cover the last few weeks.

"Are you trying to get out of this deal? Best be up-front right now, son."

Taken aback by the question, Lucas shook his head. "No,

sir. I am not. I'm asking you to explain what we agreed on for me again."

"'Spose I ought to introduce myself if you don't recall." He bowed. "Hector Alvarado, at your service. Back when your daddy was riding broncs, he and I were tight, seeing as we both had a love for the Lord." Hector held up two fingers close together in a sweeping gesture. "I was at his memorial service, though I doubt you recall. Long time ago. Still miss him and your momma."

Lucas nodded, acknowledging the sentiment, and finding himself intrigued and curious about a rodeo friend of his father's. "It's an honor to meet you, sir. Were you a bronc rider as well?"

"Oh no. I'm a bulldogger. Sometimes your daddy worked as my hazer."

From behind Lucas, Trevor cleared his throat, reminding him of his presence. "This is my brother, Trevor. Trev manages the ranch."

"Pleased to meet you." The clanging and squeaking of a horse trailer opening had the men turning. "That's my eldest," Hector said. "Rode with me from Skiatook."

Lucas smiled as Hector's son brought a sorrel mare around the trailer. "So I bought a horse," he said. Every day brought a new surprise. If his life were a novel, no one would believe it was all possible.

Hector nodded. "Paid cash and everything. I've got a copy of your bill of sale in the truck, if you need it."

"No, that's fine. I probably have my copy in the house." With all the other papers in the office that he hadn't read yet.

"Mighty fine-looking animal," Trevor said.

When the mare shook her reddish mane and snorted, Hector's son ran a hand over the animal's flank and murmured soothing words.

"Della is a beauty. Good-natured as well," Hector said. "I was supposed to have her down to your ranch in August, but

I ran into some problems. Like I said, I tried to call. Finally, I gave up. I figured I'd get here when I get here."

"Turns out we both had problems," Lucas said. "My phone bit the dust in the accident. Apologies for the confusion."

"Aw, no problem. I'm here. You're here. And so is Della. All's well."

"You're right," Lucas said.

"Why don't I have Slim Jim take Della to the corral and check her out?" Trevor said.

"Thanks, Trev."

"Slim Jim?" Hector asked.

"Jim is the ranch horse whisperer."

Hector nodded. "As soon as Della is checked, we'll take off."

"Getting dark soon," Lucas returned. "We've a little barbecue party about to start. Why don't you stick around? You're welcome to spend the night in the bunkhouse and head out in the morning."

Hector cocked his head and looked Lucas up and down. "You sure? Don't want to crash a party."

"It's only friends, and you're a friend, Hector." Lucas smiled.

"That's mighty generous of you." The man inhaled and smiled. "I can smell smoked pork on the grill, which means I'd be a fool to say no." The old cowboy glanced around. "You boys have done a fine job with this ranch. Your daddy would be proud."

"Thanks," Lucas said. "It's mostly my brothers."

"Nah," Hector said. "It takes a village." He grinned. "Point me to the bunkhouse and we'll get cleaned up."

"Straight up that path toward the red barn. First building on your left. And when you're ready, follow the path to the back of the house. You can't miss the tents we set up."

"Thank you kindly." Hector tipped his hat and headed over to his son, who waited at the horse trailer.

"Who was that?"

Lucas turned at Sam's voice. "That was a man I bought a horse from. Hector Alvarado. Friend of Dad's. Sound familiar?"

"Yeah, it does. He lived in Homestead Pass for a short time." Sam gave a slow nod. "Well, I'll be. That brings back more than a few memories."

"Such as?" Lucas prompted. Once again, he found himself eager for information about his parents.

"Hector and his wife held a Bible study in their home for a while. Mom and Dad were regulars. I know because I had to babysit you and Trev. I was about fifteen and you two were eleven." He grimaced and shook his head. "Yep, that was around the time you fell out of the hay loft and broke your arm. Good times."

"I was a kid," Lucas protested.

"You sure were." Sam looked at Lucas. "A horse? How does the horse fit into all of this?"

"You tell me." Lucas frowned. "Did Gramps happen to mention the boxes?"

Sam chuckled. "He did."

"There you go. I've ten boxes of merch, a ring, and now a horse. Makes me wonder what else I got myself into."

"You might find out tonight. Are you sure you're ready for that?"

"I don't have any other options. I have a couple dozen questions and zero answers."

"Did you call the jeweler to find out if the clerk that sold you that diamond remembered you?"

"I did. The clerk that sold the ring to me was let go. The owner can't even find the sale in the computer system. He blames it on their new point-of-sale software. Says the transaction has to be in there somewhere and assured me that he'd call me as soon as they figure out what happened." Lucas ran a hand over his face. "I am not feeling reassured."

"Maybe Liv will have some ideas."

"Liv? You told your wife?" Lucas gave his brother a shove. "Does everyone know about my personal problems?"

"She's my wife. We don't keep secrets."

"Why not?"

"Oh, grasshopper, you have a lot to learn."

A guitar twang, followed by the screech of a microphone and the static of a sound system setting up, interrupted the conversation. A moment later, the notes of a familiar country song floated to them from the other side of the house.

Trevor walked across the gravel to rejoin Lucas. "So you hired a band," his brother said. "Anyone I know?"

"I didn't hire a band. Gramps did. Three gals. They're Jane's granddaughters. Call themselves the Dixie Hens. Gramps said they've been on tour with L. C. Kestner."

"Who?" Trevor scrunched up his face and looked at Sam, who shrugged.

"Got me," Lucas said. "Allowing an octogenarian to find the band for a bunch of millennials may not have been my best move."

"Gramps is a man for all generations," Sam said. "Let's give the Dixie Hens a chance."

"Fair enough," Lucas returned.

"So I heard about your plan," Trevor said.

Lucas released a sound of protest as he stared at Sam. "Did you tell the whole world?"

"Aw, cut it out," Trevor said. "I'm your twin. I knew something was up. You should have told me yourself. And if you had, I'd have said this whole idea sounds risky. With your amnesia, there's about a dozen ways to put your foot in your mouth. Bad idea, Luc."

"It's not a bad idea. It's a very efficient plan. Besides, it's Sam's idea. He's the one who mentioned Cinderella. That prince should have worked smarter, not harder. Gathering all the women I know in one place saves time and money."

"Do not blame me for this fiasco," Sam said.

"It's not a fiasco. And I'd appreciate a little help tonight. I need ears in the crowd. Once the party starts, mingle. You might hear something important."

"You expect us to mingle and chat up twenty single women in front of our wives?" Sam asked. "That is the second dumb thing you've said in ten minutes. Man, you really don't understand women, do you?"

"No. He doesn't," Drew said as he joined them.

"You told Drew too?" Lucas glared at Sam. "Big mouth."

"I forced it out of him," Drew said.

"For the record, I invited the ranch wranglers as well." Lucas shook his head, eager to change the subject. "So have you seen my new horse?"

"And what's with that?" Trevor asked. "Though I will admit Della is a fine animal. Do you need another horse?"

"I'm starting a training school. Makes perfect sense."

"And another thing…" Trevor continued. "How come I was the last to hear about your training school? Good thing Sam keeps me in the loop." Trevor eyed Lucas.

"Trev, I told you I planned to retire first of the year. I also told you I planned to start a training center."

"First of the year is January. This is September. The way I hear it, construction starts soon."

"Since I'm grounded, we moved up the timeline." Lucas shrugged.

"'We'?" Trevor asked.

"Me and Harper," Lucas said.

"You're fortunate to have her on your team," Drew said.

"Oh, she's more than on his team," Sam said. "She's his business partner."

Trevor shook his head and looked at Lucas again. "We need to have a sit-down chat. I've learned more in the last three minutes about my own brother's life than I have in six months."

"Welcome to my world," Lucas said. "I don't know what happened the last six months either."

"Are you able to recall anything?" Trevor asked.

"Not a thing." He shook his head. "I've signed a contract, taken on a business partner, and am about to break ground on my parcel. Can't remember planning any of it."

"If you're using your parcel for the training center, where do you plan to live?" Trevor asked.

"I'm doing fine at the ranch house with Gramps."

"You're gonna live with Gramps forever?" Trevor asked. Both Sam and Drew had amused smiles on their faces.

"Are you trying to make a point here?"

"Yeah, I am. You have a ring and, somewhere out there, you have a future Mrs. Lucas Morgan. She won't want to live at the main house with your grandfather."

"How do you know that? Seems to me like my timing is pretty spot on. You left and got married. I'm there now. Gramps isn't alone in that big house." He looked at Trevor. "Why are you looking for trouble where there is none?"

"I'm just saying."

Lucas shrugged, hesitant to admit that Trevor had a point. What if his bride didn't have warm feelings about the Morgan homestead? The white-clapboard home had been around for over forty years. The place had been added onto more times than he could count. Most women wanted a new modern house when they started their married life.

He kicked at a rock. Nope. Not going there. He had bigger fish to fry right now than worrying about where he and his mystery bride would live.

"I want to know about that horse," Drew said.

"Nothing to know. It's a horse. A man can always use another horse."

"When did you have time to buy a horse since you've been home?" his eldest brother persisted.

"I didn't. I bought it sometime while on the circuit."

In the distance, the sound of vehicles crunching over gravel could be heard. Headlights skipped over the large moss-covered pillars that stood like sentries at the entrance of the ranch drive and lit up the drive as they approached.

"Mind if we finish this conversation later?" Lucas asked.

"Not a problem." Drew pinned him with a look. "We have a lot to talk about."

"Looks like your guests are arriving," Sam said. "You better go get changed."

"I did change." Lucas looked down at his black T-shirt and Wranglers. "Showered too."

"Aren't you going to shave?"

"I shaved yesterday." He ran a hand over his stubble. "If there's a woman out there willing to wear my ring, she likes me just like I am."

"Oh brother." Sam groaned and rolled his eyes. "That's not exactly how Prince Charming works."

Lucas grinned. "It's how Lucas Morgan does."

A luxury sedan parked and a dark-haired woman carefully stepped out of the vehicle. Despite the setting sun, oversize white sunglasses obscured her face. She wore a red blouse, its collar raised, along with a white skirt and red peep-toe shoes. Removing the sunglasses, she moved carefully over the gravel toward him.

"Is that Claire Talmadge?" Drew asked.

"Sure is," Sam said. He gave a nod to the cute brunette. "Didn't she leave for New York to model or become an actress or something?"

"That's what I heard," Trevor added.

"It's showtime, fellas." Lucas waved his brothers off with a hand. "Time for you to disappear."

"Claire Talmadge. Tough job, but someone's gotta do it," Sam said. "Never understood why she gave you a second glance and ignored the handsome Morgan brother. Me."

Drew gave Sam a light smack on the back of the head. "That's because you were head-over-boots in love with Olivia, goofball."

Lucas ignored his brothers as he crossed the yard to meet his old flame. For the life of him, he couldn't pinpoint the exact details surrounding why they'd parted ways. He did recall that while Claire was one of the most beautiful women he'd ever dated, they hadn't had much in common.

"Claire, thanks so much for stopping by."

The brunette smiled and glanced over his shoulder. "Did I scare off your brothers?"

"Nah, they have someplace to be."

Claire put a hand on his arm. The gesture set off the tinkling of a dozen silver bracelets on her wrist. She smiled. "It was so nice to run into you in San Antonio. I told my mom we had dinner. Mom considers you the one that got away."

"I, uh…" Lucas swallowed, panic choking him as he searched for a response. Could Claire be the one?

"You can breathe, Lucas." Claire's laughter trilled. "I think you're wonderful, too, but my fiancé is pretty special."

"You're engaged." Relief hit like a welcome rain.

"A gal can't wait around for Lucas Morgan forever." She raised her left hand and wiggled the fingers to show off a rock the size of Texas.

"Congratulations," he said.

"Thank you." Claire paused. "What about you? As I recall, you mentioned a special woman on your mind that evening."

Lucas did a double take at the comment. "I did?"

"Yes. Though you never said who it was."

They chatted for a few minutes and when Claire sashayed off to the party, Lucas spent a few minutes trying to recall dinner with the brunette. Dinner where he'd mentioned another woman.

Ninety minutes later, the party was in full swing and Lucas did the math. He'd ruled out ten of his twenty female guests. He'd tried to locate Harper, but every single time he tried to find her, another of his former girlfriends managed to corner him for a one-on-one chat. He may have lost a chunk of memory and couldn't recall the names of a few of them, but the reason why some of these women were exes came back to him within a few minutes of conversation.

"Lucas!" a singsong female voice called out.

He turned to see a perky redhead in a short-sleeved plaid shirt, Wranglers and cowboy boots approach. A redhead he'd never seen before in his life. Her long strawberry hair swung, kissing her shoulders as she walked his way.

She grinned. "I'd say long time no see, but I did see you at the Lawton rodeo."

"Lawton," Lucas murmured. That was where he'd left six months of his life along the roadside. He prayed the deer fared better.

"It was so lovely of you to invite me. How are you doing? I heard you hit your head pretty hard."

He glanced down at her and squirmed. Was she really batting her eyelashes? "You know me. Hardheaded."

"Did you get the flowers I sent?"

"Sure did. Thank you." Her flowers had to be among the dozen or so arrangements delivered from the Elk City florist.

"That's why I decided to have this shindig," Lucas continued. "To thank everyone for their kindness. A man finds out who his friends are when he's laid out."

"This is very generous of you. I was more than surprised to get that message inviting me. How did you get my number?"

"I called the florist and asked them to reach out to you."

A phone started ringing and Lucas glanced around.

"Your phone is ringing."

"Is that mine?" Lucas chuckled. "Guess so." He pulled his device from his pocket and stared at the screen. *Harper.* "If you'll excuse me a moment, I better take this." With a nod, he stepped away from the redhead.

"This is your friend Harper saving you from Ginny Malone."

"Who?" he asked.

"Ginny Malone. Trick rider. That's the woman you're chatting with. We met her in Lawton in August. Be careful. She's half in love with you and only needs a bit of encouragement to push her over the line."

"Oh?" Lucas looked back at the redhead and offered an awkward smile when she cocked her head and batted her eyelashes again. "*Oh!* That's not good." He glanced around again. "Where are you?"

"Over by the band."

Lucas eyed the band area where Harper stood next to the makeshift stage. She grinned and waved at him.

"You better get back to Ginny," she said. "Let her down easy, Lucas."

Let her down easy? He couldn't recall who she was. The only thing he was sure of was that the redhead was not the woman who held his heart. No way. No how.

It took a good fifteen minutes to convince Ginny that he couldn't come to Lawton to visit her next week. By the time he'd directed her interest to the dessert table, Harper was nowhere to be found.

"Having fun?" Gramps asked. His grandfather sidled up next to him with a can of Dr Pepper in his hand.

"Define fun," Lucas asked.

Gramps chuckled. "This was your idea."

"So it was." The night wasn't a total failure. It was good to see his friends and former girlfriends. Though, so far, he didn't have a clue who the woman he'd fallen in love with could be.

"Appreciate you letting your brothers help with the party."

Lucas turned and looked at his grandfather. "Huh?"

"You let them help you. Normally, you're all about doing everything yourself."

"Am I?" He frowned, letting that information sink in.

"Yep. Nice of you to invite Hector and his son to the party too."

"Friend of Dad's. Seemed like the right thing to do." Lucas

glanced at his grandfather once again. "Did you know Hector back then?"

"Ran into him a time or two. 'Course, I was living in Tulsa when your daddy was on the circuit."

Lucas nodded, his scrutiny spanning what he could see of the ranch in the moonlight. The silhouette of the old barn stood out against the black-velvet night sky. Hector was right. His daddy would be proud of how his brothers had built up the Lazy M. The ranch was their father's legacy. Once again, Lucas asked himself what his legacy would be.

"Your brothers are having a good time on the dance floor," Gramps observed. "Good for them to get out without the kids on occasion."

He looked in the direction of the band. Drew and Sadie, Sam and Liv, and Trevor and Hope all moved to the slow strains of a ballad. Lucas's heart clutched at the sight. He longed for what his brothers had.

"Here comes Harper," his grandfather murmured.

Harper walked across the grass, illuminated by the overhead lights that Sam and Drew had strung from the tent to the path leading to the drive. His eyes followed her the entire time. She wore a peach dress that swished around her legs as she moved. When their gazes connected, Harper's mouth lifted in a sweet smile that warmed him.

There was something comforting about his old friend's presence. Something that said everything was going to be all right.

"Doesn't she look pretty tonight?" Gramps continued.

"Yeah. Real pretty," Lucas murmured, surprised at the thud of his heart. For a moment all he could think about was how she'd felt in his arms when she'd nearly killed herself on those steps at the cabin.

"Maybe you oughta think about falling for someone like Harper," Gramps said.

"Harper?" Lucas blinked. "We're just friends."

"Keep telling yourself that," his grandfather said. The elder Morgan began to wander in the direction of the band.

"Where you going, Gramps?"

"Going to find someone to chat with who doesn't need glasses." He waved a hand. "Make sure you talk to that eye doc about your vision problems."

"I have."

Gramps shook his head. "You're not getting any better, son. I'll be praying."

Lucas chuckled. Once Gramps got an idea in his head, he hung on to it like a dog with a bone.

Fact was, there was nothing he'd like more than to find someone like Harper. Sweet, smart and beautiful.

That person didn't exist and, as he reminded himself half a dozen times, there was no way he'd cross the line and ruin the special friendship between himself and Harper.

HARPER REACHED LUCAS as the band started its second set of the night. The song was the cover of a popular romantic country ballad. A warm breeze mussed her hair and she pushed the long locks away from her face. She eyed the dance floor where twinkling lights woven through the trees cast a soft glow on the event as the cowgirls and cowboys paired up.

"Are you dancing tonight?" Harper asked.

"Ah, no." Luc's eyes were shuttered as his gaze skimmed over her. He ran a hand across his face and nodded. "Nice dress."

Harper took his expression as a positive indicator. Lucas rarely commented on her appearance. Maybe his hit on the head had changed that. She could only hope he'd start seeing her as a woman and not just his buddy.

"I got it at that little boutique across the street from Sam's shop, next to the bookstore. Glitz and Glam."

Realizing that all of Luc's exes would be here tonight, she'd gone into the boutique and bought an overpriced stunner of a dress. She refused to give up without a fight. Once upon a time, she and Lucas had connected. Harper had waited a long time to see tenderness reflected in his eyes. Maybe what she saw tonight was more than tenderness. Whatever it was, she hadn't imagined it.

"Are you having fun?" Harper asked.

"You're the second person to ask me that." Luc smiled. "I'm enjoying the food. That's for sure. Did you try the mac and cheese? Loretta says it's a blend of Asiago and Cheddar. I want to know what the crunchy stuff on top is."

Harper looked up at him. Sometimes he was so dense. "I'm not talking about the food, Luc."

"What are you talking about?"

Suddenly irritated, Harper waved a hand around. "This reality show you staged. Was there some kind of plan here inviting all your girlfriends? I mean besides the excuse of needing to return their dishes?"

Lucas shrugged and looked away. "Yeah, there was. I can't remember stuff, Harper. Important stuff." He cleared his throat. "I've spoken to nearly all the women here…well, except the ones that got married or engaged in the last six months."

"Are you going to get to the point soon?"

"Did you happen to notice…? I mean… Did I say something that might lead you to believe that I was maybe seeing one of these ladies before I lost my memory?"

Harper groaned aloud as she clenched and unclenched her hands. "No, Lucas, you did not. We've discussed this before. I do not keep track of your love life."

His eyes popped wide at her response. "Easy there. Just asking."

"And I'm just telling."

"Whoa. I'm sorry. It wasn't my intention to annoy you, Harp." He took her hand and held it gently. "I apologize."

He looked down at her, concern in his blue eyes, his lips a worried line. His caramel-colored hair curled at the nape of his neck and the stubble on his angular face had her itching to lay her palm on his cheek.

"Fine." She pulled her hand free from the torture of touching his. "Try to remember that I'm here to support you, and not to analyze your love life."

"Okay, got it. No talk about women." He offered a half smile. "Let's start over. How about if we chat about horses?"

"Horses. You're going to have to be more specific than that. Why do you want to talk about horses?"

"A fella from Skiatook just delivered a pretty mare. I bought her a few months ago. Turns out, he was a friend of my father's."

"You bought a horse."

Luc sighed. "Yep. I bought a horse, just like I bought the pens and mugs and other merch."

"You don't remember buying this horse?"

"Nope."

"Well, you were going to have to pick up a horse or two once the training center opened."

"Yeah, there is that. Except if my timeline is correct, I purchased the horse when I thought the center would open next spring."

"True," Harper said with a nod. "Did you know this fella was a friend of your father's before you bought the horse? I mean it probably doesn't matter in the scheme of things, but you have to wonder."

"Hmm." Luc cocked his head and rubbed his chin. "That's an excellent question. I don't know." He nodded at the grills. "Hector Alvarado. That's him, with the big smile, talking to Gramps."

Harper's eyes followed Luc's to where Gus Morgan and an older cowboy stood deep in conversation.

"I'll ask him."

"Luc, wait. I want to meet your horse."

"Stop by tomorrow after church?"

"Sure."

"Great." His smile broadened. "Now, don't go away. I'm going to talk to Hector and then I'll find you."

Harper nodded. *Do that, Luc. Find me.*

He walked away and her gaze followed him. Would she always be following Luc? Attending this party was a terrible idea.

Maybe her father was right and she was fooling herself. After fourteen years of friendship, was she simply another Lucas Morgan buckle bunny, hoping for his attention, pretending to herself she meant more to him?

"Some things never change. Do they? Lucas Morgan is as handsome as ever."

"What?" Harper spun around at the comment. "Jackie! I didn't expect to see you here. What a nice surprise." The tall, smiling brunette had been Harper's close friend in her early days on the circuit, as they were both from Oklahoma. Over the years, their paths had crossed less and less, a regrettable result of their nomadic lifestyle.

"I heard through the circuit grapevine that Lucas won't be going back to bronc riding. I had to stop by."

"He'll be thrilled to see you." Harper smiled. "What about you? Are you still team roping? I heard you won in Vegas last year."

"Can't do it forever. One more year and then I'll retire." She shrugged. "I always feel a pull to settle down come autumn. The leaves turn and the air smells like change. I long to find a place of my own to burrow into. My partner retired, which compounds things. I don't suppose you'd be interested in joining me part-time next year."

"I might be. Everything is up in the air right now," Harper returned. "Luc and I are working on a training center. We'll be hiring instructors come early spring, and the facility will allow for private instruction. Maybe I could give you a call when things fall into place and I know my schedule with the training center."

"Do that, and think about roping, will you?" The other woman grinned. "If you have time with being the president of the Lucas Morgan fan club and all."

"Am I?"

"It's pretty much common knowledge."

"I guess there are worse things," Harper said with a laugh. Except it wasn't funny. Not at all. She didn't want to be the needy woman in the shadows waiting for crumbs from Luc's table and she sure didn't like the idea that was what others saw when they looked at her. "Mind if I ask you a personal question, Jackie?"

"Go for it."

"Why did you and Luc break up? You dated for a while, as I recall."

"Luc's a great guy, but I can't say he ever let me see past that charming smile. I wanted more." Jackie lifted a shoulder. "Luc is one hundred percent wonderful, but he holds back. What he's thinking, what he's feeling."

Harper nodded. The words were a fair assessment, though she had been allowed to see behind the curtain a few times. Luc wore a mask that he rarely removed. The emotion he'd shared at the cabin after the Kids Day Event had been rare. Would he ever drop his guard completely?

"I'm guessing you're closer to him than anyone," Jackie said.

"We're friends. If that's what you mean."

"Oh, don't sell yourself short, Harper." The other woman offered a kind smile. "You mean much more than that to Luc."

Harper remained silent, unmoved by Jackie's words. She meant a lot to him, but not in the way she'd hoped.

Jackie stepped closer and peered at Harper. "Oh my. You're in love with him, aren't you?"

She looked at her friend and nearly crumbled as the question hit the target with surprising accuracy. Jackie cut through all the layers of excuses Harper so readily spouted day after day, year after year.

"Is it so obvious?"

Jackie nodded, her smile gentle. "Have you thought about telling him how you feel?"

Harper swallowed. "If I tell him, I run the risk of losing his friendship."

"Maybe it's worth the risk, Harper. You can't go on in this limbo forever."

"You're right." Harper sighed. "You're absolutely right." It occurred to her that Jackie's insight wasn't much different than her father's. The difference was that her friend had been there and done that and knew what it felt like.

Silence stretched between them for a minute as forlorn strains of a ballad filled the air.

"So you two are starting a training center. That's why you're back in Homestead Pass," Jackie said.

"I'm working with my father short-term and planning the training center with Luc. Like you, I'm trying to figure out what to do with the rest of my life."

"A lot of that going around." A woman's laughter rose above the chatter of party guests. Jackie turned to Harper, brows raised. "Claire Talmadge is here?"

"Yes, she's in town visiting her folks."

"This is like old home week, isn't it? Remember how the three of us used to run around?"

What Harper recalled was that Luc had dated all her friends.

"I'm going to go give Claire a hello and find Lucas."

"Do that, and don't forget to check out the buffet."

"I will." Jackie squeezed Harper's hand. "Hang in there, honey."

"Oh, that's my specialty."

For minutes, Harper replayed what Jackie had said. When the band burst into a fun tune, she began to tap her toes.

"Nice party." Harper turned to find Slim Jim, the ranch horse whisperer, standing nearby with a soda in his hand.

"It is. Do you want to dance?" she asked.

Jim dropped the soda and stumbled while working to pick up the can as it spewed its contents. "I, uh… Not right now. Thank you."

Harper's jaw sagged at the cowboy's response. Deer in the headlights was an understatement.

"What is with that look?" she asked. "Am I repulsive or something?"

"No, ma'am. You look fine. It's Luc. I don't want to get him mad at me."

"Luc? What does Luc have to do with me asking you to dance? Maybe you didn't get the memo. Luc and I are friends. Best buds. Amigos."

"That may very well be true, but I don't think he'd be a fan of me dancing with his friend."

"Is that right?" Harper's breath came out in short staccato bursts as she worked to control her anger.

"I gotta go." Jim raised his palms and started to slowly back up. "I'm pretty sure my mother is calling me."

"Your mother?"

"Yes, ma'am. If she's not, she ought to be. I told myself I was going to keep out of trouble this month, and you're not helping matters."

Harper looked around for Luc and spotted him standing with a woman on either side of him, a grin splitting his face. She turned on her heel and headed down the drive toward her truck. It was time to end this fun and games. She was so over being Luc's sidekick.

It was time for her to prayerfully make decisions about her future. A future that didn't include waiting on Lucas Morgan.

# CHAPTER EIGHT

LUCAS LEANED AGAINST the corral fence. Inside the fence, Slim Jim worked with Della. The animal allowed Jim to rub her neck and add a rope halter. Jim walked the mare through a series of exercises. Each time the animal proved to be docile and cooperative. Perfect for training students at the soon-to-be training center.

Pulling out his cell phone, Lucas called Harper again. For the third time, it went to voice mail, so he tried texting.

Looks like you aren't coming by to see my horse. Let me know if you're okay or I'll have to come looking for you.

Harper's response was immediate.

Sorry. Busy day. I'll catch you later.

"Who're you texting?" Sam angled himself around from his perch on the top rung of the fence, doing his best to peek at the screen of Lucas's phone.

"Harper. She was supposed to come by after church."

"I heard she left the party early last night. Jim said she was upset about something."

Lucas glared at his brother. "Remember how I explained that Harper and I don't discuss our personal romantic business?"

"Yeah."

Lucas shoved the phone back in his pocket. "Thanks to your advice, I tried to pick her brain about that very topic. It didn't go well at all."

Sam pushed back the brim of his hat and shook his head. "Uh-uh. That's not my fault. I said you don't know a thing about women, and I stand by that statement."

"Me? Your idea. Your fault."

"Nope. I warned you before you sent out invitations to that train wreck."

"It wasn't a train wreck. I figured out that not a one of those women from my past were in the running for my future."

When Cooper and Patch, two of the family ranch dogs, barked and whined, Trevor and his son, Cole, turned from the fence to see what the fuss was.

"Lower your voice," Trevor said. "You're upsetting the dogs and spooking the horse."

"What are you two arguing about anyhow?" Drew asked.

"Discussing. Not arguing," Sam said. "Lucas is in hot water with Harper."

"I don't know that for sure," Lucas said.

"I think she's mad at you," Sam continued.

"Not surprised."

Lucas turned to Drew. "What's that supposed to mean?"

"It means you can't invite nearly two dozen women to a party without expecting some fallout."

"That's not a fair assessment," Lucas protested. The party hadn't provided the results he'd hoped for. However, chatting with his guests had filled in a few more details on his activities over the last six months. That had been helpful.

"Well, boys, we're heading out," Hector called. "Thanks for

the hospitality and good food. It was a pleasure to sit in the pew and listen to Pastor McGuinness again."

Lucas and his brothers turned at the words.

"Thank you for bringing Della to the ranch, Hector." Lucas offered a handshake.

"My pleasure." Hector looked from Drew to Sam and then to Trevor and Lucas. "Your daddy would be proud of what you and your brothers have built here on this ranch. As I recall, when he left the circuit, your father was about Luc and Trevor's age with a pocket full of dreams. You and your brothers have kept those dreams alive. This place will be here for generations."

Lucas and his brothers were solemn at Hector's impactful words. They waved as the older cowboy and his son drove off, pulling the horse trailer behind their dually. The empty trailer clanged rhythmically as it moved over the gravel drive.

"Wow, that man sure put everything in perspective, didn't he? I forget that the ranch isn't just our job. It's our legacy. It all started with Mom and Dad. Now the Morgans have doubled. A powerful reminder of how a dream can start out small and grow, touching so many lives," Drew said.

"Reminds me of the parable of the mustard seed," Sam said.

"Exactly," Drew responded.

For a moment, Lucas let the words roll over him. Would it be the same with the training center? Would his dream grow into a reality that blessed others? He sure hoped so.

"How did you find Hector anyhow?" Trevor asked.

"I asked him the same thing. He didn't know, and I can't recall." Lucas shrugged.

The response had Drew frowning. "That has to be frustrating."

"Tell me about it."

"What do the doctors say about your memory?" Trevor asked.

"The usual. My memory is a waiting game."

"You know…" Sam said with a grin. "In the movies, a hit on the head always restores memories when someone has amnesia. Happy to oblige, Luc."

Lucas ignored Sam and turned to Trevor. "I'll be cleared to drive as soon as I complete therapy. Hopefully, in a week or two. I'm not holding my breath on the horseback riding."

"Hey, you got time," Trevor returned. "You said early spring is the target to open the facility. A lot can happen in six months."

"Yeah. A lot has happened in the last six months."

"True that," Trevor said. "Did I see excavation going on at the construction site?"

"Yeah. They'll be laying foundation rebar and column starter bars soon."

Construction had begun. He couldn't believe he was saying those sweet words. Yet somehow things felt off without Harper sharing the milestone.

"How about if we all go check it out?" Drew asked.

"Good idea," Trevor said with a nod. "I'll take the pickup and bring Cole and the dogs."

"Wait up," Sam said. "I'll go with you, Trev."

"Let's grab a UTV." Drew nodded to Lucas. "You can ride shotgun."

"I've got news for you," Lucas groused. "Shotgun is my life now."

A short time later, his brothers walked the construction area, interest evident on their faces. Excitement and pride stirred in Lucas's gut as he explained the project details and Sam and Trevor asked questions.

"This is where the outdoor arena will be." Lucas pointed to the area marked off with string and flags where trees had been removed to be transplanted elsewhere on the property. He glanced around, imagining a sunny day, the air filled with the scents of popcorn, horses and dirt. The arena would be filled with cheering spectators when the First Annual Homestead Pass Training Center Rodeo began opening ceremonies. In his mind's eye he saw Harper leading barrel racers while he took over as the arena announcer as the festivities began.

"You already have an inside arena planned," Sam said. "Wouldn't a corral work as well and be a whole lot cheaper?"

"Nope. An arena outside gives us options for future growth. When we open, we don't have to expense seating right away. If we decide to launch a rodeo-type event as a conclusion to training sessions, it'll work well. It'll also be good for anyone interested in the training center in the future."

"He's right," Trevor said. "It's cheaper to do it now than to drag equipment in here at a later date."

"Think of it as another passive income opportunity. We can rent out the space too."

"When did you get so smart?" Sam asked.

Lucas looked at Drew. "Wasn't me. It was Drew."

"Nope." Drew gave an adamant shake of his head. "Not me. This was all Harper's planning. She hired the first architect. Most everything had been researched when I picked up the ball."

"Maybe you oughta find out why she's mad at you," Trevor said. "Sounds to me like Harper is a partner you don't want to lose."

Yeah, Trevor was right. Lucas had realized that, when the bank loan had been approved, he'd better adjust to the fact that Harper was the brains of the operation.

Just the same, he glared at Sam.

Something was up with Harper and what he was going to do about the situation was the question.

"Send her flowers," Trevor said as though reading his mind. "A dozen roses will cover a lot of missteps. Trust me, I know."

Lucas nodded, mulling Trevor's suggestion. Yeah, flowers might be a good idea, but not roses. Harper wasn't a roses kind of gal. He'd ask Bess. She'd know.

"Whether she's mad or not, you oughta thank her for her support," Drew added.

Drew was right. She had supported him through all this and, in return, he'd been a big jerk about the partnership issue.

Sam walked to the cabin. He crouched down, assessing the building from different angles. "What's going to happen here? Looks like one strong gust of wind and this place will be kindling."

"Nah," Lucas said. "It's solid. Needs a little work, is all."

"A little work?" His brother grinned. "If you say so. Want some help?"

"No. I got it."

Sam's expression said he was doubtful. He opened his mouth as if to offer more advice and then closed it again.

"That cabin sure has some good memories," Trevor said.

"For Drew and me as well," Sam said.

"Dad brought you two up here?" Lucas asked.

"Yep. You two were only babies when Dad started the tradition." Drew nodded to Lucas. "You had colic. I suspect Dad needed a break. Or maybe Mom did. Dad would grab sleeping bags, drive on up here, and we'd camp."

Sam eyed Lucas. "It's possible you still have colic."

"Real funny," Lucas said. His gaze spanned the area as he recalled what the finished project would look like. "Think Dad would approve of the training center?"

"Approve?" Drew laughed. "I'm surprised he never thought of it himself."

"Yeah?"

"Lucas, this is nearly as solid a plan as the Lazy M Ranch," Drew said. "I'm assuming you'll invite your brothers to teach at your training center."

"I didn't think you'd be interested," Lucas returned, dumbfounded at his brother's comment. He hadn't ever entertained the possibility that they'd be so enthusiastic.

"Are you kidding? Between us, you've got three bronc riders and a bulldogger. Whatever you need, we'll be here for you."

"Don't forget Jim," Trevor said. "He could teach a class or two on his horse whispering techniques."

"Yeah. Okay, I like what I'm hearing. I'm guessing Harper will too."

"When will this be finished?" Sam asked.

"Drew's buddy is our contractor, and barring bad weather, we should be done by the end of the year. Ready to start classes in the spring."

Lucas looked at the cement foundation of the indoor arena building, his gaze taking in the land and the trees before finally settling on his brothers and his nephew.

"The training center name has already been registered. But what do you think about naming the outdoor arena after Dad?"

He looked at each of his brothers. In turn, a grin lit up their faces.

"Gus Morgan Jr. Arena," Lucas murmured. Emotion caught him by surprise and he swallowed hard.

"Ha! I love it," Sam said. "More importantly, Gramps will too."

"Let me run it by my business partner," Lucas said.

"Think Harper will mind?" Trevor asked.

"Nah. She gets what this is all about."

"How'd you get Harper to go into business with you anyhow?" Sam asked. "I always thought she was smarter than that."

Lucas gave Sam a shove. "I don't have a clue. But it's a sore subject, so don't bring that up either."

"What do you mean 'sore subject'?"

He stared at Sam. "I'll explain when I figure it out. Like everything else that happened in the last six months, the details are a little fuzzy."

"Okay, but your business partner is currently mad at you," Sam persisted. "Did I get that part right?"

"Maybe. But, if she is, Harper never stays mad for long. I'm not worried."

*Except, he was.* She'd avoided him for an entire week. That wasn't normal. Harper was real good about letting him know if there was a problem between them. Things felt different this time, and he didn't understand why. So yeah, he was worried.

HARPER SLOWED THE truck at the sight of the Homestead Pass town limits.

"How's Lucas?" her mother asked from the passenger seat. "You haven't mentioned him at all lately."

"I've been pretty busy." She snuck a peek at her mother. The query seemed oddly random.

"Too busy for your best friend? That's a first."

"I saw him at that barbecue party at his house." Harper reached for her sunglasses and slid them on.

"Today is Saturday. That was a week ago. You haven't chatted about the training center either. Have you visited the construction site this week? Didn't Edgar mention breaking ground?"

*Edgar again.*

"There's nothing for me to do at the training center, Mom. Construction is underway. Drew is an architect. He's Luc's resource person."

"I disagree. If you're a partner, you ought to be at the construction site. This isn't like you, Harper."

"Mom, I thought you and Dad were opposed to me being in business with Luc."

"You're father's simply upset that you aren't feasting at his table."

"What does that mean?"

"He was so sure you'd fall in love with the family business. I think he's more hurt than anything." Her mother paused. "I've explained to him that this training center project is a good thing because it keeps you close by, and it makes you happy."

"Aw, thanks, Mom."

"Now, about Luc. The man sent you flowers. A lovely gardenia plant. And you haven't said a thing about what's going on. Why would he send you apology flowers?"

Harper gasped. "You looked at the card."

Her mother picked a spec of lint off her black slacks and primly folded her hands in her lap. "Of course I did. I'm your mother." She shrugged. "Clearly, you two had a falling out."

"We didn't. Not really. I've simply decided to step back a bit while I make decisions about my future."

The party had been a wake-up call. Things were all messed up, and it was her fault for expecting more from Luc than he could give right now. The barbecue had made her realize that she had to let go of the notion he'd ever feel the same about her. That ship sailed when he'd hit his head and forgot six months of his life. And hers.

It was time to slip back into the role of Luc's pal and forget about what happened before he'd hit his head.

Could she do that? Could she let go of what might have been? Ignore the longing in her heart that said Luc was the one?

The only way that would work was for her to set a few boundaries.

"Are you listening to me, Harper?"

"What?" Harper's gaze slid from the road to her mother and back again.

"I asked if he'll still be attending Dana's party?" her mother asked.

"I haven't uninvited him, so I suppose he's still coming." The party. She forgot about the anniversary party.

"It seems very odd that you went into business with Luc and now you seem to be backpedaling on the project and him."

Harper gripped the steering wheel tightly. "I am not backpedaling. I have a short-term interning position at Reilly Pecans, just like everyone wanted. I work nine-to-five, five days a week. I don't have time to micromanage Luc."

"You've always multitasked in the past."

"I'm not as young as I used to be," Harper said.

At that, her mother chuckled. "Oh, that's nonsense. I heard you on the phone. You've still got your finger in the pie with your rodeo friends. Do you plan to take off to compete one of these weekends?"

Harper groaned loudly. "Mom. I can't believe you eavesdropped. I expect that from Dad but not from you."

"You were right there in the kitchen talking loud enough for the housekeeper to hear. I can't help it if I overheard as well."

"I haven't made any decisions about the rodeo. That was my friend Jackie on the phone. I ran into her at the barbecue party. A mutual friend is getting married in two weeks. The wedding happens to coincide with a rodeo."

"Really? A wedding that coincides with a rodeo? They planned it that way?"

"It was sort of a spontaneous decision."

"Spontaneous." Her mother cocked her head. "Dana's wedding was two years in the making. Maddy's eighteen months. You aren't going to have your wedding at a rodeo, are you?"

"My wedding?" Harper grimaced. "I haven't had a date in months. You don't have to worry about marriage. Although, I can say with certainty that when I do get married, it won't be an event two years in the making."

"Now, now. Let's not disparage Dana. Your sister's quirks are what make her unique. Just like yours are. As for your unconventional invitation… Go. It sounds like fun, and you deserve a break."

"I'm thinking about it."

"Where is this wedding-slash-rodeo?"

"A small town north of Tulsa. I could leave right after work."

The wedding was an opportunity to chat more with Jackie about replacing her partner. Harper ought to be excited, but she found herself loathe to attend another wedding. It would bring up memories of Trevor and Hope's wedding, and how she'd thought her life was finally making sense, and that she and Luc might have a chance at a future together. A future that didn't look like best buddies.

Only a few weeks ago, she was so full of hope. Now, she wasn't certain about anything. Oh, she knew what she had to do; the problem was that she was loath to do it. Putting distance between herself and Luc might be the hardest thing she'd ever done.

Harper directed the vehicle down Main Street while searching for a parking spot near the post office where a shipment of art supplies waited to be picked up. When she spotted Gus and Luc walking down the street toward Sam's shop, she hit the brakes reflexively.

This was the downside of Homestead Pass. You couldn't get mad at someone and attempt to avoid them, because the town was too small.

Her mother reached a hand to the dashboard to brace herself. "Oh my. What was that? Did you see something in the road?" She leaned forward, glancing up and down the street.

"I might have," Harper offered innocently.

Her mother's gaze landed across the street and she scoffed. "You saw the Morgans on the sidewalk." She sighed and turned to Harper. "What on earth is going on, sweetheart?"

"Nothing." Harper pointed to a parking spot next to the barbershop. "Will that work?"

"That's on the other side of the street and almost to the corner. I have fifty pounds of sculpting clay at the post office. We have to park closer to the post office."

"Okay. Fine. I'll find something closer."

Harper dutifully circled the block and backed into a spot right outside the post office.

And as they exited the vehicle, Gus Morgan hailed them with a friendly greeting.

"Great," Harper muttered, grateful for traffic on Main Street that delayed Gus and Luc crossing the street.

Usually, a trip to town was a treat. She'd take a moment to enjoy the beauty of downtown Homestead Pass, the pretty canopied shops and the foliage planted by the town council.

This time of year not only meant pecan harvesting, but it heralded her favorite time of year. Autumn. The trees that lined Main Street would be the first to spread the news of changing seasons and Harper always made a point of assessing them when she came to town.

One or two nights of dipping temperatures would start the redbud leaves turning from green to canary yellow. Soon the maples would shed their summer colors for plum and orange.

Today she eyed the door of the post office and calculated how fast she could dash inside before Gus and his grandson crossed the street.

Too late. The light changed.

"Well, look who we have here," Gus said as they joined them on the sidewalk. He tipped his hat.

Harper checked her phone. Anything to avoid looking at Luc.

"Why, Gus and Lucas, what a timely surprise," her mother said. "I don't suppose you'd mind helping us load a couple of boxes into Harper's truck."

Harper dropped her head to her chest. "I brought a hand-cart. I can handle the boxes, Mom."

"Luc is happy to help you," Gus said. "Right, Luc?"

"Yes, ma'am. Whatever you need. Happy to help." Lucas nodded and offered Maureen a generous grin. Her mother smiled right back at him as though he could do no wrong.

When had Mom joined Team Lucas? By sending Harper

a gardenia plant, Luc had somehow transformed into Prince Charming in her mother's eyes.

"Tell you what?" Gus said. "Why don't we let the youngsters handle those boxes? Have you seen Sam's shop lately, Maureen?"

"I have not, and I've been meaning to. I read that article about his woodcrafts in the newspaper." She took the arm Gus offered and turned to Harper. "You'll need to check the box, dear. We have mail too."

Harper nodded. She was silent as she entered the post office and picked up the mail. Luc was right behind her, watching her beneath hooded eyes. When the clerk brought out two boxes, Harper and Luc reached for them at the same time. Harper quickly jumped back and let him slide the handcart beneath the cardboard.

"You aren't supposed to lift. One of those has fifty pounds of clay and is very heavy," she commented.

Luc ignored her and rolled the boxes out the door and to the truck. "We can do it together. Teamwork. You remember teamwork. Right, Harper?"

"Whatever."

"Whatever?" He arched a brow. "We had a meeting with the contractor this morning. You didn't show."

Harper froze. The meeting with the contractor. She totally forgot, though there was no way she would have made it to the Lazy M in time. Sleep had been elusive of late. "You handled it, correct?"

"Yeah, but that's not the point."

"Yes. I get the point. You're calling me out." Harper released a breath. "I'm sorry that I missed the meeting." She paused. "I've been busy." Busy and confused.

"So you say. Mind telling me why you're mad at me? Why you left the party early?"

"It wasn't that early."

"You didn't even tell me you were leaving."

"Luc, you didn't even notice I was gone. I looked around for you before I headed out. You had a woman on each arm and a smile on your face."

"I was trying to be a good host, and you were supposed to be my support buddy."

"You clearly didn't need my support. I hardly saw you," she muttered.

"Is that why you're mad?"

"I'm not mad." She was hurt, and disappointed. Okay, and mad. Mad at herself for allowing herself to fall for a cowboy who would never settle down. Harper lowered the tailgate on her truck and crossed her arms.

"You sure are cranky."

"I am not cranky. However, for the record, if I were cranky, it's a known fact that accusing a cranky person of being cranky only increases the cranky level."

Luc seemed to find that amusing. His eyes sparkled as he looked at her, though he wisely bit back a laugh.

She stared at him. "Are we going to put the clay in the truck or not?"

"Yes, drill sergeant. On the count of three," he said. "One. Two. Three."

Harper lifted her end and they easily slid the box filled with clay inside. Then she picked up the lighter box and tossed it in before closing the tailgate with unnecessary force.

"I thought you were going to come and see the horse," Luc said. He crossed his arms, his stance mirroring hers as he eyed her like she was a petulant child.

"Is there a rush? Some sort of deadline?" Harper asked.

"No. I guess not."

Harper glanced up and down the street as the silence stretched between them. Where was her mother?

"Look Harp, I apologize." He kicked at the cement with the toe of his boot. "I should have been a better host to you. I'm sorry."

She looked at him, softening at the words.

"I was so sure that party would help me figure things out. I guess all I can do is pray and wait for my memory to come back. Until then, I'm grasping at anything that might help me break through this black void. If I messed up, I'm really sorry."

Harper stared at him long and hard. If only she could tell him that when he'd lost his memory, she'd lost everything as well. Instead, she nodded at his words.

"I, um… I got some news from the eye doctor this week," he said. "Glasses are ordered. I'll be driving soon too."

"Congratulations. I'm happy for you. But you don't have a truck."

"The insurance check showed up. Want to go truck shopping with me?"

She would have jumped at the opportunity to tag along in the past. Spend the day with Luc, looking at trucks.

This wasn't the past. Luc would always be her friend, but the only way to move on was to put a little distance between them.

"Oh, I don't know. I mean you're going to buy another black truck, right? All the same bells and whistles."

"Sure, yeah. I get that. Kind of boring." He paused. "There's something else."

Harper lifted a brow in question.

"I've been talking with my brothers, and I'd like to name the outside arena after my dad." He looked at her, his expression hopeful. "Would that be okay with you?"

"Of course. That's a wonderful idea."

"Thanks." He shoved his hands in his pockets and nodded. "You left the barbecue early. Does that mean I don't have to go to your sister's party with you?" He grinned and wiggled his brows as if hoping to make her laugh.

She wasn't amused. Harper opened her mouth, about to tell him he didn't have to attend. Then she stopped herself. She had purchased a new and expensive dress and spent two and a half hours of her life to support Luc at his ridiculous party.

Time that she'd never be able to recoup. And she never even danced. Why should she let him off the hook so easily?

"Seven p.m. sharp."

He groaned and ran a hand over his face.

"You're going to need to shave and get a haircut."

"Aw, come on."

"Proper attire as well."

"Paybacks, huh?" He eyed her. "Could you at least stop by the ranch and meet Della sometime?"

"Della?" Her heart clutched. Another girlfriend?

"The new mare I told you about."

"Oh. The horse. You know what? Let me look at my schedule and get back to you." She couldn't keep running every time Luc called.

"Your schedule?" He raised a brow. "Since when do you use excuses like your schedule?"

"Things have gotten complicated, Luc. I don't know if we can go back to the way things were."

The admission saddened her. Life was about to change whether she liked it or not. Yes, it was time for boundaries if she was going to be able to put the pieces of her heart together and move on.

# CHAPTER NINE

LUCAS EXAMINED THE hors d'oeuvre in his hand and grimaced. Harper was almost back to her old self tonight, so he wouldn't complain about the unidentifiable food at her sister's party. He was grateful they seemed to have moved past the bump in the road of their friendship and knew it would be wise not to overanalyze things.

"Goat-cheese-and-salami-stuffed dates with a bit of honey and pepper," Harper said.

He looked at the cracker, unconvinced. "If you say so. I don't understand why Chef Moretti wants to make this fancy stuff when clearly home cooking is her forte."

"Don't judge. Try it. I promise you'll change your opinion."

He took a bite and his eyes snapped wide as the flavors exploded in his mouth. "Ooh. That's music to my taste buds."

"I told you. Loretta Moretti can do barbecue and haute cuisine. When the Homestead Pass Training Center opens, we'll hire her for the open house."

Lucas chuckled. "You're always six steps ahead of me, Harp. Have you noticed? My brothers sure have."

"Have they?" She shrugged. "It's Reilly Pecans. I'm now officially in the marketing department as assistant to the department head. It has reawakened my creative side. Literally.

Sometimes, I wake up in the middle of the night with ideas."
She smiled.

"Here I thought the training center was your future. Maybe
pecans are."

"My stint with Reilly Pecans will be over in four weeks,
Luc. It's been interesting, but the prospect of sitting behind a
desk on a regular basis has zero appeal. I'm excited about the
prospect of marketing the training center. I'm already working on a social media platform, along with a newsletter. I did
some research and talked to a few training schools around the
country to see what they're doing that's effective. They were
more than willing to answer my questions."

He stared at her. "You're amazing."

"Not really. It's all part of marketing, and I can do it with
my laptop sitting in the middle of an arena if I choose." She
waved hello at someone across the room.

Lucas followed the direction of her gaze, finding himself
counting the number of guests in the Reilly ballroom as he did.
"Thought you said this was an intimate get-together. There
are at least fifty guests here."

"And they keep arriving." Harper nodded to the doorway
where another couple stepped into the room. 'You always knew
I wasn't like my sisters. This is more evidence that I'm the
cowgirl to their debutante."

"Good thing your father built a mansion with a space that
can accommodate a small kingdom. Imagine that. Right here
in the middle of Homestead Pass.

She glared at him. "Don't start. Olivia's father has a gated
mansion and you don't give her grief."

"That's so the cattle don't escape. And Mr. Moretti's castle
is a starter castle compared to your house."

"Not true. It's huge."

"Either way, two wrong millionaires don't make a right."

"What's wrong with a big house?" She took a sip of the
soda in her hand as she looked up at him.

"Not a thing. I'm all for big houses filled with kids."

A stunned look raced across Harper's face. "I had no idea you wanted a houseful of children."

"I do. Don't you?"

"Yes. Dogs and cats and a small herd of horses as well." She laughed, choking a little on her soda.

"There you go. We agree on something." He glanced up at the ostentatious crystal chandelier that lit the room. "Bess would never be able to clean that thing."

"We have a service to do that." She reached out and adjusted his tie. "Nice suit, by the way. With that haircut and a shave, you could pass for a banker or an attorney."

"I'm still one-hundred-percent cowboy deep inside." He patted his heart with his palm. "Speaking of attorneys..." Lucas cocked his head in the direction of the buffet table. "I see the House of Usher is here." He nodded at Edgar and Allen. All that was missing was Poe.

Harper burst out laughing. Loud enough to cause her father to turn from his conversation with someone who appeared to be important and shoot her a critical glance.

Lucas nearly laughed himself at the expression on Colin's face. He recognized that look. His father and grandfather had one exactly like it. Lucas had found himself on the receiving end more often than his brothers.

"Oops," Harper murmured. "I'm in trouble again."

"Welcome to the club." He nodded at her sisters' spouses once again. "What do you think the boys are talking about?"

"The stock market or golf. Did I mention that Edgar threw me under the bus at dinner a few weeks ago? He told the family about our project."

"You did." Lucas shrugged. "They had to find out eventually, right?"

"Yes, but..."

Lucas glanced down at her and a light bulb lit up. "You said your father was furious. It's because you've gone into business with me, isn't it?" He sighed when she didn't answer.

That explained Brett, Allen's cousin, another attorney, whom Lucas now realized had been invited for Harper. He shot a glance at the tall, serious fella talking with Dana.

Lucas didn't like the guy. Not one bit. He was too smooth, and he reeked of eau de money in his bespoke suit and shiny wingtip shoes. Yeah, good old Brett could definitely keep Harper in the Reilly tax bracket. That thought bristled Lucas.

Earlier in the evening, when introductions had been made, Brett had claimed he had always been fascinated by barrel racing. That had kept him and Harper conversing at length while Lucas had considered ways to legally get rid of the guy. He'd barely resisted rolling his eyes at Brett's inane questions about horses.

When he'd noticed Colin across the room, nodding as he observed his daughter and the attorney chatting, Lucas had dialed back his ego to see the situation from her father's eyes.

Brett would fit right in with the family and Harper's plan to settle down.

Could someone like the slick attorney make her happy? It wasn't his place to make that determination. The thought caused a tightness in his chest. It seemed with each day he was coming closer and closer to losing his friend. The strange stirrings in his heart when he considered the inevitable left him confused.

"Lucas, so lovely to see you here."

He turned to see Harper's mother, Maureen, and smiled. He genuinely liked the woman. Most of the time, a ball cap hid her blond hair, and she wore linen smocks with as many pockets as clay stains.

Tonight, she looked like the moneyed matriarch that she was. She wore a sleek black dress, and her hair was expertly coiffed and adorned with a silver clip. A glimpse at Maureen foreshadowed what Harper would look like in a couple of decades. Even more beautiful than today.

For a passing moment, Lucas tried to imagine himself and Harper decades from now. Old friends exchanging witty repartee. Would he always wonder if there could have been more between them?

*More between them.* Lucas nearly jerked back at the unexpected question that hit him between the eyes. Where had that come from?

They were just friends. A mantra he'd repeated over and over again over the years. So what had changed, leaving him longing for more? Could it be the whack on the head he'd sustained?

"You look lovely, Mrs. Reilly. Thanks for inviting me. I hear you're working on a top-secret project these days."

Maureen chuckled. "All my projects are top-secret. It's the only way to keep my darling husband from coming in every five minutes asking if I've seen his glasses or golf socks."

"Good plan. I ought to try that with my brothers."

"You won't tell anyone. Will you?"

Lucas crossed his heart with a finger. "Your secret is safe with me."

"Good. Now that we are coconspirators, you can tell me all about your and Harper's business. How did that develop?"

"Truthfully, Mrs. Reilly, I don't remember how that happened, so I can't tell you much."

"You're still having memory issues?"

"I've lost six months of my life." He raised a palm. "One minute, I'm on the circuit planning to open a training center when I retire in January. The next, I'm in a hospital bed and I've a business partner, a thousand pens and a new horse."

Along with an engagement ring. That part he would not mention. He already sounded pathetic.

"A thousand pens?"

"Long story."

"I see." She clucked her tongue and sipped her sparkling water as though she did see, which Lucas found comforting. Now he understood where Harper got her empathetic side from.

"You aren't happy about the situation?" Maureen asked.

"The pens?"

She laughed. "I meant having Harper as your partner."

"I'm adjusting." He rubbed his chin, debating how much he should say. "I don't know how much Harper has told you about the circuit, but she's a rising star, and I don't want to stand in her way."

"She doesn't discuss the rodeo much with her father and me. I generally have to eavesdrop if I want to know anything."

"Yeah, well, since we're sharing secrets, I'll tell you that she's had a few small endorsement deals. Each one a little better than the next. I wouldn't be surprised if she were the next face of Lady Bootleg." He leaned closer. "I heard a rumor she's on the shortlist."

"Excuse me?"

"Bootleg Western Wear. It's a brand of women's fancy Western boots and clothing. They use real barrel riders and ropers to endorse the brand."

"Oh, that sounds like quite a serious opportunity."

"It could open doors. That's for sure, and Harper deserves to have doors opened. She works hard, and she's talented."

"So you don't see her future with Reilly Pecans?"

Lucas chuckled. "I'm smart enough not to go there. All I can say is that I want to see Harper doing what brings her the greatest joy."

"You do care about Harper, don't you, Lucas?"

"Harp has always been there for me."

"She's fortunate to have you in her life. I'm glad you got over your disagreement." Maureen smiled. "The gardenia is lovely. It takes a wise man to send a woman a gardenia."

"You think so?"

"Oh yes. Roses are unimaginative." She looked up at him.

"On another note, how long has your brother Sam been creating those beautiful pieces from wood?"

"A long time, though he's sort of kept it under a bushel until recently."

"He's a talented artist. I'm glad to see him getting the recognition he deserves as he steps into his own."

"Yes, ma'am."

"What about you, Lucas?"

"Me?"

"What do you want to be when you grow up?"

The question gave him pause. "I don't—" He nearly said he didn't want to grow up but reconsidered the joking remark. He'd been playing the jokester for far too long. "I want to share my love of horses and the rodeo with others."

*I want to make my daddy proud.*

Maureen's eyes met his. "I pray your venture is a success. Especially if it keeps Harper close to home."

"Thank you."

She turned and frowned. "Would you please excuse me, Lucas? Ms. Moretti is flagging me down."

"Yes, ma'am. Good to chat with you. Tell her hello from me."

"I shall." She put a hand on his arm. "It was good to visit with you, as well."

Downing his soda, Lucas searched for a refill. From the corner of his eye, he saw Colin Reilly moving in his direction. The last thing he needed was an interrogation by Harper's father. Thankfully, the tall French doors to the patio were open, inviting guests for a stroll around the pool. Lucas ducked behind a tall potted ficus and slipped outside, where he stepped behind a pillar.

He peeked around the base of the massive column. Colin continued to peruse the crowd for a minute, frowned, shrugged and turned away.

*Whew.* Close one. Nope, he wasn't ready for one-on-one with the king of the castle, though he recognized that it was inevitable.

Lucas took a deep breath and relaxed for a moment, his attention going to large round globe lights strung on poles to illuminate the yard around the pool area where the skimmer siphoned water over and over. Tall, narrow fir trees surrounded the pool on two sides, their branches woven with more lights whose reflection shimmered on the surface of the water.

The temperature had dropped once again, as it usually did near the end of September. Another week and it would be October. Would his memory be restored by then?

Turning, he could see Harper across the ballroom. Her auburn hair had been pulled back into a low ponytail with a few loose tendrils framing her face. She wore a dark green dress with a fluttery kind of hem.

He wasn't the only one who noticed Harper looked beautiful tonight. While he watched from the patio, what's his name joined her. A surge of something twisted his gut, once again confusing Lucas. After a moment, he chalked up the feelings to protectiveness. When the attorney's regard moved from her face to her figure, Lucas clenched his jaw, working to remind himself that Harper deserved the best. A fella who loved her unconditionally and appreciated all she had to offer. Trouble was, he wasn't convinced the attorney checked those boxes.

Lucas frowned.

Admittedly, he was a tough critic. But this was Harper.

Harper bit into a cracker as Brett said something. She laughed and then coughed, her face becoming red. Then she stopped coughing and pounded on her chest with an open palm.

Lucas stared, horrified as everything slowed down to half speed and voices blurred. Edgar and Allen turned from their discussion to see what was going on. Dana cocked her head, confusion on her face. Harper's father, across the room, stared, his face a frozen mask of surprise.

No one moved, even as Harper continued to pound her chest, croaking an unintelligible call for help. The attorney didn't move either.

Lucas shot into the ballroom, knocked over a chair and shoved Brett out of the way to get to Harper, whose pleas had turned into a wheeze as her lips turned a flat shade of blue.

Breathing hard, he circled her waist with his arms from behind. His right hand covered his closed left hand as Lucas delivered a sharp upward abdominal thrust.

Immediately, Harper coughed, dislodging a piece of cracker that flew into the air and landed on Brett's lapel.

A low gasp spread through the guests. Relief and adrenaline had Lucas's pulse throbbing like a drum in his ears. He ran a hand over his face and sent up a silent prayer of thanks.

"You. Saved. My. Life." Harper panted each word.

"Yeah, I guess so," he said. "I'm sure someone would have jumped in there. I just reached you first."

Of course, she'd probably be limp and on the floor by the time anyone else reacted. Lucas shuddered at the thought. He'd taken first aid in high school when one of his best friends had had an anaphylactic reaction to a bee sting. He'd never wanted to go through that helpless feeling again.

As it turned out, that class had come in handy today.

Lucas stepped out of the way of the rush of people now surrounding Harper.

He looked up to see Colin Reilly staring at him a lot less like he wasn't good enough for his daughter.

So, yeah, if it made Harper's father see him through a new lens, which was a plus, though he would have preferred a different approach. One that didn't leave his heart pounding and his hands trembling.

As guests and family continued to crowd close to Harper, verifying she was okay, Lucas retreated to the safety of the pool area unnoticed. He was still shaking when Harper found him minutes later.

"Lucas, you saved my life. Thank you."

He turned and looked her up and down to verify that she really was all right. "Wasn't that part of the buddy contract? Section seven, paragraph two, I believe." Joking was the only way he could deal with what had just happened.

Harper laughed, a squeaky sound.

Lucas stood there, unable to move as it hit him. He could have lost Harper, like he'd lost his folks. Panic welled up inside, clogging his throat and threatening to fill his eyes.

"You going to be okay?" His voice sounded raw to his ears.

"Yes." She nodded. "I need a moment. I'm going to stay here for a bit. Everyone was staring at me inside. I certainly didn't mean to steal the spotlight away from Dana."

"Your sister will survive."

For moments, they stood together yet apart, attention fixed on the tiny ripples that rolled across the water's surface with each passing breeze.

Harper wrapped her arm around herself and he heard a sniffle. He turned to see a single tear trailing down her face. Always strong and capable in any storm, Harper wasn't now. Her green eyes were round with fear.

"Hey, hey. What's going on? Are you okay?"

Wordlessly, she shook her head.

Lucas didn't think. He simply pulled her into his arms.

"That was terrifying," she whispered against his shoulder. Her soft breath touched him through the fabric of his shirt and he held her tighter.

Yeah, it was terrifying. Lucas pressed his lips to Harper's forehead and whispered soothing words as the scent of her perfume wrapped itself around him. He realized that holding Harper felt like the most natural thing in the world. Like he'd waited his entire life for her to fill his empty arms.

All this time he'd spent pushing her away and denying they were anything but friends. What if he'd been wrong?

Harper raised her head and looked up at him. Her soft lips parted and she sighed. The temptation to touch his lips to hers overwhelmed him and he stepped back, away from the warmth of her body. This wasn't good. Not good at all. And he was more confused than ever.

Leaping over the boundary lines could not only ruin that friendship but complicate their business partnership.

Lucas swallowed.

Maybe it was the emotion of what had happened. The adrenaline high.

Sure. That was it.

He had imagined the tug of emotions and the longing in his heart? Because this was his best friend he was talking about.

You weren't supposed to fall for your best friend. That was definitely not in the rule book.

Yet that's exactly what he felt right now. Like he was falling hard. Lucas's mind raced as he recalled that back home there was a ring waiting for him to figure out whose finger it belonged on. Could it be for Harper?

HARPER DRAINED THE cold coffee in her cup. She picked at her salad and then pushed it away. A glance at her phone told her that her lunch hour was nearly over. It also reminded her that Luc hadn't answered today's text.

She'd texted him Monday and Tuesday, and he'd offered staccato responses. A single word each time. Yeah. Nope.

Yeah, the plumbing crew had shown up.

Nope, the cabin repair hadn't started.

They'd connected on Saturday after the alarming choking incident, and it had further cemented her belief that she and Luc had a chance at a future.

She hadn't imagined things. That moment of connection hadn't been lost in the abyss of his amnesia.

There was a rightness to being in his arms that she couldn't explain. Harper had seen something in his eyes when he'd looked at her as they'd stood together that said he'd felt the same way.

Unfortunately, now he was avoiding her. That didn't bode well. Maybe he regretted almost kissing her—and she was absolutely certain that he had had been about to kiss her.

"You still insist upon eating with the employees, I see." Dana plopped down across from Harper.

"You're corporate, Dana. I'm not. I prefer to eat with the other regular folks."

Besides, the executive dining room was one of the only areas of the company where the décor had Harper shuddering. From the platinum-colored ceiling to the hanging metal birds flying south for the winter, the room held zero warmth. She suspected Dana had helped with the vision.

"No need to get testy. I'm here to remind you that the chef has prepared the Tuesday special. If you want to miss that, fine by me."

"What's the Tuesday special?"

"Roasted Atlantic Black Bass. He serves it with a potato pancake and horseradish crema." Dana offered a chef's kiss.

Harper glanced at her prepackaged salad. "Maybe next week."

She wasn't ready to join the ranks of the Reilly privileged. Despite her last name, she hadn't earned the right to eat in the executive dining room. However, roasted Atlantic Black Bass might prove to be the tipping point.

"Great. I'll save you a seat. It gets busy in there." Dana smiled. "So...that was some quick thinking by Lucas on Saturday."

"Yes, it was."

"What did you think about Brett? Allen thought you two looked cute together. Maybe we could double date."

"He's nice enough, but I'll pass on the double dating. Life

is busy right now…" Harper hedged. She found it humorous that she hadn't heard from Brett, though he'd insisted on getting her phone number before the incident. She suspected Colin Reilly's daughter had lost her appeal when she'd spit on his Italian-silk suit.

Harper chuckled.

"What's so funny?" Dana asked.

"Nothing." She waved a hand dismissively while recalling the cracker sailing through the air and the expression of horror on Brett's face.

"Earth to Harper."

She looked at Dana. "Huh?"

"I asked how you feel."

"My throat is a little raw, and I think my ribs were bruised when Lucas did the Heimlich. He's stronger than he looks."

"Oh, that Lucas. What a hero. So swoony. Daddy was so grateful. I think he's going to name one of our value-added products after him." Dana grinned. "Lucas Divinity, maybe."

Harper burst out laughing and immediately clutched her middle. "Very funny. Try to remember that you're married. You aren't supposed to notice Lucas Morgan."

"Give me a break. Who doesn't notice Luc or any of the Morgan men? They're all from the same mold. Tall, dark, and delicious. It must be the influence of their grandfather. Gus cuts quite a dashing figure for a man of his age."

"How are you and Allen?" Harper asked. Turning the focus to Dana's favorite topic, herself, always worked as a distraction technique.

"We're wonderful. Except for you nearly dying, it was a fabulous party. Allen surprised me with a trip to Napa Valley next weekend. You should see the itinerary." She sighed. "I love that man."

"I'm happy for you, Dana." While her sister's sappy stories of marital bliss got old after a while, Harper was pleased to see her sister so in love.

"It's our last chance to escape before the triple threat."

"Triple threat?"

"That's what they call it around the office, but don't tell Dad. Thanksgiving, Christmas and New Year's. You haven't been around long enough to appreciate how overwhelming things get over the holiday. I mean you seriously need to stay far, far away from Maddy."

"You're right. Thanks for the reminder. She was a pecan-zilla last year. I didn't connect the dots. I thought it was the usual holiday harriment."

"Harriment." Dana chuckled. "Good one. But this is much more. It's what happens when you're the senior vice president, of value-added products. The holidays are a triumphant nightmare for her division. All those gift baskets and new products introduced for the season are a huge responsibility. And Daddy is oblivious because October is the start of harvesting."

Harper nodded. A lifetime of pecan harvesting had taught the Reilly girls that their father would be MIA once the season began. Colin Reilly was hands-on and spent most of October and November in the orchards. By December, he reluctantly allowed his field managers to complete harvesting and marketing, all the while claiming he wasn't a micromanager.

"Anyhow," Dana continued, "we were discussing Luc. I talked to Daddy this morning, and he went on and on about Saturday night. That's all I'm saying."

"It's good that he finally appreciates Luc," Harper said. "Even if it's for the wrong reason."

Dana rested her chin on her hands and eyed Harper. "Are you really his business partner?"

"Yes. Why do you say it like that?"

"You could have everything if you stay with the company, Harper. You'd be a vice president in five years. Why would you want to invest yourself in a rodeo school?"

"First, my life is not lacking." *Except someone to share it with.* "Second, it's not just a rodeo school. I'm really excited about this project."

Harper's phone buzzed on the table. "Speaking of Daddy." She picked up the cell. "Yes, Father dear."

"Harper, I need Lucas Morgan's phone number."

"Why?"

"That's my business."

"If you'd tell me, I might be able to find it for you."

"Harper Elizabeth Reilly. I am your father and your boss. I'd like the number now please."

She groaned. "See, this is exactly why I knew working for Reilly Pecans was a bad idea. You have no boundaries."

"Fine." He paused. "You're probably right. This is a personal matter, and I should leave you out of it. I'll call Trevor Morgan's wife. She won't give me a hard time."

"What was that all about?" Dana asked.

"He wanted Luc's number."

"Why?"

"I don't know." Harper shook her head. "But you know Daddy. He's definitely up to something."

Harper immediately called Luc, but it went to voice mail. She tried again during her afternoon break. He didn't pick up.

Harper eyed the clock on her phone half a dozen times, praying for the day to hurry by so she could call Luc and find out what her father was up to.

At 5:00 p.m., she strode to the parking garage. Her phone rang as she reached her truck. Harper prayed it was Luc. However, the number was unfamiliar.

"Hello?"

"Harper Reilly? This is Katrina Bednar with Bootleg Western Wear."

"Hi. How may I help you, Ms. Bednar?"

"Our executive committee met last evening, and, by a unanimous vote, we've selected you as the next face of Lady Bootleg, our boots and apparel brand for women."

"I'm speechless and honored."

*Bootleg Western Wear. Stay calm, Harper. Stay calm.*

"I'd love to hear the details," Harper said.

She nodded as Katrina outlined the publicity appearances associated with the position. When she summarized the financials, Harper dropped her tote bag on the ground and leaned against her truck. "That's quite an offer."

"It's a one-year contract that begins in January with a very rigorous schedule. Though I'm sure you're accustomed to traveling on the circuit. This commitment includes, at minimum, twenty days of travel a month."

*Twenty days of travel. Minimum.* Katrina was correct. That was as many days as her circuit schedule. Driving from rodeo to rodeo took time. Even if the events were on the weekend, the driving sucked up a lot of miles. The difference was that this included all major holidays. She'd be away from family and friends for the better part of each and every month for an entire year.

On the other hand, an endorsement deal would be a huge opportunity to bring attention to the training school.

"May I have some time to think about your generous offer?"

"Sure. I'll need your decision within thirty days."

For minutes, Harper sat in her truck thinking. The exposure would be great, and so would the money. But would it take her any closer to her goals? Would accepting the offer be in her best interest? She'd be forced to really become that silent partner to Luc that she'd talked about to her parents.

Her phone rang and she jumped, startled by the sound. The screen displayed Luc's number.

"Luc, I've been trying to reach you."

"Sorry, I've been monitoring the contractors. Lots of noise. Must have missed your calls. Um, everything okay?"

Did his voice sound nervous? Or was she imagining that? Was that almost-kiss going to make things awkward between them?

"Has my father reached out to you?"

Then Lucas laughed, and she relaxed.

"He sure did. Your father wants to talk. He invited me to a round of golf at the Elk City country club with Edgar and Allen on Saturday." He paused. "I guess that makes me Poe."

"Golf?" She blinked. "I wasn't aware that you play golf."

"I do not, and I have no plans to play in the future. I suggested lunch at Liv's restaurant on Saturday."

"Oh, that's a good idea." She nodded. "Wait. Wait. Why lunch? What is he up to?"

"He's falling over himself to thank me for saving your life. Even mentioned something about my entrepreneurial spirit."

"Your entrepreneurial spirit."

"Yep. He wants to talk business."

"That sounds promising." She paused. "Be careful, Luc. My father is a shrewd businessman."

"It'll be fine, Harper."

"Will you be around if I stop by to see the progress on the training center Saturday? I mean after you have your lunch date?"

"You sure you can squeeze me into your schedule?"

"It wasn't easy, but that's the kind of friend I am."

Lucas laughed again, the sound assuring her that they were okay. Hopefully, more than okay.

"Oh...and, Luc?"

"Yeah? Bootleg Western Wear offered me an endorsement deal."

"Woohoo! Congratulations. I knew that was going to happen. You can tell me all about it on Saturday."

"Yes, it's wonderful, but we have to talk about what that means for the training center." Harper paused. "What it means for...us."

"You have to do what's best for your future. Those endorsement deals are time sensitive."

"Yes. See you Saturday, Luc," she murmured.

She'd dared to use the word *us* and he hadn't responded. Was there an *us*?

Harper sat in the truck a little longer as she realized there were serious decisions to be made.

Should she accept the offer? What would it mean for her partnership with Luc? And what about what she'd glimpsed in his eyes at Dana's party? Had they made a breakthrough, or would she be disappointed again?

Harper rested her forehead on the steering wheel. "Oh, Lord, I have to give all to You, because I don't know what to do."

# CHAPTER TEN

"YOU SAVED MY daughter's life."

Lucas looked up from his ravioli to meet Colin Reilly's anguished gaze.

For a brief moment, Lucas relived the nightmare of Harper's choking incident. He shook his head to clear the image.

*Well, sir, it was the least I could do since I'm pretty sure I've fallen in love with her.*

"Heimlich maneuver. First-aid class." Lucas looked from Harper's father to his pasta, unsure of what his next move should be.

"My apologies," Colin said. "My plan was to allow you to enjoy your meal before I spoke. My emotions have gotten the best of me."

"Gentlemen, you aren't eating." Liv Moretti Morgan stood next to their table with a frown on her lovely face. She stared pointedly at Colin. "If that isn't the most delicious eggplant parm you've had in your entire life, your meal is on the house."

Harper's father raised both hands as if in prayer. "My apologies, chef. This is absolutely primo."

"It is." She turned to Lucas and lifted her brows as if to ask what his excuse was.

Lucas scooped up a ravioli. "The best."

"Very good." Liv nodded as a satisfied smile touched her lips. "Enjoy."

For minutes, Lucas was left to do just that. He savored the rich tomato sauce with hints of basil and the pillows of pasta filled with a creamy butternut squash and sage-laced Italian sausage mixture. Bess's cinnamon rolls ruled the world, but Liv's pasta could bring an army to its knees.

Colin wiped his mouth with a linen napkin and pushed his plate to the side. He folded his hands and stared at Lucas thoughtfully. "I'd like to apologize, son."

Lucas finished chewing and carefully swallowed, lest there be a repeat of the choking incident the other night. He glanced fondly at his ravioli, making a mental note to get a to-go box.

"What for?" Lucas eyed the older man nervously.

Harper's father leaned across the table. "I underestimated you. For that, I humbly apologize. You and my daughter are more alike than I gave you credit for. The unfortunate event the other night and a few strongly worded comments from my dear wife have helped me to adjust my attitude."

"Oh?"

"I think you're a fine match for Harper. Joining the Reilly and Morgan family would be a sound plan."

"Joining our families?" Lucas coughed.

He didn't know what to say. One minute he's feeling like he's not good enough for Colin's daughter, now... Well, he expected to hear the details of the dowry. Two cows, three pecan orchards and a tractor would work.

Nice of the man to offer his approval. That almost-kiss the other night was the only inclination Lucas had had that Harper might consider moving him out of the friend zone. And that near miss seemed to be based on emotions riding high.

He'd spent the last few days mulling his relationship with Harper. Could he convince her that they had more than a business relationship?

"I'd also like to invest in your project."

Lucas stared at the man once again. Colin Reilly gave new meaning to the term "steamroller." He kept talking as though his was the only voice in the room.

"What project is that, sir?" Lucas frowned. One way or another, Colin seemed determined to ensure that anything that touched his daughter would be a success. Apparently, he didn't have confidence that Lucas could do that on his own.

"The business you and Harper are launching. Obviously, I'd prefer my daughter committed to a long-term position at Reilly Pecans. Since the training center is her plan, I'd like to support her. Besides, always good to invest locally."

"Thank you, sir. I'll make note of your interest for our next meeting." They didn't have meetings, but he wouldn't accept any offers until he spoke to Harper.

"Do that. I want to be your primary corporate sponsor. I know you're related to Anthony Moretti by marriage, and cattle might seem like a closer product match, but remember that I spoke to you first. And I am Harper's father. That's even fewer degrees of separation if you two make a merger on a personal level." He winked.

Colin really was bartering his youngest daughter. Harper would be furious if she knew.

Lucas nodded as he spoke, while debating whether he should throw more competition into the mix.

What would Harper do?

He knew immediately

"Actually, sir, I've had another offer for corporate sponsorship." His brothers would love to sponsor the training center. They just didn't know it yet.

"You have?" Colin's brow knit. "How is word getting out so fast?"

"Your daughter does have excellent marketing skills."

"Yes. She does. I ought to hire her." The other man laughed.

Lucas chuckled as well.

"Are you going to tell me who the other sponsor is?"

Lucas clucked his tongue and gave a slow shake of his head. "That's confidential at the moment."

"I'll double their offer and go a step further. Harper mentioned that cabin on your ranch. As your corporate sponsor, I'd like to help you renovate the cabin Harper told me about. Underwrite the cost."

"The cabin is already under renovation."

Okay, not yet, but it was on his to-do list.

"I can donate some type of swag with both of our logos. How about pens or mugs?"

"Those have already been delivered. I have more pens than I know what to do with."

Colin's eyes rounded as though both surprised and impressed. "Talk to Harper. Let her know I support you and the business. Especially since it means my daughter will remain in Homestead Pass."

"I understand." Oh boy, did he understand. This meeting was all about keeping Harper close, which was fine by him, except there was no way would he hold her back from the endorsement deal. Clearly, Colin didn't know about that offer.

"Out of curiosity, do you mind if I ask why you chose the Lazy M for this project?" Colin asked. "Seems to me that Harper's property might have been the better choice."

"Harper's property?"

"Yes. The one she used as collateral on the loan application. Probate was completed on her grandmother's estate…" He paused, as if thinking. "Must have been three months ago. That property has better egress and room for expansion. Didn't she suggest Bettie's land as an option?"

Lucas froze at the reveal, working not to give away his surprise at the information Harper had failed to disclose. There was no way he would let Harper's father know he didn't have a clue what he was talking about.

"I, um…she may have, but as Harper probably mentioned, I've lost a few memories in late August."

"Still. We're days from October. I would have thought they'd be back by now." Colin picked up his water and downed the liquid.

"I feel the same way."

"That has to be a nuisance."

"Yes, sir."

"I have a friend who's a top-notch neurologist at a hospital in Texas. Maybe I should give him a call."

"I appreciate the offer, however I'm under the care of a board-certified neurologist in Oklahoma City."

Colin gave a thoughtful nod. "Fair enough."

Lucas's phone buzzed and he pulled it from his pocket. Harper. No doubt offering a get-out-of-jail-free card. It looked to him as though she didn't believe he could handle her father. He hit Decline.

It took another thirty minutes to extract himself from Colin. On the ride back to the ranch, he mulled over his conversation with the man.

Irritation threatened though he did his best not to jump to conclusions as to why hadn't Harper mentioned the collateral.

Once home, he shoved his to-go box in the fridge and strode to his father's office. He had picked up his glasses yesterday. That meant it was time to read the contract with the bank line by line.

Gramps popped his head into the room about the same time that Lucas finished a first pass on the paperwork.

"Nice glasses. They make you look like a college professor."

"That would be Sam. I'm the cowboy with the memory issues."

"Aw, knock it off. No feeling sorry for yourself."

"No? I don't get it, Gramps. Why couldn't the Lord have healed me completely and returned my memories? I feel like I'm taking the long way to get to my destination."

"Isn't that why it's called faith? Someday, I trust we can ask Him all those questions. In the meantime, faith and trust go hand in hand." He offered a lift of one shoulder. "Oh, and Harper is here to see Della. I told her to go on down to the stables."

"Thanks, Gramps." Lucas stood and stretched, removing his glasses.

He dreaded the confrontation with Harper, dreaded hearing from her that she had used the land as collateral when she'd known how important it was for him to launch the training center himself. His gaze went to the picture of his parents on the desk, and he sighed.

"Everything okay, son?" Gramps asked.

"No. Everything is totally messed up."

"Can I help?"

"Yeah. Time for a chat with Harper. Pray I can lead with my head and not with my heart."

"I can do that. As I recall, that's a favorite prayer for all you boys." Gramps chuckled. "Remember, when in doubt, close your mouth." He ran a hand over his chin. "I've never found that to be particularly useful for myself, but who knows? It might save your bacon."

"Sage advice, as usual, Gramps."

Minutes later, Lucas found Harper outside Della's stall, talking to Jim.

The sound of his boots on the stables' flooring had her turning. She smiled as he approached. "Della is a beautiful animal."

"That she is. Trustworthy as well."

Jim cleared his throat. "If you'll excuse me."

Lucas barely heard the words as he stared at Harper. She stroked Della's mane while he struggled to push down the memories of how she'd felt in his arms and how he'd thought he might be in love with her. Just looking at Harper had his heart hurting.

*Why didn't she tell me about the collateral?* He'd made peace with his business becoming their business. This news made the training center one-hundred-percent her business, and she hadn't bothered to tell him.

"I had an interesting lunch with your father."

Harper whirled around, the reddish-brown hair swinging. A smile lit up her face. "No doubt," she returned. "What's he up to now?"

"He wanted to know why we're starting the training center on Morgan land instead of the land you put up for collateral."

She opened her mouth to speak, but he kept talking. So much for Gramps's advice.

"You put up your inheritance. The land your grandmother left you."

"Yes. That's true." She nodded, her eyes wide with concern.

"I don't know what that other Lucas Morgan told you, but I thought I'd been really clear. I wanted to launch the training center without someone else holding me up." He took a breath. "Why your property?"

"Because I don't have a use for it, and it made sense to ensure that the loan went through." She looked at him. "Luc, you came to the realization that we likely were not going to get the loan on our own. We were rejected once. Our options were limited as neither of us wanted to ask our families."

"So you stepped in with this plan?"

Harper crossed her arms. "I decided it couldn't hurt to have the property valued by an inspector. Turns out it ticked all the boxes. Available for residential use. It has a well on the property too." She frowned, her eyes meeting his. "I went over our financials half a dozen times and there wasn't any other way."

"Did I agree to this?"

"Not officially."

"You submitted the paperwork without telling me?"

"I planned to tell you. Over dinner in Lawton. We never made it that far."

"So you decided to keep it from me."

"Decided?" Harper sucked in a breath. "Seriously, Luc?"

He recognized her gestures to control her temper. "You said your glasses would be ready this week. Read the contract. It's there in black and white. I didn't hide anything from you."

"I just read the contract. The thing I'm struggling with isn't in print."

"Oh?"

"You didn't tell me because you knew I'd be annoyed. And I am."

"No, I didn't want to push you or stress you, like the doctor said." She huffed and kicked the ground with her boot. "Was I wrong not to tell you sooner? Yes, I can see that I messed up. But deceiving you was not my agenda."

"What was your agenda?"

"There is no agenda. Once upon a time, two friends realized they had similar dreams and decided to work together." She paused. "What a horrible person I am to want to make both our dreams come true."

He scrubbed a hand over his eyes. She didn't get it. Nobody understood why he had to do this himself.

"Luc, using the land for collateral is not the end of the world. It got us the loan, didn't it?"

"Not the way I wanted."

"If I hadn't put up my grandmother's land, we wouldn't have gotten the loan." When she looked at him, he had to look away. "Sometimes you have to compromise. That's what a partnership is all about."

"I don't want to compromise."

Her jaw sagged. "So you'd rather the project tanked than accept my help?"

That wasn't what he'd meant. But to tell the truth, he didn't know what he meant right now. Nothing was working out the way he'd expected.

Harper paced back and forth a moment and then stopped, inches from him. Her perfume mocked him, so he stepped back.

"It's amazing that you can walk with that giant chip on your shoulder and that pride hanging around your neck, weighing you down. I applaud your efforts so far."

Her expression faltered for a brief moment and then her face became red, signaling Harper was full-on angry. "You know what? There isn't room for my opinion in a conversation with you and your ego. From today on, you can consider me your silent partner."

"How can you be a silent partner when you pretty much own the training center on paper?"

"I'm strictly your cosigner on anything necessary to the functioning of the business. Call my attorney when you need my signature." She waved a hand and marched to the entrance doors. "I'm out. I'll be on the road with Bootleg next year anyhow."

"That right? Well, good for you. You earned it." The words were hollow and flat.

"When the business turns a profit, which it will since it's a brilliant plan thanks to me, you can pay off the loan. Eventually, the land will be removed from the title as well as my name. I can always start my own training center on my property."

"Wait. Did you say you have an attorney?"

"That was your takeaway? That I have an attorney." Harper gave a shake of her head as she slipped out of the stables, leaving him standing there alone with the horses.

Della whinnied and stared at him with an accusing glare as he paced back and forth, trying to figure out how things had gotten so out of control.

"She's right, you know."

He turned around to see his grandfather in the doorway.

"You heard."

"Hard not to." Gramps stepped into the stables. "Lucas, you've let this whole memory thing make you bitter. What happened to the happy-go-lucky grandson you used to be before you whacked your head?"

"Pretty sure that fella is long gone. Not before he spent all my money on swag, a horse and a ring."

"A ring? I haven't heard anything about a ring."

"Never mind. The point is that everything that's happened in the last six months is playing out in real time. I feel like I'm reading the biography of Lucas Morgan."

"Why get angry about the situation? Maybe the solution is to relax and laugh. Nothing you can do about things anyhow."

"Gramps, Harper used her land as collateral for our business. Head injury or not, I would never have approved that move."

"Even if it was the only way to launch your dream?"

"Yes." He paused. "No. I don't know. All I'm saying is that maybe the fella I was before my accident is the real fraudster here." He poked himself in the chest with a finger. "I'm the legit Lucas Morgan."

"That may be so. But, son, you owe Harper an apology. She's an innocent bystander in your battle with yourself."

Lucas released a long breath and shook his head.

"Yeah, Gramps. You're right. But I don't have the emotional energy to do anything else today. It can wait. Maybe Harper and I can find a solution somewhere in the middle of this muck."

"You better pray she's still around when you pull your boots out of that muck."

A SICK FEELING settled in Harper's stomach as she looked out at the orchards from her position on the horse. She sniffed back tears that threatened, refusing to allow them to fall.

The vibrations of the hydraulic arms that shook the pecan trees provided a white noise in the background. Harper had grown so accustomed to the sound that she barely noticed it.

Her dad was right. A terrifying thought, indeed. She couldn't spend the rest of her life following Lucas around. Reilly Pecans wasn't so bad, except for the whole desk-in-an-office-with-tiny-windows thing. The pay was good, and she had a flair for marketing.

Maybe she'd sign the contract for the Bootleg Western Wear, stash the funds in the bank and call it quits after she'd fulfilled her year of obligation. She'd have enough cash for a down payment on a house.

A place of her own.

And there she'd be, alone in her house.

Katrina Bednar had given her thirty days to accept or decline the offer. Harper intended to lift the situation up in prayer rather than risk repenting in leisure over a bad decision. There were plenty of doors opening. She simply had to walk through the right one.

Wasn't that what Pastor McGuinness's sermon addressed this morning? "Liminal space," he'd said. The transition place from where we are to what He has for us. "That takes faith. It's not about jumping into our future, it's about being still and waiting."

Harper wasn't very good at waiting or with change. She liked to have the map in front of her with everything laid out.

That's what had made this last week torturous. Not knowing. Not knowing what she should do next. Not knowing if Luc would get his memory back or realize he was a jerk and apologize.

None of this would have happened if Luc hadn't lost his memory. The continued rub was that he still remembered nothing from the last six months. No wonder he thought she'd usurped his dream. It had been their dream once.

Harper slipped off her horse and they walked across the field to the stream that cut through this portion of her father's property. She stood at the bank as the water sloshed over the stones in a frothy haste. The smell of water and tall grass filled the air.

Her phone pinged with an incoming text.

*Maybe it's Luc.*

She pulled it from her pocket, fumbling and nearly dropping the device. It was not Luc.

*You have to stop. Luc is over. He's never going to feel the same way about you as you do about him.*

The text was from her mother. A reminder that chef would have lunch ready in fifteen minutes. Harper typed back that she'd be there shortly. She wasn't hungry, but it would behoove her to show support for the newest hire as it kept her mother out of the kitchen.

First, she'd call her friend Jackie about her invitation to the rodeo and the wedding. Harper punched in a number. "Jackie?... Yes, it's Harper... I'll be in Tulsa next Friday. You have yourself a date for the wedding."

It was time to get out of Dodge and clear her head. Harper smiled. She'd mark today on her calendar. Her father was right and now she recalled her mother's words. *Go. Have fun. You deserve a break.*

Yes, Mom was right as well. She'd been walking on broken glass for two months since Luc's accident. The last few days she'd functioned by rote, driving to Reilly Pecans and home again. Hardly eating or sleeping, living on coffee while trying to figure out how everything she had banked on had fallen apart. The thing was, she couldn't fix it. That was the real issue.

Her entire life, she'd been an overachiever, determined to do things herself and not rely on her family name. She'd succeed, too, by being strong, goal-oriented and focused. It had gotten her a scholarship for college and a successful career in rodeo. But it couldn't get her what she wanted most.

For her best friend to see that they had a shot at a future together. Yes, if the last six or so weeks had taught her anything, it was that she couldn't make Lucas Morgan love her.

## CHAPTER ELEVEN

"YOU SURE YOU'RE supposed to be doing this?"

Lucas grabbed the keys for the UTV off the wall of Trevor's office and turned to face Slim Jim.

"Yeah. Didn't I say so?"

The doc had okayed him to drive yesterday and recommended short distances to start with. Lucas strode to the vehicle. It was Friday, the sky was blue, and his brothers weren't around. The construction on the training center had paused while the crew allowed the concrete to dry.

It was a perfect day to work on the cabin.

He'd convinced Jim to pick up a load of lumber in town for him, so he didn't have to answer any nosy questions. Now, they transferred the 2 x 4s from Jim's truck to the UTV.

"Where you headed with this lumber and those tools?"

"To the cabin on my parcel."

"Sam's a carpenter. Have you thought about asking him for help?"

"Ever thought about minding your own business?"

Jim transferred another 2 x 4. "Sure are a lot of cranky people around here lately."

"That implies more than one."

"Yep. I can count. You and Harper. The woman nearly bit

my head off at the barbecue party 'cause I wouldn't dance with her."

"Harper? That was weeks ago."

"And you can see I am still traumatized." He pulled the circular saw out of the truck and put it in the UTV. "I'd have gladly taken her for a spin. Since I won that line dancing competition last year, word of my skill on the dance floor has spread. But I turned her down out of loyalty to you, my friend."

"Loyalty to me?" Lucas stopped what he was doing and looked at Jim.

"You're in love with her. Any fool can see that. Why, at Trevor's wedding, you hardly let her out of your sight."

"That was two months ago and, for the life of me, I cannot remember any of it."

"That's a problem. You sure acted like a man who lost his heart to a particular woman. That's all I can tell you."

Lucas shook his head. Had he been in love with her at the wedding? He couldn't help but think about the pretty diamond in his duffel bag. Could the ring be for Harper?

How was he going to find out?

"What are you thinking about so hard?" Jim asked.

"Nothing and everything." He looked at his friend. "She asked you to dance."

"Sure did, and that woman has a temper. Let me tell you. My plan is to never get on her bad side again."

Yeah, she did. Harper didn't get angry often, but when she did, look out. She made a rodeo bull look timid.

"Well, I appreciate the information and the concern for my safety."

"But you're still going out to the cabin by yourself."

"Yep. It's time. I've been sitting around for weeks. I couldn't lift anything because the doc didn't want me to mess with the pressure in my eyes. Couldn't read because it gave me a headache. What did that leave me? Six weeks of doing nothing. Bess felt so sorry for me, she let me make cinnamon rolls the other day."

Jim's jaw sagged and his eyes bugged out. "You saw the secret recipe?"

"Focus, Jim. I'm saying I need to do some physical labor."

"I see your point. A fella needs to work with his hands. It's therapeutic."

"Therapeutic. That's one way to look at things." Luc saw it as an opportunity to burn off his anger, but therapeutic was good.

He couldn't remember going into business with Harper against his better judgment. But, apparently, he had. Willingly.

Why was it only now that he'd discovered his partner owned the collateral which was foundational to the entire business? So much for doing it on his own. The center ought to be called Reilly Training Center because it sure wasn't a fifty-fifty operation. Nope, Harper was the real owner.

The thought chafed and embarrassed him.

He ought to be grateful to have a partner as committed as Harper.

She hadn't told him about the collateral on the loan. That's what kept looping through his mind over and over. Why hadn't she told him?

"I can stick around and help," Jim said. "Not much going on today."

"Huh?" Lucas turned to look at his friend.

"I volunteered to help you."

"The idea is for me to be alone."

"Oh yeah, sure. I get it. Man against the land." Jim dusted off his hands and nodded. "Sure hope the man wins."

"Thanks, pal. Good to have your support."

Waving Jim off, Lucas headed to his parcel. He parked the UTV near the cabin, got out and took a slow walk around the construction area. The crew hadn't wasted any time. Concreting of stub columns was in progress. He didn't know much about construction, but Drew sent him updates.

Returning to the cabin, Lucas pulled the lumber from the vehicle and tossed it on the ground. Then he got a crowbar out. First, he'd deal with the steps and then the remains of the railing had to go.

He maneuvered around the hole in the steps from Harper's near fall and two-stepped to the cabin door. When he turned the handle, it wouldn't budge. Lucas pulled hard, using his booted foot as leverage on the frame. It popped open.

Something leaped at him, causing him to stumble backward. Something big. A huge daddy of a raccoon. At least a thirty-pounder.

Grabbing the remaining railing for support, he avoided tumbling to the ground. A good move as it kept him from landing on his head. His neurologist would likely have frowned upon that. Instead, both his feet crashed through the landing floorboards and his arm hit a broken piece of railing.

Great. Wedged in and unable to free himself. He recalled when Harper had fallen through the steps. If he tried to pull his legs out, he would certainly cut himself on the edges of the wood that spiked like shards of glass.

Lucas yanked a bandana from his pocket and assessed the gash on his left forearm before awkwardly wrapping the scrap of cotton around the arm and tucking the ends in neatly. It wasn't like he was going to bleed out, but there was no point risking an infection.

Grabbing his phone from his pocket, Lucas debated who to call. It had to be someone discreet. He'd like to keep this incident from getting to his brothers.

He couldn't call Harper. Bridges had been burned there. Maybe Jim was still around.

A moment later, a rustle in the woods behind the cabin caught Lucas's attention. He prayed the raccoon hadn't returned for round two.

A horse and rider appeared.

"Looks like you have a problem," Trevor said from astride his mare.

The sound of an engine had Lucas looking in the other direction. Sam and Drew pulled up in the other ranch UTV.

"Good timing, I'd say." Drew grinned as he slid from behind the steering wheel. "What do you think, Sam?"

Sam's smile was even wider, with a little I-told-you-so mixed in. "I say that if we're going to do this, let's do it right. I brought tools."

Lucas grimaced. So much for keeping this from his brothers. "How did you know I was here?"

"Jim might have mentioned it," Trevor said as he dismounted. "Said he smelled trouble. We should probably promote him from horse whisperer to trouble sniffer."

Drew laughed at that. He reached for a hand saw in the back of Lucas's UTV.

"Whatever," Lucas said. "He's off my Christmas list for sure."

"Don't blame Jim. He might have saved your life." Trevor approached the steps and frowned. "What happened?"

"I'd tell you that a raccoon jumped me, but then you'd laugh. So I'm not answering on the grounds that this is going to be a story for the next dozen Sunday dinners no matter what I say."

Now all of his brothers were laughing. "You got that right," Drew said. "Be grateful we didn't bring Gramps along."

"There is that." He'd never hear the end of it from his grandfather.

"What did you do to your arm?" Trevor asked. "You and that raccoon wrestling?"

"Real funny."

"I'm starting to think Mother Nature doesn't like you. Those broncs stomp on you more often than not. A deer tackled your truck. Now a raccoon."

"It's a small cut."

"That bandana says otherwise. I have first-aid kits in the back of the UTVs courtesy of my wife, the RN. I'll grab one."

Sam approached the steps with a handsaw. "Don't say I never do anything for you." He knelt on the ground and proceeded to cut Lucas out of the broken boards.

"Thanks," Lucas said as he extracted one leg then the other and slapped at the dust and dirt on his jeans and boots.

Trevor removed the bandana, cleaned his laceration and dressed the wound.

"You're a pretty good nurse," Lucas said. "Got a mean mug, but your heart's in the right place."

Trevor eyed him unsmiling. "I used butterfly bandages, but you need to head to the clinic for a few stitches."

"I'll do it when I'm done here." Lucas held up his right arm where a row of scars from an incision trailed from his elbow to his wrist. "A few stiches are nothing compared to last year's accident. This can wait a few hours."

"Stubborn," Trevor said.

Sam shook his head. "Prideful."

"Hardheaded," Drew added.

His brothers formed a semicircle around him.

Lucas backed up, but they continued to move closer. "Is there something you want to say, fellas?"

"Yeah. There is." Drew pointed at him. "This gotta-do-it-all-yourself attitude is getting old."

"We're a team," Sam added. "Teamwork is what teams do."

Teamwork. Hadn't he just said that to Harper? Harper, who he'd practically kicked out of his life. Oh, the irony.

"Luc, we're like the five musketeers," Drew said. "The Morgan brothers and Gramps. All for one and one for all. We've been that way since the folks passed. You gotta stop trying to do it on your own."

"He's right," Sam said. "We're standing on the shoulders of giants at the Lazy M. Those are Mom and Dad's shoulders, and we're nothing without each other."

Emotion clogged Lucas's throat. He nodded and hung his head.

"We're family," Trevor said. "You and I are twins, and you still won't let me in unless it's on your terms."

Lucas released a breath and dared to look at Trevor. "I've leaned on you and Drew and Sam all my life. You were the ones who held me up when Mom and Dad died. Those days when I all I could do was cry."

"You cried," Sam said. "So what? We made a big mistake with our stoic responses. Trying to be strong because Gramps lost his only child." He sighed. "Gramps didn't need us to be strong. He needed a distraction from his pain. He needed to be needed. Maybe you were the only one that got that right. You were the one who helped Gramps get through that time."

"We're all we have in this world," Trevor added. "Each other. The Morgan brothers. Don't lock us out, Luc. We want to be part of your world."

Each of his brothers gave him a man hug. Though they avoided eye contact, he knew they were as glassy-eyed with emotion as he was.

"Come on. Let's get this cabin in shape," Sam said. "A couple of meetings of the Morgan boys and it will be like new."

"What are you going to use it for?" Drew asked.

"You know all those pens, hats and mugs I bought before my accident? This cabin is going to be where we sell training center merch."

"That's a great idea," Trevor said.

"Harper's idea."

"Of course it is," Trevor returned. "She's the brains of this operation."

Yeah, she was. The brains and the heart and soul, and he'd ruined everything by letting his pride get in the way. His brothers had made him see that.

The sun had begun to set by the time they stopped for the

day. The steps and the landing had been replaced. Next time, they'd tackle the rest of the porch and the railings.

Once his brothers left, Lucas stood and stared at the cabin, admiring their progress. They'd managed to restore what had been damaged. Could he do the same with his relationship with his best friend?

Lucas got in the UTV and headed to the barn. His phone rang and he quickly reached for it, praying it was Harper.

Not Harper.

He stopped the vehicle and answered.

"Morgan here."

"Mr. Morgan, this is Amy from Keller's Family Jeweler in Lawton. We spoke a few weeks ago. I'm sorry to bother you so late in the day, but I do have news."

"You have information on my purchase?"

"In a manner of speaking. We've found your order, and it seems we owe you a refund. You paid for engraving on the ring and never received it. I'm so sorry for this oversight. I can send you a check, or if you would like to bring the ring in, we'd be happy to add the engraving."

"Engraving? What engraving?"

"Give me a moment to find that." She paused. "Ah...yes. Here it is. 'LM & HR. Best friends forever.'"

Lucas's jaw dropped and he slapped the steering wheel, his heart beating against his chest. *Harper.* All this time, it was Harper.

"Are you there, Mr. Morgan?"

"Yes. Yes. Sorry." He paused, collecting himself. "Thank you. This means a lot."

"Do you want to stop by and complete the engraving or shall I issue a refund?"

"Truthfully, I'm not sure. I have your number. I'll get back to you."

"That's fine. Again, I'm so sorry about this inconvenience."

"Inconvenience. This is nothing, ma'am. It's all good."

All this time, he'd been fighting his feelings for his best friend, and somehow, even with his memory gone, he'd known she was the woman he wanted to spend the rest of his life with.

Lucas tamped back his pleasure at the discovery. There was nothing to be happy about, yet. Harper could very well be on her way to the first stop in her Bootleg tour by now.

His throat tightened as he punched in her number on his phone.

The call immediately went to voice mail.

Desperate, he called Maureen Reilly.

She picked up on the first ring. "Luc, how are you?"

"Not so good, ma'am. I've messed things up, and Harper isn't answering her phone."

"Well, that explains so much." Maureen paused. "Harper is loading up her truck right now. You better hurry. She's leaving for Tulsa shortly."

"Can you stall her?"

"I'll do my best. How far away are you?"

"Twenty minutes."

"We've got this, Lucas." He could hear the smile in her voice.

"I sure hope so." Lucas ended the call. "Lord, I'm going to need some help here."

HARPER LOOKED AT her phone. Nearly a week since her argument with Luc and he decides to call today. Nope. She was not picking up. A gardenia could not fix what was broken. The bond of trust between them had been destroyed by his failure to trust her.

She'd cried her eyes out for too many nights before she realized it was time to get away from Homestead Pass, clear her head and spend some alone time, praying about what came next.

"Harper, have you seen my car keys?" Harper closed the

tailgate and turned around. Her mother stood on the front portico in jeans and her artist's smock.

"No. I never drive your car."

"I've an appointment. Could you please help me locate them?"

Harper cocked her head and assessed her mother's clothes. "You have a Friday night appointment?"

"I do."

"What's your appointment?"

"Does it matter? I need my keys."

"Fine. I'll look for them." She glanced at her phone. "But I have to get on the road soon."

"Thank you. You know I wouldn't ask if it wasn't important."

"Let's retrace your steps. When did you see them last?"

"Hmm. In the kitchen, I believe."

"Okay, I'll look in the kitchen. You check your purse."

"I'll do that."

Harper muttered to herself as she searched the kitchen countertops and drawers for ten minutes. Her mother was a brilliant artist who functioned like an absent-minded professor when she wasn't in her studio.

The new chef entered the kitchen as Harper rummaged around the utensil drawer. "What are you looking for?" she asked. "Maybe I can help."

"My mother lost her keys."

The woman pulled a set of keys out of her pants' pocket and dangled them in the air. "These?"

"Yes. Where did you find them?"

"In the refrigerator."

Harper snatched them. "This is another reason why we never let my mother in the kitchen. Thank you." She glanced at the wall clock and raced out of the house.

"Found them," she called. When she got to the portico, she saw Luc standing next to the Lazy M Ranch pickup. She stiffened. No. No. No. Her heart couldn't go another round with Luc.

"What are you doing here?"

Her mother took the keys from her. "I'll let you two chat."

Harper's gaze went from Luc to her mother. "Did you plan this, Mom?"

"I wouldn't say that. Would you, Lucas?"

He offered a somber nod. "No, ma'am. This was all my idea."

Harper shook her head, confused. "What are you doing here?"

"Talking to you, I hope."

She glanced at the truck. "You drove?"

"Yep. All doctor approved."

She stared at him, uncertain what to do. His hair was damp, as though he'd just showered, and he sported a large bandage on his left arm. "Your arm?"

"My dumb pride got in the way." He put his hands in the pockets of his jeans. "Could we talk?"

"What do you want to talk about? How I tricked you into starting a training school and provided collateral to make it happen? Or maybe how I'm taking over the business you didn't want me to be part of in the first place."

"Guilty on all counts." He released a pained breath as his gaze raked over her. "Harper, let's forget about the training school. Close up shop right now."

"What?" She sputtered, searching for a response. "It's your dream, Luc. Besides, we already spent some of that loan."

"I'll use my truck money. I'll sell my horse. Whatever it takes." He pulled his hands from his pockets and raised them as if pleading. "I want to go back to the way things were... The way I don't remember."

"That doesn't make any sense."

"Sure it does. I've messed things up, and I'm here to say

so. To apologize. You're right. I let my pride and my ego put a wall between us. And I need to explain."

Harper sucked in a breath. She wanted so badly to believe him, but she couldn't go back to being his buddy.

"I don't know..." she began, her attention on the tips of her boots.

"Please, Harper. Give me one more chance."

Raising her head she saw something in his eyes that gave her pause.

"Go ahead. Explain," she murmured.

Lucas ran a hand over his face and cleared his throat. "I didn't know you when my folks died. It was a tough time and I struggled. My brothers... Well they've always been protective of me because of it." He hitched a breath.

"Oh, Luc." She stepped toward him, and he moved back.

"I gotta finish now. I've kept this inside too long."

Harper nodded, holding back tears for the young boy who'd lost so much.

"When I planned the training center, I figured it would be my way to show my family that I had what it takes. That I could do it myself." He cleared his throat and met her gaze. "I was wrong. I can't do it alone. I need my brothers and the Good Lord and..." He cleared his throat. "I need you."

"I can't go back to the way things were," she whispered. "Because I want more, Luc. And I think you need to figure out what you want."

"Oh, I know what I want. I just told you. I want to go back to the moment I knew in my heart that you are the one I want to spend the rest of my life with. I might not have my memory yet, but I put enough of the pieces of the past together to figure it all out. Turns out, the other Lucas is a lot smarter than I gave him credit for."

He pulled the ring box from his pocket. "You're the reason I went out and bought a diamond engagement ring. Losing my memory made it take a little longer to figure it out. But I finally did."

"A ring? What are you talking about?" Stunned, Harper licked her lips as she stared at the box in the palm of his hand.

"This ring has an interesting history. Apparently, I bought it for you. Not that I recall buying it or anything."

"How do you know that?"

"The jewelry store called me and told me."

Harper opened her mouth and then closed it, her thoughts racing.

"Is it too late?" Luc asked.

"I..." She blinked, her gaze on the ring box. Was this really happening?

"I fell in love with you twice, Harper. Doesn't that give me bonus points?"

"You love me?" Her heart soared at the tenderness in his expression.

"Yep. Twice. The first time was before I lost my memory. I didn't want to wait to start our life together. I knew you were the one before we'd even had a first date and that's why I bought the ring."

His eyes searched hers as he continued. "These last weeks since the accident, I've fallen in love with you all over again. How could I not? And, by the way, I plan to get the ring engraved this time. In case I hit my head again and forget I love you."

"You love me?" He kept saying the words she'd never expected to hear.

"Of course I do. Who else would put up with me? I finally understand why the other Lucas wanted a partnership."

"That's the nicest thing you've said to me since you lost your memory."

He laughed. "That's not true. I just said I love you."

"I love you, too, Luc. I always have."

"That's because you're smarter than me." He got down on

one knee and opened the ring box to reveal a sparkly marquise diamond.

Harper looked from the ring to Luc. Her heart began to stutter, and her hands trembled at the love shining in his eyes. Luc really did love her.

"Will you marry me, Harper Reilly?"

"Oh, Luc. Yes."

Lucas stood and slid the ring on her finger, though she wasn't sure how since she was shaking so hard. He put his arms around her, and his lips met hers.

"I love you, Harper," he whispered.

"I love you, too, Lucas Morgan."

"Please, just tell me you aren't going to get married at a rodeo."

Both Harper and Luc turned to find her mother on the portico, smiling.

"Mom, you have got to stop eavesdropping."

"That's the thanks I get for losing my keys." She rushed down the steps. "Let me see that ring."

Harper held out her hand and laughed. "Isn't it beautiful?"

"Oh, Lucas," her mother said. "You have excellent taste."

"That's the truth." His gaze met Harper's. "Would you excuse us, Maureen? Harper and I have some planning to do."

Harper waited until her mother had left and then she turned to Luc. "What planning?"

"I plan to tell you a few more times how much I love you."

She laughed and pulled his head down to hers. "I love you, Lucas Morgan."

# EPILOGUE

Lucas sat in the bleachers of the Gus Morgan Jr. Arena with Harper. They'd started a ritual of praying together each morning since the training center had opened in the spring. Each day, they took their coffee and Bibles to the site and prayed for the instructors, students, and the horses.

There was a beautiful peace to the arena this time of day. Today the scent of smoke from fireplaces mingled with the crisp smell of fir trees. His favorite perfume. Each morning, he thanked the Lord for all that had been given to them.

The chute sign advertising Reilly Pecans flapped as a breeze passed through. Lucas turned at the sound. His gaze spanned the fencing surrounding the arena, taking in dozens of colorful vinyl banners. The most prominent sponsorship banner featured the Lazy M Ranch. Lucas smiled at that.

He would raise the American flag and the familiar blue flag of the State of Oklahoma on the tall flagpoles once prayer time had concluded, officially starting another day.

"It's going to be a busy one," Harper said. As usual, they were on the same wavelength.

He nodded. Yes, tonight, the last graduation of the season was scheduled. Students enrolled in bronc-riding and barrel-riding training would circle the arena, stirring up the red dirt to entertain the crowd who filled the stands to watch their loved ones before they were awarded certificates of completion.

Harper zipped up her jacket and inched closer to him as the sun rose higher in the sky. The mornings were nippy as winter threatened to make an entrance. They would have to move their prayer time to the inside arena soon.

Opening his thermos, Lucas poured more coffee into his mug. The aroma wound itself around him. He took a long sip of the warming brew before closing the thermos lid. "Our first anniversary is coming up in a few weeks."

Harper stretched out her hand and admired her engagement ring nestled next to a white-gold band. The delicate marquise diamond seemed to wink at him as if to remind him of the day he'd purchased the ring. A day that he still couldn't recall.

Lucas shook his head.

"What?" Harper asked.

"I sure would like to remember buying that diamond."

"It doesn't matter. What matters is I'm the only gal whose cowboy fell in love with her twice." She looked up at him and sighed.

Lucas leaned close enough to touch his lips to hers. "My Cinderella," he whispered.

Harper put her arm through his. "Things have certainly changed in the last twelve months."

"You mean the fact that neither of us has been outside of Oklahoma since I asked you to marry me?" he said. "Do you regret not taking the Bootleg offer?"

"No. My days of wandering are over. This is where I want to be. With you. All my dreams are here. All my tomorrows."

"Mine too. How do you want to celebrate our anniversary?"

"I thought we could have a party like Dana did."

He groaned. "Tell me you're not serious."

"Not in the starter castle. We can use the indoor arena, hire Moretti catering, and invite all our friends and family."

"Like my exes party."

"Yes, but without the exes or the hors d'oeuvres."

"Sounds good to me."

Harper shivered as a breeze passed by. She pulled the wool cap on her head down around her ears.

"Want a sip of my coffee?" he asked. "It's hot."

"No, thanks." She wrinkled her nose.

Luc reached into his backpack, pulled out a container and popped the lid to reveal plump cinnamon rolls slathered with cream cheese icing. "Bess hid these for us."

"I'm going to pass. My stomach is a little queasy."

"What? No cinnamon rolls?" He frowned. "Maybe you should schedule an appointment at the clinic."

"Oh, I've been. The doctor tells me that it's nothing nine months won't fix."

"What?" He turned to her, confused.

A mischievous smile lit Harper's face and her green eyes sparkled. "Do the math, Lucas."

He blinked. "We're having a baby?" Joy bubbled up inside as he processed her words.

"It turns out we are. I know the timing is all wrong. The doctor recommended I stop riding when I hit my third trimester. This is definitely going to throw a wrench into our spring programming schedule."

He started laughing. "The best kind of wrench, Harp."

"I know we talked about starting a family after the business hit its second year."

"We're having a baby," Lucas murmured. "We have a nursery at the house from when Drew and Sadie lived there. Of course, we'll have to head into Oklahoma City for supplies. We'll need a high chair and a car seat for starters."

"Did you hear me?" she asked. "About our programming schedule?"

"I did. I absolutely did." He couldn't stop smiling. "Wait until Gramps finds out. This will be his sixth great-grandchild. Six. Imagine that."

"Yes, but what will we do about the training center?" She pulled out her phone and began to scroll through her address book. "I could make a few calls. Find a replacement. Jackie said she was interested."

Lucas put his hand on hers. "Harper, relax. Everything will work out. We're going to trust the Lord. Like we always do."

He pulled out his glasses and opened his worn King James Bible. He flipped through the pages until he found 2 Samuel 22:33. "'God is my strength and power: and he maketh my way perfect.'"

"Yes. You're right," Harper murmured. "Absolutely perfect."

He brushed his lips against hers. "We're having a baby."

\* \* \* \* \*

# The Cowboy's Inheritance
## Julia Ruth

MILLS & BOON

**Julia Ruth** is a *USA TODAY* bestselling author, married to her high school sweetheart and values her faith and family above all else. Julia and her husband have two teen girls and they enjoy their beach trips, where they can unwind and get back to basics. Since she grew up in a small rural community, Julia loves keeping her settings in fictitious towns that make her readers feel like they're home. You can find Julia on Instagram: juliaruthbooks.

Visit the Author Profile page at LoveInspired.com.

Rejoicing in hope; patient in tribulation;
continuing instant in prayer.
—*Romans* 12:12

Grace and Madelyn, I hope you both always
set the biggest goals, let nothing stand in your way
and pray with each step you take.

# CHAPTER ONE

RACHEL SPENCER TIGHTENED her grip on the reins as she brought Sunshine to a halt. She adjusted the wide brim of her hat to block the bright morning sun from her eyes. She still couldn't quite see who had pulled into the Circle H Ranch twenty minutes ago, but whoever drove that sporty black car evidently wanted to stick out like the proverbial sore thumb. No one in Rosewood Valley cared about money, let alone flashing their material possessions around.

Was this person the new owner of the neighboring ranch? A ribbon of remorse curled through her gut, both at the loss of her beloved neighbor and the potential loss of this prime piece of land. Oh, she had no money to purchase, but surely there was something she could do, right? She didn't believe she'd come this far and jumped every hurdle life had thrown at her to just miss her dream property. Besides, anyone who drove something so sporty and ostentatious likely had no clue how to properly care for a farm. Probably had shiny shoes that wouldn't dare go near a cow field or a chicken coop.

Rachel glanced at her own worn cowgirl boots as she pushed her bitterness aside. With a tap of her heel to Sunshine's flank, she started forward again. She had to get a closer look. She wasn't sure what her intent had been when she saddled up in her family's barn moments ago, but the unknown had been eating at her since she'd seen the sports car speeding down the two-lane road right past Four Sisters Ranch this morning.

If nothing else, she needed to introduce herself and give a stern warning about the tractors that were often on the road.

She truly wished her mood would lift, but she was human and lately there seemed to be one blow after another. She really wanted to catch a break.

Rachel actually wondered if she should turn back and not come across as some nosy town crier ready to spread the word on the newbie. In a town this small, she'd have no problem finding out what was going on with George Hart's property and who this stranger was.

But just as she had the thought to leave, a tall man came around from the side of the wraparound porch. He adjusted his dark sunglasses, then propped his hands on his hips as he stared out onto the front yard. The jeans and simple T-shirt didn't seem flashy, which was quite a juxtaposition to the black car sitting in the drive. But then she squinted to his shoes… Yup, shiny. Just like the car.

Sunshine let out a neigh and the stranger on the porch jerked his attention her way. So much for sneaking in and out.

"Thanks a lot," she muttered to her mare.

With another soft tap to her side, Sunshine took a casual approach across the field and onto the Circle H. Raking her gaze over the pristine two-story white farmhouse sent a warmth through Rachel. This was the exact type of home she'd always envisioned for herself and the family she wanted someday. Flower boxes under each window and a porch with swings and rocking chairs that just begged for family gatherings and sweet tea on a summer day. At least, that was how she dreamed of her future.

"Mornin'," she called.

No reply in return. The man remained still and didn't seem to get the memo that folks around here were chatty and friendly. Well, if he had any intention of sticking around, he'd have to learn real quick.

Considering she'd much rather figure out who this handsome stranger was than get back to her term paper due at the end of the week for her online class, she kicked Sunshine back into gear.

"You're new here."

*Way to state the obvious.*

"I'm Rachel Spencer," she added so he didn't think she was completely crazy. "From Four Sisters Ranch."

"Jack."

Rachel waited, but apparently "just Jack" had no last name. Regardless of his lack of manners and social skills, she smiled. Maybe she could get him to crack a smile as well. Not that he wasn't handsome enough with that light sandy hair and dark brown eyes. Even from on top of her horse, Jack seemed tall, over six feet, if she was guessing.

"I take it you're the new owner," she said.

"Something like that."

Rachel held on to the reins as she threw her leg over the saddle and dismounted. She led her mare closer to the porch as she tried to squelch her worries and her curiosity. If desperation and adoration could buy this land, she would have already signed her name on the deed long ago.

Being nearly thirty-five and living in a loft apartment over a barn on your parents' property seemed a little pathetic and unstable. Not to mention her parents needed that extra space for their growing farm-to-table events business they'd launched just a few months ago. Who knew offering such an experience would be such a huge success?

Her sister Jenn, that was who. The brainchild behind the operation.

Rachel knew her parents would never ask her to leave and would never even hint that they needed the space, but considering she knew the ins and outs of the daily operation—not only with the farm, but also all the growing events they'd added to bring in more income—it was well past time she move on and start her own legacy...and the Circle H was the perfect place.

Now, if she could only figure out how to buy when the bank had approved her for a certain amount and this place was worth well beyond that, no doubt... If it even went up for sale. Which was why she had to be careful in her questioning but still figure out the intentions of this stranger.

"You need any help settling in?" she offered. "My mother will likely bake something to welcome you to the neighborhood, but I'm more of a hands-on girl, if you and your wife need any help moving things."

Jack came down the steps and stood at the base. Now that they were on even ground, she could appreciate his height and broad shoulders. The lean frame and heavy-lidded stare shouldn't have her heart beating faster, but she was human and couldn't help how she felt. He had that city vibe with his polished attire, but a bit of his messy hair made him seem just a bit country, like he'd just removed his hat.

She'd never ogled another woman's husband before. She really should have turned around earlier when she had the chance. Yet here she was, unable to move her feet.

"It's just me and I won't be staying here for long," he explained.

Something about that statement both pleased and intrigued her, but she couldn't take the time to assess all her thoughts. She'd crossed property lines on a mission.

"Putting the farm on the market?" she asked, wondering if she could get some type of ballpark price to see exactly what she was working with so she could start praying.

"Soon."

A blossom of hope opened and she took a step forward. "I've always loved this place," she told him. "As a little girl I'd come visit and maybe make a pest of myself." She smiled thinking of the summer afternoons she'd spent here with her sisters. Come to think of it, one of the reasons they'd spent so many summer days here was because of their neighbor's grandson, an older boy who'd captured their interest. She chuckled as she recalled. "George Hart had the cutest grandson that would visit from out of town. I might have had a little crush, though now I can't even recall his name. I showed him how to bait a hook to fish on the pond in the back. He was absolutely terrible at fishing."

Rachel laughed and shook her head at the adolescent recollection, realizing she'd been babbling. "Sorry. I just have so many memories of this place. So, how did you know the owner?"

Jack took two slow, easy steps and stood just a few feet from her when a crooked, adorable smile spread across his face. She'd been waiting on a smile from him, but now that he presented it, she had a pit in her stomach because he looked a bit like he knew something she didn't.

"I'm the grandson and terrible fisherman."

RACHEL. HER INFECTIOUS grin faltered just enough to know she regretted her words, but her childhood secret hovered between them now.

He remembered the infamous four sisters hanging around, but it had always been Rachel who wanted to fish in the pond and help on the farm. She'd been such a tomboy, and from the looks of it, not much had changed. Her long hair fell in a braid over one slender shoulder and her white cowgirl hat shielded her eyes. Her worn jeans, even more worn boots and simple red T-shirt were all perfect staples of the girl-next-door look. Quite the opposite of the women he was used to seeing back in San Francisco. Many of them preferred heels to boots and makeup over a natural look. He had to admit, Rachel was nice to look at.

"Is this when I turn and leave and we pretend I didn't just admit my ten-year-old crush on you?"

Yeah. Quite different. Bold and assertive right off the bat. Something about that confused him. He wasn't used to women like that, but the other part of him found her intriguing and refreshing. The last woman he'd gone on a date with had giggled her way through the evening, almost trying too hard to give him attention.

Not that he was looking for a love connection—he was looking for a buyer. He had one goal in mind—to sell his grandfather's farmhouse quickly and figure out what to do with the feed store in town that had also been willed to him. Then get back to San Francisco. Finding a date wasn't even on the page of his to-do list. Gaining his father's approval and taking over the new real estate office came above all else. He hadn't worked this hard to prove himself to his only living family member just to lose this promotion to a guy who wasn't even family...but acted like the son Jack's father had always wanted.

*Forget about Brian.*

"No need to leave," Jack stated, concentrating on the here and now. "You're the only person I halfway know in this town."

He might be solely focused on his business goals, but that didn't mean he wanted to purposely embarrass her, either. Even though he'd been raised by a single father driven by money and a career, Jack still had loving nannies who'd taught him manners, morals and how to respect women.

"I'm sure my parents will remember you." She tipped her head and pursed her lips just enough to draw his attention to her unpainted mouth. "I'm not sure you'd recall them, though. Will and Sarah Spencer. Dad rarely leaves the farm, but I know my mother came over and brought food and canned goods."

Jack tried to recollect, but those summers were a blur. He did remember a few times going over to the farm next door and the girls always being around. But mostly when Jack thought back to that time, all he remembered was being happy and content and...loved. His grandfather always tried to get his work done while entertaining a growing, curious boy who knew absolutely nothing about farming. Jack wouldn't remember a thing he'd been taught, so by the time the next summer visit rolled around, he'd have to learn all over again.

Being back now, well…he hadn't expected such a punch of nostalgia. He didn't think the place would have so much feeling, especially with his grandfather not here. Jack had been so conflicted with emotions and guilt when his grandfather passed, he'd not come back for the funeral. He hadn't seen his grandfather in so long because Jack had let his life get in the way, he'd felt like he didn't deserve to mourn with all those from the town who loved him.

But now he was back, and everywhere he looked, Jack saw the man who'd helped shape his life. From the fence by the barn Jack helped his grandfather nail into place, to the old porch swing where they'd share a cold glass of lemonade after a hard day's work.

He'd known many hard days in the real estate grind. And he didn't know what he'd do if he didn't get that promotion. Out of all the deals he'd had in his career, this was the biggest. His next move up the ladder hinged on this one sale and how much he'd get from the property…the property his grandfather had willed to him, completely bypassing Jack's father.

There was no plan B if he didn't sell this for top dollar. It was time he had his own office with his own staff and his own way of running the family real estate company.

"So, why sell?" Rachel asked, pulling him from his thoughts. "Not that it's my business, but this place is amazing."

"For some," he agreed. "But my home is in San Francisco."

"City boy."

"Through and through," he confirmed.

She snickered. "The shoes and the car were dead giveaways."

He wasn't sure if that was a dig or merely an observation. He'd worked hard for his things. That didn't mean he wasn't thankful, but he wouldn't be sorry. Maybe sometimes his taste leaned on the expensive side, but he had no other responsibilities other than to himself, so what was he hurting?

"What will you be asking for the farm?" she asked.

Was she interested? Or knew someone who was? "Why? You have a buyer?"

"I need a place and I've always loved this property." Rachel shrugged, then adjusted her hat. "Depends on the price."

"All cash is preferable and I'd like to have this closed within thirty days once I get it on the market," he told her before throwing out a ballpark range. "I suppose I could wait on someone to get a loan so long as there's no setbacks."

Her brows rose as her shoulders fell, and the only word he could use to describe her would be *defeated*. Clearly she was hoping for something else, but he was here for business and that was all he knew.

"Thirty days is short," she finally replied. "Why the rush?"

Jack slid his hands into his pockets. "I don't really have a reason to stay here and I don't need a farm." No reason to keep up this property now that his grandfather was gone. Using this piece of land was the fastest, not to mention only, way to gain access to a portion of the family company, which he and Brian were neck and neck for. His father had pretty much stated this would be his best chance for success. "I'd like a quick, easy sale so I can get back to my life."

Rachel squared her shoulders and tipped her chin as she held his gaze. "I'm sure we can work something out. I fully intend to make sure I'm the new owner of the Circle H before you leave town."

If he thought she seemed defeated earlier, she had the look of a very determined woman now. But that grit staring back told him she didn't have the means to make this place hers, so his time here in Rosewood Valley was about to get very interesting.

# CHAPTER TWO

RACHEL HAD CALLED herself all kinds of a fool for the past twenty-four hours. What on earth had she been thinking blurting out such a bold, confident statement to Jack about the Circle H yesterday?

She hadn't been thinking, and that was how she found herself in an extremely awkward situation. One she couldn't stop mulling over as she drove into town to run errands. She only hoped Jack wouldn't be at his grandfather's store today and that she could avoid him a little longer. She just never learned her lesson. Her mouth often got her in trouble, but when she was passionate about something, sometimes her thoughts and words overrode her common sense.

As the oldest of four, Rachel had always let her words spill out before she truly thought everything through. Like the time she told her father she would take his early morning barn chores over the summer before her sixteenth birthday if he'd consider buying her a truck. About day three of that summer, she'd started wondering why she ever tossed out such a proposal. But that was when she truly started to appreciate the work of a farmer.

She'd really put her foot in her mouth this time. That daring, definite statement she'd left with Jack dropped a heavy weight of dread in her gut. Oh, sure, she wanted nothing more than to hand over an all-cash offer and move into that house today, but the harsh reality was she wasn't there financially. She didn't know if she ever would be, but she had every intention of trying and refused to back down.

Which was why she'd secretly enrolled in online schooling. Her business degree with an emphasis in agriculture would help her in the future. She wanted to assist young farmers or new ranchers to the area in getting a start and making smart decisions.

Now she just needed to take her own advice about said smart decisions and think before she spoke. More than that, though, she needed to pray. Relying on her own devices wouldn't get her very far in life, and she'd been taught at an early age to pray over anything and everything.

She'd prayed for her own ranch, her own future. She'd prayed for God to send the right man so she could start her family and begin making memories of the life she'd always envisioned. God's timing was always going to be better than her own... At least, that was what her father always told her. She just didn't know how long she'd have to wait to find that happy ending.

Rachel pulled into the lot of the All Good Things Feed Store and tried to focus on her mission today and not her unsettled nerves. She had offered to go get the grains for the horses today, since her mom had finagled her dad into hanging new curtains in the guest bedrooms. She needed the ride into town to clear her head anyway, but now that she was here, she was no more relaxed.

On a sigh, Rachel grabbed her purse and stepped from her truck. She adjusted her braid over her shoulder and smiled at a patron heading from the old two-story barn turned feed store. A variety of potted plants and hanging baskets deco-

rated the front entrance in a nice display that she knew for a
fact the new hire, Emily, had handled. That girl had a green
thumb and a love for animals. And that was the type of person Rachel hoped to help with her degree when the time came.

As soon as she stepped through the wide-open doors that
allowed fresh summer air to waft through, that familiar scent
of grain and hay hit her. She loved the country life and couldn't
imagine any other way of living. Rosewood Valley and all its
simplicity and beauty would always be home. The way the little
town was nestled between the rolling hills of Northern Cali-
fornia, the white church surrounded by lush evergreens, and
the farms that made up her community would always make her
smile. She wanted nothing more than to build the next stage
of her life here; she just prayed that would happen soon. She
knew she had to trust God's timing, but still, she had human
feelings and emotions and wanted to speed things along. With
her sister Jenn engaged and getting married soon, that only
made Rachel wish for her own true love to come along.

"But the grains and vegetables would be best, from everything I've seen online."

The worried tone had Rachel glancing at the lady standing
at the checkout counter. She tried not to eavesdrop as she began
to get her own things, but it was impossible not to overhear.
She didn't know who sounded more panicked, the customer
or the worker Rachel didn't recognize…which meant he was
fairly new. Her father typically did the feed store runs, and
Rachel hadn't been in for quite some time.

She checked out the endcap with its fresh supply of vitamins
and figured her own homemade holistic options were still better for her family's livestock. She always supported the local
store and bought what they needed for the farm, but she also
integrated some of her own all-natural herbs. She continued
to survey the stock, all the while listening to the duo behind
her, who both seemed extremely confused.

"I've only been here a few months, ma'am," the young worker stated. "I'm not sure on that type of supplement, though."

"Is there anyone here who is?" the patron asked.

"I'm afraid they don't come in until this afternoon, but I can call someone else if you need an answer right now. Our manager is on vacation until next week."

Rachel spun around. "I'm sorry," she intervened before she could stop herself. "I couldn't help but hear that you need guidance with some chicken supplements. I can offer my opinion if you don't mind."

The middle-aged woman's shoulders relaxed as she smiled. "Please. I've never had chickens, and my granddaughter talked me into getting some. I can't kill them already and I'm worried I'll feed them the wrong things. I've seen so many suggestions online."

Rachel returned the lady's smile and took a step forward. "I've grown up around chickens, and to be honest, there are some great at-home remedies you can supplement into the feed options you'll find here. Depending on the type of chickens you have, they can generally eat it if humans can. If that makes sense."

She didn't want to take business from the store, but she also felt that being honest about things she had at home was another great way to ensure trust in any customer. Rachel went on to explain some basic spices and pantry items the woman could use for the chickens to keep them healthy.

"The key with chickens is to start doing these things to prevent any illness from coming on in the first place," Rachel added. "They're pretty easy creatures once you get the hang of it."

"Well, that's reassuring." The lady laughed. "Since my granddaughter came to live with me, she's been begging for chickens so she can get eggs, and I bought some before thinking through the actual day-to-day care."

"I can definitely understand rash decisions." Rachel sighed. Boy, did she ever. "But you'll be just fine and the people here are always so helpful."

"Sorry about that," the new worker chimed in. "I'm still learning."

Rachel waved her hand. "No worries. Everyone has to start somewhere and you're trying. You'll get the hang of things in no time. I'm Rachel Spencer, by the way."

She held out her hand and the teen shook it. "Myles Taylor," he replied.

"Myles, my family is in here nearly every day, so you'll be seeing quite a bit of us. My father is Will Spencer."

The young boy's brows drew together. "Red suspenders?"

Rachel laughed at her father's well-known signature style. "That's him."

She took a step back and turned her attention to the customer. "Sorry I interrupted. Just thought I'd give some input from my years with chickens."

The woman nodded. "I'm quite glad you did."

Rachel offered her another smile before she turned back around. She caught someone at the end of an aisle moving away and out of sight. She didn't quite see a face, but she'd recognize those fancy shoes anywhere. Someone needed a pair of cowboy boots if he didn't want to stand out like a city slicker.

JACK MADE HIS way back to the feed store office as discreetly as possible. He'd stared at financial statements and backed-up bills all morning and they just weren't making sense. He'd decided to head out onto the floor to look at the layout and get a feel for things so he could give his eyes a break from all the disturbing numbers.

Then he'd heard that familiar voice. The woman who claimed she'd be buying his grandfather's farm. The adorable neighbor who had wide green eyes and a soft smile and a bold attitude that intrigued him more than it should.

Apparently she had to step in and assist a customer, and she did so in such a graceful way that she didn't embarrass the new hire. He shouldn't find every single trait about her so attractive—that certainly wasn't why he'd come to town—but he couldn't help himself. Jack shuffled through more files. Who in the world kept so many paper records, anyway?

Rosewood Valley truly was slow-paced and laid-back, almost in a different era. There were probably still pay phones on the corners.

"I thought that was you."

Jack dropped the stack of statements and glanced over his shoulder. Rachel leaned against the door frame and looped one of her thumbs through her belt loops. Long strands of dark and light brown hair intertwined in a braid that fell over one shoulder. She held on to the brim of her hat in her free hand as she met his gaze.

"How did you know I was here?" he asked.

She gestured her hat toward his shoes. "You're really going to need to change those if you want to blend in. What are you doing at the store today?"

He sighed and turned to ease a hip on the edge of the desk. "I figure I needed to see my other inheritance from Grandpa. I got here early and introduced myself to Myles. Good kid. Needs to learn more about the store, though."

"He will. He's nervous. Does he know who you are?"

Jack nodded. "I told him my grandfather owned the place and I'm in town to settle his affairs. I also told him I know nothing about a feed store, so thankfully you came in when you did, because I know as much about feeding chickens as I do about winning the Super Bowl."

"Happy to help," she replied with a wide grin. "I know a few new people have been hired lately, so there might be some growing pains until they all learn the ropes."

He wasn't sure there was enough time to get through everyone learning the ropes if these numbers kept declining. He'd need to talk to the manager, but the guy was out for a week on vacation. Jack didn't believe the books looked right, but he really didn't know what to think. He knew he had to be careful about how he handled this situation. Not only because he didn't want gossip spreading, but also because Jack was an outsider coming into this small town. He wanted to honor his grandfather's legacy and not leave a dark stain or tarnish George Hart's reputation in any way. His grandfather had impeccable character and Jack intended to protect that.

Though Jack had to wonder why the store and the farm hadn't gone to his father. Jack figured his grandpa knew that out of the two familial options, Jack would be the one to take the most care and do the right thing. His father never wanted anything to do with this lifestyle. Jack didn't either, but he had more of an emotional connection.

So here he sat with a bustling small-town store and a farm, and he had no idea how to run either. The farm would be sold to someone who could handle it. As for the feed store, his father hadn't insisted he sell that, so Jack was still on the fence. Maybe he'd keep this as an investment property.

"Something wrong?"

Rachel straightened from the doorway and took one step in. There wasn't much room, so he shifted around to the other side of the desk so they weren't so cramped.

"I'm not sure, honestly." He sighed, glancing down at the stack of papers. He needed to focus and not second-guess his grandfather's intentions or reasoning. "I'm a numbers guy and nothing here is adding up. Literally. It's quite a mess."

Rachel set her hat on the edge of the desk and picked up one of the statements. Jack waited while her bright eyes scanned the document. She looked from that paper to the desk, then back to him. The worry lines between her brows creased.

"Not a lot of money in this one," she murmured. "I'm sure he had other accounts."

"The other accounts are overdrawn."

Rachel's eyes widened. "What? That's just... That's not right."

"No, it's not. His name is on the account as well as the manager's."

"Walt is a trustworthy man." Rachel set the paper back on top of the others. "I've known him almost as long as I knew your grandfather. He wouldn't do anything shady, if that's what you're thinking."

"I really don't know what I'm thinking, but I don't know the guy. Until I can talk to him, I'm not sure what to do. I'd like someone to do some investigating and check things out around here. I guess I can hang around and act like I want to see the ins and outs."

Rachel's lips quirked. "And what will you do when someone asks you a question about worming medications or that their horse has a cough?"

Yeah, he hadn't thought about any of that. He only knew he needed to see if how much was coming in was actually coming in.

"I might have to stay here in the office for the most part," he amended. "The credit card receipts and the cash in aren't matching up. I feel like I need a set of eyes and ears, and I have no idea who to trust."

"No problem," she piped up. "I'll do it."

Jack jerked back slightly. "You'll do what?"

"I'll hang around the store, help customers, be discreet to see if anything weird is going on. That way when Walt gets back, he won't think anything and you won't be lurking over everyone's shoulder in your fancy shoes."

He had no clue why she was so hung up on his shoes, but he couldn't worry or think about that right now. He needed to concentrate on getting the house ready to sell and getting top dollar. He certainly hadn't expected to run into a snag at the feed store.

"Why would you offer to do this?" Jack asked, crossing his arms over his chest. "You want something in return?"

She shrugged one slender shoulder. "I would never do something for someone and expect a favor in return, but I think we could help each other for the time being."

Intrigued, he shifted his stance and leveled his gaze. The young tomboy he recalled had grown into a striking, intriguing woman who seemed to know her work and was passionate about this lifestyle. Not to mention she had a smart business mind, which was definitely something he could appreciate. Negotiations were very much in his wheelhouse, so she had his undivided attention.

"For reasons I don't want to get into, I need the money, so I'd need this to be a paid position," she added.

"Fair enough," he replied. Even though the place was in a financial disaster, if she could fix this issue, she'd be invaluable. "What else?"

"I'm sure you'll want to renovate the farmhouse, but I hope your ideas aren't too..."

He waited while she seemed to struggle with the right word. She twisted her hands together and pursed her lips, which amused him.

"Just say it," he coerced. "You won't hurt my feelings."

"Flashy."

She kept using that term to describe him, and he'd never had anyone say that before. He didn't think his style was over-the-top, but he wasn't here for a makeover of any kind, so her thoughts didn't matter—at least, not about his fashion sense.

"So I think I should help you with your renovations." She dropped her hands at her sides and shrugged. "I also want a chance at first dibs when you get done and decide to sell. Maybe we can work something out as far as a lease to own or something like that."

Jack hadn't seen that coming. Lease to own? There was simply no way. He had to sell—and at top dollar so he could get that promotion and get back to San Francisco.

"I can't do those terms," he replied. "The farm will have to be a straight sale, no lease or rent or land contracts."

That smile on her face faltered slightly, but she composed herself in seconds. With her chin tipped like he'd seen her do just yesterday, she quirked a dark brow.

"I would think that what I can bring to not only the farm but also this feed store would be worth your time to consider my proposal." She tossed out a number for her wages that he deemed fair before she went on. "I can start here tomorrow and I'll keep our communication line open. I'm sure once you see what I offer, you might just work with me on that property after all."

And with that parting statement, she tapped the brim of her hat and turned, walking out of his office like she hadn't heard his refusal. Clearly this woman knew what she wanted and didn't take no for an answer once she set her sights on something.

Which left Jack wondering if he found that annoying or surprisingly more attractive.

# CHAPTER THREE

"HAVE YOU FOUND a buyer yet?"

Jack made his way from the back porch of the farmhouse and down the stone path toward the guesthouse. He'd been making more notes of renovation ideas when his father called. Of course there hadn't been a "hello" or "how are you" but simply straight to the point.

"I've been in town two days," Jack replied. "So, no."

"It's a nice farm, if you're into that sort of thing," his father stated. "Shouldn't be too difficult to find someone to take over."

"It needs a few updates before I list it."

Jack used the old key to let himself into the guesthouse. An instant aroma of thick, musty air smacked him in the face. Growing up, Jack had played out here on occasion, pretending he had his own fortress and was a knight or maybe even a cowboy in the old West. Sometimes his grandfather would let people down on their luck stay here. But now the one-room cottage sat empty and dark. Jack turned and reached for the curtain to let some much-needed light into the place.

"Are you still there?" his father asked.

Jack slid the drapes aside and coughed as a heavy cloud of dust wafted all around him. Last time he'd been in here, he and his grandfather had hung these curtains for the new minister of their church to stay until the parsonage was ready. Jack had used his first drill to put the screw into the wall for the rod. He'd forgotten all about that nugget of time until just now.

"I'm here," he replied.

"What are you doing? You sound odd."

*Reliving the best memories of my life.*

"Just taking a look through all the property."

Once the dust particles flitted through the stale air and settled, Jack allowed another good sweep of the place with his eyes. The old worn leather sofa sat against the wall across from the small fireplace. The mantel had no photos or decor. There were a few trinkets residing on the built-ins around the fireplace, but nothing of value. An old wooden rocker sat in the corner, and a small table with two chairs divided the open space between the living room and kitchen.

The place seemed the same…yet different. Depressing, really. The life that used to be here was now gone. A place that would be open to anyone who needed it, thanks to his grandfather's giving heart. But Jack couldn't get swept away in nostalgia. He couldn't afford to lose sight of his goal.

He knew he didn't want to sink a ton of money into this guesthouse, but he also wanted to make sure this piece of the property was another positive selling feature. He wanted to do right by his grandfather and make sure his legacy lived on. Jack wanted to make him proud while making the right renovations to sell to the right buyer.

Would that person plant rosebushes around the back entrance like his grandmother had before her health declined? Would the new owner fill the pastures with horses for their children and grandchildren to enjoy? Would there be sweet tea on the front porch swings while watching the sunsets?

"Is this a bad time?"

His father's exasperated tone pulled Jack from the memories once again.

"Was there something you wanted to discuss or were you just checking on the sale?" Jack asked.

Perhaps one day his father would ask how he was doing or if there was anything he could do to help. But Jack didn't believe today was going to be that day. The almighty dollar seemed to always be Logan Hart's only concern.

And if Jack wanted that promotion he'd worked so hard for, he'd have to make that his concern for the next couple of months.

"Just checking to see if you'd had any interest yet, that's all."

*That's all.* Of course it was. Jack shouldn't be surprised, or even hurt, yet he was both. Being back in Rosewood Valley, where his core childhood memories lived, Jack wished he could see his grandfather just one more time. To see that smile that left creases around his mouth and eyes, or to get solid life advice, or even just to sit around the kitchen table in silence… Just a few more minutes to make more memories would really help soothe his heart.

But the memories he had now were all he'd ever have. He wanted to honor that… He just didn't know how.

The adorable, persistent neighbor did, though. He hadn't heard her ideas, but she knew the area, and something told him she could be trusted.

"Why don't you text me with updates?" His father's tone had shifted to annoyed. "Clearly I'm interrupting something. I hope your head is on straight and you're not getting some wild idea about keeping the place."

Jack jerked and gripped his cell. "Why would I keep it? I know nothing about farm life."

"No, you don't, so remember that."

His father disconnected the call without a goodbye. Jack sighed as he slid his cell back into his pocket. He couldn't let his father's sour mood get him down. Jack had never known his dad to be any other way, but something about being in a place that had once brought so much happiness and now created dread in his gut really confused him.

Maybe he hadn't dealt with his mourning yet, or maybe he was a jumble of nerves over this impending sale and trying to get a promotion. Perhaps all of that rolled into one weighty ball of anxiety… He truly didn't know but had to stay focused. He couldn't let his memories, or his father, divert him.

Thankfully his dad hadn't asked about the feed store. Jack wasn't sure what to think about that place, and until Rachel could find something to help him or the manager came back and they could talk, Jack would have to keep moving forward and focus on the farm. At least he could control that portion of his life. He hoped.

"CAN MY DRESS be purple?"

Rachel eased herself down into one of the salon chairs in her sister's shop. Jenn had recently come back home after three years away and now she was engaged and going to be a stepmommy to the sweetest little seven-year-old. Paisley loved all things purple and was very invested in the wedding planning.

"Purple?" Jenn gasped. "Is there any other color?"

"Well, you're wearing white," Paisley countered. "So I didn't know if I had to wear white, too."

Jenn finished braiding Paisley's hair and spun her toward the mirror to see the final result. "You can pick out any purple dress you want. This is not just my day, but yours, too. It needs to be special."

Rachel crossed her legs and watched the darling exchange between Jenn and Paisley. Paisley's parents had lost their lives in a car accident about a year ago and her uncle Luke had come to town as her guardian. He and Jenn had fallen in love, and the trio just seemed to click right into place—right along with Cookie, their stray pup. Their nontraditional family seemed like something from a heartwarming movie, and Rachel couldn't be happier for her sister, who had suffered her own loss when her husband had passed of a heart attack four years ago. All those broken hearts had somehow healed each other.

Rachel couldn't help how she felt, though. She could be thrilled for this union and still have her own hurt of waiting for the right one to come along. All she'd ever wanted was her own family, her own farm. She knew God would lead her in the right direction—she just sincerely hoped that she wasn't missing any signs or signals. Her ex-fiancé had really opened her eyes to what she wanted out of life and out of a man. She needed someone who shared her goals and interests. While love was important, there was so much more that went into a relationship, and she would be quite certain she'd found "the one" before she opened her heart again.

"So what color should I wear?" Rachel chimed in. "I know I won't look near as beautiful as the bride or the junior brides-maid."

Jenn straightened and propped her hands on her hips. "Honestly, I was thinking of having you, Violet and Erin all in either a sage green or a cream tone. I know that sounds like an odd combo with my dress being white, but I've seen some gorgeous weddings with that earthy color scheme and they were lovely."

"Jenn, you don't have to justify anything to me or anyone else. If that's what you like and you're happy, that's all that matters." Rachel blew out a sigh and caught her reflection in one of the many mirrors. "Now, what will we do with this hair of mine? I only do a braid. I wouldn't know how to do anything else."

Paisley hopped down from the salon chair and crossed to Rachel. She pursed her lips as she seemed to be studying and thinking of a new style. Rachel caught Jenn's amused gaze over Paisley's shoulder.

"What do we think, P?" Jenn asked. "Should we just let her keep the braid or give her something bold and new for the wedding?"

Bold and new. That was what Rachel wanted to be. Well, she had the bold down, according to her family and friends, but new? She'd been the same old Rachel for years. No new clothes, because she wasn't much of a shopper. No new hair, because she didn't need anything fancy for the farm. The only thing new in her life was the upcoming degree she'd been secretly working on.

"Since we're having an outdoor wedding, what if we curl her hair all down and maybe put some pretty flowers on one side?" Jenn suggested.

Rachel slid her attention back to Paisley. "You think that would work? I've never done my hair like that before."

Paisley's eyes widened and her toothless grin spread across her face. "You'd look like a garden fairy. That's so cool."

"Then maybe you need flowers in your hair, too." Rachel tapped the end of her nose. "Purple to match your dress, if that's okay with the bride."

Jenn nodded. "Absolutely. I want everyone to have a special day and feel beautiful. This is all about a new chapter in life."

Rachel eased back in her chair and pulled in a deep breath. "Well, now that my hair has been decided, what should we do for bridesmaids' dresses?"

"Go shopping," Jenn suggested. "I was actually going to see if all of my sisters were free this weekend to go on the hunt."

"And me?" Paisley asked as she bounced on her tiptoes.

"Of course my favorite bridesmaid will be there," Jenn assured her.

The clicking of paws on the hardwood had Rachel turning to see Cookie, the most adorable rescue spaniel-mix, slowly making her way into the salon.

Rachel turned her attention toward her sister. "I didn't think she was allowed in here."

"She's not when we're open," Jenn explained. "But when I'm closed, I let her roam free from the apartment."

Jenn lived in the loft upstairs. When she'd got into town,

she decided to rent this salon and living space from Luke. Fast-forward several months and now the two were engaged and building a modest home on Four Sisters Ranch. They were going to make the most beautiful life together.

"So, back to shopping." Jenn took a seat in the salon chair Paisley had just vacated. "If we can all head out this week-end and make a fun girls' day, I think we could find the per-fect dresses."

"I'm free," Rachel told her. "Are you going to have Mom come as well?"

"Of course. She needs to find something, too."

Paisley took a seat on the floor when Cookie rolled over onto her back for a belly rub. "Can we get lunch at that place that has those chocolate drinks?"

Rachel laughed as Jenn shook her head. "You and those drinks." Jenn sighed. "I'm not sure which dress place we'll go to, but I'll try to make sure we can get you a sweet treat while we're out. Deal?"

Paisley patted Cookie's belly and nodded, shaking her fresh curls. "Deal. I can't believe I have a whole family now. I al-ways wanted aunts and uncles and grandparents. Now I have more than I ever thought."

She curled her little lips in as her chin quivered slightly. Rachel started to move, but Jenn was in motion, squatting down near Paisley.

"What is it?" Jenn asked.

Paisley glanced to Jenn with watery eyes. "I feel guilty for being happy. I love my mommy and daddy. Is that okay that I love you all, too?"

Rachel's heart broke for this sweet girl who'd lost so much at such a tender age. But God had a plan for all of them and had embraced Paisley with His arms and ushered her into this new life full of love and memories waiting to be made.

Jenn wrapped Paisley in her arms. "There is nothing to feel guilty about. I didn't know your parents, but I assure you that they would want you to be happy and loved. They would be so proud of the amazing, strong young lady you have become. So never feel guilty for living a good life."

As Rachel watched this exchange, she couldn't help but be proud of her sister for moving on from her own tragedy and living a good life for herself. She'd stumbled along the journey but had come home to where she belonged. She'd made her own way.

Now Rachel had to figure out how to make hers.

# CHAPTER FOUR

JACK STARED AT the main-floor bathroom and wondered if the new buyer would love this bird wallpaper as a statement piece or find the yellow feathery friends revolting. Thankfully his doorbell rang and pulled him from the small space, because he'd also been considering tearing down the walls to make the room bigger and that would solve the wallpaper dilemma.

The bell chimed again through the main floor as he made his way down the hall toward the foyer. The glow from the porch lights illuminated a familiar face, and once again he couldn't ignore that little tug of attraction. He certainly didn't have time to consider dating…and definitely not with someone who wasn't even in his hometown. Long-distance relationships, especially with his busy life, would never work. Not to mention he'd spent years vying for his father's approval and working to get ahead. Jack just didn't have the mental space to feed into another relationship. He'd have to push aside any interest he had in the oldest Spencer sister.

Jack flicked the lock to open and eased the door wide. "Evening," he greeted her.

"Hey."

Her wide smile did nothing to help him ignore that beauty of hers. This would be a difficult inner battle, no doubt.

"Is this a bad time?" she asked. "I probably should've texted first."

"No, this is fine." He stepped aside and gestured her in. "What's up?"

"I just wanted to fill you in on the store today and see about what you were thinking as far as renovations here."

She took a step inside and Jack closed the door as he watched her study the foyer. The area wasn't big by any means. The old farmhouse had been built decades ago with cutoff rooms. No modern open concept here. Just a small entryway table with an accent lamp, an area rug, and the dark-stained staircase and railing leading to the second-story bedrooms. One delicate glass globe nestled against the ceiling to supply minimal light. Nothing fancy, nothing exciting. And this would be the first impression when potential buyers came.

"We have to start in here," he commented before he could stop himself. "This is a very dull, boring space."

Rachel turned back to him with the sweetest smile, making those green eyes sparkle. "I think it's absolutely perfect. I might just add a nice bouquet of flowers on the table, but that's it. The staircase is grand and rich in color, the shades of blue in this rug really pop, and the adorable little light, it's all exactly what I'd put in my own home. A touch of charm and nostalgia."

He'd never looked at the house this way before, but just seeing the small space through her eyes had him wondering what she thought of the rest of the house. How would other buyers, other *locals*, view the place?

The only way to find out what would actually sell well in this small town would be to pick the mind of a resident. Not to mention Rachel seemed quite convinced this place would be hers, so who better to get an idea than someone who already envisioned this as home?

"Should I start taking notes?" he asked, crossing his arms over his chest.

Rachel's dark arched brows drew in. "Notes?"

"Do you have time to go room by room and give me your first impressions of what you love and what you'd change?"

She shrugged one slender shoulder. "The fact that you want my honest opinion is almost laughable. If my family knew that, they'd tell you to run the other way."

"Outspoken, are you?" Jack asked.

Her lips quirked. "That's a matter of opinion."

"Well, I'll take that opinion so I can get this place ready to sell."

Her bright eyes dimmed, her shoulders fell just a touch, but enough that he noticed. He'd never let personal feelings enter into a business arrangement before and he couldn't start now. He had his own future to look out for. Besides, there were other farms. It wasn't like Rachel would be homeless. She just happened to have her sights set on this particular farm, and he needed someone who could buy at top dollar. If they could find a way to get her the funds, Jack would be all for this business deal. He'd worked with enough people who needed a little help. Maybe he could think of something, but he also couldn't compromise his own mission.

"I'm going to find a way to make this place mine," she assured him. "Being next to my family's land would mean everything to me. So I'm happy to tell you how to fix things I'd like changed."

Jack couldn't help but admire her determination. She didn't like taking no for an answer and had her eye on the proverbial prize. The more time he spent with her, the more he realized that while they were from two different worlds, they had a good bit in common.

"Let's start in here," he told her, gesturing toward the living room. "I know what I'd do differently, but let's hear what you think."

Jack remained in the wide arched doorway and watched as Rachel made her way into the room. She first went to the window seat and pointed.

"Do not remove this for any reason. This is the perfect spot to read on a rainy day or for a child to do homework or even have a quick nap."

"Duly noted." Though he wouldn't have taken that window seat out anyway. "What else?"

She turned toward the fireplace and smiled. "The wood detail on this mantel is so stunning. I can see Christmas stockings hanging here and a fire with a dog sleeping on the rug. I might swap out the old furniture, but that's not a must. The built-ins on either side of the mantel are a dream. I'd just have less clutter, but still homey and stylish."

As she spoke, he couldn't deny the love that came through her tone. She truly did have a passion for this old farmhouse, and that tug on his heart couldn't be ignored. His grandparents would want someone like Rachel to have this property. There had to be a way to find the right buyer for this place—someone who'd care for it—while still making the deal he needed to earn his promotion.

Jack hated that he had to work so hard for his father's approval. Each time he strove for perfection, he always thought that would be the last time and he'd ultimately win his father over. Maybe he'd even hear his dad say how proud he was.

But no. Jack still waited for that day, and he truly hoped this final thrust to the finish line would be the moment. He'd earn the respect and launch his own career and real estate office.

"Did I lose you when I mentioned the screened-in patio?"

Rachel's sweet tone pulled him from his thoughts. Jack needed to push his father to the back of his mind for the moment and concentrate on the remarkable woman before him. Yes, she might be helping him from her own desire for the property, but he needed to listen because someone like her was definitely buying the place.

Rachel's expressive gaze stared across the kitchen island as she waited for him to answer.

"Screened-in porch," he repeated, glancing out the patio doors that needed an update. "I think that's a great idea. An all-seasons patio would be a great addition, and any place someone can enjoy the beautiful views from inside would be a bonus."

A wide smile spread across her face, and Jack found himself returning the gesture. Something about her happiness and radiating light made some spark of joy burst inside him. He'd never met someone that seemed both driven and genuinely happy. Most people he knew were only happy if they were successful. Their careers drove them to find that happiness, but Rachel seemed to be the opposite. That drive inside her, even without having everything she wanted, was what made her so happy. She worked toward her goals but was content while doing so.

"Can you see a couple unwinding after a tough day on the farm?" Her voice took on a whimsical tone, and he knew she saw the scene playing out in her mind. "Maybe they've just put their kids to bed for the night and they're cuddled together on a nice cushy sofa. She's holding a hot cup of tea with honey and he's telling her of plans he's made for their future."

Jack found himself getting lost in this daydream of hers, and he could see the entire scenario, too. His mother had passed when he was just a toddler, so he hadn't seen a married couple sharing stolen moments or sharing dreams growing up. All he knew was work and reaching that next level on the proverbial career ladder. But Rachel had that picture-perfect upbringing, so she knew what she was talking about and it sounded like that was the life she wanted.

"Sounds like this isn't the first time you've thought of that moment." Jack leaned against the counter.

Rachel's eyes traveled from the window overlooking the backyard to him. That smile hadn't wavered, and the love in her eyes for this place, and for the life she so clearly wanted and deserved, said more than her words ever could. Why did she have to be so refreshing and give him a new glimpse into this land? Of all the times for an amazing woman to step into his life, now certainly did not line up with his goals or plans.

"Oh, I have," she assured him. "I mean, yes, I love this place, but in my mind, I've always seen a family and spending my days with the man I love and the life we were blessed with."

"You seem sure these blessings will happen."

Her brows drew in. "Why wouldn't I be? God has been so faithful to me through the years. Things might not happen in my time frame, but they happen in His, and I have to trust that won't change."

Jack's grandfather had always been strong in his faith, and during the summers Jack spent in Rosewood Valley, he recalled attending a little white church at the base of a hillside. The main thing he remembered were the dinners and the amazing food and how kind everyone seemed to be. Maybe that was why his grandparents always loved this town and the people here. Other than it being in the middle of nowhere, Jack couldn't recall a single negative thing about this community.

"What's causing that unusual smile on your face?" Rachel asked, tipping her head.

"Unusual smile?"

"Yeah. You normally scowl or look deep in thought."

Jack crossed his arms over his chest. "Is that so? I think I'm a pretty happy person."

"Really?" she volleyed back with a quirk of a brow. "So what were you just thinking of that had you happy?"

"Potato salad."

Rachel jerked back in surprise, then busted out laughing. "Well, I wasn't expecting that."

Jack shrugged. "You asked and that was it."

"I guess the saying is true that the way to a man's heart is through his stomach." She chuckled.

"Not necessarily," he countered. "I got to thinking of the

church my grandfather attended and then I thought of all those amazing church picnics and that one lady who always made potato salad."

Rachel's mouth twitched as she seemed to stifle her laughter. "Oh, that was my mother."

"No way."

How had he forgotten that? Another memory from this town and these people that drew him deeper in.

She nodded with a sparkle in her eye. "I promise. She had us peeling potatoes the day before, so I definitely remember. She always took potato salad, fresh yeast rolls and some type of berry pie."

Jack shook his head in disbelief. "I hadn't thought about or had potato salad in years. I don't even recall the last time."

"Sounds like you need to come for dinner one night."

Jack cringed. Family dinner? That sounded way too involved. He hadn't come to town for anything of the sort.

"Well, that sure wiped the smile off your face," Rachel told him good-naturedly. "Now you're back to scowling. Is it dinner that upset you or the invitation?"

"I don't do family dinners."

"So eating alone is how you like to live?" Rachel turned and sighed as she moved toward the dining room. "That's sad. Maybe you should just try it and see if you like interacting with people on a personal level that has nothing to do with business or working."

Interesting that she'd zeroed in on his lifestyle. He didn't do much, if anything, that didn't involve work or making that next dollar. Rachel was not only beautiful and brilliant, but she was intuitive with other people's feelings, which said so much about her character.

Jack followed her through the doorway and into the formal dining area that hadn't been used since his grandmother passed of a stroke when Jack had been about six. The room had sat empty since. Jack could still see the table set with pristine white china when someone important came over—which had usually been their pastor and his family. But on occasion Jack's father would come for Thanksgiving or Christmas and those same dishes would be on display with beautiful floral centerpieces for the season. He didn't recall much from the short time he had with his grandmother, but he did remember her roses, how she liked to host and how she loved having her family all together.

"Hey. You okay?"

Rachel's caring tone pulled him from the past. Swallowing the lump in his throat, Jack nodded. The more time he spent in this town, in this *house*, the deeper he fell into all those past suppressed memories.

"Fine," he assured her, though he felt anything but.

He hadn't expected the rush of recollections going from room to room. He'd been in the house only a couple of days, but these clips of time rolling through his mind tugged at something on his heart he hadn't known existed. He couldn't be emotionally attached. That had been the first thing his father had taught him in business. Emotions didn't make the sales.

"You seem sad." Rachel took a step toward him and smoothed her braid over her shoulder. "If this is a bad time, I can go. Or we can discuss the feed store. I don't want you to be miserable."

"Miserable?" He hadn't been called that before. "I'm not, but I didn't expect to have this many attachments to a house. I mean, it's just walls."

Her mouth tipped to a soft smile. "But it's what happens inside those walls that touch our hearts and live in our minds forever."

An uncomfortable sense of unease coupled with a balm to his heart overcame him. He'd never had anyone discuss feelings like this before. And he'd never really had anyone touch his soul like this. He had no clue what to do with this mess of confusing thoughts.

"How do you do that?" he asked, thinking out loud. "Say things to make me feel like…"

Her brows drew in. "Like what?"

Jack shrugged, suddenly feeling rather silly. "Nothing. Let's talk about the feed store. Did you learn anything?"

Silence surrounded them, and he thought she'd press the topic, but after a moment she merely nodded and rested her hand on the high back of a cherry-stained dining chair.

"I did notice a pattern with the dates on the statements," she told him. "It looks to be every five days the deposits are significantly lower than the other days."

Business. Yes. This he could circle back to and make sense of.

"Five days," he murmured. "That's odd. What happens every five days?"

Rachel shook her head and sighed. "That I don't know, but the pattern started a few months ago."

"And nobody caught it until now?"

Unbelievable. Jack couldn't wait to talk to this manager, but for all he knew, that guy was the one stealing. Rachel might know the people of the town and be trusting, but he was skeptical. Having an outsider might be what was needed to find the answers. Nothing clouded Jack's judgment because he really didn't have an emotional tie here…except apparently to this old farmhouse.

"It's confusing for sure," she agreed. "And we'd never know how much is missing because we don't know what the deposits would've been. Of course we have the credit card transactions, but no clue as to the cash."

They could look at the dates of the sales and try to come up with a rough estimate of how much had been taken, but any amount was grounds for firing, as far as he was concerned. And maybe even getting the cops involved.

"That's really all I've found so far," Rachel added.

"That's important information. I just need to figure out the other missing pieces to this puzzle."

"In the morning I'm helping Dad ride the fence lines and doing some repairs. So I can't be at the store. Ellen is working tomorrow, so I'm not too worried."

"I don't know Ellen, so I'm holding out my thoughts."

Rachel rolled her eyes as her delicate hand slipped from the chair. "Do you trust anyone?"

"I trust you."

That statement surprised him, but he realized it was true.

"That's it?" she asked.

She stared at him like she expected him to give her a whole list of names. But it was that bold green stare that had him stumbling over his thoughts. Everything about this woman intrigued him, from her larger-than-life personality to her subtle girl-next-door style. Not to mention her determination to help him find the thief from the feed store and her willingness to work with him on every bit of his inheritance.

"Don't you have a father?" she asked. "Surely you trust him."

Jack kicked that idea around for a moment before replying. "I suppose on some levels, yes. It's not like we discuss our deepest feelings or anything. But we work together, so I trust him there or I wouldn't be with the company."

She tilted her head. "That sounds more like a boss-employee relationship rather than father and son."

Jack started to say something, but Rachel waved a hand in the air, cutting him off. "Sorry. Not my business, so just ignore me. I'm sure you know by now that I open my mouth and speak before I think. I get myself into trouble sometimes."

"I'm aware, but you never have to apologize to me."

He took a step forward before he realized what he was doing, but when her head tipped up and her eyes widened, he stopped. Clearing his throat, he shoved his hands in his pockets. This woman managed to literally draw him in with just an innocent look and a concerned heart. He needed to watch his step or he could get into some real trouble here.

"I should probably go," she told him, as if sensing his unease. "I can definitely give you more ideas, especially for this main-floor bathroom, if you want."

Jack couldn't help but chuckle. "I doubt I could stop you from giving your opinion."

Her gaze flared, and she seemed to pause for a moment. "You should do that more often."

"What?" he asked.

"Laugh. Your whole face lights up and you don't look so miserable."

There was that word again. *Miserable*. He'd never thought himself to be a miserable person, but she seemed to have homed in on that for some reason.

"I'll make a mental note," he assured her.

Rachel made her way toward the other doorway across the dining room that led back into the foyer. He followed behind, not too close, but close enough to get some floral notes from her perfume or lotion.

"Thanks for coming by," he stated, reaching around to open the door for her. "I really do value this friendship we have."

Rachel tossed a glance over her shoulder and held him in place with that piercing stare. "Are we friends?"

Well, now he felt ridiculous if she was questioning him.

"I thought—"

"I'm teasing." She snickered. "So, since we're friends, I'll be sure to let Mama know you'll be coming for dinner soon. Good night, Jack."

She patted his cheek and headed out onto the wide porch, disappearing into the shadows of the night. Looked like he was going to a family dinner.

# CHAPTER FIVE

"I SUPPOSE THERE'S another fancy event here next weekend."

Rachel swung her leg over Sunshine and dismounted. "You mean a farm-to-table dinner? Yes, there is."

Her father still hadn't grasped the concept, but Rachel was so proud of Jenn for coming up with an idea to help bring more income to the farm. When it'd been on the brink of foreclosure just months ago, Rachel had been so worried. She'd even sold her house to help, moving into the apartment on her parents' property, but that hadn't been enough. Then Jenn had returned home with a great idea for an additional revenue stream.

Considering their mother made everything from scratch and they grew so much of their food and ingredients, why not tap into that by making delicious fixed-menu dinners for anyone who bought a ticket? They'd put a little work into the two-story barn behind the main house, and now the place was really starting to be a success with these dinners. They were even getting calls about booking private parties.

Jenn's fiancé had also purchased the front corner of the farm, which held a spacious barn where Luke could set up his large-animal vet office. He and Jenn were building a small cottage for them to begin their lives together with Paisley after the wedding.

Everything truly seemed to be falling into place for those she loved and cared for.

Rachel stepped up to the fence line and eased her heavy gloves on to check the barbed wire. She tugged on the knot around the post as her father checked the next post.

"Your mother was baking all night," he commented. "Today she said she was working on a new scalloped potato recipe. Sounds like a good dinner to me."

"Mom has never made a bad dinner."

"True."

Rachel moved down the line, loving this manual labor and the peaceful time with her father. She loved the sunshine on her face and making memories she'd have for a lifetime. This land meant everything to her, and she wanted nothing more than to obtain the property next door and grow their farm even more.

She couldn't help but feel a stronger bond to the place than just her love of the land. As George Hart had aged, she'd pop in to check on him. She'd bring food, claiming they had left-overs, just so he didn't have to worry about making his own. She'd worried about him taking care of such a large piece of property and all the livestock. He'd had workers that filtered in and out until he eventually sold off his animals, but Rachel felt like he needed a constant.

She'd formed a special relationship with George and absolutely adored that man. And maybe that was just another layer of reasoning as to why she felt so drawn to his grandson.

"I invited Jack to dinner," she added.

"Jack? George's grandson?" Her father let out a grunt, whether of amusement or annoyance, she wasn't sure. "Heard he was back in town. I guess he's the one driving that fancy car."

Rachel bit the inside of her cheek. "With shoes to match."

"City boy, just like his dad. George's son never did appreciate what God gave him. Always wanted more. George was so happy when Jack would come for the summers, but then he grew up and went by way of his father and rarely came for visits. Crushed his heart."

"I would imagine so." Rachel stepped over a pile of manure and adjusted her hat to shield her face. "I get the impression Jack is a little mix of both his grandfather and his father. I can tell he cares about the land and the feed store, but he is planning on selling for a profit."

"Figured as much."

There went another grunt. Definitely disapproval. Will Spencer believed in hard work and sticking it out when times got tough. Which was just one of the reasons why they hadn't sold Four Sisters Ranch when financial hardships hit them. Will and Sarah Spencer were strong people, with faith that God would pull them through.

"Not everyone has a life of farming, Dad. Jack has made his life in San Francisco, and he'd like to get back to what he knows."

Her father turned his weathered, tired eyes toward her. "Just like I said. City boy. Wouldn't last a day putting in hard work on a farm. Best he sell the place before he makes the Circle H into something fancy like one of those short-term rentals or bed-and-breakfasts."

There was no secret her father was of the "no change" generation. He liked things the way they'd always been—nice and familiar.

"Sometimes change needs to take place in order for growth and good things to happen," she offered. Like with their new event space, which he'd eventually come around to. "But I am working with him to get it ready to sell, so I won't let him go too fancy with it."

Her father straightened and adjusted his signature red suspenders. "Working with him, huh?" Yet another grunt. "And you invited him to dinner? Sounds like this is something serious."

Her heart did an extra flutter, which was absolutely ridiculous. Just because a handsome man came into town didn't mean anything. And just because he trusted her and needed her help with both of his properties didn't mean anything, either. She had her guard up. High walls had been erected around her heart after her failed engagement.

"Nothing serious," Rachel assured her dad. "We're just friends."

Friends. Just like she told him last night when she patted his smooth cheek. She should've never touched him because she hadn't realized the impact such an innocent gesture would have on her nerves.

She'd been on dates, she'd had serious boyfriends, but clearly the one long-term relationship she thought would end in a marriage had failed. No wonder a few encounters with her childhood crush and a minor touch had her completely flustered.

"I know my girls, and you have more interest in him than just as a friend."

Her father's concerned tone had her shifting from his studying gaze back to the fence.

"I promise, just friends. He's leaving as soon as the sales are final, and I'm trying to convince him to let me buy the farm on a lease or some arrangement that will benefit both of us."

"Honey, I know you've always wanted that farm," her father began with a sigh. "You've sacrificed so much helping us here and put your own dreams on hold. If I could get that place for you, I'd do it in a heartbeat. You deserve nothing less."

"I know you would." Rachel tugged on a wire and noted it had come loose. "I don't want you doing anything for me, Dad. You and Mom have given us the best life. I can make my own way."

As soon as she finished this online degree, she really felt she'd be on the right path. But the timing of that didn't coincide with the sale of the Circle H. She had to convince Jack to either let her work off some of the payments or convince him to let her lease. She didn't know his urgency to sell for top dollar; she didn't really see him as a money-hungry business-man. Something or someone else was driving him.

Maybe she could get him to open up, especially since he'd said he trusted her. If she understood where exactly he was coming from, perhaps she could find the perfect angle to get everything she wanted while he still made that sale.

"So when is Jack coming to dinner?" her father asked.

"Oh, we haven't set a day or anything. But he remembers Mom's potato salad from church dinners, so we're definitely going to have to have that."

Her father chuckled. "I haven't had her potato salad in quite some time. Sounds good to me. Maybe request ham, if you're picking."

Rachel smiled and finished her work on the broken wire. "I'll see what I can do."

As Rachel continued to work side by side with her father just like she had her entire life, she could only pray she'd be able to somehow obtain the adjoining farm so she could grow Four Sisters and have something substantial to last generations.

JACK STARED AT the email and blew out a frustrated sigh. He closed his laptop and set the device on the old end table next to the leather sofa and came to his feet. Waves of frustration rolled through him. Not only had Brian sold his intended prop-erty in record time and managed to set a company record of price per square foot, but he'd just landed another multimil-lion-dollar contract. For reasons Jack couldn't comprehend, his father seemed much too elated delivering that news.

Sometimes Jack wondered if his father loved the compe-tition and the financial gain and success more than his only child. He truly believed his father loved him in his own way, but at times like this, he wished his dad would offer support or words of encouragement. Then again, maybe telling Jack how well Brian was doing was his father's strange way of motivating him.

It was times like this that Jack thought when and if he ever became a father, he sincerely hoped he put his son's needs and feelings as a top priority. Jack hoped to have a family of his own one day, but he would have to slow down enough to meet the right woman first. Still, the idea of passing his own legacy down seemed like a logical step... There were just many more steps to take before he could get to that point.

He picked up his glass of sweet tea and headed toward the kitchen. He'd been working on a different design layout for a couple of the rooms, but nothing was really sticking with him as the right way to go. He wanted each and every detail to be perfect. Not only for the potential buyer, but to pay homage to his grandparents. Yet his mind had been a jumbled mess since he arrived in town.

Why couldn't he focus? Real estate and design were all he knew, all he was good at. How could he even compete with Brian if he couldn't get his head on straight? He needed more of Rachel's thoughts. He needed her positivity and her outlook on life. She made him feel something he hadn't felt in a long, long time. He couldn't even pinpoint what that emotion was, but he knew the moment something impacted him in a negative manner, he wanted to turn to her.

What did that mean?

Maybe he could continue to spend time with her and get work done simultaneously. He'd still like to learn a little about the farm life and what type of buyer he was looking at, and he had no doubt Rachel would be the perfect person for that job. Not to mention he didn't know anyone else to ask.

After setting his tea back in the fridge, he pulled his cell from his pocket and fired off a text.

You home?

Like a teen with a silly crush, he stared at his phone as the
three dots danced across the screen. Seconds later came the
reply.

Yes

Jack shoved his phone back in his jacket and headed out the
back door toward the garage. He slid into his car and maneuvered down the curvy tree-lined drive. The rolling farmland
did have a certain appeal and a calming presence. He could
see the draw to a laid-back lifestyle and to raising a family
here and teaching core values. His father had grown up here
but clearly didn't want any of that, though Jack had no doubt
his grandfather hated to see his family go.

Jack's parents met in college in San Francisco and his father had never looked back. He couldn't help but wonder how
different his life would've been if he'd grown up in Rosewood Valley. Would he have appreciated the farming more?
Would he be married with his own little family? His priorities
wouldn't be on the next sale or how stressed he was when his
career didn't line up with his father's expectations.

He pulled into the neighboring drive and passed beneath
the iron arch welcoming him to Four Sisters Ranch. He'd yet
to see the other sisters, but he vaguely remembered them from
his past visits. He wondered if they were all still close or if any
had moved away and made a new life for themselves.

Rachel had mentioned she lived in the second barn behind
the house, the one with a loft apartment. He really should've
told her he was coming, but he'd made a rash decision. Something he figured she would appreciate and understand.

To the left seemed to be new construction for a cozy-look-
ing cottage. He assumed that was Jenn and Luke's place, the
couple Rachel had mentioned were getting married soon. A
chapter like that in his life seemed so far away. He wasn't sure

what type of husband or father he'd make. That wasn't exactly where his mind had been over the past several years.

Jack spotted the two-story white barn with chipped paint on the black-and-white doors leading into the horse stalls. He pulled around to the side looking for exterior steps and found them on the backside facing a pond. He hadn't been on this property in so long, he'd forgotten the beauty of the place. He could easily see why Rachel was so passionate about her work. The serenity of this place took his breath away. He could see the love and care, even if a few things needed some attention. Peeling paint didn't overshadow the large maple tree with the tire swing, or the colorful flowers vining down from the window boxes at the front of the main house. Swaying porch swings and mooing from the pastures made the farm come to life, and Jack understood why Rachel would want the land next door. Family and ranching meant everything to her. She wanted to grow what they'd started here, and he could appreciate her stance.

Which only made him feel guilty about the position he was in. Business couldn't get personal, ever. His father wouldn't have the most successful real estate firm in San Francisco if he'd let his feelings hinder each and every decision.

Jack stepped from his vehicle and started to lock it but realized this wasn't the city; he figured nobody would bother his things here on private property in the afternoon. He mounted the weathered stairs and tapped his knuckles on the sturdy door with a small window across the top.

The door seemed newer than the rest of the barn and he wondered if they'd made provisions for her to live above the horses' stalls.

The door flung open and Rachel's golden-brown hair went flying around her shoulders.

"Dad, I—"

She froze, her eyes widening as she took in her guest.

"Oh." She gripped the edge of the door. "Sorry. Dad just

called and I thought he was coming to tell me something else on his never-ending to-do list."

"No, just an unannounced visitor," he explained with a shrug. He should've clarified why he'd asked if she was home. "Is this a bad time?"

Rachel tucked her hair behind her ears and turned around to glance behind her, then back to him. "Um, no. This is fine."

"You sure?" he asked when she seemed hesitant. "It's not an emergency."

"This is absolutely fine." She took a step back and opened the door a bit more as she gestured him in. "I just got done helping Dad shoe a couple of our mares and then grabbed a quick shower. It was a rough morning. I probably look a mess since I thought I'd have a boring evening alone."

She didn't look a mess—quite the contrary. Her slightly damp hair fell down her back and she looked quite comfortable in her long-sleeve gray T-shirt and black sweatpants. Her bare feet got his attention…not that he took note of her pale pink–polished toes or anything.

"You look fine," he assured her, because telling her she was just as striking as any other time he'd seen her seemed a bit much.

Actually, he'd never seen her hair down. She always had that side braid falling over her shoulders. He hadn't expected all the waves, but then again, he hadn't given Rachel's hair much thought. Now he couldn't stop staring at how stunning she was. He hadn't anticipated another side to this farm girl or thought of how she'd be in her element at home. Just how many more versions of Rachel existed?

Jack crossed the threshold and glanced around the open loft area. The raw wood beams of the peaked ceiling were exposed, the small kitchen sat off to the left, a yellow sofa with a few throw pillows and coffee table were directly in front of him, and a perfectly made daybed with what appeared to be a handmade quilt sat tucked back in the corner. He assumed the two closed doors he noted were a closet and a restroom. The place was tiny but efficient, and of course tidy. He wouldn't expect anything less.

"Let me clean up my mess," she told him as she scurried back to the sofa area.

She grabbed a notebook and closed it, then stacked several papers on top and set them all on the raw-edge coffee table. She reached for her laptop, but not before he saw the screen.

"Is that an economics class?" he asked. "Are you teaching it or taking it?"

She let out an unladylike snort. "Oh, I'm definitely not teaching it. At this point, I'm not sure my fumbling around could be called taking it, either."

Jack inched closer to get a better view of the coursework. "Do you need help? Not to brag, but I aced all my business classes."

"Of course you did," she murmured as she sank down on the sofa. "And that might be bragging, but I don't care. I do need help."

Jack laughed and circled the table to sit next to her. "Do you ever ask for help?"

"I'm not too proud to admit I'm in over my head with this class." She set the computer on his lap and crisscrossed her feet on the sofa as she shifted to face him. "We have an essay due tomorrow and for the life of me I'm not sure what this professor is asking for. I mean, I can write papers, but I'm getting confused."

Her frustration was something he hadn't seen before. The Rachel he'd seen so far was determined and fearless.

"Let's have a look." Jack scrolled down and read the assignment. "So, what are you studying? What's your degree going to be in?"

"Business with an emphasis in agriculture. I want to help farmers make the most of their land, and I want to be in a position to educate new ranchers on proper setups and how to establish a firm foundation. There's nothing like building a legacy and passing down something so important as land and livestock. That's something that will last for generations if done correctly."

Jack shifted his focus from the computer screen to Rachel. Legacy. That was something that his grandfather had stressed as well. He'd wanted his farm to stay in the family and had passed the property down to Jack. But that was where the legacy would end. Another family, another lineage, would take the reins from here. A layer of guilt settled within him. He wanted to make his grandfather proud, but he honestly didn't know how, other than to find the perfect buyer who would appreciate and take care of the Circle H. At the same time, he also had to find a buyer willing to offer the highest dollar. He planned to make a legacy of his own in real estate.

Rachel shifted on the sofa and pulled his attention back to the present problem.

"You're so knowledgeable," he told her as he glanced from her to the screen. "I can't imagine people wouldn't trust you without a degree."

"Maybe not." She shrugged. "But I want to be seen as a professional and my degree will only help me."

"What does your family think about this?"

Rachel's gaze darted away as she sighed. "They don't know I'm doing this."

Surprised she'd keep anything from them, Jack eased farther into the sofa and forgot all about the essay. He'd been under the impression they were all very close-knit.

"Why don't they know?" he asked. "Aren't you proud of what you're doing? I'm sure they would be encouraging."

She blinked those wide eyes and his heart clenched. How did she keep affecting him in such a way that had his heart somehow getting involved? This girl next door, literally, had worked her way into his personal life, and with his concern and curiosity, he seemed to have worked his way into hers.

"I never thought to be proud," she admitted. "I'm doing this to better myself while helping others. I know I have the knowledge to help people, but I need that extra business sense to make better decisions for them and for our own farm. We almost lost it, and I won't let that happen. Ever."

There was that drive and determination once again. Not only did she have that strong will, but she also possessed an independence he hadn't seen in the women he'd dated.

Wait. He couldn't go down this road. He shouldn't be thinking about dating at all around her. His life wasn't here, and her life wasn't anywhere else. Besides, what did he know about relationships other than in the business sense? Other than his grandparents, he didn't really know people who stayed committed to each other in the name of love. Did people even marry for love anymore?

"So you're trying to earn a bigger income to provide for your family?" he asked.

"Partly so we have some security, but I think we'll be fine now. Luke helped by purchasing some land for his new large-animal vet clinic, and when I sold my house last year—"

"You sold your house to save the farm?"

Rachel jerked at his abrupt question. "I sold my place to help, that's why I live up here now, but even with that, my parents still struggled."

She'd sold her house to live in a barn…all to save her family's legacy. The love she had for her family and this land continued to impress and surprise him. This type of commitment and concern went well beyond anything he'd ever experienced with his father. Jack wondered if she'd had much interaction with his grandfather. He had no doubt the two of them would've really hit it off and discussed all things farming.

"You seem speechless for the first time," she stated with a soft laugh. "I didn't mean to just let all of that out. Not many people know why I sold my house, and now you're the only one who knows about my online classes."

He truly felt humbled and touched that she'd opened herself up in such a vulnerable way. "Thank you for trusting me with all of that."

While she might be tough when it came to her goals, something he could appreciate, she had that soft interior that made her relatable. Actually, he could relate to her on all levels... which was starting to concern him.

"You already know I open my mouth and speak before thinking." She cringed, scrunching up her cute little nose. "It's a flaw."

"I don't see one flaw in you," he replied. "You're honest, which is refreshing, and you love deeply. Never apologize for being who you are."

That tender smile of hers spread even wider, and Jack had a sinking feeling that if he stayed in town for too long, he'd lose himself in this amazing woman. Why was she still single? Did she date or did she throw herself into her work and now schooling?

Yes. The schooling. What he needed to shift his focus back to.

He adjusted the computer on his lap and scanned the assignment once again.

"Okay. Let's do this," he told her.

"Wait—you didn't come here to help me with a term paper. I'm sure there was something on your mind."

Rachel started to reach for the laptop, but he held it out of her reach.

"No, I didn't come for this," he agreed. "I came over because I was having an off day and you're the only person lately who makes me smile."

Her lips shaped into an O. Apparently his honesty shocked her, but he wasn't going to play games or pretend she didn't intrigue him. Even in their short time together, her genuine heart had opened wide and shown him just how he deserved to be treated.

Maybe if they'd reconnected like this under different circumstances, he'd attempt to see if they could start something beyond a friendship. But he had too much going on, and she was the settling-down type. Their life goals couldn't be more opposite.

"I don't think anyone has ever given me such a compliment before," she admitted after a yawning pause.

"I find that hard to believe," he countered. "Surely you've had boyfriends."

Rachel nodded. "And a fiancé."

Surprised, Jack set the computer on the coffee table and adjusted so he could face her better. He stared into her striking green eyes.

"You were going to marry a man who never told you that you make him smile?" Jack asked.

Her brows drew together. "I never really thought about it. I mean, he would tell me he loved me and that I was pretty, but we weren't meant to be."

"What happened?" he asked, then immediately shook his head. "Sorry. That's just me being nosy. You don't have to answer."

"It's fine." She offered him another one of her sweet smiles as she smoothed her hair over one shoulder. "Of course I was heartbroken at first when we split, but I can look back and see that God had another plan for me. I don't know exactly what that looks like, but He was protecting me from a marriage that would've failed. Tyler and I were too different. He didn't appreciate the farm life and this is my one true passion."

Jack couldn't imagine a man walking away from someone so vibrant and full of life. Had this Tyler guy not even tried to compromise to keep Rachel? From what he could tell, she had simple needs. She valued her family and the farm. She didn't need flashy expensive things to make her happy. Perhaps that was why he found her so refreshing, as she breathed a new aspect of life into him. In fact, spending time with her had made him more and more curious to reconnect with farm life, the way he had during those summers with his grandpa.

"How soon is your term paper due?" he asked, gesturing to the laptop.

"Friday. Why?"

Jack came to his feet and extended his hand. "Care to show this city boy a little more of this farm life?"

A bright sparkle shimmered in her eyes, and he didn't think she could be more beautiful, but her entire face lit up at his suggestion. And the moment she slid her delicate hand in his, he knew he'd got in deeper than he'd ever intended.

# CHAPTER SIX

SURE, RACHEL NEEDED to work on her paper, but she'd felt some unexpected connection with Jack after telling him all her secrets—why had she gone into so much detail about her class and followed it up with her failed engagement? When he'd asked about her farm, there was no way she could turn him down.

"Ever ridden a horse?" she asked, leading him through the aisle between the stalls.

"A few times with my grandfather, but that was long ago."

She glanced down to his shoes and stopped. "You want me to find you something else to put on?"

Jack's eyes followed hers as he rocked back on his heels and chuckled. "My shoes have never been so offensive as they are to you. But I think I'll be fine."

"Suit yourself," she muttered as she turned to head into the tack room. "I've just never met someone who wears dress shoes for everything."

"And now you have," he joked.

She searched for the right saddles and blankets for the two horses she wanted to take out. Sunshine was hers, no question. She thought about putting Jack on Starlight but decided Champ would be a better fit.

"How many horses do you all have?" he asked.

Rachel passed him a saddle and he took it with a grunt. She smiled as she turned back for the other one.

"We have seven now. We used to have twelve but had to sell some for financial reasons."

Rachel set everything down in the aisle before she opened Champ's stall. She slid her hand down his velvety nose. The soft hair against her fingertips always calmed any nerves or fears. Animals were so trusting and loving; no matter the type of day you had, they were always a constant friend.

"You'll be riding Champ." She glanced over her shoulder to find Jack next to her. "He's four and gentle. Definitely good for a beginner."

"Beginner?" he scoffed. "I bet I can remember everything without you telling me."

Rachel stepped aside and held her hands up. "By all means. Help yourself. Just watch you don't scratch those shiny shoes."

"Would it make you feel better if you got me some boots?" he asked.

"Oh, I don't want to take you out of your element," she joked as she moved to the next stall with Sunshine. "You do your thing and I'll do mine."

He muttered something beneath his breath while Rachel grabbed a blanket and moved into Sunshine's area. She smoothed her hand down the mare's back and gave her a good pat.

Jack's soft words to Champ warmed Rachel's heart. Any man who loved animals had a good soul. She'd learned quite a bit about her ex when he'd not really cared about her world or the care of the livestock. He assumed others would take care of everything, and horses and farms were glamorous. She'd had such tunnel vision while looking ahead to being a wife and mother, she hadn't considered he'd been the wrong man for her. It wasn't until she came to the realization he didn't have a servant's heart that her world had crumbled. God had given her signs all along, from his excuses to avoid family dinners, to his drive for working above spending a quiet Sunday afternoon with her. She hadn't wanted to see the negativity since she knew nobody was perfect.

Letting Tyler go had been the most difficult decision, yet the only one she could've made. The growth from that time in her life had prepared her, she hoped, for when God sent the right man her way. But he would have to be above and beyond for her to let those walls down ever again. At times she wondered if she was just climbing a mountain with no peak in sight.

Not that she *needed* a man to fulfill her, but she wanted someone to come home to. She wanted someone to share her days with and make a lifetime of memories. She hoped there was a man who was just waiting on her as well.

Jack groaned and muttered something beneath his breath, snapping her attention from her thoughts.

She glanced through the bars on the wall separating the stall.

"Problem?" she asked.

He glanced down and shook his head. "Oh, no. Just stepped in a pile because I wasn't paying attention."

Rachel couldn't suppress her laughter.

His dark eyes came up to meet hers and his own lips twitched in amusement. "Go ahead—laugh it up."

"Hope you don't lose the shine on those." She chuckled.

"I have shoe polish."

Rachel rolled her eyes. "Of course you do."

"Are you even going to comment on how well I saddled Champ?"

She shifted her gaze to the blanket and saddle and nodded. "Well done. You do remember a few of the things you learned from your grandfather."

"I didn't think I would, but I could hear his voice in my head guiding me through."

Rachel's amusement slipped as nostalgia slid into place. "That must be special to still know the sound of his voice."

Jack's hand smoothed down the chocolate mane on Champ's neck. "That's something else I thought I wouldn't remember. It's nice to know I still have that memory. I guess coming back has tapped into those core childhood moments."

"Are you comforted by that or do they make you sad?"

He paused as if trying to gather his thoughts. Sunshine neighed and bobbed her nose, more than ready to get out into the wide-open fields.

"I'm a little of both, I think," he admitted.

"I guess that's just the emotions that come with losing someone you love dearly."

Rachel led Sunshine from the stall and held the reins in her hand. "You ready to go or do you want that pair of boots now?"

He mimicked her as he and Champ came out into the aisle. "At this point these shoes might be done for. No need to change them. I've never worn cowboy boots anyway. I wouldn't even know how to walk in them."

"One foot in front of the other," she joked.

"But if I started that cowboy swagger, I wouldn't be able to keep the women away, and I don't have time for a relationship right now."

He winked and her heart fluttered again. He didn't need the boots or the swagger to make her want to get to know him better. She'd gone well beyond that point, but he'd made it clear he didn't have time for anything, and hadn't she learned her lesson once already? Workaholics didn't make time for the necessities in life, and her core values all hinged around God, family and her farm. Everything else was just an added bonus.

Her ex hadn't made her family a priority in his life. In Rachel's eyes, they were a package deal and anyone would be lucky to have her sisters and her parents in their lives. Not only would the next person she considered letting into her life need to be in tune with her love of the farm, but he would also have to love her family as much as she did.

"I'll be sure to keep the ladies away from you," she assured him with a laugh. "But it's not like Rosewood Valley is crawling with bachelorettes. I mean, there's my two sisters, Erin and Violet, then me and a few others, but most women get married pretty young here, and we have a very low divorce rate."

Rachel headed toward the wide opening at the other end of the barn and Jack followed behind her. She didn't recall a time when her ex asked about her farm or anything to do with the livestock. Jack had a caring heart or he wouldn't have asked. Maybe because he wanted to sell and wanted to know more about the lifestyle, but she was going to pour her soul into showing him why Rosewood Valley was heaven on earth anyway.

"This town is like something from an old movie," he stated once they stepped into the field. "Or stuck in time perhaps. Perfect marriages, picturesque town, family traditions."

Rachel stopped and pulled her hair over her shoulder to start her braid. No way could she ride with her hair flying in the wind. With expert fingers, she wound her strands together and pulled the band from her wrist to secure everything.

"First of all," she stated after her hair was in place, "no marriage is perfect. There are imperfect people who find someone who complements their flaws. And, yes, our town is amazing and our values really make us stand out. We like our little pocket of the world."

"I can admit Rosewood Valley is an amazing place." He glanced around the open area toward the hills in the distance and shielded his eyes from the afternoon sun. "I definitely don't see this much sky back home."

Rachel gripped her reins as she placed one hand on her pommel and slid her foot into the stirrup. She slung one leg over the saddle and settled into her favorite worn spot. As far as she was concerned, this was the best seat and view in the world. Rachel glanced down and offered Jack a smile.

"We're growing on you," she informed him. "You're never going to want to leave."

He put his foot into his own stirrup and did a bounce to get up into the saddle. He took a couple of tries, but ultimately got it right. The fact he was trying, that he was open to this part of her life, shouldn't have her so happy. He wasn't staying and he wasn't some date. But still, it was nice to get out and not be working or doing school stuff. She could relax and just enjoy what she'd been blessed with.

"Nice job," she praised. "You aren't as rusty as you thought."

"Oh, I'm sure I'll feel this in the morning."

Rachel nodded in agreement. "No doubt, but for now, let's enjoy this gorgeous evening. There's nothing like a sunset on the farm. Plus, fall and winter will be here before we know it, so I want to soak up all of this beautiful weather."

"Does it get cold here?"

"Pretty cold." She tapped her heel on Sunshine's flank to get her moving. "We have all seasons, but that's just another reason I love it here. I wouldn't want to live somewhere it's cold or hot all the time. I like the difference the mountains have to offer."

Jack and Champ fell into a cadence beside her, and Rachel lifted her face to the sun.

"I couldn't imagine living anywhere else," she added as she pulled in a deep breath of fresh air.

For a moment, the peaceful silence enveloped them. Rachel wondered where his thoughts had headed and if the town was indeed getting to him. She couldn't imagine anyone stepping foot here and not falling in love. Who wanted to live with stress and high-rises and crowds?

"Tell me about your sisters."

Jack's statement broke the silence, and a warmth instantly spread through her. He wanted to know her better. But he could also just be filling the quiet space. Rachel really didn't think so. She hadn't known Jack long, but she knew George, and Rachel saw so many similarities between the two. Kind and considerate, to name just a couple.

"Well, I've told you Jenn came back to town after being gone for three years. Her first husband passed, and she ran from the pain. Now that she's back, she has Luke and his niece whom he has guardianship of. Her name is Paisley. And as you know, Jenn and Luke are getting married next month. That's the very short version of her story."

"Good for her," Jack replied.

Rachel smiled and gestured toward another open pasture. "Head that way. And, yes, I'm thrilled they all three found each other. Then there's Violet. She's a small-animal vet in town and single. My other sister Erin is an elementary teacher. She's also single, but she was engaged once, and then he left town as a missionary and he's been gone for years. My sisters and I don't know that she ever got over him, but we don't bring up that sore subject."

Jack made a soft hum beneath his breath as if taking all that in. He genuinely seemed interested in what she was saying, so she went on.

"We've always been close," Rachel added. "Other than the few years Jenn was gone, but now that she's back, our family is stronger than ever. And we've started a farm-to-table event business that has really taken off, so that's something we all work on together as well."

"Are you all always together?" he asked.

"Not all of the time. We definitely have our own interests and hobbies."

Jack glanced her way. "What are some of yours?"

"I love the farm and the livestock and—"

"Outside of farm life," he corrected.

Rachel pursed her lips as they headed toward one of the

ponds on the property. Outside of the farm…did she have hobbies?

"I like to eat. Does that count?" She laughed.

Jack's soft chuckle had her heart clenching once again. How did he make all these dormant feelings rise to the surface?

"We'll start there," he replied. "You have a favorite food?"

"Anything I don't have to make." Their horses came to a stop at the edge of the pond and Rachel shifted to face him. "I'm not a bad cook, but cooking for one is depressing. I guess that's why I love this new event business my family started. Cooking for a crowd is fun, and I love to see people come together and fellowship in whatever way brings them joy."

"You can cook for me anytime," he informed her. "I'm sick of eating grilled cheese sandwiches."

Rachel quirked a brow. "You're still coming to family dinner sometime, but I'll make you something. What's your favorite meal?"

He shook his head. "Let's not do the family dinner. Remember? I don't do those. But I wouldn't turn down a meal from your kitchen. Do you have a specialty?"

"I can make some pretty good chicken and dumplings." Rachel swung her leg over the saddle and hopped down. She led Sunshine to a small nearby tree and secured the reins. "Go ahead and have a seat with me. We'll take a rest from riding so maybe you won't be too sore tomorrow."

Without a word, Jack dismounted, led his horse near hers and tied his own knot. Certainly not like she had, but Champ and Sunshine wouldn't go anywhere regardless. Rachel always tied her horse to be safe.

When Jack eased down on the grass beside her, Rachel stretched her legs out and leaned back on her hands. She closed her eyes and pulled in a deep breath.

"Do you hear that?" she murmured.

"Hear what?"

"Exactly. Just the peaceful evening." She kept her eyes

closed, trying to lock this moment inside. "We aren't worried about the missing funds or how I'm going to get the Circle H. Sometimes I just need to ride out here to pray and clear my head."

"And do you do that often?"

Jack's question had her turning her attention back to him. His dark eyes held hers and she felt another jolt of attraction.

"Well, I pray all the time," she informed him. "Multiple times a day, but I don't get here as often as I'd like with all the work on the farm and schooling."

"And I've thrown the feed store into the mix," he added.

"I agreed to take that on," she said. "I wasn't forced. Besides, I'm hoping we can still work something out for the ranch. Maybe a lease or rent or anything until I can gain my footing and buy it outright."

Jack started to open his mouth, but she held up a hand to stop him.

"I know—you have some reason to get this sold soon and for a lot of money and I'm not in a position to help you right now." She weighed her next words carefully. "I'm also not helping with the feed store and renovation ideas because I want you to do me a favor. I'm doing all of this because I loved your grandfather. But I am confident we can come to some type of agreement that will benefit both of us regarding your inheritance. I just... I can't be this close to something I've always dreamed of and watch it slip through my hands."

Jack didn't say a word. He simply stared back at her with a look in his eyes she couldn't quite label. Maybe guilt with a little bit of worry. She wished he'd just tell her the bind he was in so she could see if there was any chance she could help.

But when he remained silent, Rachel directed her gaze back to the pond and the glistening sun on the water and started that praying she always came here for.

# CHAPTER SEVEN

"YOU DON'T THINK the entire wall should be one large open shower?"

Jack waited for Rachel's reply, but she leaned against the door frame with her arms crossed and her brows drawn as if trying to imagine the space.

"Sounds very modern," she finally stated. "I mean, I haven't seen anything like that, but maybe in the main bedroom it wouldn't be a terrible idea. But there has to be a big soaker tub. I mean, if you're going to go all out in here, you might as well. Farmers are worn out and sometimes just need a nice hot bath at the end of the day."

Jack already had that on his mind as well, but he welcomed all input that would be great selling points.

"What are your thoughts on a set of patio doors leading out back off this main suite?" he asked.

Rachel turned to look at the bedroom in question and he followed her back into the small space. Boxes sat atop the bed from things he'd been storing up to give away. Books and old collectibles that didn't have any sentimental value were ready to be donated.

"I think it would make this room look larger," she agreed,

then pointed toward a narrow window. "I assume you'd put it there?"

Jack nodded. "Between the doors letting more light in and a brighter paint color, it would help make the space look larger."

"A pale yellow or pale blue," she murmured. "We could paint this furniture to save money."

"Buying will be quicker and easier."

Rachel snorted as she turned back to face him. "What if I paint the furniture while you focus on other things?"

"I think you're busy enough, and I'm positive you didn't think that through before you offered." He chuckled.

Her little nose scrunched, and he decided it might be the most adorable gesture he'd ever seen.

"You already know me well," she stated. "I just hate buying something when I know I can do it myself. But you're right. Between the store and the farm, plus my schooling…"

"And you might want to have a social life."

She crossed her arms over her chest. "Do you have a social life?"

He spread his hands out wide. "This is it. You and me. That's all the social life I've had since coming to town."

"And what about back home?" she asked. "Do you get out and do something not work related?"

"I take potential clients to dinner."

Her arms dropped to her sides as she shook her head. "I rest my case. All work. My ex-fiancé never took time for anything he loved to do, either."

Her ex. She'd touched on him before, and Jack didn't care for the faceless man. How could anyone not adore Rachel and this daydream life she wanted? Granted, this wasn't a life for him, but for someone who lived here and knew the town and the people, he couldn't imagine letting Rachel slip from his life if he was engaged to her.

But he wasn't engaged and he wasn't getting tangled in a relationship or farming.

They needed to discuss the main bath, so Jack started toward the door to the hallway and Rachel followed.

"How recent was the engagement?" he asked casually as he crossed the landing to go downstairs to the first floor.

"A couple years ago. He hated farm life and always wanted me to move away. I kept hoping and praying he'd see the beauty here and want to be part of the world I envisioned."

The sad tone that slid through her words made Jack wonder if she missed the man or just the life she'd dreamed of. A short burst of jealousy hit him, and he had no idea why. Jack had no ties to Rachel and he certainly didn't know the man in her past. So why did he instantly have this need to compare himself to a stranger?

"You want to raise your family here and carry on traditions and grow your property." Jack stopped in the foyer before heading down the hall toward the main-floor bath. "You love livestock and being there for your family. I can't imagine you ever leaving, and anyone who tried to get you to is foolish."

Rachel stopped on the bottom step and rested her hand on the wooden banister. Those green eyes fixed right on him, and he couldn't move if he wanted to. How could someone be so down-to-earth, yet so amazing and brilliant and captivating at the same time? There were so many layers to her, yet he thought he had her figured out…and he was fascinated and attracted to everything he saw.

He was no different from her ex, though. He knew nothing of how to feed a relationship, and he certainly hadn't a clue about farming.

"You've only known me a short time and already know my heart," she murmured.

His chest tightened as he moved toward her, closing a bit of the gap between them. That one step beneath her put them at eye level…as if he needed another reason to find himself utterly entranced by her. Those emerald eyes had a darker ring around them that he shouldn't care about, but suddenly he cared about every single thing when it came to Rachel.

No, not suddenly. Since she'd ridden up on that horse and professed her childhood crush. There was no denying that pull, yet frustration gripped him because he couldn't explain it. He'd always had control over his emotions—over everything in his life, really.

Or so he'd thought. Then Rachel swept into his neat and tidy world and completely disassembled every thought he'd had.

"Why are you looking at me that way?"

Her whispered words snapped him back to the moment and the fact that he was standing extremely close to her now.

"I'm just amazed that anyone who professed to love you and spend his life with you could simply walk away."

Her gaze traveled over his face. "I'm not sure how simple it was, but the parting was definitely for the best. I guess I walked away, too. At least, mentally."

Jack found himself resting his hand on top of hers, giving a reassuring squeeze. "Loss is still difficult," he explained. His heart squeezed for the hurt she must've felt at her broken engagement.

"I have to look at that experience as a life lesson and learn from it." She offered another one of her signature sweet smiles. "That's the only way to overcome heartache of any kind."

"I'm figuring that out," he told her. "I didn't realize how much emotion I had after my grandfather's passing, but being in town and surrounded by his things has really made me think and reflect."

Rachel took that final step down and tipped her head to keep eye contact.

"George was an amazing man," she told him. "The town definitely misses his presence."

Jack eased his hand from hers, not wanting to make her uncomfortable. She dropped her hand to her side, and her warmth beneath his palm left a void. That simple, innocent touch had been a mistake, but he hadn't been able to stop himself. She hadn't jerked beneath his touch and she'd smiled, so apparently she hadn't been bothered.

And the way she stared right back at him, like she could see into his soul, seemed to pull that string binding them together even tighter. This couldn't happen, *shouldn't* happen. He'd be no different from the guy who walked away from her, and hadn't Jack just called him foolish? Keeping their relationship strictly working and friendly was the only way he could move on from his experiences in Rosewood Valley with a clear conscience.

"Speaking of my grandfather, anything else on the store?" Jack asked as he turned to head toward the main bath.

She paused a moment. "The manager is due back tomorrow, so I'm going to casually discuss how business is doing since George's passing, whether the numbers are up or down, and just see if I can get him talking."

Jack reached into the powder room and flicked on the switch. "That's great. I'll be interested in what he has to say."

He stepped aside so Rachel could look into the small space without being crowded.

"What are you thinking in here?" he asked.

"Don't touch these amazing floors," she commanded, pointing to the black-and-white hexagon tiles. "Not only are they classic and timeless, but anything will go with them."

"Buyers like that touch of nostalgia and original charm," he added.

"Buyers might, but I'm the only buyer you need to impress."

That guilt gripped at him once again. For the first time in his business career, he was letting his heart get involved in his decision. And doing that would only leave him at a standstill and unable to advance to the ultimate real estate mogul he'd always striven to be. He didn't know how to be anything else other than a businessman and he was good at his job. He had no shame in wanting more success or to make his father proud.

"What do you think about a walk-in shower and making a glass wall so it looks more open and the space doesn't feel so small?"

Jack nodded. "I'm impressed. I like that idea."

"I might be country, but I have good taste."

"You definitely do. What else?"

She moved in and stared at the wall with the vanity. Her braid fell over her shoulder and he found himself following the lighter strands weaving in and out all the way down to the tip.

"What about making this an accent wall with a bold paper?" she asked, glancing back at him.

"I think that would be a nice touch. Is that something you want to pick out?"

The brightest smile spread across her face as her brows shot up. "Oh, I definitely do. I might not have time for the furniture painting, but I can online shop like a champ."

Jack chuckled. He had no doubt she'd put her all into this project, and if they were using his dime, all the better for her.

"Get me a few suggestions in the next week or so. I've got a contractor coming in the morning, and I'd really like to push through and have this for sale in the next month."

Rachel turned to face him fully and crossed her arms over her chest. "I really want to discuss a lease with the option to buy. I know you are hard-pressed to sell, but I can't come up with a solution if I don't really know what's going on."

He didn't think she'd ever come up with a solution to appease both of them unless she had a good chunk of money, and from her own account, she did not.

"Are you strapped for cash?" she asked. "Because I'm sure we can figure something out. George would want someone to have this property who would take care of it and make it thrive."

Yes, he knew all of that but needed to address the most important thing.

"I'm not strapped for cash," he assured her. "I'm trying to

get a promotion with my firm. No, I'm not trying. I'm *going* to get that promotion."

"And how many people are vying for this position?" she asked.

"Just one other."

Rachel pursed her lips and ultimately nodded. "You'll get the job and I'll be able to get the house. We just have to put our heads together on this."

She didn't know his father very well. The man didn't bend or break for anyone...not even his own son. Jack wasn't about to get into the dealings with his dad right now. Rachel seemed too sweet a person to associate with Logan Hart.

"It's getting late," she stated with a sigh. "I should probably get going and work on that paper of mine. It's not going to write itself."

"When you're done, email it to me and I'll double-check everything to make sure you ace it."

Rachel jerked as her arms fell to her sides. "You don't have to do that. I mean, I would take your help, but you're just as busy as I am."

Jack shrugged. "I'm not working on anything tonight. I'll text you my email. You're doing the grunt work. I'm just going to make sure it's polished."

Rachel's gentle laugh echoed in the small bathroom. "You really are a great guy. I don't know anyone else who would offer to spend free time working on an econ assignment that wasn't even his. But I'm a little overwhelmed with the topic and afraid I'll sound like I don't know what I'm talking about."

"All the more reason to let a friend help."

She took a step forward and patted his cheek. "Perfect, friend. I'll send that over later and you can come to my place for dinner tomorrow. Deal?"

"I won't turn that down and I'm definitely getting the better end of the deal," he joked.

She eased by him and moved into the hallway. "You won't say that once you dig into the globalization on emerging economies."

He cringed. "Ouch."

"Exactly."

Jack followed her to the foyer and reached around to get the door for her. His arm briefly brushed against hers and she gave a slight jolt, then a soft smile.

"Good night, Jack. See you tomorrow about seven."

Jack watched as she went out and untied her horse from the post near the porch. His grandfather would never want that hitching post removed, and Jack had no intention of taking anything away from this farm that made it special and operational. Rachel would rather travel by horse than car anyway, and since she lived at the neighboring farm, her horse just made sense.

He couldn't wipe the smile off his face as he closed the door once she'd ridden away. He kept thinking he'd never met anyone quite like her, and the more he was around her, the more he figured he'd never meet anyone this extraordinary again.

So now where did that leave him other than torn between his family and his heart?

# CHAPTER EIGHT

RABBIT AND SWINE feed orders were placed, and Rachel felt quite accomplished with her first order. With Walt still out, she didn't want the shelves to start looking bare and she knew enough about feed to know what was sold here. Granted, she'd never placed an order before, but after a couple of hours spent searching through invoices and then getting on the phone to customer service of a supplier, the deed was done.

Rachel leaned back in the old creaky office chair and blew out a sigh. Her first real task down since starting her part-time employment here. She wasn't going to go overboard with re-stocking, but the feed in a feed store was a rather important part.

"Busy?"

Rachel glanced from the computer screen displaying her email confirmation to the open doorway where Jack stood with a smile.

Rachel returned his pleasant gesture with one of her own. "Just restocking a couple things. Did you come to check up on me?"

He shrugged as he stepped into the office. The dark jeans and long-sleeve black button-up shirt still seemed dressy and a little fancy, but she didn't mind. She was growing rather fond of his upper-class style.

"I thought I'd hang here today while I'm waiting to hear from a couple contractors," he explained. "Maybe you can show me a bit more about this place since I do own the store."

Interesting that he wanted to discover more. She wasn't sure of his intent on this part of his inheritance, but the fact that he wanted to soak up more information warmed her heart. This was definitely an area she could teach. She'd been coming to the feed store with her dad since she was a kid and knew the floor like the back of her hand.

"Maybe we can put our heads together and figure out these off-putting numbers as well," he added.

"That would be great," she agreed. "I'd hate to have Walt come back to terrible news and no answers."

Rachel pushed the rolling chair back and came to her feet. "Well, let's get you started on a grand tour and Feed Store 101 lesson."

Jack stepped forward and glanced around the somewhat messy desk. He grabbed a pen from the old mason jar and rifled around until he found a notebook. Rachel glanced at the items in his hand, then to him.

"I need to take notes," he explained.

Stunned, Rachel shook her head in amazement. "I've never met anyone like you," she murmured.

"Probably not," he agreed as he led her from the office.

Not only was he eager to learn more, but he wanted to absorb the information given. She truly hated when she compared Jack to Tyler. They were two completely different men with totally different roles in her life. But she was human and couldn't help herself. Lately, she couldn't help but wonder if they could be more if they weren't from completely different worlds and didn't have totally opposite goals.

Rachel stepped into the hallway behind Jack, but he stepped aside to let her through.

"Let's start with some basics that our customers come in for," she started as she headed toward the open sales area. "Feed is obviously the biggest seller. We supply farms from all over, not only this county, but surrounding counties as well. George really had a knack for customer loyalty, and he made solid relationships with the farmers. I'm sure he'd want generations to know they can rely on All Good Things."

"That's what I hope to accomplish," Jack replied. "I want my grandfather's legacy to live on whether I remain the owner or someone else takes over."

Yeah, Rachel really wanted to know this place was secure, too. And maybe selfishly she wanted him to keep this part of his inheritance for himself. She wasn't ready for him to leave town with no reason to return. Which only proved as a reminder that the last time she let her guard down, she'd got her heart broken. She was going into this with her eyes wide open and her heart behind a shield of protection.

"Let's start in the front and work our way to the back," she suggested.

Jack followed her down the aisle that led to the front display of seasonal items.

"This display right inside the door is always done with whatever is hot at the moment," she explained. "Obviously since summer is sadly coming to an end, mums and fodder are center stage."

"Summer is your favorite season?" he asked.

Rachel turned to focus on him and not the rust and yellow mums. "I love all the seasons, but I definitely love the warmth of summer. Too bad you won't be in town to see all the gorgeous foliage in about a month."

Why did she let that slip out? She didn't want to think about him leaving, let alone talk about it.

He opened his mouth to say something just as the chime on the front door echoed through the old two-story barn. Rachel turned to greet the customer. She assumed Myles was around here somewhere. She'd seen his car and heard someone puttering around in the back of the store.

But her mother breezed in with a smile and a plate of something from her kitchen. The woman never went anywhere without some gift or treat for whomever she was visiting.

"Mom. What are you doing here?"

Rachel crossed to her mom and gave her a hug.

"Well, you've been so busy lately, I feel like I never see you." She extended the covered plate. "I made some cranberry orange muffin tops. I know they're your favorite."

Rachel loved her mother's giving, thoughtful heart. Sarah Spencer never had a negative or unkind remark and was always finding ways to bring others joy. Rachel couldn't think of a better role model to look up to.

"I'm sorry I've been so swamped," Rachel told her mom. "I promise to come by the house this weekend. Dad and I have been a little busy on the farm and then with trying to help out here while Walt is gone, and I'm showing Jack a few things."

Not to mention her schooling, which she hoped to surprise her family with once she was all done and a success.

"Yes, that's another reason I stopped by." Her mother's bright gaze darted over Rachel's shoulder to Jack. "George's grandson. I remember you as a little guy."

Jack stepped forward and extended his hand. "I remember you as well. Nice to see you again."

Rachel stepped aside as her mom shook Jack's hand. "You're all grown up. I see why Rachel wants to spend so much time with you lately."

"Mom," Rachel murmured. "I'm just helping out."

Her mom had the audacity to wink at her before her focus went back to Jack. "Well, it's great to have you in town. I'm sure George would be so proud of the nice young man you've become."

The muscle in Jack's jaw ticked as he dropped his arm and nodded. Rachel wondered if emotions were getting to him. He couldn't escape the memory of his grandfather between the farm and the store. But she highly doubted Jack was one to discuss his feelings, especially with virtual strangers.

"How about the two of you come to dinner this weekend?"

Rachel stilled at her mother's proposal. Granted, Rachel had already told him about family dinner, but she didn't realize her mother would be so bold. Though Rachel wasn't surprised. Sarah Spencer was the quintessential hostess.

"I'm not sure—"

"We'll be there." Rachel cut off whatever excuse Jack was about to give. "And Jack has a potato salad request."

Her mother's eyes widened, as did her sweet smile. "Well, I can certainly make that happen."

The chime sounded again as another customer came through the old doors. Before Rachel could greet them, Myles came out from the back.

"Good morning," the teen stated. "Welcome to All Good Things. Is there anything I can help you with?"

Rachel noticed Jack turned to watch the interaction. The customer asked about cedar shavings for their landscaping to deter late-summer pests. Myles promptly motioned for the customer to follow as he led the way toward the appropriate aisle.

"He's a hard worker," her mother muttered.

"He is," Rachel agreed.

"Well, I'll let you two get back to work." Her mother smiled. "I just wanted to see my girl and bring her some goodies."

Rachel held up the plate. "I'll be sure to share."

Sarah moved forward and pulled Jack into a brief yet no doubt hearty embrace. "It's just so good to have you in town again. You definitely favor your grandfather."

She turned and walked out, leaving Rachel and Jack with the homemade treats.

"Let me put these in the office and then we'll continue the tour," she told him.

"Aren't you going to eat one?" he asked, following.

Rachel laughed. "Of course I am, and so are you. Nobody can turn down Sarah Spencer's kitchen creations. Trust me."

They each took a muffin top and left the rest in the office as Rachel continued the tour of the store. Jack took his notes and Rachel loved each time he asked a question because he wanted to learn more.

Rachel's cell vibrated in her pocket and she pulled it out and noticed not only the message, but also how late in the day it had got. Her father was asking if she'd be able to help him in the main barn for about an hour.

"I'm sorry." Rachel turned to Jack. "I'm going to need to head back to the farm."

"Don't be sorry," he told her. "This has been a huge help for me to understand this lifestyle better. I'll walk you out."

As they made their way into the hallway leading to the back door, Rachel's cell vibrated again, but this time it was a call from her mother. Rachel swiped the screen as she followed Jack toward the exit.

"Hey, Mom. What's up?"

"I didn't want to say too much in front of Jack, but I'm so excited for you to bring him to dinner," her mom all but squealed. "A new boyfriend is so exciting."

Rachel froze at the back door and clutched her cell as she met Jack's confused gaze. "First, Jack is not my boyfriend. He's a friend passing through town."

"Same thing, dear," her mother went on. "I saw how you two tried not to stare at each other. That speaks volumes, so we need to make this a special occasion."

Rachel pinched the bridge of her nose and prayed for patience.

"You haven't brought a boy to dinner since Tyler."

Rachel pushed the old wooden door open and stepped into the sunshine, still willing that patience from above. She never thought her family would think Jack was *that* important. Of course he was important, but they weren't dating or anything else. Just because she still had a flutter in her belly after his hand touched hers last night... Such a simple gesture, innocent and sweet, yet she'd felt the warmth all the way to her heart.

He'd made no promises and had been very clear he had no intentions of staying. She knew what was happening, yet she couldn't stop herself from being drawn to him.

"I haven't brought a boy since Tyler because I haven't dated anyone," she said in a low voice.

"Well, we'll see where things go. Let's do a meal tonight instead of this weekend," her mom stated. "I'll see you both at six."

When the call disconnected, Rachel laughed at the way her mom informed her instead of asking. And that was how Sarah Spencer earned respect and got things done.

Rachel headed toward her truck parked in the alleyway, but Jack had walked on ahead. She stopped short when she spotted a cat curled up next to her wheel. Jack bent down and was trying to coax it away from the vehicle.

Stray cats weren't uncommon around town, but she'd never had one cozy up next to her tire before. The dark gray animal seemed to be more kitten than full-grown cat. He had a paw curled in and was licking it over and over.

"He seems pretty comfortable here," Jack told her as she came to stand beside him.

When she unlocked her truck and opened the door, she assumed the cat would get scared and dart away, but it just kept licking its paw.

"Go on," she shooed. "I need to leave."

Jack chuckled and reached for the cat. He cradled it in the most adorable way against his dark shirt. He was going to be covered in hair, and she wondered if she should offer the lint roller she kept in her console.

"I think he's hurt."

Jack's concerned tone pulled her closer to the animal and Rachel noted the way the little paw curled in as the cat continued to lick. Rachel reached forward, still amazed at how gentle Jack was with this adorable cat.

"Oh, no. He does look hurt," Rachel agreed. "Let me wrap him up and I'll take him to my sister."

The amber cat eyes came up to hers and she saw the pain. She loved animals of all types and couldn't stand to see any hurt. Thankfully she knew the right person to help.

Rachel went to the cab of her truck and grabbed a hoodie from the passenger seat. She came back and wrapped the cat, careful of the injury. Jack handed the animal over with such a delicate manner that Rachel's heart melted a bit more. As if she needed another reason to fall for this man who wasn't staying.

"I'll take him straight to Violet," she repeated. "Do you want to stay and watch over Myles?"

"I can do that."

"And my mom changed dinner to six tonight," she remembered as she laid the cat on the passenger seat. "See you then."

"I'll be there," he assured her with an affirmative nod.

Rachel started up her truck as Jack closed her door. She didn't even bother texting her sister. She would be at the clinic in less than two minutes. Rosewood Valley wasn't large by any means, and the actual "town" part only had one main road that ran parallel to the park. Directions were easy, and even newcomers couldn't get lost here.

Thankfully the parking lot wasn't packed, but Rachel still pulled to the side door where the employees went in. She gathered the kitten back up and used the passcode to let herself inside. Barking and phones ringing immediately hit her. The place always seemed to be bustling with patients, and Violet wouldn't have it any other way.

Her younger sister had a knack for treating both animals and people with tender care.

"Oh, hey, Rachel."

She turned to find a familiar face heading down the hallway. "Callie, I'm so glad you're working today. I found this hurt cat behind the feed store."

Callie took the animal and nodded. "Follow me. I'll put you guys in this back room and go see if Vi is done with her current patient."

"I don't want to cut in line if others are waiting," Rachel stated.

Callie shook her head, sending her fiery red ponytail swaying. "No worries. We're slow at the moment."

She laid the cat on a metal exam table and turned around. "Wait here. Let me go get Vi."

Rachel took her place by the cat and waited on her sister to come in, which only took a few minutes. Vi swept in the door with her hair piled in a knot on top of her head and wearing a pair of red scrubs.

"Find a stray?" her sister asked.

Rachel nodded, but remained next to the table as Violet went to the other side.

"Behind the feed store. He's hurt his paw, but I didn't look for any other injuries."

Violet eased the hoodie away to examine the kitten. With her delicate hands, she felt around while the animal's eyes stared up.

"I hear we're having a guest for dinner tonight," Violet murmured as she lifted the injured paw. "Jack, who I am not allowed to call a boyfriend, according to Mom."

Rachel groaned. "Mom called you?"

"Texted," Violet corrected, then met Rachel's gaze. "Jenn, Luke, Paisley and Erin, too."

Rachel didn't know if she should cancel or tell Jack to run fast and far. But she'd never disrespect her parents that way. Still, it felt like she was throwing Jack to the wolves. Although she was rather impressed at the hotline her mother seemed to have with the rest of the family, considering she'd told them the plans and they'd only been changed about twenty minutes ago.

"I should've told her to keep it just Jack, Mom, Dad and me."

Violet laughed. "We'll be on our best behavior with your not-boyfriend."

Rachel started to respond, but Violet shifted back to work mode.

"There's a small laceration, but I don't think anything is broken."

"That's good," Rachel replied. "Do you have a place you can keep this kitty until we find him a home?"

Vi quirked a brow. "Oh, you're the home now. Don't you know that's how it works?"

Rachel shook her head. "Very funny. I don't have the time to care for a pet. You know my schedule on the farm and now with helping Jack. Surely you know someone who has a kid who would love a cuddly pet."

"Your lack of time is no excuse," Vi retorted with a grin. "Cats are easy. Leave them some empty boxes to sleep in and play with, keep their litter fresh, and have food and water. Pretty simple."

It wasn't that Rachel didn't want an animal. She lived on a farm. Animals were her life. She just didn't have the mental capability to care for anything else right now. She'd tapped out for the time being. She needed to live by her mother's motto of pouring into yourself before you could pour into others. Sarah Spencer had even bought each of her girls a gold chain with a white pitcher charm to remind them of this. If they didn't take care of themselves, how could they be the hands and feet of God?

"You can keep him for now," Violet stated, clearly not taking no for an answer.

Rachel sighed. "I don't know why I bothered arguing."

"Me, either. Now, I'm going to give you some ointment to put on his paw twice a day for a week. Let me go get that, and when I come back, I want to know about Jack."

Left alone with the kitten, Rachel had no idea how her day

had gone from making a simple thank-you dinner for Jack after he'd read her paper, to having him meet the entire family and gaining a new pet.

# CHAPTER NINE

JACK BROUGHT HIS car to a stop at the Spencer home and glanced at the other vehicles. He'd been a little surprised that the dinner had been moved to tonight, but it wasn't like he had plans, so this was fine. Besides, when she'd dropped that bomb on him, she'd been so worried about the cat, he wasn't about to question anything. The animal's care had to come first.

All the other guests who seemed to be here did give him pause, though. He hadn't expected such an ordeal, but he wasn't going to be rude or disrespectful and cancel last minute.

He wasn't sure if he was about to come for an interrogation or what was going on. The only thing he knew was he'd had that delicious muffin top Sarah had made, and once Rachel left with the cat, he'd stuck around the feed store a bit longer before he'd had to meet with his contractor. He wished she'd given him a heads-up if the whole family was here, but there was no fixing that now.

It was time to really get this renovation ball in motion. After much consideration, he'd decided to leave a good bit of the home's charm like Rachel had suggested. He'd update the bathrooms and make the kitchen more efficient, but overall, there would be more cosmetic fixes than anything else.

Now that he had a clear picture of what was to be done and

a proposed end date, he'd called a local homeless shelter to donate old clothing and some of the furniture that didn't have sentimental value. Now he just had to figure out what to do with those sentimental items. His father hadn't shown any interest in claiming them, so Jack assumed if anything was kept, it would be going home with him.

As he stepped from the car, Rachel came walking from the direction of her loft apartment. She had that signature side braid falling over one shoulder, a pair of worn jeans, cowgirl boots and a fitted cream-colored sweater to ward off the chill from the late-summer evening. The wholesome yet adorable style she had made him smile.

"So I need to confess something," she stated as she closed that distance between them. "My whole family is inside."

He offered a smile because she looked like she was ready to turn and bolt in the direction she'd just come from. "I can't wait to meet them," he assured her.

"No." Rachel shook her head and blew out a sigh. "I mean, like, the whole family. My three sisters, my soon-to-be brother-in-law and his niece, plus my parents."

He'd assumed as much from the whole drive full of cars, but knowing so many people waited just on the other side of the door did have a little bit of panic racing through him. The dinners he usually attended were with associates or potential clients. He had no clue how to handle a large, loving family and never really thought he'd find himself in this position.

"Your silence is concerning."

Jack reached out and laid his hand on her shoulder. "I'm just processing. The largest dinners I've been to have been business meetings."

She scrunched her little nose. "I should've warned you when I found out earlier, but I was afraid you wouldn't come."

"To a homemade meal?" he scoffed. "I wouldn't miss it."

"You sure?"

After a reassuring squeeze, Jack dropped his hand and gestured toward the house. "Let's go. I can't wait to meet the crew. I barely remember your dad and sisters."

"You're a good sport," she commented. "My mom's rhubarb pie will be worth all of the chaos you're about to endure."

"You're not selling this evening well at all," he joked as they made their way up the wide gravel drive and around toward the back door. "It's like you want me to run in the other direction."

"Just warning you. This is your last chance."

He took her hand and gave a gentle squeeze before letting her go. "I'll be fine and so will you. Just relax."

Rachel stopped at the top of the steps and reached for the door handle before throwing a glance over her shoulder.

"It's hard to relax when my mother thinks you're my boyfriend."

Before he could reply, Rachel opened the door and stepped inside. He couldn't leave now, but why on earth would her mother think they were in a relationship? Jack had heard Rachel address that earlier on the phone, but then he'd got sidetracked by the injured cat and forgotten about it.

The moment Jack stepped into the screened-in back porch, the delicious mixture of scents hit him and he almost forgot Rachel's words, too. The chatter from apparently the entire family, the laughter echoing from the kitchen, was all so new to him, he wondered if he shouldn't go ahead and turn around.

But he'd never disrespect the Spencer family. They'd extended the invite, and surely he could endure one evening with a loving, close-knit family. Just because he didn't have experience with such things didn't mean he wouldn't enjoy himself...he hoped.

"Oh, you're here."

Sarah Spencer, donned in a yellow apron, rushed over to him with arms wide open. He found himself in a tight hug before she eased back with her hands on his shoulders. This was the second hug by this woman today, and he had to admit, the simple gesture left him feeling warm and welcome... like family.

"I'm so happy you came!" she exclaimed. "Rachel hasn't had anyone here since Tyler."

"Mom." Rachel's groan only caused laughter from her mother.

"I know. I'm just happy to have you guys here," Sarah went on. "George was such a special neighbor and we can't wait to catch up with his grandson."

The love his grandfather had for him had always been evident to him. But the more he hung around this town and the people, the more he realized just how special a man George truly was.

"Honey, let the man breathe. He just got here."

Will Spencer stepped into the kitchen and crossed the space to his wife. George always spoke so highly of Will, and Jack knew the two had been friends for years. He imagined them sharing a great many stories about farm life and family.

"Glad you could join us," Will greeted him. "Nothing more my wife loves than a reason to have all her girls and our growing family under one roof."

"I'm Paisley." A little girl with purple glasses and a matching bow around her ponytail came bouncing up. "You're really tall," she added.

Jack laughed and squatted down. "It's nice to meet you. I hear you're going to be in a wedding soon."

She bobbed her head and smiled, revealing a few missing teeth. "Toot and Jenn are getting married and I get to wear a purple dress."

"I have a feeling that might be your favorite color," he replied, then stood back up. "So, who is Toot?"

The only man other than Will and Jack waved a hand. "You can call me Luke. P always calls me Toot because when she was younger she couldn't say 'Luke.' It's stuck and does seem confusing at times."

"Nice to meet you," Jack told him. "You're marrying Jenn? Right?"

Luke nodded and wrapped an arm around Jenn's waist. She leaned into him with a smile that so resembled Rachel's. But it didn't incite the same spark in him that Rachel's did. He shook Jenn's hand and glanced at the other sisters, who also shared that smile and those green eyes. They were clearly related, but there was something different about each one that made them unique.

"I'm Erin." The shortest sister, with her hair down in curls, stepped forward and extended her hand. "I hope you like chaos."

He chuckled and shook her hand. "Funny, that's how Rachel described this, too."

Jack turned his attention to the sister over by the oven taking out a casserole dish. She had her hair piled on top of her head, and once she set the dish on top of the stove, she turned to meet his gaze.

"You must be Violet," he greeted her.

She nodded. "That's me. I know you're not a boyfriend, but we're really glad you weren't scared off from a big family dinner."

Oh, he was scared all right, but he wasn't a coward and didn't run from a challenge. Besides, being in this room with everyone didn't make him want to turn and run. Surprisingly he felt as if he was in the midst of one gigantic hug. And he couldn't recall when he'd felt that way before.

"Can I do anything to help?" he offered, not really knowing what else to say or do with so many sets of eyes on him.

"You and Rachel can go have a seat in the dining room," Sarah told him. "We can bring everything in."

He might not know how family dinners worked, but he

knew manners and he wasn't one to sit and watch while everyone else handled things.

Jack shook his head and moved around the island toward the empty glasses on the counter. "How about I fill these?" he offered.

Will whistled beneath his breath. "You're a brave man for not taking orders from my wife."

Jack glanced around the room and it seemed everyone was shocked. When his attention turned to Sarah, he found her smiling.

"I like him. Helpful and a gentleman." She winked at Rachel. "Maybe you can slide him into that boyfriend slot after all."

Jack couldn't help but laugh at her tenacity. He saw where Rachel got her bold and determined personality.

"I'm just doing the tea," he replied, reaching for one of the pitchers. "I'll be heading back to San Francisco in just over a month."

"Then you have to come to the wedding."

Jenn's statement had him pausing. A family wedding was much more personal than a family dinner. He couldn't flat-out refuse, though he didn't feel comfortable crashing such an intimate family moment, so he did the only thing he could think of. He looked to Rachel for help.

JACK LOOKED LIKE he wanted to flee, so Rachel took pity on the poor guy and offered up a reply.

"I thought you wanted to keep the guest list small," she stated, giving her sister *the look* to stop pushing.

Jenn lifted a shoulder. "I do, but what's one more? We'd love to have you, Jack."

"I'll see what I can do," he told her.

Rachel needed to change the subject to not only get the heat off Jack, but also remove any question that they were anything more than friends or business associates at this point.

Regardless of how she felt in her heart, regardless of the fact she wished she could explore more with him, she had to face the harsh reality that he wasn't staying and his lifestyle was no different from her ex's. Why did she have to keep falling for men who didn't have that sticking factor?

Jack was so different from Tyler, though. Yes, he was a workaholic and worried about making money. But he had a heart for this place and the animals. He seemed genuinely interested, and there were times she was convinced he might talk himself into staying. She knew he'd enjoyed their ride and the peaceful moment they'd had at the pond.

But the fact remained that Rachel would want a partner in her farm life. While Jack seemed interested, this certainly wasn't the lifestyle he was used to.

"So I'm the proud new owner of a cat."

She really didn't know what to say, but she needed to change the subject and that was the most exciting thing in her life at the moment. Her family still didn't know about her online degree and they didn't know about the feed store issues she was helping Jack figure out.

So that left the stray cat.

"Did you remember the ointment before you came over?" Vi asked.

Rachel reached for a couple of the glasses Jack had filled and started toward the dining room. "I did," she confirmed. "And left the box and food and water just like you told me."

Violet grabbed glasses as well and followed. "And did you name him yet?"

"No. We're not getting that attached," Rachel said.

Jenn laughed from the dining room and called in, "That's what I thought and now I'm the proud owner of Cookie."

Jenn had come back to town and found a dog, a fiancé, and became a mother figure in record time. Rachel wasn't quite that far along in her life, but there wasn't a reason to name the cat. She'd find the animal a proper owner as soon as she had time. But for now, she'd care for him as best she could.

At Vi's gesturing, she and her sister grabbed more glasses and placed them on the dining table, passing Jenn as she crossed back to the kitchen. "So how serious are you and Jack?" Vi whispered once they were alone.

The bustle and chatter from the kitchen covered anything Rachel would want to reply, but she had to go with the truth and not her daydreams.

"We're just friends," Rachel assured her sister. "He's only here to sell the farm and possibly the feed store."

Violet's brows shot up. "And you're trying to get the house, right?"

"Trying, but I don't know if anything will work." More truth she couldn't deny. "He has reasons he needs to flip and sell quickly, and you know my financial situation."

"Well, he wouldn't have come to family dinner if he didn't like you, so I'm sure there's something stronger than a friendship there."

Rachel set the glasses down and shook her head. "Don't read anything into this. I thought Mom and Dad were going to be the only ones here until you told me otherwise. I'm sure Jack would've politely declined had I given him a proper heads-up."

"From the way that man was looking at you, don't bank on it." Violet's smile widened as she winked. "I'd say you have a little more control than you think."

The way he was looking at her? What did that mean? Did Violet see something that Rachel hadn't noticed? Her mother had hinted at something as well, so what was her family seeing?

"I wouldn't use an attraction to get favors," Rachel whispered since family started to filter in. "I need to do something to make everything fair for both of us. I'm just not sure what that is yet."

The moment Jack stepped through the arched doorway, his

dark gaze met hers. That familiar flutter in her belly seemed to be a default feeling that accompanied his stare. The longer he remained in town, the deeper he got into her soul… into her heart.

"Go ahead and have a seat."

Sarah Spencer came in carrying one dish while Will carried another. Luke brought a casserole and Paisley held a basket of rolls. Once the meal was presented on the table, Rachel took a seat and Jack came to sit next to her. Her parents took their spots at each end of the long farm table, which her mother had had made specifically in the hopes that her girls would marry and their crew would expand.

"This is just so perfect," her mother stated, clasping her hands. "I hope I made enough of everything."

"This is more food than I've seen on a table since my grandmother made Thanksgiving." Jack chuckled. "I appreciate you having me, but I hope this wasn't too much trouble."

"Trouble?" Rachel's mother waved her hand. "I love to cook and I love my family under one roof. You were a great excuse, and we're happy you're in town. I hear Rachel is helping you with the renovations and working a bit at the feed store."

"I wouldn't be able to do either without her," Jack assured them.

Her heart warmed once again. "I'm sure you'd be fine, but I'm glad I could be here for you."

Rachel's father reached for her hand. "Let's pray for our meal and then we can discuss the Circle H."

Everyone around the table joined hands, and the moment she reached for Jack's, her heart kicked up another notch. She'd been so used to this common family tradition, but from the look on Jack's face, he had no clue what was going on.

As her father said the prayer, Rachel gave Jack's hand a gentle squeeze. When he returned the gesture, she had a difficult time focusing on her father thanking God for all their blessings. She wanted to be that supportive friend for Jack and knew she was his main anchor in town. There was a line she simply couldn't cross no matter how much her heart was telling her to do just that.

Her father ended with an "Amen," and she released Jack's hand. Immediately the dishes were passed around and the family chatter commenced once again. She stole a glance toward Jack and noted for the first time since she'd known him that he looked absolutely terrified. She took the bowl of potato salad and lifted a spoonful.

"Here," she leaned in and whispered. "Start eating and you won't feel obligated to join in."

He blinked and shifted his eyes her way. "Thanks."

Once their plates were full, Rachel wanted to keep the mood off interviewing Jack.

"Other than shopping for our dresses this weekend, what else is left for the wedding?" she asked, meeting Jenn's gaze across the table.

"Honestly, nothing. That's why we wanted something small and just here on the farm." Jenn slathered a pat of butter on her homemade roll. "The ladies from the Women's Missions at church are doing the food in lieu of a gift, which is perfect. I don't need anything for my house anyway."

"Are the contractors still on time?" Rachel asked.

"Surprisingly they're ahead of schedule," Luke replied. "With the dry weather we've had, they were able to get everything under the roof sooner than expected, so the interior is nearly finished."

The low hum of a vibrating phone caught Rachel's attention, and Jack slid his hand into his pocket and pulled out his phone. Rachel didn't miss the name on the screen, even though Jack tried to hold his device beneath the table so as not to be rude.

"I'm sorry," he stated as he eased his chair back. "Excuse me while I take this. It's my father."

"Of course," Rachel's mom said.

Rachel didn't miss the worry in Jack's eyes as he stepped

from the room. She heard him answer, but nothing after the
back door opened and closed. Rachel didn't know the dynamics of that father-son relationship, but she knew enough to
know there wasn't anything warm and cozy.

While wedding and house discussions went on around her,
Rachel tried to concentrate on the delicious meal and not what
Jack was dealing with regarding his father.

Moments later he stepped back in, his face impassive. Whatever had taken place with that phone call had put a look on his
face she'd never seen before.

He took his seat next to her once again and she leaned over.
"You okay?"

He paused a minute before quietly saying, "Not really."

Rachel knew that admission cost him. He had his pride and
he was a strong man. Whatever his father had said had knocked
the wind from Jack's sails. Not only that, but this was also a
much-needed dose of reality to remind her that Jack was only
here for one purpose…and it wasn't to fall in love and live happily ever after as a farmer.

# CHAPTER TEN

HE'D STAYED LONG enough to not be disrespectful or rude. Dinner tasted amazing, as did the homemade pie, and the potato salad was exactly how he remembered. Jack probably would've enjoyed the whole evening even more if only he'd ignored that call from his father. He should've let it go to voicemail and then he could've been in the moment with the Spencer clan instead of smiling and trying to fit in with the small talk after the news from his father.

He let himself in the back door of the Hart farmhouse and flicked on the light to the kitchen. He set his keys on the island and maneuvered his way around a stack of boxes he'd brought down from the upstairs bedrooms.

The emotions whirling around inside him couldn't be described, not when they were all over the place. Hurt, confusion, anger…betrayal.

The tap on his back door had Jack turning around and suppressing a sigh. He should've known she'd follow him back home. Rachel wasn't dumb, and she worried about those she cared for. And as much as he just wanted to be alone in his misery, he wouldn't turn her away or be impolite to the one true friend he had at the moment.

Jack maneuvered around the boxes once again and slid the

lock open. The moment he stepped aside, Rachel let herself in and closed the door behind her. She tipped her head and those worry lines deepened between her brows.

"You don't have to tell me what happened at dinner if you don't want," she started. "But I'm a pretty good listener and I feel I owe you for all the whining I've done to you."

"You haven't whined one bit," he corrected. "And I'm happy to listen to you anytime."

She reached out and placed a hand on his arm. That tender touch calmed him and he found himself taking a deep breath. There was nothing he could do right now or even tomorrow. He had to move ahead with his plans just like he'd been doing. He still had a goal within his reach and every intention of obtaining it.

Jack blew out a sigh and turned to get out of the congested area by the back door.

"What are all the boxes?" she asked, following him into the den.

He pointed toward the now bare built-in shelves. "Nearly all the books from in here and several things from the guest rooms upstairs. Artwork and knickknacks. I haven't found too much that I'd want to keep, and anything I do keep, I have no clue where it will go."

He moved over to the desk and tapped his fingertips on the scarred top.

"I can still see him sitting in here," Jack murmured, staring at the old leather chair. "He'd go over his livestock and the trading he'd do with other farmers. He'd study rain patterns and droughts and read all the history to figure out the future of farming. I never understood half the stuff he talked about, but he'd tell me like I was going to be the one to take the reins one day."

Rachel's boots clicked on the hardwoods behind him, then muffled as she stepped onto the area rug. He didn't turn around, didn't want to remove himself from the memories.

"I remember him sitting behind this desk when Grandma passed away," Jack went on. "The only time I saw him cry. He wondered how he'd go on living here without her. I never really understood the love between a man and a woman until that moment. My mother passed away when I was little. I don't even remember her. My dad doesn't date, or if he does, he keeps it quiet. He's all in with his work, so that's all I know."

Jack turned to face her, finding her closer than he'd thought. She had that concerned look once again...or somewhere between pity and concern. He didn't want pity, but he knew that was just Rachel's giving heart.

"I see how your family all just meshes together and that's so odd to me," he went on, then shook his head. "That didn't come out right and I didn't mean to sound ungrateful or insulting."

"I didn't take it that way," she assured him. "My family is loud at times and we love hard. If that's not something you're used to, I can see how it would be overwhelming. I promise I only found out a little before dinner about the whole crew."

"Don't apologize for having an amazing family." He didn't want her to be sorry for anything when clearly he had some things to work through. "You were fortunate and I didn't realize what I was missing until I got that call and my world came crashing into yours."

"Was the call from your father?" she asked.

Jack nodded. As much as he didn't want to get into this, he owed Rachel an explanation for not staying longer and for mentally checking out of the dinner with her family. They had all tried to include him in the conversation and made him feel so welcome. Maybe that was what had him so cranky now. His father had interrupted one of the purest, most enjoyable moments Jack could remember. Rachel's family didn't expect anything from him. They had all seemed genuinely interested in what he was doing to the house and his plans for the feed store. Not once was money mentioned or who would be his top-dollar buyer.

"I'm sorry he upset you." Rachel's soft tone pulled him from his thoughts.

"I don't even know if I'm upset," he stated honestly. "Angry, frustrated, maybe annoyed. I guess *upset* is a good blanket term for all the emotions my father evokes."

"Why do you let him do that to you?" she asked, her brows drawn in as she took another step closer.

Confused, Jack asked, "Excuse me?"

"If you get so angry, why don't you remove yourself from a situation that will cause so many negative emotions?"

Remove himself? How on earth could he just remove himself from his father's life? They worked together—they were really all the family either of them had left.

"I don't mean ignore him," she corrected. "I'm saying put some distance between you, and try to focus on what makes you happy. When was the last time you did something for yourself that had nothing to do with work or your father?"

Jack took a moment and tried to think of his life lately. He'd been so focused on getting those few house renovations set, and now trying to figure out the missing money from the store, he hadn't done much for himself.

Except that ride.

"I went out with you on the horses around the farm and the pond," he finally told her. "That was fun and had nothing to do with work."

Her face relaxed as her lips lifted into a soft smile. "We did have fun and I think you even let your mind take a rest for a bit."

"I did. Must be the company I've been keeping."

He sat on the edge of the desk and laced his fingers together as he continued to stare back at her. Rachel was the type of person who could make a man want to open his heart fully. The type who wouldn't judge but would listen and try to put your needs ahead of her own.

No, she wouldn't try—she *would* put others' needs ahead

of her own. She'd already proved that by helping at the store. Granted, he was paying her and she wanted to get this property, but she didn't have ulterior motives. Rachel Spencer was one of the most honest and trustworthy people he knew.

"My father called to inform me that Brian has been working out of the new office," Jack explained. "The office that wasn't supposed to be open to the public until after the promotion decision was made." His stomach clenched as he recalled the phone call earlier.

"Brian is the other guy up for this position?" she asked.

Jack nodded. "Dad has always considered him another son. He applied to the firm straight out of college, so we started about the same time. Dad tried to mold both of us, but Brian has my father's work ethic and mindset. Their lives are all about money. Maybe he would've been a better son for my father. They are similar in the way they think and will do anything to make a sale. Sometimes I wonder why I'm trying so hard."

"Because you want your only family member to be proud of you," she explained. "And there's nothing wrong with that. But when you're not appreciated for the work you're doing or constantly trying to prove yourself, then maybe you need to reevaluate why you started this work in the first place."

Jack glanced down at his hands, not quite sure what to say at this point. Rachel seemed to have the right words and the perfect understanding tone for Jack to wonder if he should be doing something different. But what? He'd never known anything else in his life, and he'd been climbing that invisible ladder for years.

"If you love real estate, that's great. But make sure you're doing it for you and not because it's expected." She reached for his joined hands and covered them with hers. "Does that make sense?"

Jack turned his hands over in hers, wanting to feel that connection and draw from her amazing strength.

"I've never thought of my career as doing something I love," he replied. "I'm good at it, so that's all I know. But I do enjoy what I'm doing. I meet all sorts of people and help them find the perfect home or business."

"You're making dreams come true. That has to feel good."

He couldn't help but smile at her outlook. "You think of things in ways I never would have."

She lifted a slender shoulder. "Because I'm on the outside with fresh eyes looking in. You're submerged in this life."

"Have you ever thought of becoming a therapist?" He chuckled. "If the farm life doesn't work for you."

"There's nothing else I'd rather do with my life."

She eased her hands from his and slid them into the back of her jean pockets, but she didn't step away and her eyes never wavered from his.

"So, what can we do to make this better?" she asked. "We can come up with a way for you to tell your dad how he's making you feel or we can put that topic to rest for the night. Whatever you need, I'm here."

Why did he have a feeling she'd always be there for him? Even when his time in Rosewood Valley came to an end and he went back home, he knew without a doubt that he could always call on her.

"Let's table this discussion," he told her. "Dad has sucked enough of my mental energy out for one day."

With a curt nod, Rachel glanced around the room. "I hope there's no change planned in here."

"None," he said, pushing off the desk. "Well, the built-ins could use a sand job and fresh stain. I decluttered but the rest of the furniture and rug will stay for staging. I definitely want the desk, though. Not sure where I'll put it, but that piece is important to me."

Rachel turned back to him. "Does your father want anything from the house?"

"He's never shown interest or asked what I was doing with the contents, so I have to assume he doesn't."

"When are the contractors starting?" she asked.

"Monday, and they claim they'll be done in three weeks."

"That's good." She moved toward the built-ins on either side of the fireplace. "I'm not giving up on getting this place, just so you know. I can't be this close to my goal and watch it all slip away."

The ball of guilt tightened in his gut. He had the exact same thoughts on his end. He had his own goals, and this house would be the final step to reach everything he'd been working for. At least, he had to hold on to that promise. Just because Brian was working from the new office didn't mean anything. He hadn't been given the title or the lead.

Selling this farm would prove so much. Not only would this be his biggest sale of the year, but knowing he could market and successfully find a buyer in an area outside of his wheelhouse would prove to his father that he could do more than sell just inside the city.

"I get where you're coming from," he offered.

After trailing her fingers over the spine of his grandfather's Bible, she shifted back around. "There has to be another way to get your promotion where I can get this land."

Jack said nothing; she'd already figured out his predicament and he honestly couldn't see a way for them both to have what they wanted.

"Okay, then." Rachel blew out a sigh of frustration that matched his current mood. "That's quite a stumbling block, but I have faith. God didn't lead me through all of this with my family for me to end up with nothing."

Her faith astounded him. She didn't get flustered; she just kept moving forward. While his mindset told him to keep moving toward his own goal, his heart had started pulling him in the opposite direction.

"It's getting late. I should go. I just wanted to check on you and make sure you were okay."

Rachel started toward the door and he wanted her to stay, but for what? He could invite her to watch a movie or sit on the patio and enjoy the starry late-summer evening. But his emotions were all over the place where she was concerned, and he wasn't sure how to get them back under control...or if that was even possible at this point.

Jack crossed the room and replied, "You could've just texted me."

She stopped in the doorway and turned. "When someone I care about is hurting, I won't text."

He stopped directly in front of her and he couldn't ignore his attraction. Far beyond her physical attributes, she had an inner beauty that he'd never quite seen before. Each time they were together, he wanted to find more and more reasons to cling to the way she made him feel. A light inside him had been flipped on in the most unexpected way, but he had no idea what to do with his newfound emotions or if he should do anything at all.

"You're remarkable," he murmured.

Her smile had his heart doing another flip. "You've said that before, but thank you. I like to think you would've come to check on me if you knew I was sad."

She came up on her tiptoes and placed a soft kiss on his cheek.

"Good night, Jack."

For reasons he couldn't explain, he remained in the doorway while she let herself out. Her delicate touch warmed him, and he put his hand on his cheek like that moment shifted something inside him. How silly could he be? He and Rachel couldn't be more opposite, and they had entirely different goals...with this house being right between them.

Jack snapped out of his trance. He had a sinking feeling one or both of them would get hurt when he had to leave, because this property couldn't go in two different directions. He could either work a deal with Rachel and lose his promotion or he could stick with his plan and sell, leaving Rachel's dreams crushed.

Either way, someone was going to lose.

# CHAPTER ELEVEN

"THE OFF-THE-SHOULDER DRESS is stunning."

Rachel turned from side to side in the three-way mirror as she stood on the platform at the dress shop. She liked the strapless one she'd had on earlier, but Jenn loved this one, and since the wedding was for Jenn, Rachel didn't mind one bit.

She met Jenn's reflection in the mirror. "It's the perfect color," she told her. "I think it will match the flowers beautifully."

Sarah clasped her hands on the edge of the pale pink velvet sofa. "My girls are going to be stunning."

Rachel lifted the flowy skirt of her plum-colored dress and turned to her mother. "What about you? I saw your dress on and you are going to be the most breathtaking mother of the bride ever."

Her mother waved her hand and scoffed. "Oh, please."

"You think we'll get Dad out of those red suspenders?" Jenn asked, wrinkling her nose.

Their mother chuckled. "I had to make him a compromise. He could wear them beneath his suit jacket."

"He wouldn't be the same man without them," Rachel agreed.

Violet stepped out wearing the same dress as Rachel, and

Rach had to admit the design did look romantic and elegant. The deep color would be perfect for the season and in the gardens on the farm.

"I love it," Vi stated. "And I don't need any alterations."

"I think I just need a hem," Rachel replied, fluffing out her skirt.

Erin slipped from behind a curtain and had on her own dress as well. They were doing the same color, but their own choice of style. She'd been the first one to dress before helping Paisley.

"Who's ready for the most beautiful flower girl to ever exist?" Erin asked, holding the curtain shut. "There are no alterations needed for this one, either. Just accessories and a great hairstyle."

"Let's see our girl!" Sarah exclaimed.

As they each turned to face the closed drape, Erin did a little drumroll with her lips as she slowly pulled the thick material aside to reveal Paisley. She came out of the dressing room in her own purple dress with her arms spread wide and did a spin, earning a clap and a few whistles.

"I love it," Paisley declared as she went toward the mirror. "I feel like a princess."

Rachel stepped off the platform to give Princess Paisley her shining moment. Violet and Erin came to stand behind the girl, and Jenn came up beside them.

"I will have the best wedding party in the world," Jenn exclaimed. "What kind of shoes do you want, Paisley?"

"Am I too young for a heel?"

"Not at all," Jenn replied. "I'm sure we can find something the perfect size for your age."

One of the young workers who had been helping them popped back in and the shoe hunt was on. Violet went to change from her dress and Erin went to help Jenn get some jewelry for Paisley.

Sarah Spencer patted the seat beside her as she looked up at Rachel. "Sit down for a minute."

Her mother wasn't asking, and Rachel knew when her mom had something on her mind. She gathered the material of her skirt and sank down onto the plush sofa.

"How's Jack?"

As always, her mother wasted no time getting to the point.

"He called the following day to thank me for dinner, but he seemed almost sad when he left that night," her mother went on.

Of course he'd called. Jack might be a business mogul from a big city, but he didn't lack manners and morals. They'd had dinner three days ago and she'd sent him some wallpaper links, but she'd been so busy with the farm and the feed store and school, she hadn't seen him.

And she missed him more than she should.

"He had gotten a call from his father during dinner," Rachel explained. "I don't know what all he's dealing with regarding his dad, but I don't think they have a healthy relationship."

"I assumed they didn't," her mother stated. "At least, if I had to guess. I remember Jack coming during the summers, but his dad rarely made an appearance. I know that always seemed to upset George, and I never asked, but figured there was a disconnect somewhere."

"I really don't know what happened, if the problem was with Jack's dad and grandfather or Jack's dad and Jack." Rachel pulled in a deep breath and tried to make sense of a situation she knew very little about. "I went to the farm after dinner because I could tell he was stressed. I just wish he'd let me help more than he is."

"You care quite a bit for him."

Rachel jerked back at her mother's bold statement, and none too quietly, either.

"He's a *friend*," Rachel insisted. "Of course I care."

"The best ones always start out in the friend category." Her mother patted Rachel's hand. "It's okay to admit you have feelings for him. He's a handsome young man with a nice personality, and he seemed to be quite taken with you."

How did everyone see something she didn't? What looks was Jack giving her for her family to be so in tune?

"Mom, don't get so excited," Rachel warned. "He's a friend that I am helping and he's going back home in about a month."

"A great many things can happen in a month."

Yes, they could, but she wasn't about to get her mother's hopes up. If Rachel started thinking in terms of something beyond a friendship with Jack, she'd get hurt, and she'd already been down that path. Another career-minded man who stole her heart and attention, another man who wasn't cut out for the farm life.

But everything about Jack seemed to be so different and completely...right.

Yet it wasn't. God wouldn't send someone who wasn't staying. The man who was meant to be for her would have her interests and share the love of this town.

"He's not like Tyler."

As if her mother could read her mind, her words broke into Rachel's thoughts.

"No, he's not," Rachel agreed. "But they do have some similarities."

"Not the ones that matter."

There was no arguing with Sarah Spencer once she made up her mind. Obviously her family liked Jack, and Rachel loved that he'd got along so well with everyone. She would talk to him privately about attending the wedding, but she had to make it clear to her entire family that Jack was only a friend and temporary in town.

Rachel came to her feet and stared down at her mother. "I know you mean well, and I know you only want the best for me, but we have to be patient. And as much as I want a wedding day and a family of my own, I have to face the real possibility those things might not be in my future for a bit longer."

Her mother came to her feet and pulled Rachel into an embrace. Was there anything more comforting or loving than a mother's hug? Rachel returned the gesture and held tight for a moment.

"I know God has a special plan for you," her mom whispered. "He always looks out for His children."

Yes, He did. Rachel kept reminding herself of that, and honestly, she was beyond blessed. She had more than she'd ever need and well beyond anything she deserved. Her family farm had been saved, her sister was marrying the love of her life and bringing an adorable little girl into their world, and in less than a year, she would have her degree. Life was moving forward for everyone, maybe not the way Rachel had hoped, but forward in a positive direction nonetheless.

She prayed for Jack and the situation with his father. Maybe Jack coming to Rosewood Valley had nothing to do with her and everything to do with his personal and spiritual growth. And if her only part was to help him with his walk with God and his difficulties with his father, then so be it.

JACK STEPPED THROUGH the back door of All Good Things and inhaled the scent of grain and wood. The more he hung around town and this place, the more acclimated he became to country life. Maybe he didn't fully understand it all, but he did appreciate how hard people worked and how they all seemed to be supportive of each other. Small-town life was not only more laid-back than the city, but it also wasn't as competitive.

He'd yet to meet the manager, and he really needed to introduce himself. Now that the contractors were at the house, he needed reasons to step out and get out of their way. Always trying to hang with Rachel seemed odd, and a little pushy, since he'd made it clear they were friends and he had no intention of staying in town.

The thought of leaving didn't appeal to him like it had when he'd first come to town. Maybe he'd just got used to all the friendly people and the homey place. Or maybe there was one certain woman who had changed his entire thought process.

Regardless, he still had to move on with his plans, and the farmhouse was going to be absolutely amazing once those few rooms got a little facelift. He'd already ordered one of the wallpapers that Rachel had suggested for the main bath. He had to admit, she had a serious eye for design. Maybe farming was her passion, but she had many talents that she could tap into if she truly wanted some extra cash. He knew she wanted a place of her own, *his* place, but that wasn't likely. Still, she deserved something of her own, and he wanted to help her in any way he could.

For now, he had to deal with the feed store. Walt was back from his vacation, so this meeting had to be his top priority.

The office door was closed, but not latched. He tapped his knuckles on the door and waited for someone to call him in. Just because he was the owner didn't mean he didn't respect privacy. This place was more Walt's than Jack's and that was okay.

"Come in," a gruff voice called from the other side.

Jack eased the door open and stepped over the threshold. "Is this a bad time?"

An elderly man with silver hair and denim overalls covering his rounded belly came to his feet.

"Not at all if you're George's grandson."

Jack nodded. "I am. Thought it was time to introduce myself. Rachel has told me a good deal about you."

"Has she now?" Walt came around his desk and held out his hand for Jack. "She's told me about you as well. Gotta say, I thought your grandfather would live forever. He seemed to be a staple not just in the store, but also in the community."

"I've heard that." Jack shook Walt's hand, then released it and slid his thumbs through his belt loops. "I just wanted to let you know I haven't quite decided what I'm doing with this building yet. I had intentions of selling because I don't live here and have no need for a business, but I might just keep it and continue to let you manage. No matter what happens, I will make sure your job is secure. This place wouldn't be what it is without you, according to Rachel."

Walt gripped the straps on his overalls and rocked back on his heels. "That's not true. Your grandfather is the one who gets the praise. All I do is inventory and people managing. Nothing too hard. He did all the grunt work making a name for the place."

Jack couldn't help but accept the burst of pride that spread through him. The way people talked about his grandfather like he was some type of superhero to Rosewood Valley really had Jack wishing he would've spent more time here. While he appreciated all the summers he'd been here, he just wanted to have more memories stored up. Did he appreciate his grandfather enough? Did his grandfather know how much Jack loved him?

As he'd got older and into high school, sports and girls took up his time. Then Jack would call, but that also got few and far between. He just hoped his grandfather never doubted how much he meant to Jack. Now was his chance to honor the most remarkable man.

"I'd like to see what I can help with or if you have any concerns about the store in general."

Jack laid that out, hoping Walt would address the funds. Maybe he'd been doing his own investigation. While Walt might also be the one pilfering the money, Jack trusted Rachel when she said no way would something like that have happened. He also trusted his grandfather, and George Hart wouldn't have put someone in charge if they weren't trustworthy. But Jack wouldn't reveal what he knew quite yet.

"My biggest concern would be my job and my employees," Walt replied. "I want to do right by them. I'm old enough to retire, but I love what I do and will continue to work as long as the good Lord allows."

"I'm happy to hear that because I certainly couldn't keep this place running without you," Jack replied. "So, aside from that, is there anything else that concerns you? Anything with the staff or how well the store is doing as a whole?"

Walt hesitated and then let out a long sigh. "Close that door, would ya?"

A private conversation? Maybe they were getting somewhere.

Jack reached behind him and closed the door with a soft click before focusing on Walt again.

"What's up?" Jack asked, crossing his arms over his chest.

"I'm not sure what all you know about the store or how far you dug into things while I was on vacation," Walt began. Then he circled his desk and took a seat. "The store isn't bringing in what it used to when George was alive."

Jack moved closer to the desk and made himself comfortable in the old wooden folding chair opposite Walt. He'd let the guy take the lead here and reveal anything he knew or suspected.

"You think his passing caused the decline in sales?"

Walt rested his forearms on the desk and shook his head. "No. I'm afraid someone is taking money from the store. I don't want to just accuse anyone, and I don't have solid proof, but something is off over the past few months."

Jack eased forward just a bit in his chair. "When did you first notice money missing?"

"About a month ago I had a hunch something wasn't quite right with the numbers." Walt reached into a drawer and pulled out a folder. "And I've been looking over more things since I've been back and it's still quite troubling."

"Did you have a new hire about the time you started noticing an issue?"

Walt flipped open the cover of the folder and picked up the top paper. He turned it to face Jack and slid it across the desk. This wasn't something Jack had seen before. This paper was a spreadsheet that looked like something Walt had done up since his return. Jack was impressed, quite honestly. He didn't know if his grandfather would be one to do a spreadsheet. He'd always done old-school pen and paper and kept files secured in a cabinet.

As Jack glanced over the numbers, he saw a good bit of what he and Rachel had noticed.

"I've hired three new people and then you brought on Rachel just the other day," Walt stated. "Safe to say we can rule out Rachel."

"Pretty safe bet," Jack agreed.

Not only because of the timing, but also because he'd bet his annual salary there wasn't a corrupt bone in her body.

"I know the families of the ones I've hired and wouldn't think anyone would take from me," Walt went on. "But we can't ignore facts."

No, they couldn't.

"I'll be honest." Jack slid the paper across the desk and eased back in his chair. "I noticed some off-putting numbers when I first started looking at things. That's the main reason I asked Rachel to put in a few hours a week. I figured nobody would think anything of her being here, plus she's extremely knowledgeable."

"Smart move." Walt stuffed the paper back into the folder and put it back into his drawer. He leaned back in his creaky leather chair and laced his fingers over his belly. "I trust all of this will stay between the three of us."

"Absolutely," Jack promised. "And now with all of us on the lookout, we should be able to solve this quickly and quietly. I don't want the store or my grandfather's reputation tarnished in any way."

Walt studied him. "You're a good man. I don't think any of that will happen with you in charge. Your grandfather would be proud of the man you've become."

Would he? Jack hoped so, but he hadn't seen the man in

a few years before his passing. That guilt weighed heavy on him, and perhaps that was why Jack was so torn on whether or not to keep the store or sell it. Having a link to his grandfather seemed right. Another way for Jack to keep his connection here in Rosewood Valley. Perhaps he needed a reason to return every now and then without it being so obvious he wanted to see Rachel.

What would happen when she finally found the one and settled down on her own? How would he feel then? Would he be happy for her or would he wonder if he'd let the greatest woman he knew slip away?

# CHAPTER TWELVE

JACK LET HIMSELF in the front door since the construction crew was in the back working in the kitchen. A bit of the weight on his shoulders had lifted since talking to Walt. Jack had to agree with Rachel. That man had integrity and wouldn't do anything to harm the store.

He also felt a bit better knowing the house was on its way to getting on the market. Each step of progression put him that much closer to his own branch of the real estate firm. He couldn't wait to start his own legacy, something he could pass down to his children when the time came.

He vowed to be a more hands-on father, a more loving father. Yes, money was important, but from his short time here in Rosewood Valley, he could see that money was not the bottom line. Family had to come above all else.

The moment he crossed the threshold, he stopped.

"What are you doing here?"

Rachel turned a short white vase from side to side as she adjusted the various stems of colorful flowers. She flashed him that megawatt smile and any worries he had simply vanished.

"Oh, I wasn't sure when you'd be home and I rode Sunshine over so I could put this bouquet in your entryway." She stepped back and clasped her hands. "There. That's better."

Jack closed the door and chuckled. "You rode over on your horse with a vase of flowers?"

"I rode over with a bundle in my saddlebag," she corrected. "I found the vase in the storage closet here."

The banging of a sledgehammer had him jerking his attention toward the hallway leading toward the back of the house.

"Do you normally decorate while in a construction zone?" he asked.

Rachel turned and crossed her arms over her chest. "The foyer wasn't on the list, so I figured there needed to be one room that was completely done and cheery. I also went to school with your head contractor, so I brought the guys some biscuits with homemade apple butter."

Jack raked a hand through his hair. He'd never seen a woman with so much on her plate, yet still doling out favors and niceties to others.

"How's the kitchen looking?" he asked.

"Like a disaster. There will be no meals in there for a while, which is why I put something in the Crock-Pot for us back at my place."

Jack blinked, processing the words she'd just said. She'd started something for their dinner?

"I really don't know what to say," he admitted. "You know you don't have to feed me, right? I can go into town for something or make a sandwich."

Her mouth dropped as she gasped. "You will not be making a sandwich for your dinner. That's just ridiculous. You're not camping."

He couldn't stop his laugh now. "Is that when I should eat sandwiches? When I'm camping?"

"I'm just stating there's no reason to rough it when you have a friend more than willing to cook. I have to eat, too," she explained with a shrug.

*Friends.* Yes. The term that summed up their relationship and one he needed to remember. But there were times he wondered if their situation would be different if he didn't have an established life and career somewhere else. If he didn't have things yet to prove, and goals he'd worked too hard to accomplish to abandon now. Would he come home from work and find her making their house cozy like she'd just done with the flowers? He would never expect his wife to do all the cooking, decorating and cleaning. He firmly believed in any relationship the responsibilities should be shared, but he had to admit having her greet him with that smile the moment he stepped through the door had his mind traveling down a path he couldn't keep ignoring.

"You're doing it again," she told him.

The hammering stopped and the guys in the back started discussing something he couldn't quite make out.

"What's that?" he asked.

"Staring like you want to say something but you don't know how."

She'd got that right. He did want to say something, but it wasn't that he didn't know how...more like he didn't know what to say. Did he say he was falling for this town? Did he admit he'd started feeling more for her than he'd anticipated? Then what? They'd both feel awkward because there was no future here. He didn't want her hurt, and she'd already had one guy walk away. He wouldn't be another man to break her heart. The pressure from his father to make this sale and get back to the brokerage weighed heavy on him. It had weighed heavier each day since their last phone call.

Which meant he had to suppress anything he felt, because his feelings were only going to grow if he focused on them.

"I'm just happy you're here," he told her honestly. "Thank you for the flowers."

"You're welcome. Heard you went by the feed store today."

He nodded. "Word travels fast in this town."

"Walt called me just a bit ago," she explained. "He said you guys discussed the issue, so I'm glad we're all going to be on top of this."

When the hammering started up again, Jack motioned for her to head upstairs. Once on the landing, the noise was a bit more muted.

"He said he'd been doing his own digging," Jack told her as he leaned against the railing. "He also told me he'd hired three people around the same time and he only noticed the missing funds about a month ago."

Rachel slid her hands into her pockets as she pursed her lips, clearly in thought. Her signature braid fell over her right shoulder, lying flat against her long-sleeve plaid shirt. She'd tucked her top into her jeans and had a brown belt that matched her brown boots. She was pure cowgirl through and through.

"It's just difficult to imagine any of his workers taking money," she murmured. "They all should know he'd give anything if they needed it."

Jack had no doubt Walt would do anything for anyone. That was just another aspect about this town that he loved. Everyone's willingness to step up without being asked or expecting something in return.

"I don't see any other explanation other than an employee," Jack stated.

"It would have to be," she murmured, glancing down. "And it's going to be devastating to whomever it is. It's a small town and people will talk. I just hate this."

There she went with that big heart again and her worries for everyone else, even if they were in the wrong.

"I just hope I figure out who it is first," she added, bringing her worried gaze back up to him. "Maybe then I can talk them into returning the money or something."

Yeah, he really had no clue how he and Walt would handle this once they found out who the culprit was. Stealing was wrong no matter what, but Jack couldn't help but wonder about the circumstances.

"So, when would you like to head over for dinner?" she asked. "I don't want to scare you away, but I did try a new recipe. So we could be ordering a pizza in the end."

Jack shrugged. "Fine by me. I'll eat whatever. Just let me talk to the guys downstairs first and change clothes."

"You're getting out of your businessman attire?" She nodded and gave a thumbs-up. "Nice. Can't wait to see what you dress down in."

Why did he have to find all sides of this woman appealing? The compassionate side, the giving side, and even her snarky sense of humor at his expense. He found every aspect of her adorable and much too attractive. She could make him laugh and feel things he hadn't in…well, maybe never.

"Very funny," he retorted with a mock laugh. "We'll see who's laughing once we try this mystery meal you made."

"It's not a mystery," she scoffed, barely hiding her grin with the twitch of her lips. "I know everything that's in it. I've just never done this one before."

"Give me about twenty minutes and I'll be there," he assured her. "I don't have a horse, so I'll be driving."

"You city boy." She started down the steps and called back, "See you in just a bit."

When she got to the first floor, she yelled toward the kitchen, saying her farewell to the workers. Jack always found himself in a better mood after being in Rachel's presence. Just as he started to head to the bedroom, the cell in his pocket vibrated. When he slid it out, he noticed his father's name. Jack's thumb hovered over the screen, but he didn't answer.

Never in his life had he not taken a call from his father, but right now, he was in such a good mood and he was ready to go see Rachel in a few minutes. He didn't want to be filled with anxiety and negativity.

Jack donned a pair of jeans and a long-sleeve T-shirt. He grabbed his sneakers and tied those up, too. There, now she shouldn't say anything, right?

Good grief. He truly was like a teen with a crush, all worried about his outfit and what she would think.

Jack wanted to see if the guys needed anything before he left, even though he assumed they had it all under control. He was excited to see the progress, even though with most things the rooms or buildings got worse before they got better. He knew in no time this place would be ready to sell.

And with that thought, the lump of guilt weighed heavy knowing he already had the perfect buyer...just not the one he could realistically sell to.

"THIS IS SO SILLY," Rachel muttered to herself as she took the lid off the Crock-Pot. "It's a meal. That's all."

The stray cat slid by her leg and Rachel jumped. She still wasn't used to having a pet, but she had to admit, she didn't feel as silly talking to herself with something else in the room.

The lasagna didn't look or smell terrible, but she'd never tried making it in a Crock-Pot. Her mother would not believe it. At least the sauce was homemade with tomatoes from their garden. That had to count for something. And the bread was homemade as well. So what if she'd cheated a little with using a slow cooker.

But it wasn't the meal she felt silly about. She'd made an impulsive purchase and now...well, she just had to go through with the gift giving. She didn't necessarily have extra funds right now, considering she wanted to buy a house, but she couldn't help herself. And like with most every other aspect in her life, she made the leap without thinking.

She had no idea who her guardian angel was, but Rachel had a feeling she followed her around shaking her head.

The tap on her door had Rachel spinning away from the kitchen and smoothing a hand down her braid. Should she have done something else with her hair? Something less boring?

Too late now. Jack was here and she had nerves curling through her belly like this was her first date. Only this wasn't their first date or any type of a date. It was a friendly meal where they could chat about their day, and maybe the store and renovations, and she could give him his present.

The cat scurried toward the bedroom as Rachel crossed to open the door. She blinked at the man standing before her.

"Well, you did pack casual clothes. I'm so proud of you." When he started to enter, she held up a hand. "Or did you go buy those when I laughed at all of your dressy clothes?"

"I packed them all by myself," he replied and tapped the tip of her nose with his finger. "Now, something smells amazing and I'm pretty hungry. Please tell me it turned out okay?"

She eased aside as he let himself in. "I haven't tried a sample yet, but it looks fine."

"Then it will be great," he assured her, then suddenly pulled his cell from his pocket.

He glanced to the screen and sighed before shoving it away.

"Everything okay?" she asked.

Offering her a small grin, he nodded. "Just taking a mental break from calls with my father."

"And how do you feel about that?" she asked. "Because I can give you privacy if you want to take it."

"No. That is his third call in twenty minutes," Jack told her.

"What if there's an emergency?"

Jack let out a frustrated sigh. "There's no emergency. Oh, he might think there's one, but it wouldn't be medical. It would be something to do with a listing or he's checking on the progress of the house. All of which can wait."

Rachel hesitated before adding, "You're sure he wouldn't call with an actual emergency?"

"I promise," he assured her. "He wouldn't even tell me if he had to go to the hospital until after the fact, and even then he'd blow it off. So, let's just enjoy the evening and not have my father join us as an absent third party."

She had to respect his wishes and believe he knew his father best. If he wanted a worry-free evening, then that was what Rachel would supply.

"So do you want to eat first or do you want your surprise?" she asked.

Even though she felt a little ridiculous with her gift, she still wanted to give it and see his reaction.

"A surprise?" Jack's brows rose as he took a step back. "You just put flowers in my house."

She didn't miss the way he said *his* house, but she wasn't about to call him on it. If he was getting used to being here, then so be it. And honestly, this area might be better for his mental well-being.

"The flowers were decoration," she corrected. "And because that space just called for it."

"So what's this surprise?"

"Oh, it's a necessity as well."

His warm laughter filled her tiny loft apartment and hit her right in her soul. She'd never felt more alive than when she was with Jack. Her adolescent crush had grown into something much larger and more complex than she could have ever dreamed. Part of her wanted to be completely open and honest about her feelings, but she didn't want to make things uncomfortable between them. There were too many working parts to their relationship, and throwing a wrench into any of that could jeopardize the solid bond they'd created.

"Well, you've intrigued me." He held out his hands. "Let's see this surprise."

Rachel spun around and went into her bedroom to retrieve the gift. Her cat shuffled somewhere beneath her bed, likely hiding from the visitor or curling up for a nap.

When she stepped back into the open space with her kitchen and living area, Jack was over by the Crock-Pot with the lid off.

"We can eat first," she told him. "Unless you're afraid of that lasagna."

He replaced the lid and turned to face her. "I've never

known how lasagna was made, but never would've guessed a Crock-Pot."

"Oh, it's normally in the oven in a large pan, but I wanted it to cook all day, so I tried this." She moved to the small round table that separated her living and kitchen area and set his present next to the small teacup of flowers she'd picked earlier today. "Here you go."

Jack's gaze shifted between the box and her, then back to the box.

"You wrapped it and everything?"

"Well, it is a gift."

Should she have just given it to him out of the shopping bag? That didn't seem proper at all. If she was going to do anything, she was going to do it right.

Jack closed the distance to the table and lifted the box. "It's heavy."

Rachel merely smiled as she waited for him to tear into it. She would've already had paper flying at this point if someone had presented her with a surprise.

He set the package back down and went to one of the folds on the end. Moving much slower than anyone should with a surprise, he lifted the flap.

"You know you didn't have to get me anything, right?" he asked, pulling the paper completely away.

"I'm well aware, but you needed this and I couldn't pass it up."

The paper fell to the floor and he stared down at the red box with a logo on the top that was so familiar to her but probably not to him. He glanced up once again with a crooked grin, like a kid on Christmas morning. Rachel didn't realize how special or exciting this would be, but she wanted to lock in this exact time and the look on his face. She hadn't seen him caught off guard or genuinely happy too often. So even if she felt silly about giving him something a touch extravagant, she would do it again in a heartbeat if that meant he was carefree for a short time.

"What's this?" he asked.

Yeah. He didn't know that brand or logo. Rachel merely shrugged.

"Lift the lid and find out."

He pulled the cardboard top off and shifted the tissue paper aside before stopping. Then he stared back up at her.

"You're kidding."

"Do you hate them?" she asked, now worried at his reaction.

"Hate them?" He chuckled as he pulled one dark brown cowboy boot from the box. "I never thought I'd say that I love these boots."

Relief replaced the worry, and she found herself smiling and taking a step toward him. "I'm so glad. When you stepped in the pile the other day, that pretty much convinced me you needed some farm-appropriate shoes. They'll be stiff at first, but once you wear them a bit, they'll be your favorite pair of shoes."

Jack pulled out one of the wooden chairs and took a seat. He immediately went to untying his sneakers and toeing them off. He set them aside and pulled out both boots, taking the stuffing out of each one and tossing it back into the box. Rachel waited while he slid into them.

When he came to his feet, she clasped her hands and did a little hop of excitement.

"Look at you," she declared. "You're practically a native now."

He walked around the table with an extra-exaggerated swagger that had her laughing even more.

"Is this how I do it?" he asked. "I feel like I need something plaid."

"We do not walk like that," she snorted.

"I did after I got off that horse the other day," he told her.

"Well, you look fine without anything plaid. And I hope

you don't think I want to make you somebody that you aren't," she said. "I thought I'd buy them as a joke. Then that thought morphed into the realization that you might actually need them if you're going to come back from time to time. We don't want any more muck to tarnish that shine on your big boy shoes."

He stopped just before her and propped his hands on his hips. "Rachel, I would never in a million years think you were trying to make me into anyone else. Your gift came from the heart, and I can't tell you how much I love that you thought of me and were worried for my other shoes."

His smile and teasing, and his compliment, had those giddy emotions swirling through once again. But had they ever stopped? Since she'd ridden over to the Circle H that first day, she'd been in a constant state of awareness and attraction.

"You don't have to wear them right now," she told him. "You can put your sneakers back on."

He snapped his head back in mock shock. "Are you kidding me? I don't know the last time I received a gift. I'm wearing these all night."

"You don't know when you received a gift last?" she repeated, her chest tightening just a bit. "Christmas? A birthday?"

"I'm too old for birthday gifts, and for Christmas my father typically puts extra money in my bonus for the end of the year commission," he said matter-of-factly. "So, if that counts."

"No, it doesn't."

And she was truly starting to see why Jack seemed so happy here. No expectations, no one bribing him or trying to use him for gains. She might not know Jack's father, but she didn't like the man. Which just proved to her she needed to pray harder for him. Anyone who was that absorbed with the ways of the world and hungry for more power needed guidance and God. It wasn't her place to judge, but it was her place to look out for her friend.

"How about we eat?" she suggested. "You sit and I'll get everything ready."

"I can help," he offered. "Let me mosey on over and I can get our drinks."

Rachel held up a hand to stop him. "You can't just throw on the boots and turn instant cowboy with a swagger and the lingo. You've got to ease into this lifestyle."

He hooked his thumbs through his belt loops and tipped his head. "I've been here a couple weeks now. I think my next step is a big hat and a horse."

She dropped her hand and snickered as she made her way to the open shelving above her counters. She grabbed two yellow plates and set them next to the Crock-Pot.

"If you were staying, I'd help you shop for the perfect horse." She lifted the lid and scooped out a healthy portion for Jack. "But you can borrow Champ on your visits."

"I'd like that."

She wasn't sure what the future held for either of them and the farm, but for tonight, she was going to enjoy their time together and not worry about the outside world or tomorrow. God had a plan, and this was where her faith and her trust had to take over.

# CHAPTER THIRTEEN

JACK FIGURED SINCE several rooms in the farmhouse had turned into a construction zone, he might as well decide what to do about all of his grandfather's things in the main barn. He unlocked the side door and slid the key back into his pocket. He reached in and felt for the light switch and flicked it on.

The old space had that musty smell from being closed up for a while, and Jack hadn't made it down here since his return. He'd been busy with more important things and figured when he sold the place, nobody would care if the barn looked all glitzy. The house was a different story, though, so he'd kept his focus on that.

His booted heels clicked on the concrete floor, echoing throughout the empty space.

Jack merely stood and took in his surroundings. It had been years since he'd been in this area and he needed a moment. The memories came rolling in one by one. The first time he learned how to groom a horse, the first time his grandfather taught him how to clean a stall. Grunt work was all part of the life of a rancher. His grandfather always told him you had to put in the work to reap the rewards.

So many life lessons learned on this farm and here in this barn. Jack wasn't sure he fully appreciated the moments at the time, but looking back, he loved all that his grandfather had instilled in him.

He also couldn't help but wonder why his father was so anti–farm life and shunned anything to do with the Circle H. Clearly something happened between his dad and grandfather, something that had driven a wedge between them. Thankfully, Jack hadn't been pushed out of his grandfather's life.

Jack headed toward the office area and turned the knob. The moment the old wooden door swung open, Jack was faced with another old desk, where his grandfather would pour hours into his work. Jack was taking the one from the house and knew he couldn't take this desk, too. There would be no need for two desks, so he'd probably leave this one in the barn for the new owner.

An instant image of Rachel sitting in that rickety old chair gave him pause. Everywhere he looked at the Circle H, he could see her making her mark and continuing what his grandfather had started.

And for the first time, Jack wondered what his grandfather would want done here. Jack knew money never mattered to his grandfather, not the way Jack's father coveted it. Traditions and morals and his faith were the staples in George's life up until he passed.

Had Jack inherited all of this because his grandfather wanted him here? Did he want Jack to carry on the Circle H into a new generation? How could Jack decide between his father and his grandfather's wishes?

Or maybe he was supposed to do what felt right to *him* and no one else. He could really use some of that faith Rachel relied on. He needed guidance because he was so utterly confused.

Swallowing the lump of remorse and guilt in his throat, Jack moved around the desk to see if there were any personal items left. He had no clue what his grandfather kept in here. All of the actual business paperwork was up in the study at the farmhouse.

Jack rolled the old chair aside and started with the top middle drawer. A few random pens, some blank sticky notes, a few unwrapped pieces of hard candy that made Jack chuckle. Cherry, of course. Jack recalled finding those little red candies all over the house. His grandfather always said being outside so much made his throat dry. Jack remembered sneaking pieces for himself until he found an entire bag on his nightstand one morning and knew his grandfather had been onto him. He'd never said a word and Jack only told him thanks.

He closed that drawer and reached for the top right and gave a tug. A variety of worn notebooks and journals were all that was in this drawer. Jack reached in, pulled out one of the books and flipped it open. He stilled at the familiar sight of his grandfather's elegant cursive writing. On closer inspection, Jack realized this wasn't a business journal but a personal one. Why would he have such a thing out here?

Jack felt for the chair he'd shoved away moments ago and sank onto the creaky leather. He flipped back to the first page to start at the beginning. This journal was dated about twenty years ago. Even though the pages weren't too worn or torn, he still turned them carefully. He had a feeling he'd be getting nothing else done today except reading these journals. Perhaps that was what his grandfather had been doing at this desk for hours. He'd been pouring his thoughts out onto paper.

Part of Jack felt like he was violating his grandfather's privacy, but the other part wanted to feel closer to the man who'd had a small part in shaping the person he was today.

*Spring is the most exciting time. All the babies are born and bringing new life to the farm. This year I will try to hire a couple boys from the local high school to help around the place. Jack will be here in just over a month, and I can't wait to see him. He's the brightest point in the year for me. The house gets lonely without Bonnie here. Jack really fills a void, and he's growing into such a nice young man. I can't wait to see how much he's changed and what he remembers from last summer.*

The words blurred and Jack realized his emotions were getting the best of him. He hadn't cried since coming back. He'd been in work mode and caught up with Rachel, and maybe there was a part of him that simply didn't want to face that hurt.

Jack turned the page and blinked away the unshed tears. He wanted to concentrate on each word and knew without a doubt he'd find a special place for these journals. Nobody needed to know about these, and honestly, Jack didn't feel like his father deserved to know. Likely he wouldn't care anyway, but Jack planned on keeping this precious secret to himself.

"I THINK THE rosemary bundles need to go on top of the napkin on the plate," Sarah Spencer stated as she came up to the long dining table in the barn.

Violet rearranged the place setting and stepped back. "Like that?"

"That definitely looks better," Rachel agreed from the other side of the table. "I like the look we're doing on this dinner."

She set a tall bundle of pampas grass in the middle of the table and adjusted a few of the pieces to balance out the simple arrangement. Tonight they were having another farm-to-table event, but this one was for a bridal shower. A small, modest gathering with only about twenty-five people, but no matter the size of the party, the Spencer ladies always wanted each guest to feel like they were special.

"I do, too," Erin agreed as she slid the white slipcovers over the chairs at the opposite end of the table. "The bride requested neutrals and elegant, so I think we did pretty good."

Rachel loved the gift table with a nice photo of the couple and a large prop initial *B* for the last name they would share. The letter had been made of wood and brought from the bride to use with the decor. The piece had been hollowed out and Erin had placed gorgeous cream and white flowers stuffed neatly with various pops of greenery.

Rachel turned from the table where her mom and sisters were working and went to the food tables. She could go ahead and get the cupcake stand set up and the macarons displayed. The bride had also sent over her great-grandmother's white serving platter, which she wanted incorporated, and Rachel thought the pistachio macarons would look perfect on that piece.

She couldn't wait to have her own bridal shower one day. Maybe she'd do one just like this, here on the farm. She definitely wanted small and intimate. Just a cozy gathering for her family and closest friends.

"Need help?"

Rachel turned as Jenn came up to her side.

"If you want to do the cupcake stand, I can get the macarons ready," she told her. "The boxes are in the kitchen."

They'd transformed this barn space into something amazing over the past several months. The town had really embraced the farm-to-table idea. What had started as a prayer to help save the farm quickly turned into something bigger than they ever could have imagined.

Rachel hoped this venture would last generations and continue to bring families and the community together. She yearned for a family of her own to pass her own traditions down to.

"You seem lost in thought," Jenn stated. "Everything okay?"

Rachel tucked a wayward strand that had slid from her braid back behind her ear as she turned toward her sister. "I'm fine. I just love all of this. Your wedding coming up, this bridal shower. It just leaves me feeling so happy and hopeful."

Jenn reached for her hand and gripped in that tender way she had. "Rach, you will find the right one at the right time. You have so much to offer, and just because Tyler didn't have the same vision doesn't mean he was your only chance at love. He was a great guy, just not the right fit for you."

"I know," Rachel agreed. "He wouldn't have been happy

here and I wouldn't have been happy in a big city where he wanted to be. I think I just worry because I'm the oldest sister and what if I get too old?"

Jenn let out a soft laugh. "Too old for what? Love has no expiration."

"For children," Rachel admitted. "What if I get too old to have my own family?"

Their mother and other two sisters were chattering about which drink glasses to use while Rachel was having a slight pity moment.

"What if you meet someone with a child already?" Jenn countered. "I met Luke and his sweet niece and we will raise her together. I'm not sure if we'll have children of our own or if Paisley will be it, but I know that God's plan worked out perfectly after my husband passed. I never thought I'd be happy again, let alone find love."

"You don't know how glad I am that you're back home." Rachel pulled her sister into a hug, because they still had a three-year gap to make up for. "You're right where you belong, and Luke and Paisley are lucky to have you."

Jenn eased back and nodded. "We're lucky to have found each other. And may I say something and not be offensive?"

Rachel pulled back slightly but held on to her sister's hand. "That's a loaded question."

"I just can't help but wonder if Jack came into town at this precise time for a reason," Jenn stated. "I mean, he wasn't here for George's funeral, but he's here now and he seems to be quite attached to you."

*Attached?* That wasn't quite the word Rachel would use.

"First, I'm not offended," Rachel started. "Second, he's here now because he has to sell the home and get back to his life in San Francisco. His father tasked him with the Rosewood Valley properties."

"All in God's timing," Jenn repeated.

Rachel's heart fluttered. If Jack even had an inkling of an

idea of staying, she would embrace every part of that. She could see him here in ways she could never see Tyler. Jack seemed happier and more relaxed here, and frustrated when he discussed his life back home. Was he in a hurry to get back to the stress and day-to-day rush?

No matter what he was feeling, Rachel couldn't help but have a sliver of panic with how fast her emotions had grown toward him. Try as she might, she couldn't seem to get control over how she felt toward her childhood crush. But she needed to slow down; she needed restraint over her thoughts and the direction of her heart. She could only pray she didn't get hurt again, but she was human and couldn't help who she was drawn to.

"Well, right now we're going to concentrate on this bride," Rachel told Jenn. "And in a couple weeks, we're going to concentrate on you. My time will come. I'm going to believe that. Until then, I will celebrate you."

Jenn gave her one final hug before going to the kitchen to retrieve the boxes. Rachel blew out a breath and wished she had the courage to just tell Jack how she felt. But if she did and he left like he said he would, she'd look and feel like a fool again. Risking her heart wasn't something she was ready for. So until or unless Jack indicated he wanted to remain in Rosewood Valley, she'd have to keep those thoughts and feelings locked deep inside her heart.

# CHAPTER FOURTEEN

JACK FELT RIDICULOUS now that he was here, but he'd already pulled into the drive and been spotted by Will Spencer, so there was no backing out now.

He put his car in Park and killed the engine. He'd spent all night reading his grandfather's journals, and this morning he wanted to talk to the one person who might have been the closest to the man he'd lost. Will was not only a fellow farmer but a close neighbor. No doubt they'd shared stories and confided in each other over the years. After seeing Will's name multiple times in the journals, Jack realized those two had to have had a special bond.

"Mornin'," Will called through the barn opening.

Jack waved. "Morning. Is this a bad time for a visit?"

"Rachel is in the house with Sarah, if you're looking for her."

Jack wouldn't turn down a moment to see Rachel, but that would have to wait.

"I'm actually here to see you."

Will gripped his red suspenders and nodded. "This is a good time, then. You want a cup of coffee? We can head to the house."

"No, no. I'm good." Jack really didn't know what to say

now that he was here, but he wanted another connection to his grandfather. "I know we don't really know each other—"

"I feel I know you pretty well," Will stated. "George spoke about you pretty often, and when you were young and visited, I recall a few times when you all came over."

Yeah, Jack remembered coming to the barns here and discussing livestock.

"I just wanted to talk to you about the Circle H and the direction I'm going." Jack shrugged and looped his thumbs through his belt loops. "I plan on selling as soon as the minor renovations are complete. I guess I'm feeling a little guilty about it, and I just want to make sure the right person gets it and I make my grandfather proud. I figure you knew him best from anyone in town, other than Walt at the store."

"Your grandfather and I were pretty close over the years," Will agreed. "I valued our friendship and continue to mourn the loss."

George Hart had made his presence known in Rosewood Valley—that much was certain. Jack was proud to be the grandson of a man who had been so highly thought of.

"I also think he'd want you to do what is best for not only the farm, but for you as well," Will added. "He loved you and was so proud of you. He wouldn't want anything to be a burden."

No, he wouldn't. Jack could definitely agree with that. His grandfather wanted others to be happy, and he constantly put himself second...much like Rachel. Maybe that was why he felt such a connection to her. That giving spirit inside her and the compassion and bright light she projected made him feel so at home in ways he never would have imagined.

"The property isn't a burden," Jack replied, crossing his arms over his chest. "I just don't have a need for it and I do need to sell it for top dollar."

"Money never mattered to George."

"No, just my father," Jack muttered. "It's important that I

get the most I can from the land and farmhouse for reasons I can't get into."

Or didn't want to get into.

Maybe if Jack was honest, money had mattered more to him at one time, too. He couldn't deny the thrill of success and accolades from associates. But since coming to this small, humble town, Jack realized maybe money didn't always have to be the end goal.

"Rachel has wanted that farm for years," Will stated. "Her dream has been to join the two properties and ultimately pass down her part to her family, because this land will always be Spencer land."

"She told me she wanted the property," Jack confirmed. "I just can't lease or rent it to sell. It's a long story."

Will nodded and blew out a long sigh. "If I could buy that place for her, I would in a heartbeat. That girl does everything for everyone else. Sold her own home not long ago to help her mother and me around here. She puts those around her first and herself last."

"I've noticed that."

Will's bushy silver brows drew in. "You and Rachel have gotten close since you've come to town."

Jack didn't want to make anyone believe they had anything beyond a friendship. He wasn't staying, and no matter what feelings he might have developed, it wouldn't be fair to her to express them.

"She's become a great friend," Jack replied honestly. "She's been a huge help with ideas on the house, and I know nothing about a feed store, so she's been putting in a few hours there helping as well."

"That girl." Will shook his head. "She told me she was working some for extra money. She'd do anything to get her own place. She's wearing herself too thin, if you ask me."

Jack agreed, but he hadn't come here to get Will worked up

over Rachel's hectic schedule. He truly wanted advice. Maybe he wanted fatherly advice he couldn't get from his own dad.

Jack glanced around the barn and noticed it was smaller than the one his grandfather had used the most. Will's had four stalls where the Circle H had eight. Both properties had more than one barn for livestock, but his grandfather's sat empty now, just waiting on a new owner to bring in their chosen stock. George had sold his animals a couple of years ago as his health started to make the hard work more difficult. He'd kept his focus on the store, which was easier to maintain, especially with Walt's help.

"I respect you guys so much," Jack stated as he moved toward the first stall, where Champ stood. "The hard work ranchers and farmers put in typically goes unnoticed."

"That's not why we do the work." Will turned to face Jack and adjusted his worn cowboy hat. "We love the tradition and the land. We love knowing we are providing for our families and instilling morals and work ethic that will be passed down."

Jack reached through the wrought iron bars and slid his hand over Champ's velvety nose. Tradition and tight family bonds seemed to be the theme through Rosewood Valley. Jack couldn't help but wonder if his grandfather had been depressed or upset knowing Jack's father would never take over the land. Had George Hart wanted the Circle H to go to his only child and a new generation to grow with the times while still keeping those values and traditions?

"I just wish I knew the right thing to do for everyone, including my grandfather." Jack dropped his hand and glanced back at Will. "Believe me, if I could gift this to Rachel, I would. There's just more to it than that. I know she'd take care of the land like my grandfather would've wanted. And I know there's nobody better fitting to work it and run it."

"You don't have to explain yourself to me," Will chimed in. "You can't just give away something like that, and I know you are a city businessman. You all think differently than rural folks do and that's okay. The good Lord made us all different or this would be a boring world."

Jack chuckled at the accurate statement. "I guess if we were all working from an office, nothing much would get done by way of agriculture."

Will nodded. "You got that right. But I couldn't work in an office, so there's a reason God made all the variety. We all have our strengths."

"I'm wondering if I even know mine anymore," Jack muttered.

"What's that nonsense talk?" Will grumbled. "George followed your career and would brag how well you were doing."

"Did he?" Jack asked. "Once I graduated college and tried making a name for myself, all I could focus on was work. Being self-employed is difficult, as you know. If I don't work, I'm not getting paid. I guess I got so wrapped up in trying to lay a firm foundation, I didn't get back for those visits like I'd always done."

"I won't lie," Will added. "George sure did miss seeing you, but he knew you'd grow up and get a life of your own."

A life of his own? Jack wondered lately who he'd been living that life for. He'd always wanted to make his father proud, but the constant jumping through hoops was starting to wear on him. Maybe once this farmhouse was complete and on the market, his father would see the hard work he'd put into his childhood home. Jack hoped, anyway.

"If you don't mind my saying, you look torn or worried."

Will's observation had Jack blinking back to the moment and stepping out of his thoughts.

"I'm both," he answered. Why lie? "I have no need for a farm, but it's difficult to say goodbye to a place that holds so many core childhood memories."

"I've never had to let go of something I loved before," Will admitted. "I don't know what I'd do without the Four Sisters, and I hope I never have to find that out."

Jack wasn't sure what to say. He didn't have any more clarity than when he'd walked in here.

"I wasn't sure what would happen to the farm once your grandfather passed," Will went on. "But I'm not surprised you were the beneficiary. George loved the summers you spent here."

As if Jack needed another dose of guilt. But he couldn't deny that those summers had been some of the best moments and fondest memories of his entire life.

"What happens if you don't sell right away?" Will proposed. "I'm not sure of your circumstances, but if you prayed over your situation and waited for God's guidance, that might help."

Pray over this? Jack didn't recall praying over any business dealings he'd done in the past. Maybe he should give that a try. It wasn't that he didn't believe in God. He knew all the good things in his life came from above. He'd just got so busy climbing that invisible corporate ladder that he'd put his faith on the back burner.

Being back here, though, reminded him of how important faith was.

"I'm not sure if I helped your decision," Will went on. "I know George wouldn't want you to be torn up over this, but he definitely would want his farm going to someone who would love and appreciate it like he did."

Jack nodded and attempted a grin. "I appreciate your advice. I will pray on my decision. I guess I just needed someone to guide me in that direction."

"I'm here anytime you need to talk," Will offered. "And Rachel is a great listener, too."

"She's pretty amazing," Jack agreed. "I'll let you get back to work."

Jack started to walk out of the barn when Will called his name. Jack turned to look over his shoulder.

"I know you both say you're just friends," Will started, gripping those red straps once again. "But you're both so quick

to remind people of that, it makes me wonder if you're keeping those real feelings buried. Maybe add that to your prayer
list as well."

Jack couldn't help but bite the inside of his cheek as he tried
to suppress the grin. Will was of the generation of the wise
and observant.

"I need to add quite a bit to my prayer list," Jack replied,
then turned on his new boots and headed back to his car.

He pulled his sunglasses down to shield the sun, and movement from the kitchen window caught his eye. Rachel stood on
the other side, waving with a wide smile spread across her face.

Yes. He had quite a bit to pray about.

"I CANNOT BELIEVE THIS."

Rachel glanced up from her laptop as Violet burst through
her loft door. Rach never expected family to knock, and she
left her door unlocked unless she was asleep.

Since she'd just submitted an online quiz, she shut her laptop
to focus on her sister and the paper she was waving in the air.

"Calm down," Rachel said as she came to her feet and set
her laptop on the coffee table. "What happened?"

"A fine from the new sheriff." Vi shut the door behind her
and stepped forward, thrusting the paper in Rachel's direction.
"I mean, this is how he wants to introduce himself?"

Rachel took the paper and ran her gaze across it to see what
the fine could be about.

"It's just a parking violation," Rachel explained. "So park
somewhere else."

Vi scoffed and snatched the paper back, crumpling it in her
hand. "I've been parking in the same spot for eight years. The
old sheriff didn't have a problem with it, nor has any other law
enforcement officer in Rosewood Valley."

Rachel slid the band from the bottom of her braid and loos-
ened the strands. "Did this come in the mail?"

"No. He hand-delivered it to my office staff," she explained. "Didn't even wait to hand it straight to me or introduce himself."

Rachel tried not to laugh at how worked up Violet seemed to be. Out of all the sisters, Vi had very little patience with people, but all the patience in the world for her pet clients.

"I've been so busy with everything, I forgot I heard we were getting a new sheriff," Rachel stated. "Do you know his name?"

Violet carefully unwrapped the wad in her hand and glanced at the page. "Dax Adams. Dax. What kind of name is that?"

Rachel couldn't help the snicker that escaped her, but then she remembered her morals. "Be nice. He's new and just doing his job."

"I'm sure there's other things he can be doing other than harassing a local business owner."

Rachel tucked her hair behind her ears and held her sister's frustrated gaze. "I wouldn't call this harassing," she replied. "He didn't even speak to you."

Violet's brows drew in as she shoved the paper back into the pocket of her gray scrub top. "Why are you coming to his defense?" she asked, crossing her arms. "I thought you had a thing for Jack."

Rachel jerked. "I most certainly do not."

Vi rolled her eyes. "Rach, it's me. I know you better than anyone, except Erin and Jenn. None of us can lie to each other. You know that."

Rachel shrugged and turned to sink back onto her vacated nook in the corner of her small sectional sofa. "So what if I like him? That means nothing."

Violet remained unmoving, but that intense stare locked in on Rachel.

"What?" she asked. "I admitted I like him. What more do you want from me?"

"Did you tell him?"

"Why would I do that?" Rachel retorted. "He's a great guy

and he's made it clear this isn't the life for him. I wouldn't tell him something to make him feel guilty or pity me."

Violet moved around the end table and took a seat on the sofa. "Did you ever think he might have grown feelings for you, too? That maybe it's not fair to either of you to keep how you feel a secret?"

Rachel glanced away and stared at her closed laptop…which held another secret she'd been keeping. Maybe she didn't want to be rejected again if she told Jack how she felt. That was a very realistic outcome and one she never wanted to face again.

"He's not Tyler," Violet murmured, taking Rachel's hand in hers. "I think you need to give him a chance. Jack could be keeping his feelings bottled up as well."

Rachel wasn't naive. She knew Jack liked her, but did he *like* her? Should she tell him how she felt and just take a chance? Did she want to risk her heart again?

"Let me ask you this," Violet added. "If he leaves town, will you regret not saying anything? You have to think about that."

Rachel's heart swelled and she pulled in a deep breath. Yes. She would have regrets if Jack left and her feelings remained locked tight inside. Maybe being completely open and up-front was just how she'd have to handle this and then leave the decision to him. She wouldn't beg and she wouldn't want him to compromise who he was. That wouldn't be any type of relationship.

So now the question was, when would she tell him?

# CHAPTER FIFTEEN

THE PROGRESS ON the house was coming along faster than he'd thought, but Jack wanted to step away. He hadn't seen Rachel since the day before yesterday. They'd texted a few times, but nothing of real substance. He was torn and confused and really just needed to see her. Something about Rachel gave him peace and clarity when his world seemed to be complicated lately.

Before he'd arrived in Rosewood Valley, Jack figured he'd get into town, have a few rooms painted and staged, put the house up for sale and leave with a record number sale. But life had a weird way of showing who was in charge...and it wasn't Jack.

He'd taken the past day and a half and really tried praying like Will suggested. And although Jack was still confused, he felt better knowing he had God on his side. But he still wished he knew the right answer and where to go from here.

He mounted the steps to Rachel's loft and tapped on the door.

The door burst open. "Are you still upset about the violation?"

Rachel stopped abruptly. "Oh, sorry." She laughed. "I thought you were Vi again. She just left a bit ago."

"Just me," he stated, holding his hands out. "Bad time?"

He glanced at her long, flowy dress and her hair around her shoulders. This wasn't the Rachel who worked around the farm or feed store or the one who helped him brainstorm renovations. This Rachel looked quite different and equally as stunning.

"Not at all," she told him. "Come on in. I was just trying on my bridesmaid's dress again since it got hemmed. I'm trying to decide on the right shoes."

He stepped inside and closed the door behind him. "Well, you look beautiful."

Her smile spread across her face, and just that simple gesture calmed him and soothed his soul. How did she do that? He'd never met a woman who managed to have such a hold over his emotions and she likely didn't have a clue.

"Thank you," she replied. "Are you hungry? I haven't made dinner yet, but I can change and whip something up."

"I didn't come by so you'd feed me again," he explained. "I came by because I missed you."

Her mouth dropped open. "Missed me? I don't think anyone has ever missed me before. Or if they have, they've never told me."

That was a shame. The gap in their nearly two days apart had left him a little unsettled...so what would that lead to once he went back home and didn't see her for what would likely be months?

"Let me get changed and then we can talk." She started to turn toward her bedroom, then tossed a glance over her shoulder. "And I missed you, too."

As she walked away, a cat darted from beneath the sofa and straight into her room just before Rachel closed the door.

He raked a hand down his face and glanced around the small living area. Granted, she lived alone, but his penthouse apartment had to be five times this size. Yet the more he looked, the more he realized she had everything anyone needed. Fully stocked kitchen, table and chairs for dining, a small sectional sofa, coffee table, television. Her bedroom had a bath off it and she was happy and content. Yes, she wanted her own farm, but Jack knew in his heart she didn't care about the size of the house she lived in. All Rachel wanted was land for animals and to raise a family. Her dreams and wishes would seem simple to most people, but they were everything to her.

Moments later she came back out with her jeans, a plain long-sleeve red T-shirt and her hair back in that signature braid. Her pitcher necklace hung around her neck, and he loved how she and her sisters and mother shared that symbol of giving and love. What would that be like to have such a wholesome foundation? To have love and unconditional support from so many family members?

"Hey. You okay?"

Rachel's concerning tone pulled him back to the present. But instead of nodding and playing everything off, he shook his head.

"Not really," he admitted.

Instantly she crossed the space between them and took his hand in hers as those green eyes came up to meet his. "Talk to me."

Jack reached for her other hand so he securely held on to both. "I don't even know what to say except I'm just glad I met you. You've given me some reprieve from the stress of the house and the store. I know I can talk to you about anything and trust it stays between us."

"Of course."

That sweet grin of hers hit him straight in the heart once again. How could life be so complicated? How could he meet and fall for a woman who led a completely opposite life and lived hundreds of miles from him? Was that how God's plans worked? He presented His plan and you had to figure out how to make a go of it?

"You look more stressed now than I've ever seen you," Rachel stated. "Do you want to have a seat?"

She led him to the sofa, and the moment he eased down, she sat right next to him, still holding on to one of his hands.

"Did you find out something with the store?" she asked.

"Not yet."

"Is there a hiccup with the renovations?"

He shook his head. "We're actually ahead of schedule."

"Something with your dad?"

*Something with you.*

"No. I actually haven't talked to him in a few days. I texted and told him I was busy and I'd get back to him once I got the house on the market."

"Well, if it makes you feel better, you got an A on that essay you helped me with."

A sliver of relief slid through him, and he hadn't even realized how much he cared about her grade until now.

"That's good to hear," he replied.

"We make a pretty great team with several things," she informed him. "Are you sure I can't fix us something for dinner?"

"I don't expect that."

"So you already told me," she reminded him. "But I'm getting hungry and you're here and could clearly use some company and comfort food."

Yes, but he could use clarity more than anything. And being closed up with Rachel only made him more confused about what he wanted.

"Isn't there a good place in town to grab home-cooked food?" he asked.

"There are a couple of places." She narrowed her eyes and tipped her head. "Are you asking me on a date or are you afraid of my cooking?"

"I'm not afraid of your cooking."

She blinked and her hold on his hand relaxed. "Oh, um… yes. We could do that. I need to put on something else and—"

"You look beautiful just like always," he interjected. "You

never have to get made up to do anything with me. I like you just the way you are."

There. He'd placed those delicate, loaded words right between them. She could interpret that as friends or more. He wanted to gauge her reaction before he could figure out his next move.

But again, he needed to pray on it. No matter what he wanted to do, he had to go to prayer to make sure that was what God wanted him to do.

"Can I at least grab my boots?" she asked with a chuckle.

"You can do that, but you don't need anything else."

When he came to his feet, he took her hand and pulled her up with him. He didn't know what he was thinking or how to label his emotions, but leaning in and placing his lips against hers just seemed right. With their hands trapped between their bodies, Rachel relaxed against him and sank into the kiss. Jack hadn't been sure of her feelings, but that one simple gesture said more than any words ever could.

Now he had even more to think about. Rachel had feelings for him just like he did for her.

When he eased back, her lids fluttered open, revealing those expressive green eyes that he'd come to love.

Love?

Yes. Love. He was falling for her, and he wasn't sure when that had happened. Had the transition been slow or had he fallen the moment she'd professed her adolescent crush that first day she rode up on her horse?

"I hope I didn't overstep," he murmured.

"I'm wondering what took you so long to make that move," she threw back with a slight grin.

His heart swelled, and he couldn't dwell on everything that could go wrong if they pursued a romance. He didn't want to dwell on negativity. For his time in town and with Rachel, he wanted his sole focus to be on her. Maybe through his new prayer habits and spending more time with her, his answer would become clearer.

RACHEL WASN'T SURE what was happening, but she also wasn't going to question it.

She and Jack had grabbed dinner at Fork 'n' Finger. She'd had the chicken and noodles and Jack had gone with the steak and fried potatoes with green beans. Definitely some comfort food, and Rachel didn't know if it was the tender kiss or the hot meal that had perked up his spirits.

And somehow they'd ended up in the den sanding those built-ins.

"I have no clue what I'm doing," Jack muttered. "I always hire for this work to get done."

Rachel laughed and dropped her sandpaper to the drop cloth beneath her feet. She moved to the other end of the wall where Jack worked on his section. She glanced at what he'd done and nodded.

"Look at you for excelling at yet another thing outside your comfort zone," she joked. "First saddling a horse, then the boots and now sanding. Better watch yourself. You'll want to keep this place for yourself and you'll be buying a horse next."

Jack shook his head. "I don't see me buying a horse anytime soon."

"Sanding and staining is grunt work." Rachel ran her fingertips over the lighter area that he'd already smoothed out. "It's time-consuming, but so worth it in the end when you sit back and see your finished product."

"You've done this before, I take it?"

She turned her attention to him, noting again how those dark eyes could draw her in and mesmerize her. The invisible pull between them only seemed to grow stronger, and the thought of him leaving made her heart ache.

"I did the table in my living room, and I helped my mom

with the old bookshelves she put in my bedroom when I was a teen."

Jack reached up and swiped the pad of his thumb across her cheek. "You had some sanding dust," he explained as he dropped his hand to his side.

That brief, innocent touch had a whole host of new emotions running through her. She was falling for him and there was absolutely no denying this fact anymore. She'd promised herself she'd try to keep her feelings in check, that she'd put up an emotional barrier, but her human tendencies had taken over and now she had herself a predicament.

"Thanks," she murmured. "You're doing a great job. It's just not going to be done tonight or even tomorrow. But we'll get it."

A smile flirted around his mouth. "I like the fact you're helping me. With everything, really. The farm, the store."

"Maybe we make a good team," she suggested, forcing a smile when her heart was beating much too fast and her stomach was in knots.

"I'm starting to think we do."

His gaze dropped to her mouth, but the chime that echoed through the house pulled her attention away from the tender moment.

"Was that the driveway alarm?" she asked.

Jack nodded. "I'm not expecting anyone."

He started from the room and Rachel pulled in a deep breath as she followed him. She had no clue who this unexpected guest was, but she should probably be thankful because she had a feeling he'd been about to kiss her and all that would do was make her fall even more.

As they reached the foyer, Jack glanced out the sidelight to the drive. The porch lights and the glow from the barn lights lit up the space and Jack came to a halt and gasped.

"Is that a worker?" she asked. "It's kind of late for them, isn't it?"

"That's not a worker."

Jack's words had a whole new tone—one she didn't recognize.

"That's my father."

# CHAPTER SIXTEEN

JACK WISHED HE was home alone. Rachel shouldn't have to be here to see his father, whom Jack had certainly not been expecting. He hadn't told Jack he was coming, and Jack imagined this little surprise was exactly how Logan Hart wanted it to be. To catch Jack off guard and check in on progress. Great. Just great.

"I can't wait to meet him," Rachel stated as she started toward the front door.

That was such a Rachel comment and gesture. Always looking for the positive, but Jack wasn't feeling so warm and fuzzy. What had gone from a beautiful evening could very well go south quickly.

"I can run you home," Jack offered.

"No. I'd like to meet your father. I loved George and I... I adore you. It's only fitting I meet your dad, too. What's his name?"

"Logan."

Jack reached around her to unlock the door but didn't miss that she'd said she adored him. With all the turmoil rolling around inside him over his decisions and now facing his father, he couldn't quite delve into what she'd just revealed.

And maybe a slipup was all that was. But he'd have to figure that out later.

Rachel was already stepping onto the porch, ready to greet his father. Jack pulled in a deep breath as he moved ahead of her. With a gentle grasp, he took her elbow. He didn't know if he was wanting her to stop here and wait on his father to come up or if he just needed to cling to her for a little emotional support. Either way, he was glad she was here. Even if he wasn't quite comfortable with his father meeting her, Jack had come to rely on Rachel for much more than he could've ever imagined.

"Just keep in mind, he's nothing like people around here," Jack warned. "He's harder, no-nonsense."

Rachel turned and patted his cheek. "I can handle myself."

Looking into those wide eyes, Jack truly believed she could, but he still wanted to wrap her up and protect her and give her all the good in life she deserved. He only hoped his father wasn't too harsh and only talking business.

"Dad," Jack greeted him. "I wish I'd known you were coming. I would've been here or made sure a room was ready for you."

"When you weren't taking my calls and only resorting to texts, I assumed something was wrong, so I had to come out and see for myself."

"Everything is going according to plan," Jack replied, leaving out the part about the sidetrack of his plan with Rachel. He certainly hadn't expected to find someone to throw his entire world for a proverbial loop.

"I thought this place would be on the market by now," his father practically grumbled as he stepped up onto the porch.

Jack took a step forward, but Rachel stepped in front of him. "Hi. I'm Rachel Spencer. I live on the farm next door. Your father was an amazing man and we definitely miss him."

Jack waited, holding his breath, hoping his father would turn on some sort of manners.

"Yes, he was an amazing man," his dad agreed, his eyes darting between them. "Are you and my son dating?"

"Dad."

"No."

Jack and Rachel spoke at the same time, but Jack stepped up next to Rachel.

"Even if I was dating anyone, that has nothing to do with the house," Jack started. "Rachel has been helping me with renovation ideas, and she's extremely knowledgeable with the town, which will help with finding the right buyer."

Rachel tensed beside him. Jack shouldn't be surprised at his father's business-only approach. The only reason his dad had asked about dating was because he wouldn't want it to interfere with the progress and sale. Jack didn't have to ask; he knew Logan Hart better than anyone.

"Why don't we go inside so you can see some of the progress and Jack's ideas?" Rachel suggested.

While Jack appreciated her big heart and peacemaker ways, he didn't want her in the middle of this. But they all three moved into the foyer and Jack closed the door behind them.

His father glanced around, down the hallway, trying to see toward the kitchen, and then to the right toward the family room.

"How soon will the farm get listed?" he asked. "Have you scheduled an open house for after the renovations or anything yet?"

"I don't think an open house will be necessary," Jack replied. "Rosewood Valley is pretty laid-back and everyone around here already knows this farm well and what a prime piece of real estate it is."

His father unbuttoned his suit jacket and sighed as he rested his hands on his hips. "You know how this business works, son. There's a method to flipping and selling. I hope you're not getting caught up in sentimental memories and delaying listing this place."

Jack ground his teeth and pulled in a deep breath as he sent up a prayer for patience. He'd dealt with this type of behavior from his father his entire life, but it wasn't until coming to Rosewood Valley and seeing the dynamics of the Spencers and dealing with a home that housed so many precious moments that Jack came to the realization that there was more than the almighty dollar. Yes, he still wanted that promotion, but all of this had become a learning experience. Money wasn't everything and he could still get that office he'd worked so hard for.

"I'm well aware how the business works," Jack replied. "Which is why I also know my market in this area, and wasting money on an open house is not what I plan on doing. The home will be on the market in less than three weeks. I'll have it sold in less than a week once it is listed."

"Brian recently sold a commercial building." His father rattled off a staggering number. "I'm sure you know that's a company record."

"Good for him."

Jack truly was happy for Brian. They were all on the same team for Hart Realty. Jack still felt like he deserved the promotion over a man who had only been with the company for three years.

"I need this project wrapped up and you back in the office," his father went on. "We have bigger listings and the new location needs someone in it full-time."

"Isn't Brian there?"

"He's going back and forth. If you would have answered my calls over the past few days, I could have saved this trip." His father glanced around and then back to Rachel. "But I'm glad I came, because I'm starting to see what the holdup is."

Jack opened his mouth, but Rachel beat him to it.

"Mr. Hart, Jack has been extremely hands-on with this home and the feed store. He's been taking the time to get to know the people of the town just like your father did. While the contractors are here, Jack is planning the best way to market this land to not only get the best price, but also to make sure your father's legacy is still honored. It's quite a feat for such a short time."

Of course Rachel would continue to come to his defense. And while he shouldn't be surprised that she'd hyped him up and mentioned putting the house on the market, he still was because she'd not once mentioned herself or that she wanted the land yet couldn't afford it.

She didn't have to say a word, yet she did on his behalf.

When his father continued to stare at Rachel like she was insane for coming to his defense, Jack wanted her out of here.

"I'm going to run her home and then I'll be back," Jack said.

His father gave a curt nod.

"It was nice to meet you," Rachel stated with one of her signature smiles that could warm anyone's cold heart.

Logan actually cracked a grin. "You as well."

Jack turned and placed his hand on the small of Rachel's back as he led her out the door. The moment they were both in the car, tension surrounded them. The unspoken words, the obvious worry and the end of a happy evening all seemed to settle right between them.

"Well, that didn't go too bad."

Rachel's words sliced through the quiet, and Jack gripped the wheel as he pulled out of the drive. He couldn't argue with her, knowing that brief meeting could've been a whole lot worse.

"You didn't have to stand up for me," he stated. "I can handle my father."

"Oh… I just…"

Jack turned into Four Sisters a few moments later, frustrated at the man he'd become after just a few moments in the presence of his father.

"I didn't mean to sound ungrateful," he amended. "I appreciate what you're trying to do, but Dad doesn't always play nice. He wouldn't care if I sold the land to a developer who planned to tear it down and make a mall out of the property."

Rachel's gasp filled the vehicle. "Are you serious? That would be... Well, that would be horrendous. I'm starting to see why you seem so relaxed here and why you need a break."

Yes. Jack was starting to see those same things. Yet he'd worked so hard to have his own company under the umbrella of Hart Realty. An already established firm and a dynasty from his father that someday Jack could pass to his own children was all he'd ever wanted.

But Rosewood Valley calmed him, and he couldn't describe it, but he felt like home here.

"I just need to talk to him on my own." Jack pulled the car to a stop and glanced her way. "Sorry this night didn't end as nice as it started."

"No worries. Hope you and your dad have a nice talk." Rachel blinked and looked away as she reached for the handle. "I'll see you tomorrow, and we can work more on those built-ins. Good night, Jack."

She stepped from the car and Jack thought for certain her voice had cracked on those final words. Had he also seen a shimmer of unshed tears in her eyes before she stepped away?

Had he upset her with his gruff reply a moment ago? Or was she upset that she thought her own dream of the farm was slipping away? Either way, he didn't like this sinking feeling that he'd ruined the only bright spot in his life. The last thing he ever wanted was for Rachel to be hurt by anyone, most of all him. But now he had to go talk to his dad and hope Rachel wasn't too upset with him.

RACHEL LOCKED HER door behind her as soon as she got into her loft apartment. She was going to grab a shower and head to bed. This evening had mentally drained her. Between the unexpected kiss that left her more hopeful than ever, to meeting Jack's father, to admitting Jack would be getting the home on the market soon, tonight's events had really torn into her emotions. She had to face the harsh reality that Jack was in charge of the farm and he had to sell it to appease his father and get that promotion. She couldn't ask him to keep waiting on her or try to give him less than it was worth. That wasn't fair because what if she was never in a financial spot to give him what the place was valued at?

There was a family out there who needed the land and the big house. A family who would love the place and care for it and fill the empty stalls with livestock. Rachel could still have her own farm someday; it just wouldn't be next door to her family. But she knew God would bless her in His time and not hers. She had to hold on to that.

Still. She was human and had feelings and a heart that hurt for what she thought she might obtain. Granted, Jack had never promised her anything. He'd been clear on what he needed to do, but she'd thought for certain they might be able to work something out.

Maybe she'd been too naive or too hopeful.

Right now, her head hurt and she just wanted to freshen up and put on her cozy pajamas.

As she made her way toward her room, her cat sprinted ahead of her. Clearly this was their new game. Her cell chimed from her pocket.

There went that sliver of hope again as she pulled it out thinking Jack had texted her.

But no. The message was from Walt in a group with her and Jack.

Can you both be at the store tomorrow at 8? I figured out who's been stealing. We're going to deal with it.

Well, at least this was something moving in the right direction. Rachel replied she'd be there and put her phone on her nightstand to charge. She didn't wait to see if Jack would reply. He was taking care of his own issues right now, and Rachel needed to spend her evening trying to relax and pray. She needed God more than ever now.

# CHAPTER SEVENTEEN

JACK HAD NEVER felt so depleted and confused in his entire life. He'd barely slept for all the thoughts filling his mind. Lying in the darkness in his grandfather's home with all the memories to keep him company had really weighed on him last night. Those middle-of-the-night hours when there were no distractions and all he could do was think left Jack wondering what to do at this crossroads he now faced. Nobody could make this decision for him, and no matter what he decided, these next steps would be life-altering.

Rachel's truck was parked out back when he pulled up to the store, so he knew she'd beaten him here for this meeting. He hadn't spoken to her or texted since they parted ways last night. His last image of her was with those unshed tears in her eyes, and each time that thought pushed its way to the front of his mind, his heart clenched with a grip of guilt like he'd not ever experienced before.

He never wanted to hurt anyone, yet he'd done just that with his harsh reply and virtually stealing her dream right out from under her.

If he left town today and went back home, he'd have regrets for the rest of his life. Yet he'd still not come up with a solid answer. Even after discussing the ideas for the farm and timelines and price points, his father still had reservations and thought the land could go for more. When his father had broached the subject of the feed store, Jack circled back to the farm, not at all ready to discuss the store. Every part of him really felt like he wanted to keep this one piece of his grandfather. This final tie to the man who'd instilled these small-town values in him, and Jack had all the confidence that Walt would keep this place running while Jack was in San Francisco.

Jack made his way down the narrow hallway leading to the office. Chatter filtered from the open doorway and he recognized Walt's and Rachel's voices. Just that familiarity from her had his gut in knots. But he had to deal with whatever Walt found out first before he could deal with his own problems.

"Morning," Walt greeted him as soon as Jack stepped through the doorway.

Jack nodded his greeting, then turned a quick glance to do the same to Rachel. Her forced smile was all the proof he needed that he'd messed up.

"I figured having you both here would be best," Walt started, clearly oblivious to the tension. "I put in a small camera behind the counter the day Jack and I talked about the missing funds. Since then, I've seen a few instances with the same person and it's quite disheartening."

"Who is it?" Rachel asked.

"Myles."

Jack pulled in a deep breath and sighed. "I was hoping there would be some mistake or explanation. I hate having to fire someone so young."

"Maybe we don't have to fire him," Rachel chimed in. "I mean, we don't know the story."

Jack jerked his focus to her. "Not fire him? We can't have a thief working here."

"We don't know his side of things yet," she defended.

"Which is why I asked him to meet us this morning," Walt added. "He should be here any minute."

Rachel nodded and looked back at Walt. "I just don't want him to feel like we're attacking him."

"We're not attacking," Jack stated. "We're firing."

"Careful," Rachel muttered with a side-eye. "Your father is coming out."

Shocked at her reply, Jack could only stare as she completely turned her attention to Walt. Maybe his father was coming out in him, but stealing was stealing. How could there be a defense to that?

The chime on the back door cut through the strain in the room and the soft echo of footsteps filled the space.

Jack shifted aside to make room for Myles. The office wasn't big by any means, but add in four people and an awkward situation and things were going to be quite uncomfortable for a bit.

The moment Myles filled the doorway, his eyes took in the group and his jaw clenched.

"I'm in trouble." He remained in the doorway, but his shoulders dropped and his head hung just a bit more. "Did you call the cops or can I explain?"

Clearly the boy knew why they were all here. He wasn't stupid and had to have known he'd get caught at some point.

"Come on in, son," Walt invited. "We're not the firing squad."

Myles took one step in and stopped. He glanced around the room again and shoved his hands in his pockets.

"I want to hear why you took the money," Rachel told him. "We need to hear your reasoning. You were given a job and one that Walt trusted you with."

"I know."

The teen's head hung just a bit more, but Rachel's compassionate gaze never left the boy. Jack was having a difficult time focusing on anything or anyone else but her. He wanted a redo of last night, and he wanted to be alone with her to apologize. He couldn't leave things the way they had.

"I never intended to steal," Myles said. "I was so thankful to get a job to help out at home. My dad left and my mom is recovering from her chemo. I just thought my paycheck would go further than it does and then that cash was there and I thought just this one time."

Myles closed his eyes and shook his head. "But that one time turned into more. I was the only one bringing in any money after Dad left and my mom can't work for a while. I didn't want my sister to have to quit her dance lessons and..."

His voice cracked as he trailed off. Jack didn't know what to say. He'd had no clue the boy faced such hardships at home and was handling his life the best way he thought he could. And all he wanted to do was step up and provide when nobody else could. How could Jack be furious with that? How could anyone with a heart not empathize with this young boy's situation to care for his sick mother and younger sister?

Rachel moved and instantly wrapped Myles in an embrace. Jack met Walt's eyes and the older man had a sheen of tears. Clearly they all felt bad for Myles, and honestly, Jack had never been put in a position like this before.

"It will be okay." Rachel comforted the teen, then eased back from their hug. "But you cannot steal anymore. If you want to keep working, we want you here, but no more stealing."

Myles wiped his damp cheeks and looked between Jack and Walt.

"You're not calling the cops or firing me?" he asked.

Walt looked to Jack for guidance, and Jack crossed his arms as he weighed the right words to say here. This would be a pivotal point in this young boy's life, and Jack knew the final decision would be up to him.

"You're not fired and you're not going to see any cops," Jack confirmed. "But Rachel is right. You can't take any more money or we will have to take action."

Myles met his gaze. "I promise. You have my word."

Rachel's eyes darted to Jack, then back to Myles. "Why didn't you tell anyone you needed help?" she asked.

The boy shrugged and glanced away as if he had to protect his pride. "It's embarrassing, honestly. I never thought my parents would split up, especially while my mom was so sick. I left the football team so I could work, but I told everyone that I was tired of playing because I didn't want to explain myself."

Jack couldn't even imagine the heaviness this teen had been carrying around for months.

"Here's what I'd like to do if you and your family are okay with it," Rachel chimed in. "I'd like to host a fundraiser at Four Sisters. We do so many farm-to-table events, and I can't think of a better cause."

Myles blinked back more tears. "You'd do that for us?"

"Absolutely," she confirmed with that soft smile of hers that could bring peace to anyone's soul. "Sometimes you just have to ask for help. You have such a wonderful community. Anyone would rally around you guys, and there's absolutely nothing to be ashamed of."

Jack knew for a fact that if Rachel had known just how dire this situation was, she would have intervened long before now. She truly had a heart for giving and loving.

She deserved nothing less in return.

"I thought I could do it all for them," Myles stated as he squared his shoulders and composed himself. "But it's been hard. I don't want my mom to be angry with me or disappointed, and you can take what I stole from my wages."

"Consider that a donation from the store," Jack stated before thinking of his reply. But now that the words were out, he was pleased with his answer. "We would have helped anyway had we known. But next time you need help, whether you work here or you're out in life, don't be afraid to tell someone. You'll find for the most part people are generous and willing to step up. You never know—you might be in a position one day when someone asks you for help and you'll be able to return the gesture."

Rachel's eyes met his and she gave a soft nod, silently approving everything he'd just said. He didn't know why, but he wanted to have her approval. To know he was making the right decision. And she'd been right to have patience with Myles and find out his side of the story before jumping straight to removing him from the workplace.

She'd also been right when she'd said his father was coming out in him. That was nearly all he knew—business and money. The low percentage of compassion and tenderness inside him came from his grandfather—and now he'd like to think from Rachel. She brought out that side of him, the side that had been buried by years of hustle and grinding in the city, trying to obtain that next level of success.

But there was so much more out there than money and success. There were feelings and real-life problems that required attention. If he was solely focused on himself and his next career move, how was he helping others?

"Your mother does need to know everything."

Walt's words cut through the room, and Jack nodded in agreement. "We will explain to her that you were only trying to help and that you're not going to be in trouble with us, so long as this is an isolated incident."

"I promise if you give me another chance, I will not do anything to betray you again," Myles insisted. "I need this job. Please."

"You can stay," Walt confirmed. "I'll call your mother later and have a talk with her and make sure she's not upset with you. I've known your family a long time, and I know your heart was in the right place."

"Thank you guys, so much."

Myles went around the room and hugged each one of them. "Can I still work this evening for my regular shift?"

"Absolutely." Walt nodded. "We need you here."

"I can't thank you enough for understanding. This is so embarrassing and—"

"You have no reason to be embarrassed for just trying to help your family," Rachel all but scolded. "I think you've learned your lesson, and I think you're going to grow from this."

"I've definitely learned my lesson and I can't thank you all enough for showing me grace."

Jack knew that was all Rachel. If he'd been in charge, he would've gone in leading with anger, while she went in leading with love. He could learn, and had learned, so much from her.

Once Myles left, Rachel also excused herself, leaving Jack and Walt alone.

"That went better than I thought it would," Walt stated as he sank back into his creaky old chair.

Jack nodded in agreement. "Let me know what his mother says. And I'm going to think of other ways we can help. That poor boy has too much responsibility when he should be enjoying his last year of high school."

"We'll figure out something for the family," Walt said. "We can do a silent auction or have something here at the store after hours as well. We'll put our heads together and come up with something."

And that was why Jack loved this town. He'd yet to meet one selfish person. Everyone was constantly looking out for others, which was what life should be about, right?

The more these thoughts rolled around in his head, the more he wondered if God was speaking to him through a variety of outlets. All Jack had to do was be silent and listen.

# CHAPTER EIGHTEEN

RACHEL STEPPED INTO the barn and glanced around for her father. Odd that he wasn't there, but that gave her a minute to send off a group text to her mother and sisters explaining the upcoming event she wanted to have to benefit Myles's family.

Once she was done, she shoved her cell into her back pocket and figured she might as well clean out the stalls. She wasn't sure what her father had planned for the day, but stalls always needed freshening up to keep the horses healthy.

Rachel adjusted her hat as she turned to grab a pitchfork but stopped short. Jack stood in the doorway. Hands in his pockets, in no hurry to speak or move inside, he just stood there.

"Are you trying to decide if you're staying or running?" she asked, also not moving any closer.

"We need to talk."

Rachel crossed her arms but said nothing. If he wanted the floor, she'd let him have it. But she had a feeling she wasn't going to like what he was about to say.

"I'm going back to San Francisco," he started, his words coming out slowly, as if he didn't want to be saying them at all. "My father left this morning."

Her heart started to break, but she had to remain strong. She knew from the beginning he wasn't going to stay.

"Short trip for him," she replied.

Jack shrugged. "He came for what he wanted and needed to get back to work."

"And is that what you are doing?" she asked. "Getting back to work before the farm is done?"

"I trust the contractors and I'll be back to see the final product and get it on the market. I'll pay you to finish those built-ins we started or I can have the guys do it."

"I'll finish it."

She didn't know why she agreed to that, because the only outcome from that project would be a reminder of something they'd started and couldn't finish…like the relationship she'd so hoped they'd have together.

"I'll make sure to compensate you for the time, especially now that I realize how tedious it is," he stated.

Rachel nodded, not quite sure what to say now. Whatever he and his father discussed last night had clearly thrust Jack back into mogul mode, and whatever she and Jack had shared was gone. Her heart sank realizing that in less than twenty-four hours, she'd lost any chance of every dream she'd ever had.

"Good for you," she replied. "I'm sure someone will be very happy there and love the changes you've made."

Jack nodded. "The new owner will love it, I'm certain. I just didn't want to leave town without telling you I'm sorry for last night."

"The kiss or the ending?"

He took a step forward but stopped. "The ending. I never intended to hurt you, Rachel. I hope you know that."

She kept her arms crossed for fear if she dropped them, he'd either see her hands shaking or she'd try to reach for him. She had to remain strong. She'd been through this before, right?

Well, they weren't exactly dating or engaged, but did it matter the label once the heart got so involved? She'd gone into this with her eyes wide open… Unfortunately her heart had been wide open as well, even though she'd tried her hardest to keep it closed.

"I believe you," she replied. "You were nothing but honest with me. God has other plans than what I wanted, and I'm sure it's something better than I ever could have imagined."

He opened his mouth but closed it and shook his head. She had no idea what he'd been about to say or what was truly on his heart. There wasn't a doubt in her mind that he was indeed sorry. Jack had a good heart; she'd seen it over and over. He wanted to do right by his grandfather and his father, and he felt torn. The two most influential men in his life were of two very different personalities and it was no wonder Jack was so conflicted.

"I feel foolish for asking, but can you keep on at the store for a bit and help Myles?"

There was that big heart she'd come to know and love. Even with all he had going on in his life right now, he still wanted to look out for those in need. How could she not be in love with him? But how could he be the one who felt so right and the one she thought should be in her life and still not fit in? Did he not feel the same? Did he not have any emotions after that kiss they'd shared?

"I'll be sure to keep Myles on my priority list," she assured him. "So you're keeping the store?"

Jack nodded. "For now. The farm is going to be my focus and then we'll see where life leads."

Would that path ever lead him back here for good? Or would he just pop in and out—or worse, call or text to keep tabs on the feed store from afar? She had a sinking feeling that once he got back into his element, he'd forget all about Rosewood Valley…and about her.

"Well, thanks for letting me know."

She really needed him to go so she could have a good, healthy cry while mucking stalls.

"If there's nothing else, I really need to get to work," she told him when he simply continued to stand there as if he wanted to say more.

When the silence became too much and he still remained standing, that bold mouth of hers took over. Her words spilled out before her mind could tell her to stop.

"Did that kiss mean nothing?" she asked. "Was that a spur-of-the-moment reaction?"

"It meant something." His soft tone only caused her heart to crack more.

"I don't know why I let myself think you had changed since you arrived," she murmured, unable to stop her thoughts from spilling out. "I thought there was more between us, that maybe you would consider staying. I know you promised nothing—in fact, you were quite honest about your plans and I didn't want to face the truth."

Yet again, Jack opened his mouth, then closed it. Whatever his response was, he clearly had more self-control than she did.

She so wished he'd say something, though. Like maybe he'd fallen for her and they could try this long-distance thing or that he'd come back and try to give them a chance.

But he merely nodded.

"Thanks for everything. You don't know the impact you've had on my life and how I wish things were different right now."

Before she could ask him what he meant, Jack turned on his booted heel and walked out.

She realized for the first time he had on the boots she'd given him. Clearly she *had* left an impression on his life, and maybe she would be hard to forget.

The moment tires crunched over the gravel in the drive, Rachel blew out a breath and pulled off her hat. She curled the brim between her fingers and closed her eyes, trying to block out the additional hurt that threatened to creep in.

"I take it you and Jack are no longer a thing, from the way he tore out of here?"

Rachel jerked her head up to see her father striding toward her with a concerned look on his face.

She couldn't speak as emotions clogged her throat. Rachel closed the distance and thrust herself into her father's open arms. The moment he embraced her, she used his strong shoulder to pour her sadness onto. She knew he'd always be there for her, just like she knew she'd get through this. But sometimes, a girl just needed a hug from her dad.

JACK PULLED IN front of the office he'd called his home away from home for nearly his entire adult life. As he stared up at the black-and-white sign above the double doors, the words HART REALTY stared back at him.

How many times over the years had he walked beneath that and taken this for granted? More importantly, how many times had *he* himself been taken for granted?

Far too many to count, in his opinion.

Jack glanced down to his boots and a ball of dread curled in his stomach as a lump formed in his throat.

Yeah, he knew where he was most appreciated. Leaving Rosewood Valley had been one of the most difficult decisions he'd ever made, but he'd known all along he belonged back here, where his job and his home were. He couldn't abandon his goals now. Not when he'd worked so hard and for so long to see them come true.

Or could he? Since leaving yesterday, he'd felt nothing but worry and anxiety and a healthy dose of guilt. When he'd first arrived in Rosewood Valley, he felt confident that when he finished his business there and returned to San Francisco, he would be elated and ready to take that promotion he knew should go to him.

Yet the whole drive back home, all Jack could think about was Rachel and her parting words. The sadness in her voice, the unshed tears she'd so desperately tried to hide. He'd only wanted to bring her joy and happiness like she'd done to him, but he'd broken her heart.

And he hadn't lied. Their kiss *had* meant something. In the short amount of time he'd been with her, his entire life had changed, and he could honestly say he was a better man for it.

So if he noticed that much of a difference in just a few weeks, what would happen if he spent a lifetime with her?

Jack had no idea why he was thinking long-term with Rachel, but the idea didn't scare him. In fact, for the first time since leaving, he had a burst of hope and a positive outlook on his future. While he had no clue what that looked like right now, he knew who he wanted in his life.

Jack took the steps leading to the doors and let himself in. The modern design of metal and leather with black accents was a far cry from the country life he'd been living. Walking back in here now, the office seemed almost…sterile. There were no pops of color, no flowers, nothing cozy at all.

His father stepped from the back, where the coffee bar was tucked into a small nook.

"Son. What are you doing back?" he asked, holding a black mug with the company logo on the side. "I thought you were seeing the project through to the sale."

Jack eyed the row of clear tables with industrial legs that lined either side of the room. There were enough desk areas for eight Realtors and each one had an occupant that would be in later. Thankfully they were alone as Jack moved toward his workspace. He eyed the photo on the edge of the desk, the one where he stood in front of the first home he'd ever sold. He always wanted that reminder, but the main thing he remembered was that his father hadn't been there that day. He'd been at another listing and said he couldn't make the open house where Jack had finally sealed his first deal.

"I plan on seeing the farm renovation through completely," he stated, glancing back up to his father. "I needed to come here and settle a few things first."

"I didn't see that you had a closing scheduled today."

"I meant business with you."

His father's brows rose slightly, and for the first time Jack could recall, Logan Hart was speechless and surprised.

"If this is about the promotion—"

"It is," Jack confirmed.

"You know it's all going to depend on the sale," his father told him, then took another sip of his coffee. "Brian has quite a bit in the works and has already made some great progress working out of the new office to get a jump start before our official grand opening."

"Good for him." Hearing this didn't bother Jack, and he realized he wasn't jealous of Brian and didn't want to one-up him to get that office for himself. "I'm taking myself out of the running for the promotion."

The coffee cup lowered slowly as his father's gaze narrowed. "Excuse me?"

Just admitting those words out loud lifted a weight from Jack's shoulders. He couldn't imagine how he'd feel once he put his thoughts into actions. The chains were breaking, and he had one family and one town to thank for opening his eyes.

He also had to thank God. Those prayers hadn't gone unnoticed or unanswered. Jack simply had to be open to God's plan.

"I've been praying and doing quite a bit of calculating in my head, especially on my drive here. At this time in my life, I'm going to step away from San Francisco and from Hart Realty."

His father set his mug on the closest desk and propped his hands on his hips, never once breaking eye contact with Jack. Jack knew this conversation wouldn't be well received, but it was long overdue.

"What did that woman do to you?" his father demanded.

Instead of being angry or defensive as he probably would've been in the past, Jack merely smiled when he thought of Rachel.

"She showed me there's more than money and there's more

than working all the time," he replied. "There's family and peace and a laid-back way of living I didn't know existed. I mean, I experienced it as a child when I would visit Grandpa, but to embrace that culture as an adult is a different story."

"You're just like him," Jack's father muttered. "My dad never could understand why I was here in the city, never understood why I ever wanted to leave Rosewood Valley. But once I went to college, I knew I'd never live in that small town again. I needed people and the hustle I could only find here."

"And that's what works for you and makes you happy," Jack replied. "That's what works for Brian, and I thought that's what worked for me. I see things so much differently now. There's a calm inside of me that's been brought to the surface, and I don't recall being happier."

Well, if he didn't completely mess things up with Rachel. He wanted to go back and tell her how he felt, but he had to settle all of this first. He wanted a clean slate and nothing in his way once he presented his future to her.

"I thought I'd lose you," his father admitted, blowing out a sigh. "I've been hard on you because I wanted you to always be here with me. I wanted us to be a team, and I thought if I made you work harder day after day, you'd take over the company. But I've always known you were more like my father than I ever was."

Jack wasn't sure if this was his father's attempt at an apology, but the man seemed almost tired. Like he'd been waiting for this moment to come and now he could breathe.

"I don't resign to hurt you." Jack needed him to know that above all else. "The city is not for me anymore, and if Brian wants to take over, then he should. He's great at what he does."

"So are you," his father retorted. "So what will you do in the country? I'm not sure you're knowledgeable enough about farm life."

Jack laughed and shook his head, loving the way this conversation had turned. His dad seemed understanding, which completely caught Jack off guard in the best way.

"I actually thought about still doing real estate and maybe opening my own office there. You're right, and I am good at what I do."

"Would you use the Hart name?" his father asked, reaching for his mug once again.

Jack blinked, surprised at the question. "I didn't think I would. I mean, you have two offices here in the city and Rosewood Valley is hours away."

"Doesn't mean we can't have another office and one that you deserve to run."

Never in Jack's dreams had he thought his father would offer another branch, but his father likely had never considered another town outside the city. Maybe they could still continue to work together, to keep their bond, and perhaps Jack could show his dad some grace and pull him around to seeing that there was so much more than just a top-dollar sale.

"I admit, this isn't how I thought our talk would go," Jack stated, circling the desk to get closer to his dad. "I thought you'd be angry and push back about my decision."

Logan merely shrugged. "I'm not thrilled you're leaving, and I never understood the draw for that slow-paced lifestyle, but I guess there's something for everyone. And if we can tap into that market, then that's a good thing."

Of course they circled back to money. If Jack was going to use the Hart name and open another branch, there had to be some ground rules set in place first.

"Rosewood Valley is quite a different demographic than San Francisco," Jack explained. "If I use the Hart name under our umbrella, then I'll be running the office how I see fit and I have final say."

His father merely studied him as if weighing the proposal. Jack crossed his arms once again, determined to stand his ground. He could open a space on his own. He wouldn't need to use the company at all, but having his father's support would make a difference. He knew without a doubt he could make a go of things on his own. This was what he knew, what he was good at, and how he could provide for Rachel. He didn't want money to be the driving factor, not like his dad did.

Ultimately, his father nodded. "I would trust you to start up an office within the company. I think you lead more with your heart, and from what I can tell, that's how business is done in that small town. They'll probably love you for it."

Jack hoped. He didn't have an office space and he didn't have anything in place other than the seed planted in his head. But he knew just like with this initial decision, once he prayed over it, God would lead him to the right place and be with him the entire way. Jack only hoped Rachel would be at his side.

"I won't exclude you from business dealings, and I'll make sure the line of communication is always open," Jack added, taking another step toward his father. "We can have our attorney draw up any documents and get this next chapter started. I just truly feel my home is in Rosewood Valley."

Logan nodded. "You seem at peace right now."

Jack couldn't recall the last time he'd had a sense of calm wash over him and through him. He wanted to rush headfirst into this next phase, but he had to take his time and make sure each stone was set in place before taking that next unknown step.

"I'm proud of you, son."

His father's words jerked Jack's focus back. "You are?"

He nodded, put the cup down again and reached for Jack. As he pulled him into a firm embrace, Jack welcomed the love his father rarely showed. Jack didn't think the man knew how to show too much emotion, but deep in his heart, Jack knew his father did love him. This display of emotions no doubt had Logan Hart feeling vulnerable and out of his comfort zone, but Jack would remember this moment forever.

"You're stronger than I ever was," his father stated with a

firm pat on the back before easing away. "You want that balance of family and career, and I believe you will pull it off. I'm afraid I put career above all else because I tried to compensate for your mother being gone. I thrust myself into work to ignore the pain, and at times I forgot how to be a father."

Jack stared back into his father's dark brown eyes, noting the fine wrinkles fanning from the corners. They'd both suffered when Jack's mom passed, and he hadn't known how much his father hurt. He always attributed his father working to uncaring emotions, but clearly it was the opposite. Logan Hart had tried to push away his pain, to mask it, by keeping busy and ignoring reality.

"About my penthouse here," Jack started. "I'll be putting it on the market as soon as possible."

"And you'll be living at Circle H, I presume?"

Jack smiled. "I can't think of anywhere else I'd rather be. I'd love for you to come visit. I'll keep a room ready for you at all times."

"I'd like that," his father stated with a smile that reached his dark eyes. "What about Rachel?"

His heart soared at the mention of her name. "I'll be asking her to marry me."

His father blinked. "Already? Are you sure she's the one?"

"I'm as sure of that as I am about this move." He'd never been more positive of any other decision in his life. "This is right for me, Dad."

"Then I can't wait to get to know her more. She's really changed you, and as much as I hate to see you go, I'm glad to see you so happy."

Jack gave his father one more embrace, feeling like maybe they'd turned over a new chapter in their family life as well. Full of hope and love, Jack had a feeling his entire world was just about to begin.

# CHAPTER NINETEEN

Autopilot.

Rachel had heard that term over the years, but she'd never fully understood the concept until now. For the past several days, she'd been working at the farm, at the store, on her schooling, and trying to organize a fundraiser for Myles and his family. But staying busy had kept her mind off a certain someone. Not that it had helped. Thoughts of Jack continually rolled through her mind, and she wondered what he was doing. He'd been gone for what seemed like forever, but in reality, it had been four days.

She'd pulled her cell out countless times to text him, but what would she say? She certainly didn't want to look desperate or clingy; she just genuinely missed him. She was a bit surprised he hadn't reached out to check on anything, but maybe once he hit the city, he'd opted to go into full work mode.

Rachel made her way toward her barn and barely had enough energy to climb those stairs. She'd put in ten hours on the farm and four at the store. One of these days, when she got her new home, she would make sure there was a large soaker tub for days like today. For now, she'd have to settle for a hot shower to ease her sore muscles.

Maybe some hot tea would help, too. She'd add some local

honey for a bit of sweetness. Maybe she'd try to find a new book, curl up on her sofa with a thick blanket and her cat, and attempt to get lost in a fictitious world where everyone got a happy ending.

The moment Rachel pushed her door open, she stilled. Her eyes landed right on the most obscene bouquet of flowers in a vase on her kitchen table. She glanced around and found Jack sitting on the sofa with the cat in his lap.

"We've become friends," he stated, stroking his fingertips between the cat's ears.

Rachel stepped inside and closed the door behind her, shutting out the cool fall evening air. "What are you doing here?"

He remained unmoving while he continued to pet the cat. How could he be so casual like he wasn't affected by being here again? Her heart beat much too fast, and she wished she'd had some heads-up that he was here.

"I didn't see your car," she mentioned.

"I hid it around back so I could surprise you."

He'd definitely done just that.

"And did you bring in this arrangement?" she asked, moving to the table. "I've never seen such a variety, and it's nearly as large as the table."

She couldn't help but laugh the more she looked at it. "I mean, thank you, but why all these flowers?"

Jack carefully lifted the cat and sat him on the couch cushion next to him before standing. "I figured you put an arrangement in my house—it's only fitting I return the gesture."

The wound to Rachel's heart healed just a bit as hope smoothed over her like a balm. She didn't want to get her hopes up or assume, but the fact he came back sooner than he'd mentioned did make her wonder.

"I'm not as good as you with flower arrangements, so I admit I paid for that." He chuckled, sliding his hands into his pockets.

"It's perfect." She reached to touch one buttery-soft pale

pink petal. Then her eyes landed on something. "Is that a card?"

"Is there a card tucked in there?" he asked. "Hmm. See what it says."

She eyed him, but he gave no clue as to what he was thinking or that he even knew a card had been placed there. Either he was a good actor or he truly had no idea the florist had put a message inside all these stems.

Rachel pulled the white card from the bouquet and started reading. She didn't get far before her heart clenched and her eyes started watering. She blinked away the moisture and started over so she could take it all in at once.

*Rachel, I want to start a new life with you. I want to make the Circle H our home.*

*I want to marry you if you'll have me.*

When Rachel looked back to Jack, he was on one knee holding a velvet box, and her stomach curled into knots as her heart leaped to her throat.

"I might have taken a couple wrong turns in life," he started. "But I can't be upset about any of them since they all led me here and to falling in love with you."

Too many emotions clogged Rachel's throat. She couldn't believe this moment was happening. Having Jack here proposing went far beyond anything she'd ever hoped or dreamed of.

She swallowed. "When I didn't hear from you at all, I thought you just shifted back to work mode and forgot all about this place."

"You're kidding, right? I could never forget the farm that shaped me or the woman who opened my eyes to faith and love. I belong here, and I'm hoping you'll give me an answer soon because my knee is hurting."

Rachel laughed and nodded. "Yes, of course I will marry you."

"You haven't seen the ring yet." He lifted the lid as he came to his feet. "What if you don't like it?"

"I don't even need a ring. I just need you."

When he pulled the ring from the box, she stared down at the simple round stone in a gold band. Nothing fancy, but delicate and absolutely perfect.

"This was my grandmother's," he explained. "And if you want something different, we can go pick it out—"

"No. This is the ring I want."

She didn't know what she loved more, the fact he had his grandmother's ring or that his hands were shaking as he slid the band onto her finger. Clearly she wasn't the only one with nerves here.

"You know I'm not a flashy girl," Rachel went on, admiring how perfectly the ring fit and looked on her hand. "With all the work I do, this ring couldn't be more perfect. I hope your grandmother would've liked me."

Jack gave her hand a soft squeeze. "I don't remember too much about her, but I don't know how anyone couldn't fall in love with you. I did in record time, and I know my grandfather adored your family. I imagine he's smiling down right now on both of us."

Rachel hadn't known such a level of happiness existed. She hadn't known that God's ultimate plan far exceeded anything she could have ever planned for herself. All she'd had to do was wait and trust in His timing.

"I have no doubt your grandparents are proud of the man you've become and that you'll be living on the farm to start the next generation."

How had their vastly different dreams turned into the same one? To know she'd be getting each dream she'd ever prayed for while honoring the memory of Jack's grandparents absolutely made Rachel more fulfilled than she could have ever imagined. Her family would be so thrilled for them, and she couldn't wait to tell them everything. But for now she just wanted to enjoy her time with Jack and discuss all the plans and dream of their life together.

"What did your dad say?" she asked. "I assume you told him."

Jack sighed but continued to hold on to her hand. "I told him and at first he was hesitant, but then he said he knew I was heading in this direction. He's happy for us."

"Really?" Both shock and elation filled her. "That's great. I'm sure you were nervous for that talk."

He took her hand and led her to the couch. Once he took a seat, she sank next to him and curled her feet to her side as she leaned into him.

"I was, but I was more nervous about the idea of not coming back here and taking over the farm and asking you to marry me." He took her hand and covered it on his lap. "I had to get some things in order before I came back, so that's why I wasn't in touch. I didn't want to waste a minute. I put my penthouse on the market and I've already had some interest."

"That's wonderful," she stated.

He offered her one of those grins that never failed to make her heart flip. "I plan on using that money to help Myles with his family, if that's okay with you."

There went another flip. "More than okay, but you don't have to run that by me."

He toyed with the stone on her ring as he held her gaze. "I do. We're a team now."

"I think they will be grateful, and your heart is so big. It's no wonder I fell in love with you."

That grin turned into a beaming smile. "You love me?"

Rachel jerked back slightly. "Of course I love you. I wouldn't have agreed to marry you if I didn't."

"I just hadn't heard you say it."

She rested her head on his shoulder and laced their fingers

together. "I can't wait to say it every single day for the rest of my life."

"I look forward to that. There's also another part of my plan that I need to discuss with you."

Rachel lifted her head and narrowed her eyes. "You've been doing quite a bit of soul-searching since you left here."

"Praying," he corrected. "And I was doing plenty of it while I was here, but I wanted to make sure I had my old life in order before I came to you asking for a new life together."

Wow. She knew nobody was perfect, but she couldn't help but think God had created the perfect mate just for her.

"So what's the other part of your plan? I hope it involves buying a hat if you're going to live on a farm."

His laughter rumbled against her, filling her with more love and adoration.

"We can go hat shopping anytime you want," he confirmed. "But I plan on opening a real estate firm here if you're okay with that."

"Okay with that? I think that's a great idea. You're good at what you do, and people will love having George Hart's grandson selling them homes."

"I hope so. I want to provide for you the way you deserve."

Rachel swatted at his chest. "I don't need you to provide for me. We're in this together, remember? We'll take care of each other, and I have total faith in you that you will do amazing."

"I suppose we need to get some animals," he suggested. "I have no clue on that, so it's definitely your call."

"First, we're getting you a horse."

He held her tighter against his side. "I can get on board with that. But I think our first order of business is to talk to your family. How do you think they'll receive this?"

Rachel could already imagine the hugs from her sisters and mom and how thrilled her father would be that the adjoining farm would be part of their family from now until forever.

"They will love every bit of this," she assured him. "How soon can we get married?"

Jack laughed once again and held her close as the cat jumped onto his lap and walked across to hers.

"In a hurry?" he asked.

"I just want to start our forever," she said.

He tipped her chin up and stared into her eyes. "Our forever started the moment you rode up on your horse and professed your childhood crush."

When he laid his lips softly on hers, she knew in her heart she had followed God's path and waited for the one. There was no doubt in her mind that she and Jack would have a beautiful life together and she would thank God in every one of her prayers for this blessing and all those to come.

\* \* \* \* \*

# WESTERN

*Rugged men looking for love...*

## Available Next Month

**The Maverick's Christmas Countdown** Heatherly Bell
**A Rancher's Return** Jen Gilroy

...................................................................

**Fortune's Holiday Surprise** Jennifer Wilck
**Cowboy Santa** Melinda Curtis

...................................................................

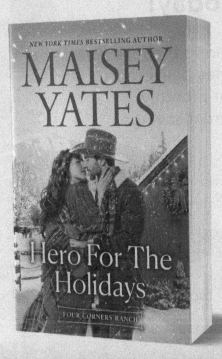

# Subscribe and fall in love with a Mills & Boon series today!

You'll be among the first to read stories delivered to your door monthly and enjoy great savings.

**WE SIMPLY LOVE ROMANCE**